PRAISE FOR *THE AVIATRIX*, BY VIOLET MARSH

"The 1920s' atmosphere and defiant characters are sure to please, particularly the scenes in which the ladies of the circus sneak out to speakeasies. Readers looking for chaste historical romance outside of Regency England will delight in Marsh's fresh, fun premise."

—*Publishers Weekly*

"Rich historical detail, endearing characters, and a tender romance bring the Roaring Twenties and the dawn of aviation to life in *The Aviatrix*—a fantastic page-turner!"

—Mary Ellen Taylor, Amazon Charts bestselling author

"I love Mattie—not even the sky is the limit for this heroine, and I'm here for it! Smart women, a brilliantly captured slice of the Roaring Twenties, and a swoony hero made *The Aviatrix* a superenjoyable page-turner."

—Evie Dunmore, *USA Today* bestselling author

"A love letter to the bravery and fighting spirit of the daredevil fly girls of the Roaring Twenties, *The Aviatrix* is a vibrant, feminist, and heartwarming romance with a playful, rebellious spirit and a sharp eye for historical detail. I adored it from start to finish!"

—Scarlett Peckham, *USA Today* bestselling author

Velocity

of a

Secret

OTHER TITLES BY VIOLET MARSH

The Aviatrix

Velocity of a Secret

VIOLET MARSH

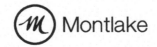

Published by Montlake, Seattle

www.apub.com

Amazon, the Amazon logo, and Montlake are trademarks of Amazon.com, Inc., or its affiliates.

ISBN-13: 9781542027632
ISBN-10: 1542027632

Cover design by Caroline Teagle Johnson

Printed in the United States of America

To my sister, Deeann Polakovsky, PA-C, who worked as an EMT during her college years; to all those who have served their communities as EMTs and paramedics; and to all the military medics, stretcher-bearers, ambulance drivers, and similar volunteers who have provided aid in times of conflict

Prologue

The pinkish glow of dawn brought danger, not hope.

American Rose Van Etten wasn't following protocol as she and her converted Model T hurtled through the salmon and golden hues. Dawn meant the return of enemy aircraft and a renewed intensity of shelling. Yesterday's casualties had been high—horribly high even for this terrible war. Rose still had patients—or blessés, as her French military superiors called them—at the poste de secours. Not only had the small field dressing station been overwhelmed, but it was equipped to handle only bandaging and the crudest, most rudimentary forms of triage. Severely wounded French infantrymen, or poilus, needed to be moved to a hospital, and she was their only means of transport.

Rose heard the angry roar of the airplane first. Energy slammed into her exhausted body—the only emotion that seemed to break through her husk of numbness. Leaning over the steering wheel, she glanced upward into the brilliantly colored sky. In the swirl of gilded coral, she spied a flash of true red: the nose of a Fokker flown by a pilot in the elite and deadly Jagdgeschwader I—the Flying Circus.

The scout was out hunting, and she was the prey.

Rose didn't have time to allow dread to freeze her like a cottontail. Instead, her muscles tensed like a jackrabbit's, and she prepared for the mad dash to the relative safety of the poste de secours.

The first bullets hit the ground to the left of Rose's Ford. Dirt struck her shoulder and rained against her tilted metal helmet. She swung to the right, thankful she was driving the nimble Tin Lizzie rather than the bulkier GMCs, Rovers, or Rolls-Royces. Her heart pumping like an overworked piston, Rose darted back to the left, knowing the airman would expect her to continue right.

She refused to contemplate her demise—or perhaps she'd just stopped considering it after being steeped in death for years. Rose didn't think about living either—at least not really. All that was inside her was the bare instinct for survival, a need that even years of war couldn't quash.

Her pursuer strafed the ground to Rose's right. Loud metallic pops slammed against her eardrums as bullets shredded the passenger side. Fortunately, none appeared to strike the engine, and the trusty Ford kept on roaring.

Rose could see the entrance to the underground poste de secours now, but so could the German scout. He knew where she planned on heading . . . or he thought he did.

Rose yanked the wheel, bringing the vehicle around in a tight turn. Her right tires lifted and then landed with a thud she felt in her chest. She yanked down the throttle, jammed the T into high gear, and shot forward like a seemingly scared, confused bunny. If the pilot had recognized her as female, all the better for her ploy.

She kept in a straight line, providing a tempting target in the desolate landscape marked only by burnt tree stumps and cratered ground. As soon as the Fokker banked and swooped in her direction, she yanked the hand brake, bringing the car to a skidding stop. A moment later, she jammed her foot on the Tin Lizzie's reverse pedal and shot backward. Rose hit a few shell-blasted divots, but she made fast progress.

By the time the scout realized what she'd done, Rose had already made it into the protected area where they kept the vehicles. Slumping back against her seat, she allowed one shaky intake of air. Just one. It wouldn't do to acknowledge what had just happened.

If Rose did, she might crumble and never collect the pieces—a sad Humpty-Dumpty brought down not by a fall but by endless tiny fractures.

Rose reached for the case where she kept her cigarettes, then flipped over the latch and cursed. She'd smoked her last ration during the endless night as she'd traveled back and forth on the road crammed with supply wagons, troops, and other ambulances. At a loss for what to do with her right hand, which normally held the roll of tobacco, she drummed her fingers against the steering wheel as she waited for the pilot to leave in search of more exciting targets.

There was a chance she knew him—this unseen German bent on extinguishing her. She had hobnobbed with many of Europe's elites before the war when she'd competed in motorcar races. Closed-circuit ones, road courses, hill climbs—she'd done them all. Perhaps she had even raced against the scout during the Herkomer Trials. Back then they would have been competitors but not enemies. They could very well have been comrades and shared a laugh. She might have even drunk a beer with him as she tried to stave off the hollowness inside her.

But then the war had come—the purposeless, endless war, which she'd joined as a relief volunteer in a misguided attempt to find meaning in her own life. But there was no *meaning* here. Just death and destruction and unspeakable violence.

Here Rose was—nearly dying to save men who might have already died from their wounds. No matter how many poilus she brought to hospitals or train stations or ports for further transport, there were still more wounded, broken souls waiting to be reshuffled among the wards of France and England.

Attempting to shake off the dismal thoughts with a roll of her shoulders, Rose shifted her body and stepped from the Ford. The pilot was likely gone, and she could make it to the poste de secours.

Alert for the sound of the airplane's engine, she cautiously stuck her head outside the shelter. The sky had lightened even more, making a drive back to the hospital impossible until the evening. She could see the grayish-brown lumps of the enemy observation balloons lurking in the blue sky like ugly behemoths ready to bring the troubles of Job upon them. Everything, though, seemed relatively quiet, so she began her dash to the field station.

The first shell hit when Rose was halfway to the poste de secours. The impact reverberated through her body, and she swore her ribs clattered together like Parcheesi dice. When the second shell sent dirt spraying all over her, a fierce need to survive surged forth, forcing her muscles into action. Holding on to her helmet, she pounded toward the safety of the underground field dressing station. Mud from yesterday's rain splashed over her uniform, and her foot slipped. Just as she was about to topple over, the door in front of her flew open, and a soldier pulled her roughly inside.

"There were to be no more ambulance runs until tonight," the man scolded in French. "Are you mad, mademoiselle?"

Before the war, Rose would have blithely said *oui*. She'd always pursued peril for the fun of it, and she'd loved every minute . . . until she hadn't.

"Je ne sais pas." Rose shrugged as she told the man the truth. She really didn't know anymore.

The dressing station was small, but she managed to find an out-of-the-way corner near one of the unconscious blessés swathed in bandages. Slumping onto the floor, she glanced around the small space filled with the smell of unwashed bodies, infected wounds, and blood.

"Why are any of us in this mess?" Rose muttered in English as she stared unseeingly before her.

"American?" The shaky, hoarse word came from the man on the cot nearest to her. White strips of material covered nearly every inch of him, and Rose could see evidence of blood, both fresh and dried, that had seeped through the wrappings. She did not know which stunned her more: that the severely wounded man had managed to talk or that he spoke with an upper-class British accent.

But those things did not matter, not when the man lay so close to death. Rose jumped to her feet, forgetting her own weariness.

"Do you need anything?" she asked. "Should I get someone? A doctor? I'm just the ambulance driver."

"You could . . . get me . . . out of here . . ." The man visibly had trouble mustering enough strength and air to speak.

"I can drive you to an evacuation hospital tonight," Rose promised, "but I can't in the daylight. It's too dangerous."

"I . . . don't . . . want . . . there. Take me to . . . German territory . . . beyond No Man's Land." The words fell jerkily from his parched lips.

Only one of his eyes was visible, but it was bright blue, filled with pain yet lucid. It was obvious that the man knew Rose couldn't take him where he wanted to go, but part of him meant the words all the same.

"What's over the line for you?" Rose asked as she reached for a sponge in a glass of water. Like she'd seen the nurses do a thousand times, she pressed it to his mouth. His tongue darted out as he sucked the moisture.

He swallowed and then answered, "What you were . . . looking . . . for . . . just now."

He gave a ghost of a grin. Rose could not make out the Brit's features, but she suspected he'd been a handsome man.

"What *I* was looking for?" she asked, confused.

"Purpose . . . a reason."

How had this man, so wrapped up in his own pain, noticed hers? It was as if he had reached inside her mind and neatly plucked out her thoughts. But then again, weren't they all searching for some lasting good or even just a simple truth in all this devastation?

"And what purpose is beyond No Man's Land?"

"Ah." The man started to chuckle, but the sound ended in a groan and a wince. "I trusted . . . the . . . wrong person with . . . that knowledge . . . it's what got . . . me . . . here."

"Oh," Rose said, both intrigued and a bit disappointed that he hadn't explained why he *was* here—a highborn British man in a French section of trenches.

"I thought . . . fighting . . . was . . . for glory . . . but it's for . . . them."

"Them?" Rose asked.

"Those . . ." The man paused and then swallowed. "Those . . . we let . . . into our hearts."

"For lovers?"

"Loved . . . ones," he corrected.

Loved ones. Two words, so simple yet so complicated. Who did Rose count as her loved ones? Who would she brave No Man's Land for? And who would face it for her? Mother and Daddy would send someone to save her, but they wouldn't set a foot in there themselves.

"Time for me to check your bandages." One of the weary volunteers broke into the conversation and fairly pushed Rose aside to reach the wounded man.

Rose instantly moved back, not wishing to interfere with the duties of those staffing the poste de secours. By the time the member of the medical staff had finished assisting the British soldier, the man had fainted from either pain, exhaustion, or loss of blood. He did not awaken for the rest of the day, but as twilight deepened into darkness, Rose was informed that he would be one of the two patients whom she was to transport to the hospital on her first run.

As a stretcher-bearer loaded the British man into the back of her ambulance, Rose leaned close to him. "I'll get you to the surgeon, and he'll see to it that you're patched up. Then you can finish your mission, whatever it is."

The corners of the man's mouth tried to lift into a smile, but he could not quite manage it. The day's wait had cost him dearly, and they both knew it. It was likely he would not survive the ride.

A leaden feeling bore down on Rose and seemed to push every fiber of her into the muck as she walked toward the driver's door. Climbing inside, she thought of the man's one blue eye—so intense with light, with energy, with *determination*.

No, she would not allow this man's purpose to die. Not on her watch.

Chapter 1

"I never would have thought I'd find Aphrodite on a quiet balcony instead of in the center of the party—especially during her own shindig."

At the sound of her best friend's voice, Rose didn't turn her gaze from the darkening surf, but she did allow a wry, self-effacing smile to grace her lips. "I've always rather thought myself a female Dionysus. Toying with mortal love is dull. I'd much rather drink and be merry."

At least she used to.

"Is that who you're dressed as, then?" Myrtle assumed a position next to Rose on the balustrade and fingered the white gossamer sleeve of Rose's costume.

The light chiffon fabric floated about Rose's body, so different from the stiff fabric of her khaki uniform. Except for the last few years, she'd lived most of her life in gowns like this—silky confections that fluttered luxuriously against her skin. But now they felt . . . wrong. Too loose. Too airy. And just not *right*.

"Nike." Rose answered her friend's question about whom she was pretending to be for the fancy dress ball.

"Ahh." Myrtle dropped the fabric. "The goddess of victory. Fitting, considering we're celebrating the German surrender."

"Yes, fitting," Rose repeated rather hollowly as she rolled her unlit cigarette between her fingers. "Although technically it is just a cease-fire. Real peace has not been declared."

It was hard for Rose to believe that all the death, all the violence, all the *devastation*, had ended, truly ended. She wondered if it ever would in her mind. She'd gone to the war searching for some type of meaning but had returned emptier than ever. What had she accomplished? What had any of them? Here she was, back where she'd started, at another glittery, gilded party. She'd thrown it *herself* in another vain and this time foolish attempt to fill her emptiness—as if a celebration of victory would make all the suffering *mean* something. Instead it just placed a magnifying glass on the futility of it all.

Myrtle gave Rose's shoulder a friendly nudge as they both leaned on the balustrade and watched the Atlantic Ocean crash against the broad white sands spread before them. "Imagine you being the one to argue semantics instead of me."

"They say war changes a person." Rose lifted the Lucky Strike to her mouth and closed her lips around it. She wanted to light it, but her lungs wouldn't take the smoke. She'd start hacking like a sick goose. Mustard gas and a bad bout of influenza tended to leave a woman like that.

"It does," Myrtle said quietly. "So it does."

Rose was glad that her old college chum didn't pry for details. She was the only one of Rose's acquaintances who didn't. Tonight had made that especially apparent when every single one of her guests had stopped her and begged for stories about her time "Over There."

There was the ubiquitous "Was the shelling as dreadful as they say, darling?"

Why, yes. Would you wish to know the details of exactly what it can do to a person's body? Because I can tell you, Mrs. Smith. Is that what you wish to hear as you sip champagne in your flouncy Bo Peep costume and make eyes at the widower Mr. Jones? Should I tell you of the deaths

I witnessed—the terrible sacrifices that allow us to continue in our own blithe folly?

And then another favorite question, especially from those of the male sex: "Is it true that you were one of the few women who drove to the front line? It must have been absolutely ghastly for you. Why the Belgians and French would allow a gal that close to the fighting is beyond understanding. No Man's Land is no place for the delicate sensibilities of women."

And you believe that dressing up as George Washington and donning a cheap white wig makes you fit to comment on military strategy? You know little, Mr. Buckley. I went only as far as the poste de secours, the field dressing stations closest to the fighting. I was never in No Man's Land. And there's a reason they call it that. It's no place for anybody—woman or man. Yet soldiers did brave it, but here we are claiming victory in luxury.

But Rose, the society darling with a reputation for a wicked tongue, had given none of those flippant answers, for she did not wish to cheapen the sacrifices and deaths of so many just to shock those who would never understand.

She'd thrown this party to forget, but it had instead forced her to remember. Rose had even donned the literal garments of victory as if she could convince herself it was all true and that she had the *right* to feel a sense of accomplishment. But she was as silly as her own guests, thinking a pantomime had anything to do with patriotism or reality. Her costume just exposed her fraud. She hadn't even been on the Western Front for the last few months but had watched the end of the hostilities as a faraway observer in Florida.

Rose sucked on her cig but not enough for the tobacco to fall into her mouth. She hated the taste of it—unlike the bitter smoke. After weeks of an illness that had brought her home from France, she no longer missed the effects of the vice but merely yearned for the physical act. Rose needed the excuse to have something in her hands, something to distract her, something to wave about or to angrily stab. She'd be crushing the butt against the balustrade now if she could.

"It was a mistake, throwing this party," Rose said, whether to herself or to Myrtle, she didn't know.

Myrtle gave a sympathetic sigh as she turned away from the ocean.

"Everyone expected it of you," Myrtle pointed out. "Perhaps even you. It is natural for you to want to return to your old routines, your old life."

What kind of frivolous person had Rose been that her old everyday habits involved throwing massive parties on a regular basis?

"Belle of the Ball, Hostess of Hilarity, Denizen of Drama, Motoriste of Mayhem." Rose didn't know why her voice sounded so bitter when she used to love those nicknames.

After Rose had fulfilled her original time commitment to the French Army, she'd stayed despite the hopelessness. Like they all had. To fight a war, despite no one really, truly understanding why they were there in the first place.

"You've still managed to hold the masquerade of the year despite just leaving your sickbed last week," Myrtle said. Her blue eyes softened before she spoke again. "We were really afraid we were going to lose you."

Rose pulled the cigarette from her mouth. Staring down at the now-floppy butt, she wished she could feel *something* about her near death from the endless, relentless fever. Yet she did not. Not joy at her recovery nor fear at what could have been.

Until yesterday, Rose had been planning on returning to France. After all, her parents' staff were the ones who had arranged for her to be transferred back to the States in the first place when she'd been out of her mind with delirium from fever. If her parents had bothered to ask her, she would have said that she wanted to stay. Yet they hadn't, just as they hadn't spent long at her bedside. They'd absently taken care of her needs in the way that they'd seen fit, not realizing that once again they'd set her adrift.

Rose didn't want just material comfort, but she didn't know what she *did* desire. Returning to her old life wouldn't grant her peace. And with the cease-fire just declared, she no longer had any plans, no chance at finding direction.

Again.

She opened her beaded evening bag and retrieved her cigarette case. After withdrawing another tobacco-filled roll, she'd just started to lift it to her lips when the sky exploded.

Charged energy shot through Rose's body as she prepared to dodge shells and to protect the blessés she transported. Her organs seemed to reverberate with the boom, and she swore she could hear pebbles and dirt pinging against her steel helmet. Her hands clutched the wheel of her Tin Lizzie, but the Lucky Strike crumpled against her palm instead, dragging Rose back to reality. Breathing deeply, she watched as red and blue sparks drifted down from the now-dark sky.

Fireworks. Not German shells. Fireworks.

Trying to calm the nervous energy charging through her body and turning her limbs into jelly, Rose exhaled as a clamor arose behind her. She turned her head slowly like a sleepwalker and distantly watched through a jittery haze as a parade of Betsy Rosses, Abraham Lincolns, Patrick Henrys, Dolley Madisons, shepherdesses, and swashbucklers invaded her formerly quiet sanctuary. Annoyed, she began to swing her attention back to the inky sea. But just then another boom sounded, and one of the Betsy Rosses let out a shrill cry of excitement.

Suddenly Rose was no longer on the veranda of her parents' sprawling beach house in Daytona, Florida, but on a shell-blasted road in France.

The boom of a shell smashed through the endless growl of traffic, followed by the hideous scream of the injured horse. Rose leaned closer to the windshield of her Model T, trying to find a space to squeeze the ambulance through the dark shadows shifting amorphously before her. She needed to find an opening. The French poilu and the British soldier in the back of her Tin Lizzie would not survive much longer without a surgeon. But the road before her was crowded with supply wagons, troops of all nationalities, and French refugees. Even with the snarl of desperate war traffic, she could not risk turning on the headlamps, not this close to the front lines. It would make her and the two patients targets for the Germans.

Another shell exploded, so close that the concussive force slammed Rose's faithful Ford to the right. She jerked the wheel left just as more inhuman cries of wounded equines surrounded her. A dark shadow was her only warning before hooves struck the left side of the ambulance. She tried to swerve, but it was too late. The draft horse's powerful kick slammed the converted vehicle to the side. Helpless to stop the Model T from listing, Rose felt the tires on the left side leave the bumpy excuse for a road.

Fragments of fear serrated her. Both her patients were near death, and she did not know if they could survive a jarring tumble.

The Tin Lizzie smashed into a ditch. Rose's shoulder took most of the impact. She hissed in pain, praying the machine would stop sliding. With another bump, the ambulance came to a rest, still on its side.

Rose adjusted her metal helmet as she crawled from where she'd been slammed against the passenger door. She heard a low moan coming from the back. Scrambling through the overturned vehicle, she managed to reach her patients. The first man she touched felt cold . . . too cold. The poor blessé had probably died shortly after they'd left the poste de secours. Each loss still had the power to twist around her heart like a relentless, ever-present snake.

The weak groan came again, and an alien sense of hope shot through Rose. The Englishman was still alive! Rose quickly moved toward the sound, her heart pumping against the constrictive band surrounding the abused muscle.

In the darkness, a hand grabbed hers. The grip on her fingers was feeble yet unbreakable.

"Spies. You. Must. Stop. Them. Now."

"Spies?" Rose felt like she'd just plunged beneath the surface of a frozen lake. "Is that what your mission was? To stop a plot against the Allies?"

"Aye." There was a surprising hint of the Isles in his polished upper-crust accent now. *"But. No. Time. To. Explain. All. Written. Down."*

Her patient's voice had grown even raspier, as if he were pushing out the words by sheer effort alone, and perhaps he was. Even more concerning, his breathing had devolved into a labored wheezing—a sound Rose recognized all too readily. She did not reassure the man, tell him that he would be fine. She had given him enough false promises already. He would not survive the trip to the hospital as she'd sworn to him.

This gentleman and she both knew the truth. He was dying.

"Give. Him. A. Message. He'll . . . help."

"Who is 'he'?" Rose asked, hearing this determined fellow's desperation. Once again, she'd failed to save a patient, and the bloody, pointless war had won.

The man did not seem to hear her. *"Talk. Only. To. Him. Spies. Everywhere. Active. Everywhere."*

The chill inside Rose turned into a ferocious windstorm. She'd heard many ravings of the blessés. Many had thought her their wife, their sweetheart, their mother, or even the enemy. She had held the hand of more than one dying man as she'd comforted him in French.

But this.

This was different.

The British soldier was more lucid.

More urgent.

More impassioned.

He had a mission, a purpose. And he was using his last breath to see that someone completed it, even if he himself could not.

But his death didn't mean this man's quest would be snuffed out as well. Rose would see it through. That was a promise she could swear to fulfill.

"Who are these foreign agents? Is this why you are wearing the uniform of a poilu?" She did not want to waste the man's precious remaining time, but if he was speaking even a bit of truth, she needed more information.

"Read. My. Notes. Find. Him. Go. To. Hamar . . ." *The patient's voice trailed off at the end.*

"Hammer?" Rose inquired.

The man's gasps became harsher, and Rose struggled to hear his next words. They sounded like a woman's name. Tamsin? Tammy? With a last name of . . . Morris? Norris?

"Tamsin Morris?" Rose asked, but once again the man did not seem to register her question. His last reserves appeared to be channeled into guiding Rose's hand to his neck. His fingers trembled as he pressed her palm against something cool and metal. A key?

"Unlocks. Notes. Give . . ." The man's voice stuttered, and he made a visible effort to swallow, the air seeming to jangle inside his chest, leaking from places where it shouldn't be escaping. "Him."

"This is the key to where you've locked up your records on the spies?" Rose spoke rapidly, trying to make sure she understood the instruction before it was too late. "And you want me to give him the key?"

"Aye." Again, that tease of a brogue.

"Who?" she asked urgently.

The man's fingers began to loosen around hers, but she kept her hand pressed against the key, sensing it would give him comfort.

"Who?" she repeated, desperate now.

His exhale shook his body, his next words sounding like the rustle of wind through dry leaves.

"Tell. Him. I'm. Sorry."

Then he was gone like so many others before. And she was left with the emptiness and the hopelessness of another soul destroyed before their time. But his words . . . they haunted Rose.

"Rose, dear heart, Rose?"

She blinked at the sound of Myrtle's voice, quiet and concerned.

With a jolt, the present returned, like a painted stage backdrop had been unfurled. Gasping a bit, Rose swiveled her head, finding herself in a secluded corner of the veranda. The rest of the partygoers clung to the railing, their wonder-filled faces lifted toward the fireworks display.

"Do you need help over there?" Mrs. Phillips asked in a booming voice. "I can get Dr. Stevens. He's here with his wife."

"No, we're fine." Myrtle waved cheerily to the woman. "It was just too much air for Rose out by the balustrade."

"Of course." Mrs. Phillips nodded, sending her white cartoonish mobcap bobbing. "Poor lamb."

Rose—whose heart was still knocking like an engine with a misaligned distributor—twisted her face at the epithet. But she did not protest. If she did, Mrs. Phillips might see past Myrtle's fib. The woman had a keen eye and an even keener tongue for gossip. Rose did not need it blabbed about that she was subject to feminine attacks of nerves— even if she *had* been jumpy ever since her return.

Thankfully, the fireworks display distracted the kindhearted but nosy busybody. As soon as Mrs. Phillips's back was turned, Rose sank against the coquina concrete walls of her parents' Spanish Revival mansion. The coolness of the facade sank into her, and her legs stopped tingling. Taking another breath to calm her pumping blood, Rose realized she was clutching the key around her neck—Viscount Barbury's key.

She'd had to call upon her famous father's connections to learn the identity of the man who'd died that night in her ambulance. He'd been a lieutenant in the British Army and the heir apparent to an earldom. No one could, or at least *would*, explain why he had been in No Man's Land in a French rather than British sector.

Rose had just learned his name when she'd fallen ill herself. She still had no idea who the mysterious "he" was, what "hammer" meant, how Tamsin Morris was connected, or whether the wounded noble had been delusional.

But now the war itself was over and, with it, the urgency to complete Viscount Barbury's mission. Rose had, it appeared, broken her second promise to him after all.

Releasing Barbury's key, Rose tried to regulate her breath. This was not the first time that she'd found herself palpably reliving the shelling, and she very much feared it would not be the last.

"Thank you," she murmured to Myrtle, knowing that her friend had dragged her into the shadows to protect her from wagging tongues. Myrtle was one of the few who knew about Rose's particular ailment. Some of her parents' staff had witnessed her retreat into the past, of course. Rose was certain they had not told her mother. If they had, Verity Van Etten would have fluttered into Rose's sickroom, all dramatic tears and protestations of how her own nerves could not handle her only child's illness. Everyone but Mother needed to be the strong one, the healthy one, the steady one.

Rose supposed the servants would have confided in her father. He abided no secret keeping from his employees. Rose had also noted that the number of nurses attending her had multiplied, and more specialists had arrived with increasingly impressive degrees. Yet her father himself had not visited her more than a handful of times. There were charities to oversee, hotels to run, and investments to monitor.

But Myrtle had been there, taking a sabbatical from her position as a professor of archaeology to push and prod Rose into fighting back against the illness racking her body. Her old college chum had also helped Rose break through those moments when the war seemed to drag her back to the pitted roadways of the Western Front.

"I need to take the Stutz out," Rose rasped. Fast driving used to be her favorite escape. Before the war, she'd enjoyed whiskey, cigarettes, and handsome men, but she'd *loved* racing. Even when everything else had felt meaningless in her gilded life, she could always feel a spark of something *more* as she sped along, the wind buffeting her.

Myrtle peered at her in concern. "Are you certain that is a good idea tonight?"

Rose allowed very few people to question her readiness to take the wheel, but luckily for Myrtle's sake, she was one of them. Instead of a withering retort, Rose just rolled her shoulders and opened and closed her hands to chase away the last of the tingling remnants of sensation.

"It is what I need, M," Rose said softly. But would a fast drive provide even a modicum of relief? Or would a race to nowhere prove as aimless as it ultimately was?

She sorely hoped not, as it was her only escape left.

⟫⟪

The Stutz Bearcat zipped across the wide stretch of beach. The pale silvery light reflected off the white sands, and Rose felt like she was driving on a moonbeam. Her headlamps provided more illumination as she sallied forth through the blankness. With the wind stirred up by her charging sports car, she couldn't hear the ocean. If she looked to the left, she could see the faint sparkle of the waves. If she glanced to the right, she might catch the faintest outline of towering cabbage palms.

But Rose maintained her focus on the white-gray-and-black nothingness unraveling before her. This stretch of beach was private, and she risked no one but herself in this mad midnight dash. She attempted a half-hearted battle cry. Hoping a second would turn into a real one, she forced more sound from her lungs. Although she did not experience the halcyon rush of her old racing days, some of the cobwebs growing inside her soul seemed to sway, as if preparing to blow away. Rose had always felt the most alive when hurtling at breakneck speeds.

Finally her heart began to pound, not from rootless fear but from excitement. In the blankness, Rose found a modicum of solace—not peace but a temporary balm. Trying out a third manufactured whoop, she spun the wheel and made a broad turn, heading back in the direction she'd come.

The muscles in Rose's back had just begun to loosen when the headlamps revealed a stack of beach chairs. Her tendons immediately retightened. It made no sense for the furniture to be in the center of the sand. She'd whizzed through this stretch of shoreline only minutes before. Swerving to avoid the collision, she stomped on the brake pedal.

But nothing happened.

Desperately, Rose yanked back on the hand brake lever.

Still nothing.

Neither the skill of the Bearcat's designers nor her own agility as a driver was a match for the physics of loose sand. The tires on the right side of the Stutz dug in, and the left lifted into the air. Rose's body shot skyward.

Fear lacerated Rose, but the raw panic slid into an instinct to survive, just like on the Front. She tucked her body, protecting her head from impact. Although she attempted to roll when she hit the sand, her back slammed into the ground with such a terrific force the displaced grit landed on her stomach. The air was expelled from her body in a painful whoosh.

This wasn't the first time she'd been launched from an auto, but nothing could prepare a person for having the wind so efficiently knocked from them. The helplessness was worse than the pain. She was truly trapped now—both internally and externally. And she was damned tired of being immobilized.

"Bloody hell!"

Rose wanted to turn her head at the words spoken with a British accent, but she couldn't manage it. She didn't want anyone to see her sprawled on the ground, especially one of her guests. Frantically, she tried to force air into her body even as her lungs protested. The low-key tension that had seemed to simmer inside her since the war burst into full-scale panic.

"I hope we didn't kill her before we find out what she knows," the voice added.

Kill her? Intense, concentrated horror bored through Rose, but she remained powerless to react.

"We don't even know how much Barbury had figured out, let alone if he blabbed anything." This new speaker sounded almost American, but the words were tinged with an accent . . . a *German* accent.

Sharp shards of alarm shredded Rose at the mention of the viscount. Spies. These men were *spies*.

The British noble hadn't been lying about uncovering espionage. Somehow, these German agents had tracked *her* down—the last person to see Barbury alive. If they had exerted this much trouble to tie up a single potential loose end, she had no illusions about their plans for her. She was a thread to be snipped and discarded.

Rose tried to draw in air, but her lungs remained painfully shut. Without them functioning, she could do *nothing* to protect herself. She couldn't even lift her head.

Desperation set in.

"I told you that wrecking her auto was a dangerous scheme. Suppose they've heard the crash back at the house? We should have erected the barricade farther away."

Oxygen. She *needed* it now. Panic clawed her, and her brain began to buzz. But her diaphragm remained stubbornly and agonizingly frozen.

"I've been watching her for weeks. I know how these people think."

"If she knows too much, it could ruin everything. Every day that treaty discussions continue in Versailles is a day closer to the end of hope."

The viscount's words blazed into her mind.

Talk. Only. To. Him. Spies. Everywhere. Active everywhere.

The spy ring was still in operation! The knowledge ripped through Rose.

She forced air into her abused lungs. It burned and ached like hell, but she'd faced worse. When she had enough breath, she screamed— sharp, loud, and chilling.

"Bloody hell. I thought she was unconscious!"

Ignoring the protests of her battered body, Rose rolled into a crouching position. Frantically, she scanned the moonlit beach, searching for deadly shadows. She saw nothing but her wrecked Bearcat and shimmering white sands. Forcing her shaking muscles to cooperate, she stayed low and slunk to the overturned vehicle. Peeking over one of the tires, she spied two dark shapes about fifteen yards away. One, to her increasing horror, looked particularly massive and brutish.

With trembling fingers, she reached inside the Stutz for her reticule. It took her two attempts to undo the latch, but she managed to pull out the trench knife that a grateful French soldier had given her after she'd driven him to safety. Forcing her hands to steady, she sliced through the straps on her silver evening shoes, the blade nicking one of her ankles. Ignoring the burn, she tossed the pumps but kept her purse.

Drawing in another agonizing breath, Rose took off in her stocking feet through the sand. The men gave a shout, and her skin prickled at their closeness. Not risking a glance over her shoulder, she dropped the knife into her beaded evening bag and searched for her gun. Instead of her snub-nose British Bull Dog revolver, her fingers found the blade again. She sliced her middle finger but not enough to slow her down. It wasn't easy searching the tight opening of the reticule as her feet pounded over the uneven sand, but finally she felt the cool, cylindrical metal of the barrel.

After pulling out the weapon, she started to cock it, but her uneven gait almost caused her to drop it. Cursing now, she pulled back the hammer with her thumb. She might have bought the little revolver as a lark to scandalize her mother, but Myrtle's relatives had taught Rose how to shoot.

Before Rose could turn and fire at her pursuers, though, she heard Myrtle shout her name. A male voice followed and then another. Rose's original bloodcurdling scream must have been heard, perhaps even the crash too. A concentrated beam of a flashlight broke through the silvery night.

Thank goodness for Myrtle and her taste for expensive, newfangled gadgets.

Rose glanced backward. The shadowy figures had gained on her, but they'd stopped now, their bodies positioned away from the bobbing glow. Clearly, they did not wish to be seen. Rose hoped they would decide that being caught was riskier than letting her go. They had admitted they had no idea if she knew *anything*.

Which she didn't. At least not much.

But she was certainly going to find out everything now.

The cries of the partygoers grew louder, and the beam of light spread around Rose's feet. The illumination seemed to prod the attackers into a decision. They stopped their pursuit and melted into the darkness, as if they'd never existed.

Rose didn't stop her mad dash. Luckily the loose style of her Greek-toga-inspired garment allowed her to employ her full stride. Soon she could make out the shapes of new figures—familiar ones, *safe* ones. The chief of police, dressed as a Roman centurion, reached her first. He was a tall, imposing man, his barrel-like chest puffed out. The fake gold helmet with its garish plumes somehow suited him.

"Two men," Rose gasped out as she gestured behind her. "Spies. One of them huge, the other of average build." She couldn't describe them beyond that, as their facial features had been shrouded in darkness.

At her third word, the chief's footsteps faltered. But he did not pause. The tinfoil that he'd used on his legs to simulate leg armor flashed in the moonlight as he pounded down the beach.

"Are you okay?" Myrtle asked, throwing her arms around Rose. "What happened?"

"There were two attackers. They tampered with my Bearcat." Rose gave her friend a brief embrace before she sank to the ground, finally allowing herself to feel the aches spreading over her body.

Thank goodness her shout had brought reinforcements. Rose had always had a knack for theatrical screams—a skill she'd previously put to use only during boarding school pageants and house party performances. She'd never thought that one day her ability to create earsplitting shrieks would save her life.

Her family physician knelt down next to her. His long and obviously fake beard brushed against Rose's bare arm. Dressed as Rip Van Winkle, the man wore tattered clothes and a crumpled tricorn hat.

"Did your car crash, Miss Van Etten?" Dr. Stevens asked. "We heard an odd sort of thud during a lull in the fireworks."

Not one to show weakness, Rose did as she'd done since she was a little girl trying to please her parents, who had no tolerance for tears or pouts: she hid her fear and pain beneath blitheness.

"The Stutz did crash, but I'm unharmed except for some bumps, bruises, and minor cuts. Sand is much more forgiving than gravel." She shook back the bangs that had fallen in her eyes. She'd been one of the first society ladies to lop off her hair. She'd done it as a lark and to stir up some minor scandal, but it had proved useful on the Front, especially given some of the spartan living conditions she'd faced.

"I still should check you over, my dear." Dr. Stevens's voice had taken on that kindly but undeniably stern tone that men liked to employ upon "headstrong" women. Rose had never done well with stern.

"No need." Rose forced herself to pop up from the ground and stretch her painted lips into a wide, carefree grin. "I'm as right as rain."

"Are you certain?" Myrtle asked.

"Nothing I haven't experienced before," Rose said, "except for the spies. *That* was novel."

"Spies?" Dr. Stevens asked, his fuzzy gray eyebrows pulling downward in concern . . . but not the kind of worry one would normally express after an announcement that foreign agents were nearby. "Are you experiencing another nervous upset, my dear?"

A nervous upset. What a domestic, prosaic way to describe the piercingly sharp memories that would slice through her consciousness without warning.

Before Rose could respond, the police chief returned, huffing a bit. His helmet listed to the right, and a piece of his leg armor had come loose, making a crinkling sound when he walked. Aside from looking disheveled from his run, he thankfully did not appear harmed.

"Did you encounter them?" Rose asked Chief Montgomery.

"The, er, *spies?*" The man's mustache twitched on the last word.

Rose narrowed her eyes, frustrated anger replacing her shield of blitheness. "Yes, the spies. The men who laid an ambush for me."

Chief Montgomery exchanged a speaking look with Dr. Stevens over Rose's head.

"I did not see anyone." The chief spoke gently, as if mere words could break her.

"What about footprints?" Rose asked between gritted teeth. "How many sets were there?"

"How fast were you driving?" The policeman's tone softened even more, making it clear he did not regard this as a true investigation. Very likely, he hadn't even believed her enough to search the scene for evidence. Rose wished she had on her tailored uniform instead of a flowy, fancy dress. Yet she doubted even that would improve her credibility to these men.

"Did you even attempt to corroborate my account?" Rose demanded. Just as it had been her duty to transport the wounded to safety, it was now her responsibility to stop these spies.

Again, the man's eyes flicked toward Dr. Stevens. The two men's gazes held, and frustration welled inside Rose. They *didn't* believe her.

Dr. Stevens gave her shoulder a pat that was supposed to be reassuring. It was not.

"Now, Miss Van Etten, you know how easily you can become overset—"

"*Overset!*" The word exploded from Rose like a shell from a dreaded Paris Gun. "My Bearcat was sabotaged, I was chased by two men speaking of conspiracy, and I am *overset!*"

Dr. Stevens glanced around nervously. Taking in the growing crowd of wide-eyed party guests, he started to steer Rose out of hearing distance. She shook off his hand, but she still followed. Although she generally didn't give a fig what high society or the press said about her, she was not about to have the gossips dissect her shell shock over canapés and cocktails.

When they had moved far enough away from the rest of the crowd, Dr. Stevens cupped her elbow again. "My dear, you have been . . . well . . . prone to . . . shall we say . . . flights of fancy. Your nerves have simply not recovered from your time in Europe."

The physician spoke as if she had simply been on a Grand Tour of the Continent.

"I believe the word you are searching for is *hallucination*," Rose said crisply. "And yes, my service on the Western Front has left its mark on me, but the attack was *no* mirage."

Chief Montgomery clasped her other arm, as if the two men were trying to prop her up like a fainting damsel in a dime novel.

"Miss, the war is over. Why would there be spies lurking about the beach in Florida?"

"Perhaps because I may know *something*." Rose crossed her arms—against both the men's words and the twinge of doubt they'd triggered.

It *had* been real. Hadn't it?

But she'd been so jumpy lately. It wasn't even just the war memories. Even an unexpected tread of footsteps could send her clambering to her feet, ready to fight.

"She has a point." Myrtle, who had been standing a few feet away, spoke quietly, and she stepped closer.

"My dear, you were an *ambulance* driver. You do not need to fear that the crippled German Reich has any interest in you. This is merely an offshoot of your hysteria—quite a common occurrence in a lady of delicate breeding such as yourself," Dr. Stevens said as he hoisted his gaslight lantern.

"It just doesn't make sense, now, does it, miss?" The chief spoke softly and earnestly. Neither of the men meant offense. Her family was too wealthy, too connected, and too powerful—and not just in Florida, where her father had practically single-handedly built the state's infrastructure. The men seemed to be trying to placate her, not insult her.

Rose, though, had listened to enough. She'd bottled up her words all evening, hoping to spare the good folks from the well of acid burning holes inside her. It was time to unleash her irritability.

She leveled her gaze first on Dr. Stevens in his Rip Van Winkle garb. "It makes as much sense as one would expect from a man who slept through the war." Then she turned toward the police chief dressed as a Roman centurion. "Or from a man who ran away from an empty tomb just when things were about to get interesting."

Wishing that she felt as certain as her words sounded, Rose marched away toward the house, her face once again turned to the sea. She grabbed a cig from her ever-handy reticule and stuck it into her mouth and sucked on it as she stared out at the pinpricks of light dotting the sky.

"If it's any consolation, I believe you." Myrtle caught up to her, matching her angry strides.

"It's more than a consolation," Rose said, taking the paper tube of tobacco from her mouth and walking it through her fingers as she tried to calm the clawing frustration. Lately it seemed that if she wasn't trying to contain her anxiousness, she was battling back crankiness.

"Rose, you always accomplish the impossible. You're capable of convincing the right people."

Myrtle wasn't entirely wrong, but she wasn't completely right either. Rose didn't persuade people. Her father did. Politicians, businessmen, leaders—they all listened to the titan of industry—or, at the very least, to the amount of wealth and influence he had amassed. And Daddy . . . well, Daddy would pull any strings to mollify his "hysterical" daughter, even if he thought her utterly mad. And sometimes she feared that she was. Just a little.

Momentarily stopping, Rose bent down and plucked a shell from the sand. After standing back up, she heaved it out to sea. She waited until the waves swallowed up the flash of white before she spoke. "Why do you believe that this wasn't another one of my hallucinations?"

"Did it feel like one?" Myrtle queried softly.

"No," Rose admitted as she remembered the pain of landing on her back, the air leaving her body. "It felt real."

"Then that's enough for me."

"Perhaps it was best that the men didn't believe me," Rose said.

"How so?"

Lord Barbury's voice echoed through Rose's mind. *Talk. Only. To. Him. Spies. Everywhere. Active everywhere.* The words seemed prophetic now . . . or was that only because they'd just inspired her latest episode of shell shock?

"My attackers mentioned the name of one of my last patients— an English nobleman who spoke of an extensive network of foreign agents."

"Surely you don't believe that the local doctor and the police chief are part of the conspiracy?" For the first time, Myrtle's voice held a hint of skepticism—not that Rose blamed her on this point.

"Heavens no, but if I look into Lord Barbury's claim, I need to be careful about what hornet's nest I poke." Rose started walking again, as if the momentum would somehow give her a sense of direction. "If what the viscount said was true and I confide in the wrong person, whatever actual evidence there is could disappear."

"Are you planning on tracking down a spy ring? By yourself?" Myrtle huffed a little as Rose set a punishing pace toward the east end of her parents' mansion, where the family wing was.

"I . . . I believe I am." Rose paused at the steps that led to a private veranda outside her bedroom.

Myrtle inclined her head toward Rose's room. "Shall we head inside so no one can overhear?"

Rose nodded and opened the french doors to a small sitting area attached to the bedchamber. Despite the rather heavy-looking armor that composed her Joan of Arc costume, Myrtle sank down onto the settee and patted a spot next to her.

Rose joined her friend. After neatly arranging her Grecian-inspired dress, she launched into how she'd first met the viscount when she had been sheltering in the poste de secours. Myrtle, who normally asked a thousand penetrating questions, remained silent as Rose recounted what had happened.

"I only found out the viscount's identity right before I fell ill. I wasn't sure how much of the truth he'd spoken . . . until tonight," she concluded.

"What do you plan to do next? You've just had an attempt on your life!" Myrtle asked, worry lacing her normally collected tone.

"Well, one botched abduction at least—that I may or may not have imagined," Rose corrected, refusing to allow shadowy figures to terrify her any further. "But now that I am aware that they may be lurking about, I can take precautions."

Myrtle snorted. "I don't think you know the meaning of caution—pre or otherwise."

Rose rolled her Lucky Strike between her thumb and forefinger. "Well, then I'll just need to discover who the spies are before they can get to me."

"On your own? Entirely?" Myrtle questioned.

"I can't see another option," Rose said.

"How in heaven's name are you going to unravel a spy ring with practically no information and absolutely no resources?"

"For someone who has devoted her life to digging through mud in hopes of discovering a hint of the habits of long-dead peoples, I would think you'd have more faith."

"But where to even start?"

"I have Lord Barbury's key." Rose tugged on the chain and laid the piece of metal on the outside of her costume. "I know that it opens a chest or safe or locked drawer that holds his reports on the spy ring. He told me to go to a place that sounds like *hammer* and that a man would be able to help me. He also mentioned a woman—Tamsin Morris, I believe. I know from my own inquiries that Lord Barbury was the Earl of Mar's son."

Myrtle arched a blonde eyebrow. "That still begs my initial question of where to begin."

"Why, London, of course."

"London?"

"Where else to find information out about a peer of the realm? Besides, his father is often in residence there. I can learn more about the late viscount from his friends and family, and maybe the clues he left will make more sense."

"I am going with you." Myrtle linked her arm through Rose's, and the gesture immediately strengthened Rose's resolve—or, perhaps more accurately, her conviction. She wasn't completely alone—neither in her belief nor in the investigation. The realization warmed her.

"This is possibly going to be a wild-goose chase," Rose warned.

"Every Sherlock needs his Watson," Myrtle countered. "Besides, I have already taken a sabbatical to help you convalesce. If you are determined to ferret out spies, then I shall be at your side."

Determined. Rose wasn't sure if that was the correct word—especially when she wasn't even certain that what she *was* chasing was real. But she definitely did feel compelled.

What I was looking for? Rose's old words drifted back into her mind—the ones she'd spoken months ago to the viscount in the poste de secours.

Purpose . . . a reason, he had answered.

It seemed his mission had become hers. Was she racing toward a real goal, though, or was she just chasing specters in her own version of No Man's Land?

Chapter 2

"One of your holdings is the Isle of *Hamarray*?" Rose nearly bobbled her fork in excitement as she stared at her dinner companion, the Earl of Mar. She had spent the London Season socializing with members of the ton and asking questions about the late Viscount Barbury. And during the last few weeks, she had been practically *wooing* the lord's father.

Now finally—just as Rose had begun to entirely lose faith in her sleuthing abilities and her own experience that night in Daytona—she'd unearthed a clue. Could Hamarray have been what Barbury had said when she'd heard the word *hammer*? She'd been gathering gossip about Mar and Barbury for months, yet no one had ever mentioned the island.

Mar's sculpted lips moved into a smile that never failed to slightly unsettle Rose. It was just too perfect, too pleasant, too *practiced*. He was a handsome man with even, chiseled features and blond hair threaded with a few strands of sparkling silver. But the earl was also the type of smug fellow whom Rose normally avoided. She liked confident men but not supremely self-satisfied ones. Unfortunately, due to the circumstances, Rose was not only enduring this particular noble's considerable vanity but actively encouraging it.

He wasn't just Barbury's father but Rose's chief suspect. His own son had warned her that spies were everywhere. According to the reliable London rumor mill, the earl was in dun territory, which was an old-fashioned way of saying flat broke. German gold would be quite tempting to a man with a clear taste for luxury, from the rich foods he ate to the expensive equipage he drove.

"My dear girl," Mar said with a touch too much familiarity, "I do not own one island but two. There's a nearby islet called Frest. It is connected to Hamarray by a sandbar when the tide is out."

"Two isles!" Rose batted her eyes like a ninny. "Land sakes alive! And I mean *land sakes*. That's a lot of property."

"Oh, they are not much—mere parcels, I assure you." The earl waved a gloved hand dismissively, but he grinned like a Cheshire cat presented with a gallon of cream.

"How is it I've never heard about them until now? If I owned two islands, I'd tell everyone as soon as I met them." Rose leaned across her plate of oysters, as if physically drawn in by the peer's presence.

Mar's responding chuckle was charming enough, but Rose didn't miss the hint of amusement at her gauche American behavior . . . or the fact that she'd flattered him. He glanced around the long dining table of their hostess, the Dowager Duchess of Waterhamden, as if to make sure no one was listening. No one was, of course. Rose was quite certain that the Society matron had arranged the seating so that her old crony could have a tête-à-tête with his latest quarry. The elderly man beside Rose was not just hard of hearing but engaged in a rather loud conversation with his equally aged dinner companion. Across from them was a couple clearly engaged in an extramarital affair with each other and paying attention to no one but themselves. Even more conspicuous, the dowager had left the seating at the foot of the table next to Mar scandalously empty.

"I do not speak of my personal paradise often. Those who are invited to it are sworn to secrecy. It's my very *private* retreat, you see."

"Oooh. A hush-hush island—how exciting." Rose puckered her lips into a perfect moue, a trick her mother had taught her. Mother would approve of her employing the technique on an earl but *not* the counterespionage aspect. At least Rose didn't have to entirely feign interest this time. Could Mar's determination to keep Hamarray hidden have anything to do with spying?

"I thought you'd find it thrilling." The earl was practically purring now. "You are just the right sort of cheeky, modern girl who's always looking for an exciting lark. Aren't you?"

Not anymore, and you're definitely not my idea of adventure anyway. But Rose's real thoughts on the matter would never do. Thank goodness she had a lifetime of blithe responses at the ready.

"Oh, as long as there is a handsome man involved, I'm your gal." Rose added a titter at the end of her statement that made her want to gag.

"It is very *secluded*." The earl turned the last word into a verbal caress.

Rose feigned a shiver of delight. "How intriguing, my lord."

"I used it before the war for hunting and more *pleasurable* pursuits."

Rose doubted that the earl would have been so bold as to drop a barely veiled innuendo in the presence of a proper, titled English miss. But Rose was an American and a notoriously wild one at that.

"The isle is very remote," the man continued, "so no gossip ever leaves. That is why my father bought the land. Even if the servants wished to speak, there is no one for them to gossip with."

"So Hamarray is not part of the entail?" Rose asked, an impolite question to be sure but not exactly unexpected from a title-hungry heiress. The earl *did* have assets to sell, but he hadn't, despite his perilous finances. Why were these islands so priceless to both him and his late son? Did Mar's attachment to their remoteness have anything to do with concealing treason?

"No. It could easily be gifted to a favorite of mine, especially a much-beloved wife."

Rose managed a doe-eyed smile. She had no intention of ever marrying and creating obligations and expectations that she didn't want. She definitely wouldn't wed into the British peerage with all its unspoken rules and requirements.

"Where are these islands?" Rose asked. "In the Channel?" Were they near any important shipping lines? Naval bases?

"Oh, much more far flung than that." Mar chuckled, clearly pleased with himself for having stumped her. "They are to the north. In Orkney."

In Orkney.

The two words blasted through Rose with even more force than when Mar had revealed his ownership of Hamarray. During the majority of the war, the home port of the British Grand Fleet—the most powerful collection of warships in the world—had been in Scapa Flow, a huge natural harbor that lay between many of the islands of Orkney, off the north coast of Scotland. Only the Grand Fleet's powerful presence had kept the German dreadnoughts harmlessly in Wilhelmshaven for the bulk of the war. The sheltered anchorage of the British had played a key role in the conflict, and a spy ring there would have been able to gather intimate details about the movements of the largest contingent of the Royal Navy.

Admiral Beatty had moved the home of the Grand Fleet to the Firth of Forth last April, but Scapa Flow still remained critical. The interned German High Seas Fleet—a naval force second only to Britain's—was now impounded in the great natural harbor and under the guard of British battle cruisers. If foreign agents wanted to restart the fighting, they would need the assistance of the remnants of the formerly mighty Kaiserliche Marine. Any attempt to free the vessels—no matter how ill advised—could explode the tentative peace and ignite the still-glowing embers of war.

"Ork-Knee?" Rose feigned ignorance, hoping that Mar would reveal more without her asking too many direct questions that might raise his suspicion. Depending on how close Hamarray was to Scapa Flow, the earl could have easily entertained both Admirals Jellicoe and Beatty, which would have given him a perfect opportunity to pry out secrets from the men. He might have even dined with Lord Kitchener, England's Secretary of State for War.

More horror detonated inside Rose as she recalled the suspicious circumstances surrounding Lord Kitchener's death. The important British leader had drowned when his cruiser, the HMS *Hampshire*, had sunk after leaving the safety of Scapa Flow en route to diplomatic meetings in Russia. Many suspected a German U-boat was responsible, and there were whispers of conspiracy plots.

What if spies *had* been involved? Did one of them include the Earl of Mar? What had Viscount Barbury unearthed? If foreign agents had arranged the death of one of England's most influential men, Rose did not want to contemplate what tragedy they could orchestrate if they managed to free the Imperial Fleet.

"Orkney is part of the Scottish Northern Isles," Mar explained patiently, drawing Rose's attention back to him. "You may have heard it mentioned during the war. It is where the British Grand Fleet had its home base. Now it is the watery prison of all the vessels of the German Navy."

"Oh, there!" Rose clutched her hands together. "To think your little islands will be part of history."

Mar bristled almost imperceptibly at the word *little*, just as Rose had intended. She wanted to provoke him into bragging.

"Both Hamarray and Frest are situated in Scapa Flow, where the ships were anchored. Why, you could see Jellicoe's flagship, the *Iron Duke*, from the window of my manor house."

Indeed. How fortuitous.

"Is it now frightening to espy the German dreadnoughts instead?" Rose faked another shiver.

Mar shifted in his chair so that he faced her, his knee almost touching hers. "I have not been to Hamarray recently."

Rose's heart kicked as she realized that he was preparing to extend an invitation to the very place she'd been searching for.

"You haven't? But don't you wish to witness the might of Germany under the control of the Royal Navy?"

Mar smiled. "That *is* a capital idea, my dear. Would you care to join me?"

"I would be absolutely delighted," Rose said—and this time she had to suppress a shiver. She might have just agreed to accompany a traitor to a remote island that he'd managed to keep away from Society's wagging tongues—a traitor who might have arranged for the death of his own son.

But Rose had also just solved one of the clues Viscount Barbury had left for her. Perhaps all the answers awaited her in Hamarray.

Frest, Orkney

Visitors to Hamarray had arrived, bringing with them both the return of the Sheep Problem and the Earl of Mar.

Thorfinn Sinclair had heard from the staff at the big house that the cursed laird had actually arrived a few days earlier, ordering his beleaguered servants into a frenzy of preparation. It marked the first time that the toff had brought women of his class to the island instead of his normally boisterous male chums and their latest selection of misfortunate painted ladies.

According to Janet Inkster, whose daughter, Ann, worked at the mansion, Mar had thundered more than once that he wanted to impress one of his guests in particular: Miss Rose Van Etten, an American heiress. Since the laird needed both a new heir and plenty of blunt, it was clear to all of Hamarray and Frest that he was in the market for a wife—and for that reason, and that reason only, Sinclair pitied the unknown Miss Van Etten.

Sinclair rose from the loamy ground to warily watch the sleek speedboat slice through the waters of Scapa Flow. In sharp contrast to the dark sense of foreboding brewing inside him, it was an unusually fair day for April in the Northern Isles. The good weather was the only reason he'd heard the purr from the pleasure craft. Normally the constant roar of the angry wind would have drowned out the noise of an engine, even a motor as powerful as this one. Of course, any guests of the earl would bring nothing but the finest, mightiest toys with them.

When the roar had first broken through the cry of seabirds and the sound of surf, Sinclair had originally thought the sound came from one of the Royal Navy's Coastal Motor Boats. During the Great War, the ever-present roar of their engines had never failed to remind him that while other men battled the enemy, he remained pushing his plow on Frest—vital to his family's survival but useless to the cause.

Now the CMBs were back—not as sentinels protecting the heart of the British Navy but as jailers guarding the decaying might of the enemy. No longer did the CMBs search for the looming masts of mighty ships of the Kaiserliche Marine or even the periscopes of the small but deadly U-boats. They knew exactly where the enemy fleet was. Its rusting hulls and skeleton crews were hostages—sureties to guarantee that accords benefiting the Allies would be reached at the conclusion of the negotiations at Versailles. It was a peace Sinclair hadn't fought for but one for which he was immensely grateful.

The vessel before him now, though, wasn't a gray CMB with imposing Lewis guns poking out like the quills of a hedgehog. It was a bonny craft with gleaming wooden sides and the words *The Briar* emblazoned over the hull. Like anything associated with the earl and his cronies, it was extravagant and showy. Even from this distance, Sinclair could spy the craftsmanship in the pattern made from different types of expensive timber. It looked nothing like his stepfather's ancient sloop with its hodgepodge of lumber, some of the "new" planks little better than the rotting pieces they had replaced. But trees didn't grow often or well on the windswept isles, and none stood on the one that Sinclair called home. Luckily, like his stepfather, he had learned long ago to make do with what he could scrounge.

The female passenger on the motorboat gestured toward the howe on Sinclair's croft, and the woman operating the vessel swung closer to shore. The craft obeyed its mistress's command with flawless precision. The women's focus seemed riveted to the peculiar mound that the old islanders had claimed was the home of an impish trow. Although not a true believer himself, Sinclair had always loved listening to the old tales, especially when his late mother had told them. No one could spin a yarn like her, although Sinclair tried his hardest to recount the old stories to his younger half siblings—just as he would attempt to describe these newcomers to them.

Knowing the children would be curious, he carefully scanned the occupants of the boat. The ladies were both elegantly dressed—the fair-haired one in a smart wool coat, and the brunette in head-to-toe fur. Almost immediately Sinclair identified which aristocrat was rumored to be Mar's intended bride.

It wasn't by her beaverpelt ensemble or even by the way she was expertly conning the ship. No. It was the way she scanned the shore, taking inventory of it. The blonde woman only studied the howe, but the other lady . . . she *surveyed*.

It was a look Sinclair recognized, and a bit of his pity for her dried up. Her expression was one of ownership, of possession, of dominion, but not one of love or even appreciation of the land stretching before her. She was obviously taking stock of the isles that would become hers upon marriage to the earl. She was like Mar, and his father before him, and the laird before that. They came during fair weather and took what they wanted. They did not reside in Orkney, nor did they work the soil or lay lobster traps in the waters. Yet they thought *they* were the custodians of the bounty of Hamarray and Frest.

Aye, the potential new mistress possessed a fae beauty, but so did Mar have a handsome face. His gilded mien hid a fetid, boggy soul. Although Sinclair had no way yet of judging the contents of this woman's heart, he wasn't about to be fooled by any outward frills—no matter how much those trappings glittered.

Miss Van Etten caught sight of him, and she steered her pleasure craft in his direction. She and her passenger waved eagerly. Sinclair reluctantly responded with a hesitant salute. It never boded well when one of the toffs showed an islander any attention. He'd much rather the newcomers ignore him, like proper misses.

"Hi!" Miss Van Etten called out in the informal, overly enthusiastic way of Americans. "You have a beautiful island!"

He just cupped his ear and leaned forward, as if trying to hear.

"I said you have a beautiful island!" she shouted even louder now. "Is that your boat you're working on? Are you a fisherman?"

Sinclair shot her a polite half smile. He added a helpless shrug and pointed toward his left ear for good measure.

The determined lass finally took the hint. Her grin slipped slightly, but she still gave a blithe wave before she revved the throttle of her fine craft. Leaving naught but seafoam in her wake, the woman guided the vessel through the water with the ease of the mythical, magical finfolk. He wasn't surprised by her skill—all the earl's wealthy sycophants had the leisure time to perfect their "sporting" affectations. It was the first time, though, that he felt a reluctant twinge of admiration for the ability of one of their kind. Proficiently conning a small vessel was much more useful than shooting imported deer trapped on a peedie treeless islet.

Turning a journey that would take Sinclair an hour to row into a matter of mere minutes, Miss Van Etten quickly reached the docks of Hamarray. As soon as she and her companion set foot on the strand, the wind began to pick up. By the time they'd started climbing the steep hill leading to the mansion overlooking the cliffs, the air began to howl, and the waters grew rough.

A wry smile touched Sinclair's lips. The finfolk were known for bringing bad weather and chasing away the fish. Perhaps Mar's intended did have a bit of dark magic in her after all.

Sea spray doused Sinclair, but he ignored it as he again set to work on cleaning the motor of his sloop. The cranky piece of machinery needed all the coddling Sinclair could give it. The cheap petrol he could afford kept clogging the filter, and he'd learned to clean it regularly even if it meant losing precious daylight during the short winter days. Though the days had lengthened a bit, he found himself now working against the weather.

Between Sinclair's focus on the task and the thunder of the gale, he didn't notice his stepcousin's approach until he spied Astrid's boots. After placing his rag in a bucket, he stood up to greet her. She'd been the only one of his stepfather's family other than her grandmother to embrace him, and over the years they'd become as close as siblings.

"Did you catch sight of the new Lady of Muckle Skaill?" Astrid asked without preamble, using the Orcadian words for *big hall*, which was what the locals had dubbed Mar's home. Even though Astrid practically shouted in Sinclair's ear, he had to strain to understand her with the loud gusts buffeting them.

"Aye. How'd you hear?" Astrid and her grandmother's croft was on the other side of Frest, and they did not have a good vantage point of this part of the sea.

"Ron Inkster saw her on his way back from bringing in the day's catch, and he stopped to tell Nana and me. He said she was a chatty one, even hollering hello to him and asking him questions he didn't wish to answer. Was the boat she arrived in as fancy as he said it was?"

"Fancier." Sinclair grunted as he leaned over to put the motor back together. A splash of rain had already hit his cheek, and he wanted to finish before the deluge. He didn't mind the rain himself, but it would do no good to get water in the persnickety engine.

Astrid sat down on a nearby stone wall. Despite being in her twenties, she bounced her feet off the side just as his young half sisters did. "He said that the woman steered the vessel like one of the finfolk."

"At least the earl's intended isn't a stranger to the sea."

"You know for certain that she was at the wheel? Miss Van Etten could have been the passenger." Astrid's expression had turned downright curious. It was the same one she wore when a rare bird decided to rest its weary wings on their isle before continuing north or south. It was also one Sinclair didn't like directed at him.

"She had the right look about her." Sinclair tried to keep defensiveness out of his voice, but a bit crept in.

Astrid quirked one of her red eyebrows as she leaned forward, her hands gripping the stone to balance her body as she peered at him. "Ron said both ladies were bonny lasses but that the woman operating the boat looked as fetching as a mermaid."

No use denying it—not when Sinclair had noticed the same. "Aye."

His response made Astrid tilt so far forward that she looked ready to topple onto her nose. Sinclair ignored her scrutiny and focused his attention entirely on cleaning up his tools. Astrid, however, did not grant his unspoken request for her to leave it be.

"You know what the old islanders say about a fair mermaid." Astrid hopped down from her rocky throne to stand near him. "They are always scheming for a way to trap poor mortal men into doing their bidding."

Sinclair snorted, even though he'd predicted that his stepcousin would allude to the old legend. It was said that female finfolk abducted human men to save themselves from lives of drudgery as finwives. If a mermaid married a finman, the ethereal beauty would turn into a hag within seven years. "A union with the earl would be worse than to one of the seafolk."

Astrid frowned. "That's why she might set her sights on someone more of her own age—someone she *thinks* she can toy with. The earl's guests are always looking to stir up trouble, and I suspect Miss Van Etten will be no different, even if she's female. She might think it a lark to make the earl jealous—or that it might bring him up to scratch faster."

"I'm sure she'd pick better quarry than the likes of me." Without thinking, Sinclair reached up and touched his face. His fingers first brushed his eye patch and then trailed over the puckered scar that ended at the corner of his mouth—a gift from the Earl of Mar.

Astrid's eyes followed the path of his hand. He froze, but it was too late. With the war having claimed Reggie's life, Astrid was now the person who knew him best. The concern in her green eyes had shifted, becoming more intense.

"You're much too good for the likes of Miss Van Etten, Sinclair. When the right lass comes along, you'll make a fine husband. Don't let anyone tell you otherwise." Astrid gently touched his upper arm.

"I suppose I'd be a sight better spouse than a finman," Sinclair agreed as he hoisted his tools and headed with Astrid toward the stone house he'd helped his stepfather build.

"You're the catch of the Northern Isles!" Astrid squeezed his arm.

He cocked his head to the side, wishing she'd stop this nonsense when they both knew the truth. His frustration made him speak a little more harshly than he'd intended. "The coward of the Northern Isles, more like."

"No one blames you for not going to war," Astrid said. "There wasn't anyone to care for the croft and your half siblings after Uncle Sigurd had his stroke. The bairns would have starved—along with some of the others on Frest whose menfolk went off to fight."

And didn't come back. But Astrid had no need to say the words that every islander felt too keenly.

"You kept this island alive and even prospering these last few years," Astrid told him earnestly. "There's honor in that too."

A vision of Widow Craigie flashed before Sinclair, her dark eyes condemning as he brought her share of the proceeds after his monthly twilight trip to Kirkwall. She'd lost her eldest son in the Battle of the Somme, her youngest at the Dardanelles, and the middle at Verdun, and her husband had died on a merchant marine vessel sunk by a U-boat.

But he, the half-English bastard of the laird, had avoided all duty to country and had skirted the seemingly endless bloodshed.

"You could not have joined the infantry or signed up for the navy, Sinclair." Astrid tugged on his forearm now, as if trying to shake him into believing her words. And this last, at least, was true. Blind in one eye, he was ill suited as either soldier or sailor.

"Everyone knows Reggie wanted me as his batman."

Astrid made a dismissive gesture with her free hand, her fingers seeming to sweep along the gentle grassy slope of the island. "As much affection as I had for Reggie, you were and *are* meant for more than being a glorified valet to a viscount."

"It was a way I could have seen action." Sinclair rubbed his thumb along his scar again as he thought of his half brother's betrayed hurt the day that Sinclair had refused to follow Reggie to war. As boys, the two of them had been inseparable . . . even after Sinclair and his mother had fled from Muckle Skaill and the Earl of Mar. The cliffs and sea caves of Hamarray had been their kingdom to rule. But their relationship had already fractured the day Sinclair had caught Reggie, a notorious rake, kissing Astrid.

"That would have been a decision that a boy would make—to run off toward a facade of glory when he was sorely needed at home." Astrid said the words that Sinclair knew to be true, but that didn't do anything to assuage his feelings of cowardice.

"Reggie was wrong to feel slighted when you rejected his offer to be his batman," Astrid continued, "and it was even worse of him to complain to the islanders. It was an action the earl would have taken. Reggie was normally better than that. In time, if he had lived, he would have apologized. I know it. I sensed his guilt when he briefly returned to Hamarray."

But even if Reggie had rarely acted like the earl, he had been the man's son . . . and so was Sinclair. Even if the old sod had never acknowledged Sinclair, the islanders never forgot his parentage. His mother might have been an island lass, but he was the living, breathing evidence of the earl's manipulation of the island and its people for his own pleasure. Sinclair was, and always would be, an interloper to this land of pastures, sea, and stone—a reminder of how foreign lairds had laid claim to the land that should be the crofters' by right.

"I am glad you see it that way, Astrid, but I fear you're in the minority."

"If that's so, then why have all the islanders chosen you to be their representative to talk to the earl?" Astrid halted their progress and released him so she could cross both arms over her chest.

Sinclair grunted and raised the hand not holding his tools. "I make a good lamb to slaughter."

"I don't see why you fail to see your importance to Frest." Astrid's expression became mulish. Normally, she appeared this way when try-ing to track down a suitable site for her rather profitable enterprise.

"I just happen to be one of the few available, able-bodied men around," Sinclair pointed out. "I am also the least likely to be missed if Mar tosses me into Scapa Flow when I ask him to extend our prewar agreement to keep sheep on his old hunting grounds on Hamarray."

"Thorfinn Sinclair—" Astrid began, but her obvious lecture was cut short by the appearance of Sinclair's half siblings—all six of them.

Freya, with her long blonde braid bobbing behind her, reached them first. The cold had pinkened her cheeks, making her smattering of freckles stand out even more than usual.

"Is it true?" She tried to walk like a lady, but she couldn't help but bounce. "Mr. Craigie said that the heiress has arrived! Is she as pretty as a fae mermaid? What was she wearing?"

"Did her boat really skim through the water like a porpoise?" Twelve-year-old Hannah was next. Her wild red hair had entirely escaped her plait, and it bounced carefree about her cherubic face. "What did it look like? Do you think I'll get to see it?"

"Is she like a fairy princess?" Mary, the ten-year-old, asked.

Her twin sister, Barbara, immediately interjected, "No, silly. Not if she's like a mermaid."

"Will the sheep have to leave their home now that the Earl of Mar is back?" Margaret, the serious one at age eight, stared up at Sinclair in concern. She had the softest heart and, unfortunately, tended to listen the most to the discussion the crofters had around her father's table, which led to endless worries.

"I want to go in a fast boat," Alexander, the baby of the family at six, announced as he took up the rear.

The stream of questions and observations didn't end as Sinclair's half siblings gathered around him. They always greeted him like this—a gaggle of excitement and curiosity. He bent down to embrace them and soon found himself in the middle of a mass of skinny limbs, constant jostling, and boundless inquiries.

As Sinclair tried to address each one the best he could, he acknowledged another truth Astrid had said. The children had sorely needed him. About a year before Britain had entered the Great War, his mother had passed away giving birth to Alexander. The shock and pain of her death had triggered his stepfather's apoplectic stroke, rendering him still bedridden in 1914. Eleven-year-old Freya couldn't have managed the care of Sigurd and her siblings, let alone the running of the croft. And their neighbors, although always ready to help, were severely shorthanded themselves with the young men gone to the trenches or to the sea.

Aye, his siblings wouldn't have survived the war without him, at least not as a family unit. And Sinclair would do anything, sacrifice anything, for his sisters and younger brother—even if it meant giving up his honor.

"Do you also have the feeling that we have traveled through the pages of a bucolic seaside fairy tale only to end up in a sensational gothic novel worthy of the Brontë sisters?" Rose shouted over the wind as she and Myrtle stared up at the towering sixteenth-century mansion. The stepped gables looked like massive gravestones against the darkening sky. It did not help matters that the entire structure had been plastered with a rough aggregate of pebbles and shells and then coated with a lifeless gray lime.

"I do, but I can't figure out whether it is Heathcliff, Rochester, or Edgar Linton who lives inside," Myrtle replied as she tilted her neck backward to study the tops of the opposing structure.

"Probably an unholy mix of all three," Rose added darkly. "The Earl of Mar seems like a typical handsome middle-aged gentleman in search of a new wife and heir, but there is just something unpleasant about his undercurrents that he just can't seem to dam up."

"As unsettling as this monstrosity?" Myrtle asked, eyeing a partic-ularly nasty gash in the ancient harling. Clearly the building had not been properly maintained for years.

"I thought you liked tumbledown old structures," Rose said as she started to climb the weathered stone-slab stairs.

"To study, not to live in, especially when the owner may or may not have had a role in his own son's death." Myrtle climbed up the first step and then stopped to point in the direction of a ruin at the opposite end of the craggy headlands. It looked as if it had once been a round, almost chubby tower. "Besides, I'd much rather explore the even more ancient edifices, like that Iron Age broch. Maybe the earl will let me study it and poke around some of those mounds that we passed on Frest. They might hold caches of Viking grave goods or perhaps something older!"

Rose glanced over at Myrtle, feeling another sharp stab of guilt for dragging her best friend along on this seemingly fruitless venture. Myrtle should be preparing to spend the summer at a real dig, not playing nursemaid to a woman playing spymaster. "You don't have to accompany me, Myrtle. I'm much stronger physically than I was in November."

"Do you think I'm going to let you face Mar and a spy ring all by yourself? Besides, you have just led me to an untouched archaeological gold mine that no man is jockeying for. Perhaps I will finally have a chance to lead my own excavation. Of course, I am sure competitors will come crawling out of the woodwork once I show any interest." Her friend quickly finished climbing the steps to join Rose by the thick, elaborately carved door full of fantastical creatures. Between its sturdiness and the wild wind buffeting them, no one inside could even hope of hearing their conversation.

"At least there is some definite benefit to our visit, then. After all, I still might have dreamed up the foreign agents in Daytona last November," Rose pointed out. "We could not find anything about what Viscount Barbury did in London after his escape from German territory early in the war other than attend Society events. Even my friend Percy couldn't tell us anything of use, and he's a Royal Air Force pilot and a duke."

"Like you've said, perhaps that is because the viscount was working for the Home Office and everything was hushed up," Myrtle reminded Rose.

"Or it is due to the fact that there is nothing to find." Rose had been in higher spirits a half hour earlier as she'd conned *The Briar* through the vibrant turquoise water and skimmed close to the reddish-gold beaches of Frest. But it seemed her mood had blackened with the sky, her uncertainties whipping up their own gale. Strong doubts had never consistently plagued Rose before the war, but it seemed they were another legacy of her time on the Western Front.

"You found out what *hammer* meant, didn't you?" Myrtle pointed out. "Have a little faith in yourself, Rose. Pretend this is like the start of one of your races. What's your strategy?"

Rose straightened her shoulders under her practical, naturally waterproof duster coat. "Three pronged. I will search for the mysterious *him*, Tamsin Morris, and Lord Barbury's papers. The first two will involve talking to residents of Frest and Hamarray, not that they currently seem inclined to converse. The last approach involves finding the likely lock for the viscount's key."

"Which could well be secreted in the very house we're about to enter." Myrtle nodded her chin toward the imposing entrance.

Rose knocked crisply on the door. "Let's hope the earl is an inattentive host who prefers to leave his guests to their own devices. Otherwise, it might be awfully difficult to explain why I keep poking my nose into every nook and cranny."

Unfortunately, Mar turned out to be a suffocating presence. He absolutely refused to leave Rose's side until well past dinner, which was why she found herself slinking out of her room, carrying Myrtle's electric lantern. Even if she wanted to turn on a light, it appeared that the generator in the basement had broken some time ago, and the earl had not ordered it fixed. Here on Hamarray, the precarious state of his finances was much more evident than in London. The draperies were practically moldering on their rods, and the curtains were brittle with dry rot. The whole building was understaffed, and Rose had spied more than one room with its furniture entirely covered with drop cloths before Mar had whisked her in another direction.

Beneath Rose's feet, a floorboard groaned in a rather dramatically loud fashion. She froze and flicked off the handheld light. The earl had given her a room scandalously close to his, especially given that the house had several wings. Rose wouldn't be surprised, though, if the other sections were in even worse repair or void of furniture. Perhaps the arrangement was solely from necessity, but Rose did not trust Mar. He was definitely scheming, but whether it was just to seduce and wed her, or whether he was keeping her close to hide treasonous activity, she did not know.

Fortunately, the loud sound did not appear to disrupt Mar's sleep. After turning on the lantern again, she concentrated the light on the old hand-knotted rug beneath her feet. Tufts of it had gone missing over the years, interrupting what must have once been a bold floral pattern. The rich colors had faded, too, and more than one place had become threadbare, exposing the coconut-husk matting below. It did little to muffle Rose's footsteps, so she proceeded more cautiously than before.

Finally, she reached the end of the long passage and made a sharp turn into the central structure of the great hall. Although the boards were no less squeaky, she no longer had to fear that her nocturnal investigation would wake Mar. Sighing, she loosened her tightened muscles and lifted the lantern . . . only to come face to face with a set of glowing eyes. Rose took an involuntary step backward, energy spiking through her. The wood beneath her slippers emitted an eerily humanlike moan, and Rose gripped the handle of her light even tighter.

Lifting her source of illumination, she released a self-effacing laugh as she realized that she'd been startled by the glass eyes of a stuffed hare perched on a wall sconce. The taxidermist hadn't even done that grand a job, and the poor creature looked a bit lumpy and not the least bit lifelike. Tarnation, Rose had indeed become the jumpy sort.

Walking a little more confidently now, Rose strolled through the rather ghastly hallway. An array of red stag heads stared disapprovingly down at her, their antlers casting shifting shadows against the peeling wallpaper. On a piece of wood high on the wall, a fox stalked a cluster of partridges, while pheasants seemed to roost everywhere, their bodies permanently frozen in positions with varying degrees of veracity.

The select pieces of artwork were either violent, overtly sensual, or disturbingly both. They all depicted scenes from ancient Greek and Roman mythology. Mar seemed particularly fond of portrayals of Zeus, especially those involving Europa, Leda, and Ganymede. There were several depictions of Persephone being dragged into the underworld by Hades and of a scantily clad Artemis at the hunt.

The uneasy feeling in Rose grew. This was not a home where a nobleman would bring a prospective bride . . . unless he meant to force her into marriage by creating a scandal. It seemed that the earl was setting a trap for her.

Irritation boiled inside Rose—an emotion separate and distinct from her now-familiar fidgetiness. She did *not* appreciate being maneuvered, especially by a smug, self-satisfied man. She'd grown up making her own decisions, and she'd always chafed when her parents had sporadically tried to create rules and restrictions. Her mother had been notorious for going through spells when she thought Rose needed "polish" before her entrance into the Marriage Mart. Fortunately, her mother had normally given up very quickly and returned her focus to her own social calendar.

A scurrying sound to Rose's left brought her back to the present. Her heart pounding like an unbalanced engine, she stiffened. Rose swung her lantern in the direction of the noise, only to find a scullery maid trying to shrink behind a rather bloodthirsty statue of Hercules wrestling the Nemean lion. The young miss's eyes were wide with fright as she clutched a rag and a strong-smelling polish to her chest. All of the earl's household staff appeared to be as jumpy as Rose, but this woman had literally begun to shake.

"I'm sorry," Rose said in her best soothing voice. "I didn't mean to startle you."

The woman dipped her chin so low that it nearly touched the top of her sternum. She emitted a sound that was more squeak than word. Rose had no idea what the poor darling was trying to say.

"Why are you up so late?" Rose asked, just as a slightly older maid appeared from one of the parlors.

"Beg your pardon, milady, but we were just getting the house polished up for you and your friend." The other woman tugged on the younger one's arm.

"No need to call me milady," Rose corrected. "Just Miss Van Etten."

"I'm Kilda." The older servant bobbed in deference. "And this here is Ann."

"Nice to meet you, Kilda and Ann." Rose inclined her head too. She hadn't expected to run into anyone, but perhaps this was actually an opportunity to gently begin to dig into what the household staff knew about the earl and the late viscount. "We must have arrived very suddenly. I'm sorry that the earl did not give you more notice so you wouldn't be working all night."

"'Tis no problem, miss." Kilda's eyes flicked nervously up and down the hallway, as if expecting a phantom to materialize.

Rose began to suspect that perhaps the women were hiding something . . . and that *something* could be linked to the spy ring. "Does the earl normally show up unannounced?"

Kilda stiffened. "I couldn't say."

"Oh, I didn't mean for you to tell tales on your employer. I was curious—that's all. It seems like such a whirlwind trip to me. I just wondered if the earl is a spontaneous man or a creature of habit. It is important to understand a man's character before thinking about coming to an understanding." Rose knew she was committing scads of social blunders by having such a frank conversation with the household staff. Fortunately, she had her reputation as a nouveau riche American to explain away her behavior.

"The earl doesn't like us to speak about him or his guests," Ann burst out so quickly that between her broad brogue and soft voice, Rose almost didn't understand her. Kilda did not appear happy with the scullery maid's outburst.

"Unless you would like us to fetch you something, miss, we'd best be getting to our beds now," Kilda said. "We'd just finished with the parlor when you came down."

"Oh no, I'm fine. I was having trouble sleeping, and I thought I'd read a book in the library."

"It is down the hall, third door to the left," Kilda said crisply before she grabbed Ann's arm and shepherded the young woman toward the servants' corridors.

Rose waited until they had disappeared into a concealed door in the wall, and then she ducked into the room Kilda had emerged from. All the drop cloths had been removed and the heavy, masculine furniture revealed. There was no lightness, it appeared, in this manor house. Rose believed the decor was to evoke a sense of might, but it just seemed unnecessarily weighty.

As she moved her lantern through the darkness, she spied nothing much of interest. The room appeared to be exactly what it was: a parlor. There was a little side table with a small drawer under it. Rose started to bend down to see if there was a keyhole, but the thud of footsteps stopped her.

She flicked off her lantern and tried to still her breathing. The tread was definitely that of a man, and there were very few male servants with so many of the soldiers still trickling home from the war's various theaters. She wasn't so much frightened as she was alert.

The parlor door scraped back, and the earl stood illuminated by candlelight. The soft glow obscured some of his wrinkles, making him look young, handsome, and somehow more sinister. He strode masterfully into the room, using his tall body to block the exit.

Unlike the night on Daytona Beach, Rose wasn't caught off guard. Although energy pumped through her, it didn't make her shake. Instead, like it had on the shell-blasted roads of France, Rose's fierce response steadied her.

Not one to hide in the dark, she flicked on her lantern. The light caused the silk fibers of the earl's dressing gown to glow, bestowing upon him an almost unearthly appearance. Yet this was no archangel but a fallen one.

The earl's gaze swept over her body, and his lips twisted slightly when he saw that she still wore her practical traveling suit. Clearly, he'd hoped to find her in a gauzy night rail.

"You needn't have traveled halfway across my home for a private moment with me." Mar stepped forward, his voice rich and soft, but it didn't warm Rose. It chilled her. "I would have come to your bedchamber soon enough."

Rose arched an eyebrow. "Is that why you think I am up in the middle of the night? I was after a good book, not an assignation."

Mar laughed, but the sound was not amused. "There is no need to play coy, Rose. We know why you came to Hamarray."

Did Mar know about her intent to sleuth around his estate? A true trickle of fear slipped through Rose, but she hid it under a familiar protective layer of blitheness.

"The sea air?"

Mar's long legs ate up the space between them. "You are to be my wife. You needn't worry about your reputation."

"Aren't you skipping a vital step?" Rose asked as she tried to dart around him. Unfortunately, her legs hit the back of an end table.

Mar had her trapped.

"We'll take our vows soon enough." The earl grabbed Rose's shoulders, his fingers digging through the soft wool of her tailored jacket. His grip hurt, but it didn't quell her. It galvanized her.

She smashed her knee into his groin, the movement quick and vicious. Before she'd gone to war, Rose had been taught to defend herself by Myrtle's grandfathers—one a Texas Ranger, the other a gunslinger. Mar crumpled over with a pained roar, but he did not drop to the ground.

"I actually was referring to the fact that you hadn't properly asked for my hand." Rose towered over the earl as he clutched himself. "And the answer is no, by the way."

Mar lunged at her. "You deceiving bit—"

The earl stopped both his forward movement and his words as Rose pressed the barrel of her snub-nose revolver against his forehead. The man's blue eyes almost comically lifted upward as she cocked the weapon.

"Bloody hell, what are you doing with a pistol!"

I don't go snooping without it was probably too revealing an answer—although Rose's hopes of sweet-talking the man through an extended stay on Hamarray were dashed. Clearly her ruse of pretending to be interested in a marriage was over. But she wasn't about to leave this island. Not after she'd just arrived.

"Protecting myself from unwanted advances." Rose pressed the gun farther into his forehead just enough to show him that she wasn't shy about using force.

"You were practically begging for my attention, you little conniving c—" He choked off the slur as she redirected her aim toward his crotch.

"No one asks to be mauled," Rose corrected. "If you'd like to stay intact, Mar, I suggest that you don't use offensive language. It makes me rather trigger happy."

"You're mad!" Mar paled as he moved his hand protectively over his lower half.

"You do realize your palm is rather ineffective at stopping a bullet? It is just sinew, flesh, and rather delicate bones," Rose said archly.

He stumbled backward. "I will ruin you for this. You shall have no choice but to marry me. Your parents will be begging for me to take you off their hands."

"Mother would be delighted by an offer from an earl," Rose replied, "but it will mean nothing to Daddy. He won't force me to marry you if I don't wish it."

"Do you think you'll have any standing in Society after this?"

"If I were worried about my reputation, I wouldn't have traveled here in the first place. I am not known by my virginity but by my dowry," Rose pointed out. The earl was hardly the first who thought he could coerce her into marriage by threatening to kiss and tell. He was the only one, though, she'd had to ward off at gunpoint. "In fact, out of the two of us, it is you who should be worried about a black mark upon your character."

"Me?" The earl scoffed, but he still watched her Bull Dog revolver carefully. "If you claim that I tried to force myself upon you, they shall simply blame you for tempting me in the first place."

Sadly that was true, and the unfairness of that stoked Rose's already inflamed temper. "Oh, my dear Mar, I am much more diabolical than that. I know which repute really matters to a man like you. It is not honor but prowess."

The earl looked as waxen as a melted candle. "What do you mean?"

"If you claim that you tupped me, I won't deny it—or at least I won't repudiate that you tried your hardest, but in the end you just, well . . . couldn't." Rose feigned a pout. "It is really not your fault that you bored me, I suppose. It is hard for a man of your age to satisfy the appetites of a young, adventurous woman like myself. Although after such a *scandal*, it might be difficult for you to find a youthful heiress to agree to be your wife."

A curious expression fell over Mar's face as he realized that he really did not have power over her. It must have been a very alien concept for an entitled man like him to even comprehend, let alone accept. His facial muscles contorted, but before he could lunge in her direction, Rose jerked her gun threateningly.

"Get. Out." The earl snarled the words, all pretense of gentlemanly polish long since rubbed away. "Get off my island now."

"No." The response was instinctual, but by the time Rose spoke again, a plan was beginning to form. "No."

"This is my land," Mar roared. "You have no power here."

"I am going to buy Hamarray and Frest," Rose said, not even bothering to demand rental rights instead. She had made an enemy out of the earl, whether or not he was involved in the spy ring. If he *was* a foreign agent, it would be better for her to have complete control over these islets.

Yes. *Control.*

The household staff and the crofters couldn't dodge her questions if *she* was landlord. It would be a perfect excuse for asking questions, and no one could stop her from poking around every sandy, rocky, grassy inch of the place. And Myrtle could finally lead her own dig into any tumbledown rock heap that she desired.

"You are what?" the earl bellowed.

"It is clear the place is falling down, and you can no longer afford its upkeep," Rose pointed out. "I shall pay you top dollar, which is more than you deserve. You can use the money to prop up your entailed estates until you can find a bride title hungry enough to marry you."

"I have no intention of selling Hamarray and Frest to *you*," Mar huffed.

"I wouldn't be so hasty in rejecting my kind offer. After all, you might have trouble off-loading it if rumors of its shabbiness start circulating, especially combined with other tales of my thoroughly unsatisfying stay."

"Are you blackmailing me?" Mar started to puff out his chest and then seemed to belatedly recall her pistol. He huffed out his breath, looking a bit like a schoolboy who'd dropped his favorite sweet in the mud.

"I'm forcing your hand. Something I'm sure you've done to others."
Rose lowered her gun to her side. She had the earl in her sights without
it raised, and they both knew it.

"Why the hell do you want these islands anyway? What good are
they to you?"

Since Rose could hardly tell Mar the truth, she gave an answer
a man like him would understand. "Because I can. Now I think it is
time for you to leave *my* island. Our lawyers can handle the transaction
from here."

The earl's jaw clenched threateningly, but he turned and stomped
from the room. Rose stood in the circle of light from her electric lantern
until she realized that she was shaking. Collapsing into the chair, she
stared out into the dark night and saw a flash of green dance across the
sky in an eerie, undulating wave.

"My word, did I just buy two islands?" Rose whispered into the
silence. "On a whim? With virtually no consideration beforehand? I
haven't changed at all, have I?"

Chapter 3

"It looks like—"

The wind swept away the rest of Myrtle's words, not that Rose had been paying much attention to her friend. Rose was standing in the middle of a row of empty, decaying pheasant coops on the edge of a steep cliff as she reanalyzed the events of the past night. Rolling her cigarette through her fingers, she realized that there was probably a metaphor in her shabby surroundings. Buying two entire islands just to chase after clues seemed even more impetuous now with the sun illuminating all the land to which Rose had laid claim.

But it was too late to stop the purchase. The earl had stormed away at dawn, and Rose hoped that she hadn't banished the very man whom she should be tracking.

From the hillcrest, Rose could easily see in all directions except the portions of the horizon blocked by the mansion. It was no wonder the previous lairds had chosen this locale for their grand home. Judging by the ruins of the towerlike broch on the other end of the headlands, the ancient inhabitants had also taken advantage of the stunning views.

There was something powerful in standing there, with the sea beating against the towering red sandstone cliffs on one side and the rolling, bumpy slope of the land on the other. It was drama and peace all in one single glance. And this land—that Rose didn't particularly want and certainly didn't need—would all be hers soon, like it or not.

Frustrated with the situation and with herself for once again jumping into something without considering the consequences, she nudged a pile of pheasant feathers caught in the crevice of a rock with one foot. The wind caught the loosened debris and sent it sailing over the cliffs.

Rose needed to literally drive off her skittering, nervous energy, but her mechanic was still readying her Raceabout. At least the new car had arrived in time. Even on a small walkable island, Rose did not wish to be without transportation, so she had made the complicated arrangements for her vehicle's transport to Hamarray even before she'd planned her own trip to the Northern Isles.

"Invaded!" Only one word of Myrtle's shout reached Rose's ears this time, but it made her immediately stiffen her spine. Her heart jerking with almost painful force, Rose instantly imagined U-boats converging on the island, their periscopes poking ominously from the choppy waters. But when she caught sight of Myrtle's teasing grin, Rose forced her muscles to relax.

Tarnation, she hated how anxious the war had made her.

Walking headlong into the gusts, Rose strolled toward her best friend, who stood looking in the other direction to observe the surprisingly lush isle of Frest across the natural sandy causeway rather than the sheer red cliffs of Hamarray beneath their feet.

"I still didn't hear all your words," Rose shouted at Myrtle as she finally fought her way to her friend's side despite the gale trying to blow her back toward the bluff.

"It appears that your brand-new fiefdom is about to be invaded!" Myrtle did not even put down her binoculars.

Although the sunlight remained low and weak, Rose still shielded her eyes as she scanned the seascape. She noted a small rowboat bobbing along in the stretch of water between the conjoined islands.

"Do you think the German Navy has been reduced to dinghies?" Rose asked lightly, her tone purposely belying the initial flash of fear that Myrtle's announcement had caused. Carefully, she tracked the progression of the wooden hull. It looked more like a cork than a vessel, bobbing up and down as it crested the waves.

"Well, yes, since the Imperial Fleet is currently moored behind our backs under the guard of the Brits," Myrtle responded. "This visitor, however, appears more Viking than Visigoth. He has the most impressive rowing technique, and given the shape of his upper arms, I'd say that he's no stranger to the sea—"

Rose plucked the binoculars from Myrtle's hands and lifted them to her own eyes. When she caught sight of the sailor, she felt an immediate—and decidedly *unwelcome*—tug of appreciation. She didn't have time for distractions of the flesh, and the visitor was carnality itself. Despite the chill damp, the man wore only a sweater. The wool pulled tightly against his back, revealing each stretch and bunch of his muscles. Although Rose had admired her share of posteriors, she'd never ogled a man's shoulder blades before, yet now she could not help herself.

"I can see why you called him a Viking," Rose told Myrtle.

"He is my find, you know," Myrtle said airily, but she made no move to retrieve her binoculars.

"It is *my* newly claimed isle that he is intent on sacking, and you've already called dibs on the broch."

"True," her friend agreed.

"I do wonder why he's rowing rather than walking here," Rose mused as she watched him give the oars another mighty heave. "The tide is out, and the natural bridge between the islands is passable."

"But the water is rising. There're already puddles along the sandbar that weren't there before."

"Thunderation!" Rose lowered the binoculars in disgust. "I was planning on driving across to Frest as soon as Harrold finished readying my Mercer. I need to *race*, and Hamarray is far too hilly to go the speed that I want. The sandy ring of beach around Frest will be perfect."

Rose yanked the field glasses back to her eyes to watch the islander bring his boat ashore. He made quick work of tying up the dinghy to the pier, perhaps even faster than Rose herself could.

The visitor rose and started up the crest of Hamarray straight toward them. The land was uneven with dips and valleys, almost like a mountain range in miniature, so he'd disappear from view and then reappear. When his features finally came into focus, Rose involuntarily sucked in her breath—and *not* because she recognized him as the man who'd been working on his boat when she and Myrtle had arrived.

At Rose's gasp, Myrtle grabbed the binoculars. Rose let her have them. She'd already taken a much longer look than prudent.

"My, my, I am not sure what real Vikings looked like, but he certainly could star in a picture show about one. He makes Douglas Fairbanks look plain." Myrtle sighed. She started to hand back the binoculars, but Rose declined with a shake of her head; she had the man's finely chiseled features emblazoned upon her memory. He had the look of an avenging angel with straw-blond hair peeking out from under a flatcap.

He was hale and fit, so different from the blood-soaked, mud-covered soldiers she'd treated—men worn down by the horrific struggle of trench warfare. This man brimmed with *life*, perhaps even adventure. He fit this wild land of wind and sea.

A damnable spark flickered inside Rose. She'd experienced nothing this electric since long before the war. But it wasn't the old excitement. It was stronger. More tempting. And definitely dangerous to a woman intent on infiltrating a den of spies.

⎯⧫⎯

Since the age of ten, Sinclair had become accustomed to strangers staring at his visage, especially young children. He paid little heed to it now, accepting it as part of him, just like the scar itself. He was neither a particularly social man nor a shy one.

But no one had ever watched him like these two lasses, especially Miss Van Etten. Her gaze swept over him, stopping everywhere, it seemed, *but* his damaged eye. It wasn't even that she studiously avoided it, rather that her attention seemed drawn elsewhere. It was deuced disconcerting. The fact that the Earl of Mar intended to marry this woman made Sinclair feel all the more unsettled.

He almost hesitated before he began to mount the last incline, knowing it would place him face to face with the lasses. But he'd stopped allowing aristocrats and their ilk to intimidate him long ago. Marching up the final rise, he prepared himself to meet Mar's chosen bride.

Then there she was—her more practical beaver coat exchanged for raccoon now that she was out of the salt spray. She was a first-rate beauty steeped in an elegance that spoke of faraway, grand cities, of a world Sinclair had never, and likely would never, see. It was no wonder the earl had chosen this lass. The toff always liked fine, pretty things . . . until he inevitably broke and then discarded them.

"I'm Miss Rose Van Etten," she announced in her clipped Yankee accent as she boldly stuck out her hand. Her forthrightness shocked him. Mar generally had preferred the shyer sort of lass.

"Mr. Thorfinn Sinclair." He reluctantly took her hand, expecting to find the touch soft and delicate. It wasn't. Aye, her kid glove was all supple smoothness, but her fingers held a strength he hadn't anticipated.

Miss Van Etten's eyes widened. "*Thorfinn* Sinclair?"

"Aye." He tugged on his flatcap with his free hand. It was a common enough name here in Orkney, where Norse and Gaelic traditions meshed, but he supposed it might be a trifle uncommon in America. And the gentry never did seem to appreciate a workingman like himself having the name of a god and legendary hero.

Still gripping his hand, Miss Van Etten turned in the direction of her companion. "Right as always, Myrtle. We have indeed been invaded by a Viking." Then she whirled back toward him. She gave his hand one firm pump and then dropped it. "Pleased to meet you, Mr. Sinclair."

He really should be excusing himself and focusing on his real purpose for visiting Hamarray—discussing the Sheep Problem with the earl before they counted the flock on the morrow. Sinclair knew better than to linger this close to Muckle Skaill, but instead of politely making his adieus, he rather inanely blurted out, "Viking?"

"Yes," Miss Van Etten said conversationally, as if they were the best of chums, "you were rowing so prodigiously that my friend here, Miss Myrtle Morningstar, likened it to an invasion."

Miss Van Etten paused just long enough for Sinclair and Miss Morningstar to nod in each other's direction before she barreled on with the explanation: "Given the recent hostilities, I inquired whether she meant German, and she assured me you seemed more Norse than Goth. She is an archaeologist, you know, and well versed in these matters."

Sinclair rubbed the bridge of his nose as he tried to follow her conversation. He had come here to talk to Mar about *sheep*. He had no idea how he had fallen into the subject of antiquity with two fae lasses. Did Miss Van Etten mean to purposely confuse him, the lowly farmer and sailor, with her mention of ancient history? It was something Mar would do—setting himself apart, ridiculing those he found beneath him, which amounted to almost everyone.

But his son hadn't been like that. No. Reggie had smuggled books from the library to Sinclair and shared with him lessons that he'd learned at Eton, from history to mathematics to classic literature.

"And what am I sacking? Rome or an Irish monastery?"

The earl's mouth always flattened into a hard line whenever one of his sharp-edged barbs had failed to sink into tender flesh. Instead, Miss Van Etten hooted good-naturedly when Sinclair dodged what he'd thought had been a taunt. The sound of her chuckle was bright and deuced unnerving. Miss Morningstar laughed, too, but it did not have the same effect.

"I—" Sinclair paused and cleared his throat, wishing he could settle his pesky reaction to the lass just as easily. "I, well, I came to talk to the Earl of Mar about . . ." No, he didn't want to tell *her* about the Sheep Problem. She wasn't their mistress yet. But she could be, which was why he had to be exceedingly polite. No use in having the new Lady of Muckle Skaill despise him too. "Well . . . welcoming you and your friend to Orkney. Officially. On behalf of the crofters. All of us."

"Thank you, Mr. Sinclair. That is quite kind of you. Miss Morningstar and I are very happy for the warm greeting."

"That we are," Miss Morningstar agreed.

Sinclair had known that the women would sense his palpable unease. Their insight wasn't surprising given his clumsy delivery, but their gracious reaction *was*.

"How are you finding Hamarray?" He hated small talk but understood its necessity.

"It is quite charming, which is why I've decided to buy it," Miss Van Etten announced as if she were pointing at a fresh pint of gooseberries at the market in Kirkwall.

"Buy it? Hamarray? You're going to buy Hamarray?" He sounded like a right gappus, but he simply could not believe her words.

"Yes. And Frest." Miss Van Etten's pink lips tightened ever so slightly.

If Sinclair's early childhood as a servant at Muckle Skaill hadn't taught him to be aware of shifts in his employer's mood, he probably wouldn't have noticed that his instinctual disbelief irked her. Miss Morningstar clearly noticed as well, for she surreptitiously backed away, clearly removing herself from the suddenly tense conversation.

"The earl is selling his holdings in Orkney?" Sinclair could not believe that Mar would part with his realm of pleasure, where he ruled absolute, far from the rules and laws of alleged civilized society.

"Mar has already departed," Miss Van Etten informed him crisply. Sinclair did not miss that she failed to use the peer's proper title, a surprising mark of disrespect toward a man who normally instilled obe-dient fear. "He will not be back."

Sinclair did not wish to further annoy the potential new "laird" of Muckle Skaill, but he simply could not believe that the earl had just scarpered off at Miss Van Etten's say-so. The man clearly had been intending to wed Miss Van Etten, and the cursed toff didn't just hate to lose . . . he never did. Moreover, people did not just acquire entire islands in less than a day because they found them charming—at least Sinclair hadn't thought so.

"So you are now the owner of all this?" Sinclair swept his hands over Muckle Skaill, where he'd been born and where he'd worked for nearly a decade. Then he swept his palm out toward Frest and over the land he'd been tilling for almost twice as long—soil that he had a part in reclaiming by digging drainage ditch after drainage ditch after drainage ditch through the muck.

Miss Van Etten waved her gloved hand as if batting away a midge in August—the gesture reminiscent of Mar's and his cronies'. Old frus-tration burned through Sinclair.

"There is the paperwork to finalize, of course, but those are just the details. The deal has been made." Miss Van Etten spoke with a finality that Sinclair could not deny. Despite her outward blitheness, he sensed in her an unbending seam of steel. As she stood there looking so fierce, so supremely confident, Sinclair didn't know whether to be annoyed, concerned, or impressed by her sudden acquisition of his and his fellow islanders' homes. This lady must be made of stern material indeed if she'd managed to wrest Mar's favorite playland away from his brutally tight grip. Sinclair would do well not to underestimate her.

"Is that all, then?" Miss Van Etten asked dismissively. Without wait-ing for an answer to her apparently rhetorical question, she turned and stomped off toward her stables. "Harrold! Is my baby ready yet?"

Baby? Once again, Miss Van Etten had managed to poleax Sinclair. As a bastard himself, he saw no shame in a babe born out of wedlock.

Most folk, however, were not kind. Perhaps this was why Miss Van Etten had chosen to suddenly retreat to such a far-flung locale. Sinclair felt himself soften toward this woman who'd chosen exile over giving up her child.

"Raring to go, Miss V. She's purring like a lion cub."

And the English thought Orcadians used odd words and idioms. Clearly, they had not encountered enough Yanks.

"She didn't give you any trouble? I was afraid the ocean trip would be too hard on her."

"She spit up all over the bonnet, but I got her patched and cleaned up."

Although Sinclair had stepped into the role of mother and father to his half siblings, it seemed odd for a woman to hire a man as a caregiver for her infant. Perhaps this chap was the father, yet their exchange seemed more like employer and employee. But a hidden relationship *would* explain why the earl's plans to marry the woman had gone utterly awry.

Miss Van Etten's dark-brown eyebrows knit together. Whatever her connection to the man, it was clear she cared for the bairn. "What happened?"

"Just a cracked cylinder, but I replaced it. She's as good as new."

Now what did that Americanism mean? It sounded like the man was talking about a machine, not a child.

"So I can take her for a spin?" Miss Van Etten asked.

She was heading toward the stables, not the house, not a nursery, but the *stables*. What *had* Miss Van Etten meant by *baby*?

"She's been idling for ten minutes now. The engine's warmed up and ready to run."

Her baby was an *automobile*?

Startled back into action, Sinclair scrambled to catch up with Miss Van Etten. Although his stride was longer, she moved with a quick lightness that reminded him of the hares Mar had imported for hunting.

"Miss!" he called out just as she was about to disappear through the open stable door.

"Yes?" She craned her neck to glance at him, but she did not stop.

"If you are indeed the new mistress of Hamarray and Frest, there is a matter of some importance that I would like to discuss. Several, in truth."

During the war, the crofters had designated him their spokesperson, a position he knew he had fallen into by default rather than by merit. His stepfather had been the leader of the islanders since the 1880s, and everyone had become accustomed to meeting in his house. Even after Sigurd's stroke, the islanders had continued the tradition of gathering in his home, with Sinclair helping his stepfather host. Now that they needed to send someone to Muckle Skaill, they'd all turned to Sinclair—the one who'd lived there once and who understood the ways of toffs better than them.

"You wish to speak to me?" Miss Van Etten seemed generally perplexed as to why he would be seeking her counsel.

"Aye. About the crofts." He caught up to her as she stepped farther into the old building.

"The crofts?" Her eyebrows turned to dark slashes against her pale skin as she stopped by the fanciest auto Sinclair had ever seen. But he had no time to admire the bonny machine.

"On Frest and the grazing rights here on Hamarray." *Grazing rights* might be too formal a term for the unwritten agreement with the earl, but he needn't let Miss Van Etten know that.

"I can't see that I'd be much help to you." Miss Van Etten opened the driver's door to her bright-yellow vehicle and slid behind the driver's seat. "I've barely been here a day, and I know next to nothing about agriculture."

Sinclair clamped his teeth together and tried not to squeeze his left eye shut in frustration. It would not do to lose his temper. When he spoke, he was proud of how measured his voice sounded, even if a bit stilted. "According to your own statements, you are now the landlady, Miss Van Etten."

"Oh." Her topaz eyes grew large as comprehension seemed to finally rain over her. "Ohhhh."

Shite, it never failed to amaze him how bloody ignorant the wealthy were of the land, the animals, the *people* who helped to support their lavish lifestyles.

"Is it urgent?" Miss Van Etten asked.

"I would rather not wait." Sinclair tried to sound polite, and he thought he managed it. Barely. If she was going to be Frest's new laird, cementing the islanders' grazing rights on Hamarray was more important than ever. "It is the cause of much concern, and I would like to put the people of Frest at ease. Some of them are elderly—"

"Then I suppose you might as well hop in."

"Hop in?"

Miss Van Etten patted the seat next to her. "We can talk while I drive."

Sinclair had never ridden in an automobile, but he doubted an open-air one would be conducive to a business conversation, especially with the high winds already buffeting Hamarray. But this was his best and perhaps only opportunity he would have today to discuss the tenancies with Miss Van Etten.

When he climbed into the bucket seat next to her, he couldn't quite stop the flash of excitement that flickered through him like the emerald-green merry dancers that sometimes appeared in the darkened sky on a winter's eve. He'd first spotted an automobile in Kirkwall, the principal town on Mainland, the largest isle of Orkney. The locals of that island had even started an auto club. Of course once the war had begun, the navy had brought lorries, motorcycles, and other vehicles to their bases. But Sinclair had admired the machines only from afar.

But now. Now he was climbing into the finest, sleekest vehicle he'd ever spied. Even the motor sounded posh. Its rich, steady roar sounded nothing like the pathetic put-put-put of the one on his skiff. The leather seat felt even softer and more buttery than the upholstery on the Earl of Mar's favorite armchair.

Part of him wanted to groan in appreciation. And he hated the weakness. Sinclair could not afford to allow the trappings of wealth to distract him, especially not when the crofters needed him.

"Have you driven a car before?" Miss Van Etten asked almost in his ear. Although the stone walls of the old stable temporarily sheltered them from the constant howl of the winds, the rumble of the engine still necessitated her raised voice.

"Nay."

"Ridden in one?" Her voice didn't sound the least bit superior, but it still chafed.

"Nay."

Miss Van Etten tapped the steering wheel with one gloved finger. "Are you good with mechanical things?"

"Passable."

"That's all we need," Miss Van Etten said. And then, without warning, she leaned over him, her fur coat pressing against his wool sweater. Her breasts brushed against his arm, and he sucked in his breath. He didn't know if she'd registered the contact, but he bloody well had.

"This is the oil pump," she told him, touching one of the tubes on his side of the vehicle before moving to the next. "And this is the petrol. Got it, buster?"

"Aye."

"Good." She pulled back, her body once again sliding across his. Seemingly unaffected by their closeness, she tapped a gauge. "When the indicator travels below this point, pump the handle. That will repressurize the tank and give the engine more gas."

"Gas is petrol?" he asked, stumbling through her Yankee dialect.

"Yep." She next tapped on the sight glass. "You can see the oil splashing through here. Give it a squirt or two if it needs more. You think you can handle that?"

If he could coax his boat motor into performing on gritty, low-grade fuel, he could certainly inject a bit of lubricant into this well-maintained masterpiece. "Aye."

"Oh, one more thing." Miss Van Etten leaned over him once again and stuck her hand between his *legs*. Before he had a chance to react, she'd opened a small compartment and pulled out a set of goggles. Tossing them onto his lap, she warned, "You'll need these. There's no windshield on your side."

"Ah," Sinclair said, glancing at the circular piece of glass in front of her. It looked a bit like a giant monocle and fit with the trim, minimal design of the yellow-and-black automobile.

Using a bright-green scarf, Miss Van Etten secured her hat around her chin. She adjusted the levers on her side of the car and then gripped the wheel. Suddenly, without any other warning, they were off, shooting through the open doors of the stable.

Sinclair quickly shoved on the goggles and adjusted the strap as they bounced through the old mews. Although he'd sailed at a fast clip when the wind was just right, he'd never experienced anything like this. The ground seemed to simultaneously rush by and rise up to greet him. Then there was the vigorous bouncing. He felt a bit like the innards of a bairn's rattle being shaken back and forth.

Miss Van Etten, however, was not the least bit bothered by the jarring ride. She waved to her friend, Miss Morningstar, who had taken off in the direction of the broch.

The road down to the docks, which the earl had installed a few years before the war, was not well maintained. That, however, did not slow Miss Van Etten. With ungodly whoops and hollers, she sped around the big craters, swerving right, then swiping left. Despite Sinclair's bulk, he found himself slipping and sliding—hitting the metal door one minute and slamming into Miss Van Etten's shoulder the next. If that wasn't enough jostling, the wind blasted him in the face with the force of an angry winter gale.

"What did you want to talk about?" the American shouted over the motor as she started to navigate a particularly sharp turn around one of the sharper rises of land.

"About the—*sheeeeep!*"

On the other side of the hairpin curve, three fat ewes meandered across the road. They were all owned by Widow Craigie, judging by the painted markings on their wool. The middle sheep released a terrified bleat so loud that Sinclair could faintly hear it over the motor. While the other two scampered away, fear rooted this one to the ground. It gave another bloodcurdling scream that almost rivaled a billy goat's.

Deftly Miss Van Etten skirted around the ungulate obstacle. Somehow, she managed not to smash the automobile into the hillside or send it tumbling over the steep slope. As she jerked the conveyance back to the center of the road, Sinclair's hat flopped off his head, catching on the brim of hers. While continuing to straighten the vehicle, Miss Van Etten snatched his cap. Without removing her eyes from the rough road spinning out before them, she dropped it squarely in the center of his lap.

Judging by the way Miss Van Etten tore over both the land and water, she was certainly talented, and Sinclair begrudgingly respected that.

"Maybe we should try this over again," Miss Van Etten hollered after they finished bouncing over a particularly deep rut. "What did you wish to discuss with me?"

"The Sheep Problem." He hadn't meant to blurt it out, but she made him feel like he was sinking into a bog with no steady ground under his feet. All his limited stores of eloquence had vanished, leaving just his natural bluntness behind.

"I'd say there *is* a sheep problem!" Miss Van Etten exclaimed as they popped over another hillock. As if on cue, another group of sheep came into sight. They lifted their heads in clear bewildered panic before they took off running. Only one intrepid ewe stayed a few feet away from the roadside to glare at them—Fetty. She was his sheep, and the children had made a pet out of her. The stubborn, surprisingly bright old girl often showed up on their croft, having walked across the exposed strand in pursuit of special treats.

"I didn't mean that the sheep were the cause of—" Sinclair tried to quickly correct himself, but the blasted air carried away his words.

"I wouldn't want to injure one of the flock while driving."

At least Miss Van Etten seemed concerned about the fate of the sheep rather than annoyed by their presence.

"Who owned that first ram who froze in the middle of the road anyway?" She shifted gears as they started to coast down the last hill. The blue of the water beyond Hamarray seemed ready to swallow them up, but at least the roar of motor and wind diminished enough to allow speech as Miss Van Etten was forced to slow a fraction.

"Ewe," Sinclair corrected.

"Me?" she asked, clearly befuddled. "I own a *sheep*?"

"I meant female sheep—not *you*."

"But I thought I spied horns on it," Miss Van Etten yelled. "Also, we need oil!"

"I assure you that it was a ewe," Sinclair shouted as they sailed over another bump while he pumped more lubricant into the engine. "In many breeds, the females have those protrusions too."

"Do they? Sheep are much more complicated than I've given them credit for."

They really weren't, but Sinclair was not eager to discuss the particulars of a sheep's general personality with someone who clearly knew little about the species. Any explanation would just frustrate both of them.

"So who *does* own that ewe?"

"Widow Craigie." Sinclair hoped that even if Miss Van Etten did get angry over the collection of woolly beasties on her hunting grounds, she would at least temper her ire toward a bereaved woman.

They'd reached the edge of the strand, and Miss Van Etten had slowed the car to a stop, making the conversation easier.

"Does Mrs. Craigie own the entire flock?"

"Nay. All of the residents of Frest keep a handful of sheep on this island. The Earl of Mar agreed that we could bring them to Hamarray at the beginning of the war since there was a bigger demand for lamb with the Grand Fleet stationed in Scapa and there wasn't space to expand the flock on Frest. His Lordship received—and now you will receive—a percentage of the proceeds of any sale of meat or wool. In fact, we'll be holding the annual sheep count tomorrow as per our agreement with Mar."

"So I *will* have a stake in sheep," Miss Van Etten said as she turned the wheel to avoid another section of collapsed road. "I never imagined myself a shepherdess. What is this Sheep Problem, then?"

"We, your crofters on Frest, want to confirm that you will extend the agreement that we had with the earl regarding our grazing rights on Hamarray."

"Give me the contract, and I'll give it a skim and see what I need to discuss with my lawyers."

Sinclair rubbed the bridge of his nose, resisting the urge to strike his head against something hard in frustration. The stone wall whizzing by to his left would do nicely. "There is no document." The cagey earl hadn't wanted anything to bind him. He'd still been bitter about the restrictions the Crofters Holdings Act of 1886 had placed on his holdings in Frest.

"Oh." Miss Van Etten waved her hand. "We'll need to remedy that in due course. If there is one thing I learned from my father, it is to put everything in writing. There are some matters that I must take care of first, but after those are resolved, I'll be happy to discuss the terms in more detail with you."

"But this is a matter of great importance for us croft—" Sinclair began to say, but the roar of the Mercer's engine drowned him out. To his astonishment, Miss Van Etten once more accelerated and steered them straight toward the exposed strand currently connecting Frest and Hamarray. Water had already begun to form large pools, and it would not be long before the entire bar was once again under the sea.

"Where are you going!" he shouted as loudly as he could, making sure that she could hear him properly.

"To Frest. The ring of sand around the island is a natural racetrack."

"But the passage will soon be flooded!"

She sped faster and tapped on the gauge that showed the air pressure in the gas tank, indicating that it was running low. "I'll wait until low tide or have someone bring me back by boat. I can have one of the servants at the big house deliver your rowboat to Frest."

Miss Van Etten was not entirely thoughtless, yet she was clearly accustomed to her whims being automatically met. She was an odd contradiction, and Sinclair was no closer to understanding her than when they'd begun this journey—nor his reaction to her.

Sinclair at least knew enough not to attempt another protest as he pumped more air into the "gas" tank. The lass wouldn't listen even if she could hear him.

The black-and-gold racer shot across the sand like an angry great yellow bumblebee. Sand and water doused them, but Miss Van Etten didn't seem to mind the deluge. Instead she shouted. He had no idea how she didn't swallow a mouthful of grit and salt. Perhaps she did and simply did not care.

He, for one, kept his lips firmly clamped together, but he had more than one reason for doing so. Not only did it keep debris out, but it kept his own shout bottled up. He was sore afraid that if he did yell, it would be in the form of a rather high-pitched scream.

Sinclair had never in his life approached this velocity either by sea or land. The turf seemed like a living creature, ready to reach out and drag them into the sandy depths. Yet it also felt as if they would take flight, losing themselves in the bright-blue April sky.

Despite Sinclair's trepidation, a thrill crashed through him. His heart seemed to tap and skitter like his fingers did over the strings of his fiddle when he played a particularly lively hornpipe. He'd always enjoyed the wind in his face—a good thing considering where he dwelled. A part of him had wanted to soar like a whirling, dipping, diving hen harrier without boundaries.

But he did not indulge this side of himself. It reminded him too keenly of his sire. Sinclair's family needed his stability. They relied on him too much for him to think about adventure beyond that of keeping the bere barley growing, the animals fed and watered, the herring barrels full, and the lobster pots regularly checked.

Miss Van Etten appeared to have no such limitations. She drove not like a mere bird of prey but more akin to a shooting star blazing across the firmament. The isle that he knew so well looked entirely different as it became a whirl of green, gray, and reddish brown. The ride was disorienting yet freeing. He did not know if he breathed. Either his chest muscles had frozen up in wonder or the wind whipped the air away from him.

Miss Van Etten did not stop with one circuit of the isle or even two. Again and again they whirled around the circumference of Frest. The islanders not at sea had come down from their houses to watch the spectacle. Their faces flashed by like pictures in the zoetrope toy that Reggie had owned. The folks of Frest would all be talking about Sinclair's madcap ride with the new Lady of Muckle Skaill over their dinner tables tonight. A sight like this might even go down in island lore.

Finally, they came to a stop.

"Now that," she said, "was the best course I've ever driven. You have a marvelous island."

It pleased him that she'd called Frest *his* and not *hers*. It did not, however, solve the primary issue of why he had sought her out in the first place.

"There is still the Sheep Problem." Sinclair crossed his arms over his chest. For some reason, he felt the need to gird himself from this fae woman.

"I told you that I would look into it as soon as I took care of some pressing matters." Miss Van Etten's mouth had tightened ever so slightly. "I am a woman of my word."

Sinclair had never trusted the word of an aristocrat—even Reggie's, as much as he'd loved his half brother. Things came too easily to them, and they treated their promises too cavalierly, not understanding what a spoken guarantee meant to those who did not have the luxury of unlimited means.

"Miss Van Etten, with all due respect, you are now the landlord of Frest and Hamarray. You are here now, are you not? This may seem like a silly annoyance to you, but we rely on those grazing rights to feed and clothe us. With the count occurring tomorrow, the future of the flock will be on every crofter's mind, and they'll all be anxious about what the new laird—meaning you—will decide."

"I am the 'laird'?" Miss Van Etten's lips quirked in wry amusement. "My dear Mr. Thorfinn Sinclair, I can assure you that as an American, I have no desire to put on airs and—"

"How are you not putting on airs when you insist that your concerns are more pressing than those of an entire island's worth of people?" He was thundering now. He really should stop, but he couldn't. "We have suffered through enough absentee landlords who only take from these isles. This may be a pleasure escape for you—be it for hunting or racing or for whatever shite toffs do—but this is our home, our livelihood, our past, and, God willing, our future."

Miraculously, Miss Van Etten did not look angry. True, her sardonic mirth had vanished, but ire had not risen in its place. Instead, she appeared . . . thoughtful and perplexed—put out, even, but not enraged.

"This isn't just about the sheep, is it?" Her question showed a surprising acuity despite her previous lack of any insight into what he was trying to convey.

"Nay." The word was expelled from Sinclair along with his righteous anger. How could he express that it was about a people now mourning the loss of a generation of loved ones—the generation who had been supposed to take up the mantle of struggling to eke out a living from a tiny plot of land, less-than-generous grazing grounds, and an oft raging sea?

Miss Van Etten appeared even more contemplative. Once again, she reached over his legs for the compartment by his knees. Although the motion was perfunctory, it affected him all the same. For a moment, he felt like he had when they'd barreled through the strand.

She withdrew a pack of Lucky Strikes. Instead of lighting one and lifting it to her mouth, she just rolled a cig through her fingers and then leaned back into her seat.

"How many people live on Frest and Hamarray?" Miss Van Etten asked.

Sinclair battled down annoyance that she hadn't thought to consider the human souls living on the islands she was buying—as if they mattered less than the amount of acreage. But at least she was asking now. He needed to focus on that. "There are fifty-three crofters, including children, on Frest."

"What about Hamarray?" She lifted the still-unlit cigarette to her lips and sucked on it. Aye, she was a woman of contradictions.

"Just the live-in household staff at the mansion. Hamarray was made into pastureland during the Enclosures, and many of the folks living there moved to Frest. It is why we are so densely populated." Of course, the Earl of Mar had only made matters worse when he'd gotten rid of the sheep and instead filled his land with wild game not native to Orkney, including hares that ate the crops on Frest.

"How big are the farms?" Miss Van Etten spoke around the thin roll of tobacco in her mouth and somehow managed almost perfect elocution.

"A few acres or so each."

Miss Van Etten whipped around in his direction. Her mouth agape, the sodden paper clinging to her lower lip. She grabbed the cigarette moments before it dropped. "A few *acres*! How is *that* sustainable?"

It wasn't.

"Isn't that just a kitchen garden plot at best?" Miss Van Etten continued. Her tone was honestly befuddled and not at all belittling. Still, her words carried an unintended sting.

"We fish the seas, too, and there are the sheep on Hamarray. We do odd jobs. Some of the women sell their knitting from time to time." And there were less legal means of earning an income that he would never reveal to any laird.

Miss Van Etten did not speak as she scanned the landscape with a sharp, reassessing gaze. Her glance stopped near his stepfather's croft, and their milch cow, Sally, raised her shaggy, reddish-brown head and lowed. Frest, like most of the islands in Orkney, was relatively low lying, so even situated on the strand, they had a good view of most of the western side of the isle. The green fields were crisscrossed with drystone walls and dotted with cattle, ponies, and a few woolly sheep. It was a bucolic view that belied the hard work the land demanded from its stewards.

"Shit," she said, her voice a bit thunderstruck, as if the full enormity of her whim to purchase the islands had finally begun to register.

Sinclair had never heard a lady of her class swear, but he fully echoed her sentiment. "*Shite* is generally the preferred term around these parts."

"Well, shite, then."

They both fell into silence as they gazed over the fields that Sinclair loved. He wondered what Miss Van Etten felt as she surveyed her holdings. She could not possibly experience the intense tug he did, the connection to the soil and to the people. But perhaps she no longer saw it as a mere acquisition, like an exquisite string of pearls for her to don and discard at will, but as a living land full of history, tradition, and promise.

Miss Van Etten began to draw in her breath, as if preparing to speak again, but before she could, his cottage door popped open, and out spilled his half siblings. Sinclair glanced over at the elegantly dressed Miss Van Etten and wondered if she was ready for an invasion of the Flett children. He did not want to disrupt the shaky accord they had just reached.

"We should do another circuit of Frest—mayhap a bit slower this time—and I can tell you more about the place and its people."

She grinned then—a short but honest flash of a smile. "I rather like that idea."

Just as she started to reach for the Raceabout's throttle, Freya's voice broke through the wind and the hum of the motor. "Thorfinn! Thorfinn!"

Miss Van Etten turned her head toward the call. Sinclair knew the moment she caught sight of the bairns racing down the hill, since her eyes widened so far that they seemed to nearly double in size.

"Your relations, I take it?" Miss Van Etten asked wryly.

"My half siblings," Sinclair answered.

Freya, who had the longest legs, reached them first. She whipped her blonde braid behind her back and smiled broadly at Miss Van Etten. "You must be one of the American ladies who is visiting Muckle Skaill."

"Mookle Skull?" Miss Van Etten slanted a confused look in his direction.

"Muckle Skaill. It means *the big hall* in Orcadian," Sinclair explained. "It is what we locals call your new home."

"Ah." Miss Van Etten nodded and then turned back to Freya. "I suppose I am, then. My name is Miss Rose Van Etten, and who might you be?"

"Frey—I mean *Miss* Freya Flett." His sister dropped into an awkward curtsy.

To Sinclair's relief, Miss Van Etten's lips did not twitch at his sister's clumsy attempt to assume courtly manners. The golden flecks in the heiress's eyes might have flashed a bit brighter, but she said with perfect solemnity, "I am pleased to make your acquaintance, Miss Flett."

"And I yours." Freya clasped her hands over her heart and dipped so low this time that she had trouble getting up.

"Have you asked her yet?" Mary shouted to Freya from halfway down the hill.

"Did she say yes?" Barbara yelled next.

Freya shot a meaningful stare at the twins. "I was getting around to all that. I had to greet her proper first." When she returned her attention to Miss Van Etten, a gracious smile once again wreathed her freckled face.

"Miss Van Etten, would you do us the *great* honor of joining us for dinner? I was just putting it on the table when we heard your magnificent vehicle outside our window."

Say no, Sinclair silently pleaded. *Just say no. Please.*

Miss Van Etten's bright-red lips stretched into a particularly bonny smile. "Why, yes! I'm famished, and a meal sounds absolutely wonderful right now."

━━━◆━━━

Rose had attended grand dinner parties held by the Astors and the Vanderbilts, and she'd dined in manor houses, châteaus, and castles of Europe's elite. Yet no invitation had instantly charmed her as much as these adolescent sprites'. Rose was generally not one to coo over children of any age. She did not dislike youngsters, but neither did she feel compelled to adore them. Since her own childhood, she'd rarely found herself in the company of young people. Yet something about this girl's unabashed enthusiasm delighted Rose. Perhaps it reminded her a bit of the joie de vivre she and so many of her generation had lost on the battlefields of the Great War.

A miss with the brightest-red hair Rose had ever seen barreled onto the beach next. Almost as tall as her fair-haired sister, she moved like a whirl of color against the blue sky and pale sand. Constant motion. Rose had been like that once herself.

"Whatever are you driving? It is the grandest thing I've ever seen—even in Kirkwall." This child was as informal as Freya had been formal.

"Hannah," Freya hissed, sounding very much like a harried nanny, "you're *not* supposed to bombard a guest with questions. It isn't polite. You haven't even introduced yourself yet."

"Oh, right." The redhead bobbed her head, but she didn't seem the least bit contrite. She pivoted toward Rose, giving a bounce as she did so. "I'm Hannah Flett. What is the model of your automobile? What type of a motor does it have?"

"It is an American brand—a 1913 Mercer Raceabout." Rose chuckled, the sound seeming less perfunctory than it had for a long time.

"It's a jolly-looking machine!" Hannah circled around it. She started to reach out, as if to touch it, but quickly snapped her hand back. Although Rose enjoyed when folks appreciated her cars from a respectable distance, she didn't generally like strangers—or anyone, for that matter—touching one of them. But oddly enough, she found she wouldn't mind if this girl did. She just seemed so reverent.

"Would you like to see the motor?" Rose asked, unable to keep a hint of amusement from her tone. Luckily, the girl did not notice as she rapidly clapped her hands.

"Oh yes. Would you really let me?"

"Every race car driver likes to show off the engine." Rose climbed out of the car and walked over to the hood, choosing the side that was facing away from the sea and its salty spray. Hannah smacked her palms together again as Rose undid the buckles on the straps holding the metal down and folded back the bonnet.

"Ohhh, it is a T-head! It is ever so much prettier than Thorfinn's dirty old motor in his sloop. His doesn't roar like yours either. It makes this sad little put-put sound, as if its piston is all puggled."

Mr. Sinclair, who'd also exited the Mercer to study its engine, made a choked sound. Rose cast a curious glance in his direction. Even the thickness of his wool sweater could not obscure how his muscles had stiffened. He was uncomfortable with her presence and clearly wanted her gone.

He was indeed a sobersides. It was obvious that he thought she purposely acted like a flibbertigibbet. But at least he hadn't treated her like a fragile doll or an ice princess during their argument in the Mercer about the Sheep Problem. He'd actually blasted her with his temper— but not as a scold, not really. She'd endured enough chiding lectures from men to recognize one.

No, Thorfinn Sinclair had challenged her. Dared her to be better. Perhaps even thought her capable of rising to the occasion as "laird"— and all that the word entailed. People always thought Rose irredeemably frivolous. Even during the war, she'd often been seen as either some sort of angel or a rich girl on a charitable adventure. No one ever took her seriously . . . she barely did herself. Yet Mr. Sinclair seemed unwilling to allow Rose to use her fecklessness as an excuse to wriggle out of what he considered to be her duty. He pushed at her outward facade of blitheness.

Although Rose wasn't exactly sure how she felt about being prodded, Mr. Sinclair's insistence that she assume an active role as landlord offered her the perfect excuse to start poking around Frest for information about the viscount and any suspicious activities. Sinclair had certainly answered all her questions about the population of the island without ever suspecting that she might have an ulterior motive.

"Are you really going to marry the Earl of Mar and become the mistress of Muckle Skaill?" one of the identical girls with strawberry-blonde hair asked as she moved closer to Rose.

Her twin followed and immediately added, "And are you truly from America? What is it like there? Are you as rich as they say?"

"Girls!" came Freya's horrified cry just as Mr. Sinclair said in a stern tone, "Barbara. Mary."

Although they seemed ready enough to overlook their sister's admonishment, they immediately looked chastened by their older brother.

"Sorry, miss," they both mumbled to her.

"No harm done, girls," Rose told them brightly. "I've faced worse questions from society columnists back home. Yes, I am from the United States, but no, I am not going to marry the earl. I *am* buying his estate, however, so I will be mistress of Muckle Skaill after all."

"The Earl of Mar will no longer be laird?" Freya asked, her voice even more high pitched with excitement as she immediately glanced at her half brother.

"He is already gone," Rose answered, and her pronouncement caused a great cheer to rise up. Clearly, the Flett family did not harbor any soft sentiments for their old landlord. Did such disdain for English authority extend to all British rule and make spying for the enemy more palatable to the adults?

The littlest member of the gaggle of children marched forward, his chest puffed out in importance. "I'm Alexander. I'm six. Can I ride in your automobile? I've never been in one. Hannah would like to go, too, but she didn't have a chance to ask you yet."

Rose did not know why, but she found herself kneeling in the sand to address the little tyke. "Why, that sounds like an excellent idea, Alexander. I think it would be even better if all your siblings had a ride."

Freya stepped forward then, opened her mouth, and then shut it firmly. Even if she did not voice a complaint, her crestfallen disappointment was palpable. Clearly, she was worried that her dinner would be ruined.

"After," Rose added loudly, "we eat the wonderful meal that Freya has prepared. Should we all adjourn to the house?"

Freya beamed, looking once again like a merry wood sprite. But she wasn't the only one shooting Rose a pleased expression. So was Mr. Sinclair.

As the brood of Fletts led Rose up the gentle slope to a gray-stone cottage with a slate roof, she felt a tug on her hand. Glancing down, she noticed the last of the children—a girl who seemed to fall in age between the twins and Alexander.

"My name is Margaret," the little girl told her solemnly. Although she had auburn hair, she reminded Rose the most of Mr. Sinclair. It was the eyes—the deep, serious eyes. "Did Thorfinn talk to you about the Sheep Problem?"

"He did," Rose said, not precisely surprised that little Margaret knew about the adult crofters' concerns. She herself had absorbed more about her father's business than anyone had ever expected. As a small child, Rose had often sneaked into his office in hopes that he'd notice her. A man of singular concentration, he rarely did. His secretary had always had a soft spot for Rose, so he had not alerted his employer to her presence but had occasionally brought her a glass of milk and a plate of cookies. Rose would sit there, listening to her father dictate letters and handle business calls until her nanny found her. More than once she'd even managed to secrete herself behind a potted plant and listen to business meetings. That had been *quite* the education.

"Will you let us keep our sheep on Hamarray?" Margaret's tiny features looked heartbreakingly mature as she stared up at Rose in worry.

"Your brother and I have discussed working something out," Rose replied carefully. She did not fully understand the details surrounding

84

the woolly creatures, but it was becoming evident that she would need to learn—at least until she had managed to root out the spy ring.

"It is very important, you know." Margaret jutted her small chin into the air, looking like an Amazon warrior of old.

"So I hear." Rose sighed. At Margaret's sharp look, Rose immediately sobered and asked, "Could you explain it? I'm afraid this is all very new to me."

Margaret tilted her head quizzically. "Aren't you the new laird? Shouldn't you know everything about your holdings?"

And that simple question sliced even more than her older brother's previous blustering. "I am afraid understanding how to run an estate is not a prerequisite for owning one."

A choking sound came from Rose's right, and she glanced over to find Mr. Sinclair listening to her conversation with Margaret. He had the oddest expression on his face as he studied her. She was accustomed to confounding people, but there was an intensity to Mr. Sinclair's look that was unusual. And she still wasn't sure if she liked it.

"The sheep have brought us a handsome income after selling the meat and hides to the navy." Margaret held up a thin finger as she sagely made each point. "And we use the wool for our clothes, like Thorfinn's sweater. I helped card the wool, and the twins practiced spinning. And the money from selling part of the flock helped some of the farmers pay for petrol and buy motors for their boats. It is all connected."

"There's not enough land here on Frest for them?" It was half a question and half an observation.

"Nay." Margaret shook her head with the gravitas of a scholar. "Especially with us needing to plant more—"

"For the cows and ponies to eat," Mr. Sinclair quickly broke in, pronouncing *cows* like "kyes."

Now it was Rose's turn to scrutinize the Orcadian. If she was not mistaken, he had strategically interrupted his sister. Could he be hiding something? Perhaps it was just a relatively innocent matter—something that a tenant would not wish his landlady to know, like poaching. Or maybe it was more serious subterfuge—the kind involving spies and ambushes on dark beaches.

The snort of a cow interrupted Rose's increasingly lurid musings. The beast shook its shaggy head as if chastising her, its liquid brown eyes reproachful. Although the creature sported two little spiky horns that protruded from its head, Rose now knew that an animal's headgear did not necessarily denote its sex.

"Who is that?" Rose asked Margaret.

"Oh, that's Sally. She's a sweetheart. We get all of our milk from her, and she is *never* bad tempered," Margaret said.

Mr. Sinclair emitted another amused snort. "Don't let Sal or Margaret fool you, Miss Van Etten—Sally has her obstinate days like we all do."

"She's only kicked you once when you were milking her!" Margaret protested.

"Once is enough," Mr. Sinclair said crisply, but Rose had no trouble detecting the surprisingly fond humor in his voice. Although Rose had met many horse-mad men, she had never encountered one who showed patent affection for a dairy cow. Perhaps he had more softness inside his prickly exterior than she'd originally suspected.

"Mind your head," Mr. Sinclair warned as they approached the low door to the cottage. It was a snug, inviting-looking building despite being made almost entirely of unforgiving rock. Although not as small as the blackhouses Rose had seen while touring Lewis in the Scottish Hebrides with friends before the war, it was not a large or even midsize home either. It certainly did not seem as if it could house all the boisterous and inquisitive Flett children, but then again, what structure could? She imagined they could easily take over her "Muckle Skaill," her family's lavish Florida mansion, or any one of her father's numerous hotels.

The smell of peat fire greeted Rose as she stepped over the threshold. The thick walls held the roaring wind at bay, making the house even more of a homey sanctuary. The main room, with the dining table already set, seemed to serve multiple functions. There was even a stone bed built into one of the walls. It reminded Rose a bit of an enlarged animal trough with the pallet situated between the wall and three stone slabs.

As she moved farther inside, a thin man rose slowly from a chair near the fire. Although he leaned heavily on his cane and his muscles seemed to hang loosely on his bones, he still exuded strength. It was not just a mere vestige left over from a robust youth but a present sturdiness melded together through stubbornness and sheer strength of will.

His pale-blue eyes studied her, and he made no attempt to hide his disdain. "This is one of the 'grand' lasses visiting Muckle Skaill, then."

Rose was long accustomed to judgment. One didn't grow up as the daughter of one of America's wealthiest men without facing preconceptions. And those assumptions only grew greater—and more pejorative—if a society darling chose to drive fast cars, drink hard liquor, seduce handsome men, and smoke like the proverbial chimney.

"So I've been told." Rose gave the man a wink, which he did *not* return. His glower, however, did not deepen. Instead, his gaze sharpened assessingly.

"And you must be . . . ?" Rose asked the man pointedly.

"My late mother's husband, Mr. Sigurd Flett." Mr. Sinclair spoke quickly, clearly attempting to stave off a confrontation.

"You have the most delightful children, Mr. Flett. They are quite bright and all very lovely." Rose could charm when she wanted to. After all, she *had* endured all her mother's haphazard lessons on poise and niceties, even if she generally chose to forgo them.

Mr. Flett grunted, obviously pleased by her compliments but not wanting to be happy with anything she said.

"Miss Van Etten will be joining us for dinner." Mr. Sinclair's tone was even, as if he expected an argument.

Mr. Flett made another abbreviated sound. His facial muscles tightened, making him appear even more rawboned than before. He cast a speaking glance at Mr. Sinclair that somehow managed to appear both disappointed and morosely self-satisfied. Having seen the look on her parents', nannies', and instructors' faces, she easily recognized it. Rose had always enjoyed living down to expectations or even far below them.

"I am the one who invited the new Lady of Muckle Skaill," Freya piped up, her eager grin a little too bright.

When Mr. Flett glanced at his eldest daughter, his entire visage softened, and Rose could see how he still made for a handsome man. Although he had none of his stepson's stunning golden beauty, his craggy face was fascinating in its own way, especially when tempered with a smile.

"Always kindhearted like your mother, even to the English."

"I'm an American actually," Miss Van Etten said, although she was rather certain the man knew that already.

Mr. Fleet's pale-blue eyes flicked back to hers, and he said rather sardonically, "Ahhh."

His jaw so tight it looked ready to snap, he glanced at Mr. Sinclair and said, "I take it nothing is resolved with his Lordship. He will *not* be happy with us entertaining Miss Van Etten."

For some reason, Rose felt the need to defend Mr. Sinclair—although she was quite sure he was more than capable of doing so himself. But she wouldn't stay silent when this earnest man's own stepfather clearly expected him to fail. "If you are speaking of the Sheep Problem, Mar is no longer your landlord. I am. Mr. Sinclair and I are well on our way to ironing out a more permanent solution that will benefit everyone. He is quite persuasive."

That might have been a bit of an overstatement, as Rose did not fully comprehend exactly *what* the people of Frest needed. But since all she desired from Hamarray was to complete Viscount Barbury's mission and to give Myrtle the chance to lead her own excavation, she had no concern that she could easily give the islanders what they wanted—at least when it came to allowing sheep to peacefully munch grass. The more Rose ingratiated herself in their lives, the more secrets she could pry apart.

The two men jerked in her direction. Despite both having piercing blue eyes, the hues couldn't have been more different. Mr. Flett's were a cold blue, as monotone as a cloudless, frigid winter morning sky in New England. Mr. Sinclair's, on the other hand, had both warmth and depth, like the waters in the Florida Keys or the French Riviera. Each fellow, however, studied her in varying degrees of surprise. Mr. Flett's disbelief was tinged with cynical interest, while a hint of embarrassment mixed with Mr. Sinclair's astonishment.

Rose was accustomed to making herself the center of attention during the rare times her parents actually ate dinner with her. A shocking disruption from her had invariably seemed like the only way to break the stilted silence that pervaded family affairs. But she didn't want to be the source of discord for the Fletts, so she whirled toward Freya in hopes of easing the rising tension. "I simply cannot wait to eat your meal. I'm absolutely famished."

"Of course." Freya immediately bustled over to the table. "Please have a seat. You can sit at the head opposite Da."

"Everything looks absolutely delicious!" Rose exclaimed.

"It is just a simple luncheon." Freya's pale skin flushed a rosy pink.

"But Freya and the younger girls made all the cheese themselves." Mr. Sinclair cast a proud look at his half sister as he pulled out a chair between her and Rose.

"We assisted with the bannocks too!" one of the twins chimed in. "And Hannah mixed the butter."

"A mechanized churn would be more efficient," Hannah commented with a deep sigh.

"I made the pickle." Margaret pointed to a dark-brown chutney filled with unidentifiable clumps of vegetables instead of the cucumbers that Rose had been expecting.

"I helped Thorfinn milk the cow," little Alexander chimed in. "And picked the turnips. I was too little to really help scythe the barley last year, but maybe I can do it next season."

"We all worked on smoking and salting the fish," Freya added.

"Sometimes I even get to go on the boat with Thorfinn!" Alexander added, his thin little chest sticking out again.

Rose gazed at the spread before her with renewed interest. During her youth, she had rarely thought about the food that appeared before her. She had little to do with the kitchens and ate most of her meals in the nursery, except, of course, for those occasional etiquette-filled and decidedly tiresome affairs with her parents. Rations during her time on the Western Front had merely been sustenance to scarf down between long shifts and little sleep.

A trickle of guilt slid through Rose as she thought about how much she had simply taken for granted before the war. She had lived a disconnected existence, as if she'd simply floated in a golden champagne bubble from one sumptuous party to another.

"That is all very remarkable. You are quite the industrious family."

"You will find us to be very self-sufficient here on Frest," Mr. Flett intoned. "We islanders have never had a need of any assistance."

The man meant the comment as a thinly veiled barb, but he was going to find that Rose's skin was a lot less tender than he expected. After all, he wasn't saying anything that she hadn't thought herself. She just smiled jauntily and said, without a trace of irony, "That is very obvious."

"*Hmph.*" Mr. Flett clearly hadn't expected her capitulation to his statement. Taking advantage of his sudden lack of words, Rose decided to try to steer the conversation to the benefit of her investigation. Perhaps she would even discover the identity of the mysterious *him*. But the easiest place to start was with the one name that she had: Tamsin Morris.

"What are some of the names of the families living on the island? I thought I heard one of the household staff mention the Morrises?"

"Never heard of them." Mr. Flett shook his head dismissively. "And my father's family has been living on Frest since long before the king of

Norway foolishly lost the Northern Isles to the king of Scotland in the fifteenth century over a failed dowry payment."

"I suppose I was mistaken, then." Rose shrugged airily, while inside she battled back disappointment at another dead end.

"There are a lot of Craigies and Inksters here in addition to us Fletts and Sinclairs," Freya added helpfully as she passed a plate of sliced cheese to Rose.

"What are common first names? So many of yours sound more Scandinavian than Scottish," Rose asked, trying to steer the discussion in a direction where she could inquire about any Tamsins.

"We are Orcadians, *not* Scots." Mr. Flett rather ferociously stabbed his smoked herring.

"We are a mix of cultures," Mr. Sinclair explained more helpfully as he cast his stepfather a warning look.

"Some of us more than others," Mr. Flett grumbled, side-eyeing his stepson.

"Is Tamsin one of the British names used in Orkney? I always found it rather a pretty one myself." It might not have been the most elegant way to ask the question, but at least Rose had managed to make her inquiry not a complete non sequitur.

Mr. Flett made a dismissive sound in the back of his throat as he heaped pickle onto a bere barley cracker. Mr. Sinclair, however, gave her a warm smile. "That is more of a Welsh name, I'm afraid."

"I've never heard of it before," Barbara piped up. "But I think it sounds wonderful."

It did not appear as if Rose would be learning anything more about the mysterious Tamsin Morris, at least from the Fletts. Biting down on a piece of the cheese, she let the sharp flavor prick her tongue. Perhaps she needed another line of inquiry.

"This is an absolutely wonderful meal, Freya. You are an excellent hostess. Did you ever entertain the Earl of Mar or his late son?"

That had not been the right thing to say. Tension swamped the room like humidity during a Floridian summer. Everyone, even little Alexander, shifted uncomfortably. Mr. Flett's dour expression devolved into something deadly. The right side of his body stiffened while his left stayed limp. He made a fist so tight that he scraped the tines of his fork against his plate. The resulting shriek was the only sound that filled the now-silent room.

"Well, I *am* flattered to be an occupant of Muckle Skaill who's been invited to eat at this table." Rose made a clumsy attempt to settle whatever dust storm she'd inadvertently kicked up.

The children dipped their heads lower toward their plates, while Mr. Sinclair half swallowed, half choked, the harsh motion causing his Adam's apple to shift. The squeaking coming from Mr. Flett's dinnerware only increased.

"I suppose you weren't well acquainted with the earl and his family. Their loss, of course. I assume Mar and Barbury mostly stayed on Hamarray when they visited."

Mary's head bounced up. "The viscount—"

"Was by all accounts a decent sort," Mr. Sinclair hastily broke into his sister's sentence, and Rose did her best not to show undo interest in his interruption. What *had* Mary been about to say? Had they known Barbury more than Mr. Sinclair was willing to let on? Why would he hide a connection like that? Was Mr. Sinclair one of the spies, and had he realized that the viscount suspected him?

Mr. Flett, the champion of disgusted sounds, emitted another one, but he otherwise did not comment. Instead, he went back to eating, chewing as if attacking his meal. At least he had stopped making the earsplitting scraping noises against his plate.

"Was anyone on Frest particularly close to the heir apparent?"

Barbara bounced in her seat this time. "He was—"

"Not as arrogant as the earl," Mr. Sinclair again interrupted. "He would at least acknowledge the presence of us locals. He would have made a better laird than his father."

Mr. Sinclair was definitely hiding something—perhaps many somethings. Unfortunately, he was also extremely talented at steering the conversation in the direction he wanted. He seemed unlikely to permit one of the children to slip and admit something that he didn't want her knowing. Rose had a feeling he had known Barbury better than he wished to admit, but again, why was he so eager to keep that fact from her? Had they been friends? Enemies? Could Mr. Sinclair be the *him*, or could he be the spy?

"I suppose a landowner should get to know his or her tenants," Rose said, seizing the chance to lay the groundwork for interviewing the rest of the crofters. "Do you think you could serve as my guide, Mr. Sinclair, and introduce me to them? Perhaps the day after tomorrow? That way you can give them advance notice so it doesn't seem like such an intrusion—more like a neighborly visit."

The best scoff yet erupted from Mr. Flett. Mr. Sinclair, however, did not make his feelings quite so apparent. He looked a little bit dumbfounded, definitely a tad concerned, and perhaps, just perhaps, a touch pleased.

"You could come to the sheep count tomorrow, Miss Van Etten," Margaret said solemnly. "Everyone from Frest will be on Hamarray helping to round up the flock. We put them in pens that we call *punds* just like they do on North Ronaldsay, except our breed isn't adapted to eating seaweed like theirs."

"I'd love to help," Rose said, eager to begin her investigation almost immediately and not wanting to give either man a chance to protest.

It seemed, however, whether any of them truly wished it, including her, Rose was about to play Lady of Muckle Skaill come hell or high water.

Chapter 4

"Don't be a gappus over a lass." Sigurd's low words carried through the small byre that Sinclair had built.

Sinclair didn't even turn from milking Sally. The sun had sunk nearly below the horizon, but he was acclimated to working in the darkness . . . just as he'd become long accustomed to being considered a fool by his stepfather. Typically, though, the older man conveyed his low opinion only with grunts and well-timed coughs.

"I have no intention to be one, sir." Sinclair tugged at one of the cow's teats, and the milk hissed into the empty pail.

"You wouldn't be the first to go daft over a pretty face." Sigurd sat heavily down on the older milking stool that the children sometimes used when they joined Sinclair.

"Aye, but I won't."

"You cannot let her go poking about Frest. There is something strange about her suddenly buying Mar's estate and the old bastard just up and leaving."

"Aye. Miss Van Etten is a difficult one to decipher."

"If you can't understand her, it isn't likely any of us other folks shall." The words were edged with the sense that Sinclair didn't truly belong to the people of Frest—not with his sire's English blood rushing through him, thoroughly drowning his mother's Orcadian roots.

"I'll make sure she stays far away from Fornhowe," Sinclair promised.

"She doesn't seem like the superstitious sort. I doubt the tales that we use to warn off the daft authorities will work on a fae lass like her."

"She doesn't seem the type to go on rambles and poke into ancient mounds either." *More likely she'd just drive her automobile over it.*

"Aye. You're probably right." Sigurd sighed wearily. "I don't like her interest in Frest, though."

Sinclair didn't respond at first as he moved on to another two teats. Sally shot him a look before she docilely went back to chewing her fodder. When he'd first learned how to milk a cow under Sigurd's tutelage, the previous bovine had been a temperamental beast and new to being milked. Sinclair probably would have had his arm broken a time or two if he hadn't been so good at dodging blows up at Muckle Skaill.

"Her attention might prove useful," Sinclair said carefully, knowing that his stepfather would disagree. But he'd watched Miss Van Etten's discussion with Margaret. She hadn't been dismissive of the child's concerns. She'd actually listened. And if she could be solicitous to a mere bairn, mayhap she would be attentive to the requests of an adult.

"If you believe that nonsense, then you truly are a gappus. You could never fully see what a danger Reginald was either."

His stepfather had despised Sinclair's friendship with his half brother almost as much as it infuriated the earl. But they'd been the best of friends . . . until the day that Sinclair had found Reggie kissing Astrid. They'd fought then with blows and words. They'd only just begun to make up when Britain had declared war on Germany, and Sinclair had refused to follow Reggie to the Front as his batman. They'd never spoken again after that, although Sinclair had spotted his older sibling from a distance when he had returned to Hamarray to convalesce after his first capture.

But Reggie had refused to see Sinclair and had barely spoken to Astrid. She'd said that the normally happy-go-lucky Reggie had been cagey and steeped in secrets and darkness. Sinclair had always wondered what had made his brother return to the Front so suddenly and if . . . and if he could have prevented Reggie's death.

"Reggie had plans for Hamarray and Frest." Sinclair didn't know why he was still making this argument to his stepfather. His brother was dead, along with the ideas they'd dreamed up together, from reclaiming boggy land to purchasing a mechanized thresher for the crofts. It no longer should matter what Sigurd thought of Reggie—but it still did. At least to Sinclair. He owed his brother that much, especially since he hadn't been there to physically protect him.

"Humph."

Aye, Sinclair's stepfather had no need to actually call him a ninny, not when Sigurd could do so emphatically with a mere sound. The elderly man leaned forward on his cane, his eyes fairly boring two holes into Sinclair's skull.

"Reginald was quick enough to drag your name through the muck when you ceased dancing to his tune."

That Sinclair could never deny. His brother had gone to a pub in Kirkwall and gotten completely blootered. Reggie had never held his drink or his temper well, and he'd complained to all and sundry about how cowardly Sinclair was. Eventually, Reggie had staggered back to Frest with a jug of Orcadian beer in his hand. He'd shared his drink with anyone willing to listen to his complaints against his lily-livered half brother. The pain of Reggie's betrayal had never quite gone away . . . neither had the feeling that perhaps Reggie had not been completely wrong about Sinclair's character. So Sinclair said nothing in response to Sigurd as he squeezed the last of the milk into the now-brimming pail.

"Outsiders are all the same, seeking to use us until they grow bored of their playthings. The tales about selkies and mermaids might just be stories, but there's a real warning in them—one you would do well to heed."

"I won't let Miss Van Etten spirit me away from here, if that's what you're worried about." Sinclair rose from his own milking stool and then pivoted slowly, careful not to spill a drop. When he faced his stepfather, he realized his blunder. The man detested his dependence on Sinclair.

"Everyone knows nothing will ever make you leave Frest. You've nary an adventurous bone in your entire body. Even if a mermaid leaped upon your boat and dragged you down into the sea, you'd find a way to pop back up like a piece of flotsam."

And there it was. The veiled accusation all the crofters felt. Sinclair was a feartie for staying while the other menfolk died. Never mind that he'd had a duty here. For if Sigurd admitted that, he would have to acknowledge his own reliance on his stepson, the offspring of a man he loathed.

Sinclair rubbed the bridge of his nose, wishing he were not having this conversation with Sigurd. They'd rarely had deep ones and certainly none filled with fatherly advice. True, Sigurd had taught him how to croft, shear a sheep, and fish from the sea. Sinclair owed him for that, but other lessons—like those involving becoming a man—those topics had never been broached.

"You've been nominated as the crofters' representative, and I don't want you leading them astray," Sigurd chided.

"I want what is *right* for the people of Frest." Sinclair stood in front of his stepfather, wishing that once, just *once*, he would be seen as one of the island folks with no ties to the Earl of Mar.

"Your notions can be troublesome at best." The tip of Sigurd's cane thudded into the sod. Even with the left side of his body still partially paralyzed from the stroke, he moved with determined authority. The man's strength and will were among the things Sinclair respected about him—along with how well he cared for his own children and how he'd practically worshipped Sinclair's mother.

"We need investment in our land if we are to modernize and keep up." Sinclair tried to make the stubborn man understand. "We will no longer have thousands of hungry and thirsty sailors at our doorstep to improve our economic situation."

"Economic situation," Sigurd repeated as he managed another stamp with his cane and good foot. "It is phrases like that that hoodwink the islanders into thinking you are the lad to parlay with the gentry."

Sinclair had never found responsibility uncomfortable—until now. The people of Frest did not really wish to trust him. They would much rather put a more favored son in charge. But many had not returned. Aye, sons and fathers were trickling back. Any one of them could theoretically take up the position of de facto leader, but none of them understood the upper classes like Sinclair did. Although they'd all attended the local school, they hadn't spent the years Sinclair had studying old, dusty tomes from the earl's personal library or treatises on everything from agriculture to mechanics.

"I shall do what is required of me," Sinclair promised. *I always do.*

Even though he had not said the last words, Sigurd had clearly sensed them. The right half of his mouth twisted downward at the additional reminder of his and his children's dependence on his stepson. The man had always been a powerful force—he still was, even if his body did not always obey his commands. Yet Sigurd saw only what he could no longer do, not all that he did. The man still worked hard, helping wherever he could and teaching his children how to survive the harsh life of a crofter. He kept his body in shape by taking daily walks to the cliffs of Hamarray when the tides were low. There was much about the man to be admired.

Unfortunately, the esteem that Sinclair felt toward his stepfather would never be returned. Most of him had long ago both recognized that fact and become resigned to it.

The other part of Sinclair . . . well, it was destined for disappointment.

"You didn't mind having the Royal Navy's Grand Fleet at your doorstep?" Rose asked Mrs. Janet Inkster the next day as they stood together with Myrtle near the base of two knolls on Hamarray. The grassy lumps evidently formed a natural barricade that the islanders used to help round up the flock. The three of them were supposed to make sure that the sheep did not break loose and scatter when they emerged from the shallow pass. Rose, however, was much more interested in what the middle-aged islander had to say about her feelings toward the British and her thoughts about Mar and his late son.

"Nay." Janet shook her head. The ends of her yellow-and-white tweed scarf tied about her head fluttered in the wind. "Those big ships were a welcome sight, made us feel protected, living so far as we do out here in the North Sea."

"The sailors didn't cause any problems with the locals? They can be rowdy on shore leave," Rose asked.

"My Texas Ranger grandpa had a few tales about drunk mariners carousing in Galveston," Myrtle added.

"They were mostly good lads," Janet said. "It was nice having so many young men around—especially with our boys off at the Fronts or serving in the navy themselves. Made me miss my Jack and William both a peedie bit less and a peedie bit more. My Davy—now, he was stationed in Scapa Flow, and he'd visit me whenever he had the chance. He'd always bring a friend or two around who were hankering for some home-cooked food. When my boy died at Jutland, his old mates who survived still came around and helped me out when they could."

Rose swallowed, thinking of the soldiers she couldn't bring to safety quickly enough. All the world carried death around with them these days, one way or another. Here, on this island, where the population had been declining since the brutal Enclosures, every soul who did not make it back threatened the continued existence of these people.

"I'm so sorry for your loss," Myrtle said gently as Rose struggled to compose herself.

"We—we lost so many good people." Rose finally managed to speak. Her voice was still thick, but at least it was steady. "I cannot imagine how you must miss your son."

"Aye." A raw pain sprang into Janet's eyes that ran deeper than tears could reach. The woman let her thin shoulders drop for just a moment, as if permitting the agony that she normally held at bay to wash through her. Then she straightened, her pale-blue eyes not exactly bright but resolved. "At least the older boys will be home soon. Others, like Widow Craigie, aren't so lucky. My Ann and I will be glad to have two more hands around the croft again."

"I'm sure it hasn't been easy without your sons." Rose thought of the work the Fletts had put into providing just one meal. She'd never considered before how vital families could be—how necessary to survival. Then again, until the war, Rose had never couched the act of living in those terms—survival and necessity.

"It has been a peedie bit of a challenge every now and then. Mr. Sinclair helped us out a time or two, but he had his own croft and the other islanders to help."

The mix of bitterness and reluctant gratitude in Janet's voice shocked Rose as she realized that Mr. Sinclair had *not* fought in the Great War. She'd originally assumed that he'd lost his eye in the trenches early in the conflict, but now she wondered if he'd received the wound in childhood. It would explain why he hadn't been able to join the cause. There was no shame in that as far as Rose was concerned. War held no glory, and male crofters had been sorely needed to keep the people and armies fed. It had been a constant struggle for the rural French farmers who were torn between their obligations to the plow and to the gun. Yet it was clear that Janet did not feel the same as Rose—at least not entirely.

"Without the income the men would have earned from fishing, Ann has had to work for that horrible . . ." Janet trailed off and then glanced out of the corner of her eye at Rose and Myrtle. "Well, it doesn't matter anymore now, does it, with the men coming home."

Rose's heart stuttered. Why had Janet paused? Had Ann found employment as a courier for the spy ring? "For that *horrible* who? Someone on Frest?"

"I shouldn't have called him horrible. It isn't my place," Janet added quickly.

"The earl?" Rose asked, not sure if that should allay or heighten her suspicions. Mar remained one of her chief suspects. Was Ann the timid maid she had met her first night at Muckle Skaill? There were not too many people from the island to choose from, but the name was common enough.

"You were asking about what it was like with the Grand Fleet here." Janet seemed eager to change the conversation. "It was good for Frest. We'd never sold so many lambs as we did in those years, and we still have a bigger flock than I can remember. It's like the times my granny would tell me about, before the Enclosures."

Although Rose knew she should not let Janet distract her from exactly how Ann was employed, the woman's words caused an entirely new flicker of concern to drift through Rose. Everyone from Mr. Sinclair to the wise-beyond-her-years Margaret had impressed upon Rose the importance of the flock to life on Frest. But what would the islanders do with all these sheep now that their primary market had literally sailed away?

"The lads themselves were always buying things from us islanders. Sweaters and scarves—some for themselves or to send home to their sweethearts. Some good boys even thought of their dear old mothers. And of course, all the sailors . . ." Janet trailed off again, looking very much like she had when she'd suddenly stopped before.

"All the sailors what?" Rose prodded.

"Mind the sheep!" Mr. Sinclair's voice boomed like an engine mis-fire. At the shout, Rose felt herself start to slide back into memories of the war. The bleating of the sheep mixed with the phantom cries of men and horses. A wall of wool bore down on Rose, and she dug her nails into her palm.

"Wave your arms, Miss Van Etten!" Margaret yelled out.

"Stop them from going left!" Mr. Sinclair ordered.

"Spread your feet, miss!" Freya called. "Make yourself look big."

But Rose was rooted in place—stuck between the past and the present. The only part of her that didn't seem frozen was her rapidly pounding heart.

Warm softness hit Rose's legs. The sensation pulled her back to reality. The pungent odor of animals filled her nostrils as she found herself surrounded by the ewes and lambs. The sheep's eyes looked wild, their mouths open wide as they *maaa*ed their protest.

"You're splitting the flock!" Mr. Sinclair yelled again.

"Rose, darling." Myrtle's voice was quiet and calm as she softly touched Rose's arm. "We're standing in the middle of a bunch of ewes in a pasture. Do you hear them? Feel them?"

Glancing around, Rose realized she was indeed like Moses parting the Red Sea—except that had been a good thing. This was *not*. Sheep seemed to spill out onto the rolling slope behind Rose and Myrtle like ticker tape at a New York parade. Although the ewes and lambs still coming through the pass were not exactly orderly, they were clumped. And Rose was scattering them.

Janet was doing her best to steer the flock as she flapped her arms like an angry albatross. But she could not counteract the obstacle that Rose and Myrtle presented.

Despite her wobbly legs, Rose pushed her way through the flocculent mass. Somehow, she managed to hop over two bucking twin lambs as Myrtle sidestepped a rather massive ewe. Out of breath and with Rose also still shaken from shell shock, they took up their positions by Janet, but it was too late. The terrified ungulates were running amok.

Mr. Sinclair stomped over to Rose, his lips molded into an unforgiving line. Irritation rolled from him in an almost palpable wave. Her own back stiffened. Rose's armor of blitheness instantly snapped into place as her limbs turned from gel back into sturdy muscle and bone. Being cavalier was much preferable to feeling useless.

"I do apologize," Rose called out. "I'm afraid I was distracted by the lovely conversation I was having about Frest with Mrs. Inkster and Miss Morningstar. I hope I didn't cause too much of a bother."

Her attempt at lightness caused Mr. Sinclair's jaw to tighten to such a degree that the scar along the right side of his face puckered even more. "This might seem like a lark to you, Miss Van Etten, but the rest of us have other work we must be getting to. We do not have time to be chasing sheep all over creation."

"So no chatting, then?"

Mr. Sinclair narrowed his left eye into a rather impressive glower, making him look more like Odin than his namesake. On the other hand, Rose wouldn't be surprised if he started hurling thunderbolts in her direction.

"No." His answer was clipped and not his usual softer *nay*.

"I do believe the sheep startled Miss Van Etten very badly, Mr. Sinclair." Janet broke into the conversation. "She looked all peelie-wally when they came running toward us. Miss Morningstar was just trying to help her friend by staying by her side. They weren't nattering once the ewes burst through the hills."

Although Rose was surprisingly touched by the woman's defense, she didn't want anyone on Frest or Hamarray knowing about her shell shock and treating her as some fragile thing to coddle.

"Is that true?" Mr. Sinclair looked at Rose skeptically, and it mollified her a bit that he didn't think her a ninny, easily frightened by *sheep*.

Before Rose could assure him that she was not in any way intimidated by fleecy dams and their frolicking babes, Janet answered, "Aye. She was like a statue when they came bearing down on us. You shouldn't be so harsh on the lass, seeing as you might understand a thing or two about being a peedie bit of a feartie."

The words, although spoken in soft tones, carried a sting that caused even Rose to wince. If she'd been directly on the receiving end, her response would have been equally cutting. Mr. Sinclair, however, did not anger—not one iota. But the blow had struck him all the same. She could see the frustrated guilt in his uninjured eye, and for one mad moment Rose wanted to reach out to him and tell him that he'd served his people in his own way—a *needed* way. But just as her fingers began involuntarily lifting, she saw something else in his gaze: concern. For her.

"You needn't feel like you must help with the herding if the sheep are bothering you, Miss Van Etten." He spoke without a hint of amusement, but she almost would have preferred being mocked. Land sakes, *her* being afraid of a bleating piece of fluff? She'd dodged *shells*.

"I am quite fine, thank you." She ran her gloved hands over the serviceable skirt that she wore. Her silk Paul Poiret outfit with its floaty pants would have given her more freedom of movement, but the thin, delicate material was hardly appropriate for running up and down hills after livestock. It really was past time for women to be able to buy practical trousers with *pockets*.

"You are welcome to watch if you would feel more comfortable—" Mr. Sinclair searched her face, and his solicitous scrutiny unsettled her.

"Just point me in the direction of the sheep that you wish me to corral, Mr. Sinclair," Rose cut in.

Mr. Sinclair's gaze held hers just a fraction longer, and she stared straight back. Then he gave her a nod—the kind a man would give to another to acknowledge his mettle. A rush went through Rose, her heart swelling at the unspoken recognition in the gesture.

"You and Miss Morningstar can head out toward the western end of the isle and flank the sheep there. I'll tell you when to start moving forward. You'll need to coordinate with us islanders."

"We can do that," Rose said. After giving him a crisp nod, she lifted up her skirts and tore across the field to get into position. She'd always been the athletic sort, much to her mother's dismay. On the rare occasions that Verity Van Etten had arranged for her daughter to accompany her on society visits, she'd wanted Rose to sit demurely with the other little girls and their dolls instead of racing around with the boys.

"We'll help the both of you!" Barbara, one of the twins, cried.

"It'll make more sense once you try it a time or two, Miss Van Etten," Margaret added gravely as she, too, headed in Rose and Myrtle's direction.

Hannah joined in, rolling her eyes as she caught up to her youngest sister. "If Miss Van Etten can race automobiles in open-road trials, then I don't think running after a few sheep will prove difficult."

"Girls, please simmer down. You'll startle the flock, and Thorfinn will be calling out instructions soon," Freya said as she and Mary plodded up to them. Rose, Myrtle, and the Flett girls spread out along the top of the small rise, a quarter or so of the flock spread out on the slope below. All around the rises and hollows of the lower half of Hamarray, the crofters were doing the same until they'd formed a roughly even-spaced perimeter around the sheep.

Little Alexander had not come along with his sisters but instead was standing next to Mr. Sinclair. Every now and again, the boy would cast up a look at his big brother, and his little chest would swell with pride. Even from yards away, Rose could feel the child's admiration for the man who appeared to be a father figure to him.

"Ann Inkster, move a peedie bit to the right. We need to give them an opening to run through," Mr. Sinclair called out, and Rose's attention flew to the figure who moved. Sure enough, Ann Inkster *was* the maid Rose had frightened. She looked a bit like Janet, and the scarf she wore around her head was clearly cut from the same piece of fabric as the older woman's. Rose would need to have another chat with the shy miss.

"Astrid, Ron, and Ann Craigie, start pushing them in from your end. Take it easy now. Don't crowd them too much. We don't want them to bolt yet," Mr. Sinclair called next. All the islanders listened to him without hesitation. It was apparent from the way that he orchestrated the roundup like a conductor of a symphony that he'd done this many times before. Some of the people of Frest might be bitter that he had not served his country, but it was clear that they recognized his innate leadership. Even Rose, who generally balked at authority—including during the war—found herself listening to him. Perhaps it was because he did not so much command as he simply expected them all to work together. It was strange, being a moving part of a larger unit, all working in tandem as one single force toward the same goal.

When they finally moved the skittish creatures into the drystone sheep pens on the beach opposite the docks, an odd sense of accomplishment filled Rose. She had no idea why it felt so fulfilling to stare down at the fleecy, *maa*ing chaos as she sat on one of the thick walls, but it did.

As she watched, one of the sheep closest to Rose tried to jump over the back of another. The poor thing looked as panicked as the rest of the woolly beasts. When the same ewe tried scrambling over another member of the herd, Rose let out a gasp. There were tiny *hooves* sticking out of the poor dam's rear.

"Mr. Sinclair!" Rose shouted, instinctually calling his name. "Mr. Sinclair! I do believe that there is a sheep with a problem!"

He was at her side within a second. All she had to do was point at the struggling ewe, and he sprang over the stone barricade, using only one arm to execute his impressive vault. A chorus of bleats met his landing. Two of the other men also climbed into the pen, and the flock's existential crises burgeoned. Wide eyed, the sheep tried to form a tight huddle but managed only to move in every direction at once. No wonder the poor beleaguered things made such easy targets for predators.

"Her instinct to herd is stronger than the labor pains," Freya explained as she rushed over and leaned close to Rose and Myrtle. "If the men cannot capture and calm her, we could lose both her and the lamb."

Mr. Sinclair wove through the fluffy chaos with single-minded intent. The pregnant ewe tried her best to outmaneuver him, but he dived down and tackled her. After a brief struggle, he managed to wrap one of his large hands around the ewe's front hooves and the other around her back feet. Cuddling her writhing, bucking body against his chest, he hoisted all 120 pounds of the frightened, fighting sheep into the air. He strode through the flock as if he were just strolling down the beach in Daytona. One of the men opened the wooden gate to the pen, and Mr. Sinclair carried the ewe to an enclosure that Rose assumed had been left empty as a place to contain the sheep as they were counted.

Rose, along with Myrtle and the islanders, moved to watch the proceedings. While the men held down the ewe, Mr. Sinclair knelt beside the animal. Gently, he moved his hand inside the dam.

"What is he doing?" Rose asked.

"Checking to make sure the lamb's head isn't turned. He'll straighten it if it is," Margaret explained. Rose turned toward the eight-year-old in surprise. The girl did seem to know everything there was about sheep, but Rose hadn't expected her to be an expert in ungulate midwifery.

"She's right," Myrtle added. "I've helped with the calving on the ranch, and this is bound to be similar."

"Don't look at me," Margaret instructed Rose, showing a remarkable lack of squeamishness as she kept her gaze trained on the rather messy proceedings. "Not if you want to see the babe being born. Thorfinn will start pulling soon, especially with how the mum is struggling."

Sure enough, Mr. Sinclair did begin to steadily help ease the newborn from its mother. In a surprisingly short amount of time, the little lamb lay on the ground. The ewe scrambled to her feet and began to nuzzle and lick her offspring. Perhaps the creatures were much tougher than Rose had given them credit for. She of all people should have known better than to be deceived by outward fluffiness.

A soft cheer rose up among the people of Frest before they and Myrtle began to drift back to the other paddocks to begin the sheep count. Mr. Sinclair headed to the edge of the sand and bent to wash his hands in the turquoise water. When he stood up, he caught Rose watching him, but she didn't look away. He strode over to her, giving her a smile instead of his normal tight-lipped frown.

"Thank you, Miss Van Etten. If you hadn't noticed that the ewe was in trouble, things might have taken a tragic turn."

"I'm just glad both mother and baby are okay." Rose nodded toward the duo, who were both making low sounds as the ewe continued to clean her offspring.

Mr. Sinclair cocked his head in the direction of the pair too. "Do you hear that?"

"I do," Rose said.

"They're learning the sounds of each other's voice and their smell. That's how they know to find each other in the flock. It's important they bond like this right after the birth, or the mother will reject her own bairn."

"Perhaps someone should tell that to society parents before they summarily hand their babes off to wet nurses and nannies." The words tumbled from Rose's mouth before she thought better of it. She didn't know why she'd been thinking about her own childhood so much lately. She rarely had in the past. But something about being on Hamarray and Frest among so many families working side by side was making her revisit her own personal history . . . and the conflicted emotions that she preferred to keep buried.

Mr. Sinclair's left eye widened in surprise, but she doubted he was as shocked as she was by her impromptu statement.

"Miss Van Etten—" he began, his tone cautious, as if he was not sure what to say. That made two of them, then.

"Sinclair!" one of the men shouted, providing a convenient distraction. "We need you over here to officially start the count!"

Mr. Sinclair paused, as if unsure if he should leave her after such a melancholy statement. Rose dismissed him with a wave of her hand. "Go. I say inappropriate things all the time. Make nothing of it."

Still he hesitated, but she shooed him away. As Mr. Sinclair dashed off, Rose drew in her breath as she glanced away from the suddenly too-precious domestic scene in front of her. She hadn't come to Orkney to learn about animal husbandry. She was here to complete Viscount Barbury's mission.

Her gaze fell on Ann Inkster, who was sitting on one of the walls, watching the men wrestle with the sheep as they and the older women checked the livestock. Rose walked over and smiled at the girl. The young lady gave her a faint grin before tucking her chin. Ann still seemed shy but not frightened like she had at Muckle Skaill.

"Ann, is it?" Rose kept her voice gentle and welcoming.

"Aye," Ann said, raising her head again. Her voice was high and sweet.

"Are you Janet Inkster's daughter?" Rose sat down beside her, keeping her eyes focused on the sheep, knowing that would make the conversation easier for the timid adolescent.

"Aye."

"She was very patient with me today," Rose said. "I'm afraid I am not a natural at sheep management."

That earned Rose a quiet chuckle from Ann. "You did all right in the end, Miss Van Etten."

"How do you like working at Muckle Skaill?" Rose asked.

"It's fine, milady—I mean miss—now that you're in charge."

Now, *that* was a telling turn of phrase. "You didn't like the earl."

Ann stiffened again, and she seemed to retreat back into herself. "I didn't know him."

"But you worked there?" Rose asked.

"The other girls told me to stay in the kitchens when he was in residence. He never stayed long. Not like he did before the war."

Interesting. What had made him cut those trips short?

"What did you think of his son?" Rose asked.

"It wasn't my place to think of him or the earl," Ann said quickly.

Rose was trying to figure out how to worm her way around that answer when Myrtle suddenly rematerialized with the Flett children in tow. Little Alexander tugged on Rose's hand and stared up at her with huge eyes. "You can run really fast. Even Thorfinn said so."

"Is that true?" Rose said, surprised at the odd rush of pride that the boy's two sentences caused. She'd received so many admiring comments over the years—most of them inspired by her wealth more than anything else—that they'd become banal. But this child's were heartfelt and wholly unexpected. He wanted nothing in return, and she suspected that his older brother would be horrified to learn that Alexander had shared his complimentary thoughts.

"You're like your race car," Alexander added, making Rose laugh in delight. She rather liked the comparison.

"I did have a lot of fun today," Rose told the boy and his siblings, realizing how much she meant the words. She *had* enjoyed herself chasing after those sheep.

"It is a shame that we're not having a ceilidh like we usually do to celebrate after gathering the flock." Barbara sighed. "Now *that* was a jolly good time."

"It has been ever so long since we had one," her twin, Mary, added just as longingly. "I barely remember the last one."

"I don't at all," Margaret said gravely.

"Me either," Alexander chimed in.

"That's because we haven't had one since the war," Hannah said. "Right, Freya?"

"That's correct," Freya said with a sigh. "I do miss them, though."

"You know," Rose said as a new cover for her investigation began to form, "I've never had the good fortune to attend a ceilidh. I've heard there is plenty of food, singing, and dancing." And alcohol, which always loosened tongues quite proficiently.

"And storytelling!" Mary said with a bounce.

"Now that sounds like a good time," Myrtle said. "I'd love to hear more about the local folklore."

"I'll be sure to see that you both receive a proper invitation to the next one on Frest," Freya promised.

But Rose didn't have time to wait for the crofters to throw a party—not if she wanted to use the affair to ferret out more information about the earl, the viscount, and whatever else the islanders were hiding. The attendees would be in high spirits . . . and unguarded. People always spoke more freely at fetes, even when not soused. And if *she* threw the event, she might seem more approachable and less the highborn lady of the manor. It seemed as if her skills at entertaining might have a broader use than she'd ever imagined.

Smiling, she turned toward Margaret, who was closely watching as the adults tended to the flock. "As you seem to know more about being Lady of Muckle Skaill than I do, would it be appropriate of me to host a ceilidh for everyone on Frest?"

Margaret swung her wide gaze away from the enclosure. Her solemnity vanished in a bubbly giggle as she gleefully clapped her hands. "Oh yes! Oh yes!"

"Well then, I'll need all of you children to help me plan it, since Myrtle and I have never attended one." Organizing the festivities would give Rose one more excuse to spend time with the crofters.

A smile touched her lips at the thought. Whoever could have guessed that a party might be the way to unravel an espionage plot?

Chapter 5

The next morning, Miss Van Etten and her archaeologist friend arrived by speedboat. As much as Sinclair admired the elegantly designed hull, he found his gaze instead drawn to the lady conning the vessel. The sun had arrived in its fullest glory today, and it shone on her upturned face. Heedless of the certainly cold spray of seawater, Miss Van Etten gazed merrily ahead. She was close enough to the shore now that he could see the rise and fall of her beaver coat as she sucked in a lusty helping of air. Sinclair felt like he was breathing the crispness into his own lungs as his chest filled with a damn curious lightness.

"They're here!" Hannah's shout bounced over the landscape.

Sinclair, who had been trimming the hooves of their pony, Charlie, as he waited for the women's arrival, lifted the beast's last leg. He had time to finish the job before they secured the boat and welcomed the parade of his half siblings.

Charlie emitted a beleaguered snort at the indignity. Baring his chunky teeth, the equine tossed his ruddy thatch of mane and turned to glower at Sinclair. When he simply ignored the ill-tempered brute, Charlie attempted to nip his shoulder. Accustomed to the horse's grooming ritual, Sinclair jerked away from the powerful chomp. Most of the time, he won this battle of wills. Sometimes, Charlie did. And whenever he did, Sinclair swore the pony watched him with a malevolent gleam in his eye as Sinclair went about his chores while nursing a throbbing shoulder.

Staying clear of Charlie's jaw, Sinclair quickly clipped the last hoof. Even though he'd just saved the ungrateful Charlie from sore feet, the horse rewarded him by sneezing in his hair. Profusely. Charlie whinnied in delight, and despite his short, bulky frame, he managed to prance away with the grace of a prize Lipizzan stallion.

"Ingrate!" Sinclair called after the whelp.

The horse only flicked his bushy tail and sent his mane rippling through the wind. The animal was likely off in search of seaweed, which the stubborn gappus preferred to grass and even to grain.

When the beastie stopped to pull a clump of bead weed from a boulder near the surf, Sinclair shook his head fondly. Turning, he saw not only that Miss Van Etten and Miss Morningstar had managed to secure the boat to the ancient stone jetty jutting into the sea but that all *six* of his siblings had climbed on board. Alexander—who was always grubby no matter how many baths either Freya or Sinclair gave him— was *rolling* on her immaculate burgundy seats. Hannah had pushed the heiress out of the way to study the controls, while the twins were petting the shiny lacquered wood. Margaret had cornered the ladies and was most likely bombarding them with a litany of questions. Freya was trying to corral the younger children, but instead she accidentally stepped on Miss Van Etten's foot.

To Sinclair's surprise, the new Lady of Muckle Skaill did not lose her temper. Even Reggie—who had generally tolerated Sinclair's younger siblings fairly well—had grumbled when any of them had touched his fine things. Although Reggie had been close to Sinclair and later to Astrid, he'd always held himself a bit apart from the rest of the islanders—friendly enough but not warm. He had not had the earl's cruelty, but he hadn't completely escaped a sense of superiority. Even in his relationship with Sinclair, Reggie had always had to be the decision maker.

"Oh, I do apologize, miss!" Freya clasped her hand over her mouth in horror, her cheeks the color of a bloodred summer sunset.

"No need!" Miss Van Etten airily tossed her hand. "I assure you that it was tromped on much more emphatically during my debutante ball."

"Were the lads *that* clumsy?" Mary's mouth spread into a perfect O.

"Oh, heavens *no*." Miss Van Etten laughed. "It was all my fault. I was forever sneaking out of dance practice to race cars instead. It was *my* feet that were in the wrong place."

Sinclair had never known toffs to poke fun at themselves. Even Reggie—who had regarded life as a grand lark—had always taken his own self-image seriously.

"I've never heard of a lassie not knowing how to dance." Barbara's lips formed the exact same circle as her twin's had.

Miss Van Etten lightly patted the girl's arm. "Darling, we just let the men *think* it is all their fault when a clumsy step happens."

The girls all tittered, but Alexander stopped his bouncing, his little face scrunched in horror. "Does that mean I'll need to learn to dance all proper like?"

"Don't worry." Mary bent over and squeezed him. "We'll teach you."

"That's what I'm afraid of." Alexander thankfully sank into the cushions instead of continuing his efforts to destroy them. As soon as Sinclair got to *The Briar*, he was going to make sure the youngest was good and well contained.

"We can start your lessons at the ceilidh!" Barbara grabbed her twin's hands, and the two twirled about as if dancing to a jaunty tune. The boat bobbed ominously, but the girls paid no heed, even though Sinclair had taught them better than that.

"Mind your frolicking, lassies. You're not on solid ground," he called out. The twins listened immediately, but he could see their knees still bouncing to the reel playing in their heads. He sorely hoped that Miss Van Etten would make good on the pronouncement that she'd given yesterday to the bairns about hosting a ceilidh. Reggie had been forever making offhanded grand promises to the children that he'd never intended to keep. And it would be more than Sinclair's siblings who would be disappointed this time. News of the impending fete had carried throughout Frest.

Although Sinclair hoped Miss Van Etten would eventually do more for the islanders than just host a party, a celebration would do them all good. They needed a peedie bit of joy in their life after the long war and the worries of what would happen once the navy's presence, and the sailors' accompanying coin, dwindled even further.

The earl would never have been so generous as to even *think* of inviting his crofters to any of his events. If anyone had presented the idea to him, he would have heartily laughed at the poor person's expense. Reggie—who'd always enjoyed a party and the attention it brought him—had attended the ceilidhs from time to time. He'd dance with the island lasses and listen to some of the old tales before he'd grab a jug of whiskey and cajole Sinclair into leaving the festivities. Reggie would get drunk and Sinclair tipsy as they sat on the cliffs of Hamarray, talking about everything from novels to old battles to animal husbandry to Reggie's misadventures in London and the Continent.

"What do you think of me hosting a ceilidh, Mr. Sinclair? Margaret assures me that it is a proper thing for a laird to do." Miss Van Etten suddenly beamed at him as he reached *The Briar*, and his heart did a curious skip jump like a young lamb in spring.

"It would be enjoyed by many."

"And will you teach me the proper dance steps?" She winked at him, and the giddy feeling kicked against his chest again.

Before he could respond, Barbara piped up. "Oh, Mary and I will have to show you, along with Alex and Miss Morningstar. Thorfinn will be too busy fiddling. He's the best player in all of Orkney. Freya's very good on the accordion that used to be Da's."

Before one of his siblings could add something unintentionally embarrassing, Sinclair scrambled to say, "Are you two ladies ready to meet the rest of the crofters?"

"I am actually here to spend the day with your sisters and brother," Myrtle said. "They promised to show me around the mound on your property. It is most interesting."

"Just *our* mound," Freya added hurriedly, knowing as well as Sinclair that the islanders didn't want anyone sniffing around Fornhowe and discovering just exactly what secrets the hill in the center of the island hid.

Sinclair thought Miss Van Etten's head jerked rather sharply, as if she, too, had picked up on Freya's emphasis. Why did the heiress seem so curious? Toffs normally ignored their tenants . . . unless they wanted something from them. But what *did* Miss Van Etten want?

Miss Van Etten must have noticed his scrutiny, because she instantly gave him an airy smile, as if she didn't have a serious thought in her head—which he highly doubted.

"Well, I am most assuredly ready to visit the crofters, especially now that I am going to host a ceilidh," Miss Van Etten said.

"Because you wish to invite them?" Sinclair asked almost hesitantly, once again hoping that Miss Van Etten was taking this event as seriously as the islanders would.

"Not precisely, as the planning for the party is just in its infancy and I don't even have a date in mind yet, but perhaps you could tell me who would be a good person to supply what I'll require. I'll pay handsomely. Musicians. Cooks. I'll even compensate the children for helping me plan."

"You're paying us money, *real* money?" Barbara's squeaked exclamation echoed Sinclair's own dumbfounded thoughts.

"Yep." The irreverent American expression suited Miss Van Etten, who seemed to sally through all conventions like a Highlander leading a charge.

Sinclair wanted to immediately protest that his family and the other crofters had no need for alms, but he did not wish to guilt the children. Yet he also didn't desire to receive Miss Van Etten's charity. It was one thing to accept her help rounding up the flock and another to take money from her. A ceilidh was a shared expense of the community, with guests bringing food and volunteering their storytelling and singing. Did this heiress view them as simple folk to be pacified with celebration and coin?

It seemed not only was it hard for him to define Miss Van Etten's true character, but his reaction toward her was just as muddled. She was not simply a rich gadabout. Yesterday had proved that. He'd misjudged her when she'd split the flock. He'd thought she hadn't been taking the proceedings seriously. Reggie had always proved to be more of a distraction than an assistance whenever he'd gotten it into his head that it might be jolly fun to join the islanders in one of their community workdays. It had invariably ended with Reggie getting bored and either pulling a prank or trying to get the younger folks to abandon their posts for a game of football.

But after Miss Van Etten's mistake, she'd wholeheartedly joined the operation, dashing back and forth like a true islander. She was observant too. They'd all missed the ewe in labor, but not her. Nor had she panicked, but she had simply directed his attention to the struggling sheep. Now, here she was, willing to pay the crofters for their labors rather than think their hard-earned bounty was hers by right.

He wasn't going to straighten out his thoughts, though, by just standing here. It was time that Sinclair saw how Miss Van Etten interacted with the islanders and if it was even possible for her to understand their ways of life and needs.

"Shall we depart for the first croft on your tour? I was thinking about visiting David Craigie's mill first," he asked her.

"That sounds delightful! Let's vamoose." Miss Van Etten slipped her arm through his before he realized her intent. There was something chummy about the way she linked their elbows together . . . and intimate.

The heiress did not amble. No, she practically marched. He found her quick, economical movements surprisingly well matched to his own. The earl had always sauntered—even during his famed hunting "expeditions" over Hamarray. Even Reggie had possessed the tendency to stroll without any regard to the time wasted.

But not Miss Van Etten. She plowed ahead with the nimbleness of a sure-footed goat.

"The wind isn't as strong today," she observed. "I don't even need to shout to be heard."

"It is unusually calm."

"I almost miss the howling. There's something about the wildness that suits me."

Aye, Sinclair could see that about Miss Van Etten.

"What about you?" she asked, surprising him. "Do you find a bit of yourself reflected in this island?"

"Its hardiness." The words slipped out of him, unintended. But he'd always felt a kinship to this land buffeted by wind and sea yet still sturdy and fruitful.

"Yes. That makes perfect sense." Miss Van Etten's appreciative look threatened to turn the strange glow inside him into an unexpected and rather unwelcome inferno.

Dousing the feeling, he said stiffly, "We are all resilient here on Frest. Although we would do well by a laird interested in improving the land, we have no need for charity."

Miss Van Etten tugged a bit on his arm as she pulled back to study his face. "I wasn't aware I was giving handouts."

"There is no need to pay us for attending your ceilidh. By agreeing to give us a venue, you've done more than enough."

Miss Van Etten's dark eyebrows drew downward. Even pensive, she still exuded an ethereal kind of beauty. "I didn't mean to insinuate that I would have a sort of reverse admission for attending. That *would* be insulting."

"Guests and performers at the ceilidh are one and the same."

"Oh," Miss Van Etten said, "I suppose that makes sense now that I consider it."

"And people might view any payment as a type of alms."

Miss Van Etten stopped abruptly. At first, he thought he'd insulted her, but she appeared neither cross nor hurt.

"Mr. Sinclair, this is not disguised charity. If I have any notoriety in the world other than for my racing ability, it is my ability to throw a rollicking good party."

Miss Van Etten's statement sounded oddly like self-recrimination. It reminded him of her rather cynical statement about the aristocracy appointing others to rear their offspring.

"Newspapers have even likened me to a hedonistic successor of *the* Mrs. Astor," Miss Van Etten continued, "but do you think *I* was the one doing the work when I threw a fete? I employ people for that, and I compensate them handsomely."

"Folks around here see helping out at a ceilidh and bringing food as just being neighborly. There's no need for 'compensation,' especially for the children helping you plan it."

"I have a skeletal staff here at Hamarray," Miss Van Etten pointed out, not so much arguing with him as being extremely logical. "Your siblings would be filling a role normally assumed by my housekeeper and her assistants, and I always give a bonus when I ask them to perform extra duties. It only seems fair."

"Although the older ones will be of great assistance, I am not sure that the bairns will be much help."

"I'm sure they will contribute something. I would have no idea how to have a proper ceilidh without them."

"But—"

"Your sisters and brother all have chores, correct? And schooling?"

"Aye." The croft couldn't be run otherwise. He'd barely managed when the children were small and his stepfather couldn't move from his sickbed.

"Therefore, their playtime is precious, and they will be sacrificing it to help me. Why should I not account for that, including the benefit that I receive from their assistance? Would it not be me, otherwise, accepting something that I have not paid for?"

Sinclair rubbed the bridge of his nose again, wondering how he could explain to Miss Van Etten how the islanders would view it. "It is just being neighborly, same with the crofters bringing maet."

"Maet?"

"Food." Sinclair hadn't meant to use the Orcadian word, but it had slipped out. "You cannot ascribe an economic value to every act."

"I'm the daughter of an industrialist. I have known from the cradle that everything is, at its root, a form of currency." Miss Van Etten spoke the words flippantly, but he could hear a seriousness in her undertone.

"Even love and affection?" he asked, partially fascinated by her cynicism and partially dismayed by it.

"Why, yes. It is the oldest barter of them all."

"You don't truly believe that nonsense, do you?" Sinclair had no idea why he cared so much about this discussion, but it seemed rather . . . well . . . tragic for one not to believe in simple, kind regard.

"It is at the root of all relationships," Miss Van Etten said, her voice curiously detached, as if discussing international wool market trends rather than what was the most profound part of human existence: the capacity to care and form bonds.

"My parents' union is a perfect example. They have a contented marriage because they each obtained what they desired. It is all very conventional. My mother received wealth and security, while my father benefited from her elite New York Knickerbocker connections. They are mildly affectionate toward each other and are not overly annoyed by each other's presence. Mother still manages Daddy's social calendar and is a famed hostess. Despite his money, his standing in society would wither without her, and he knows it. And Mother is happy to have the money to spend creating their world of luxury."

Sinclair slowed his pace at her astonishing words. How could this woman exhibit so much patience toward his siblings yet hold such cold, almost mercenary views? Sinclair's mother *had* married his stepfather out of necessity, and she had become a good wife to him. But there had been real, abiding love between them, a tenderness that, despite being a mere child, he'd noticed. Even now after his mother had been in the ground for over half a decade, both Sinclair's and his stepfather's esteem for her still bound them together despite the tension simmering between them. What but love for her and the bairns would allow them to live under the same small roof?

"Which is why," Miss Van Etten continued, "I fully intend to remain unattached to the end of my days. I have wealth, status, and independence and no need to barter any of it."

The words were not a boast but what she clearly considered a logical conclusion. Yet Sinclair still felt a need to challenge it, unable to permit such a jaded view to stand. "What of companionship?"

Miss Van Etten shrugged. "That is what the occasional lover is for—an unspoken agreement to banish the loneliness of human existence, if only for a night."

He choked and tried to cover it with a cough. Miss Van Etten ignored his clumsy reaction and simply kept walking, as if she hadn't just said something rather scandalous. He realized that she hadn't said the words to be shocking. They were merely a philosophical and exceedingly melancholy observation.

Something shifted inside Sinclair as he searched for a way to respond to her words—not just to her but within himself as well. He felt balanced on a razor's edge with the dark unknown on either side of him. Before he could attempt to understand his bearings any better, a familiar voice called out his name.

"Sinclair!" David Craigie repeated as he waved enthusiastically. Relief flooded Sinclair at the interruption. Knowing David's fondness for chatting about his mill, Sinclair expected the man would provide more than enough distraction from the unexpectedly weighty conversation with Miss Van Etten. The crofter had already unfurled the sails on his windmill, and they looked like the white, outstretched wings of a fulmar as they spun through the blue sky. Winds were low today, and it wasn't the time of the year when most of the milling was done. Nor was it the day of the week when the islanders normally brought their grain. David had the canvas fully stretched across all six wooden frames, trying to take advantage of any current. Generally, the gusts were so high David had a devil of a time keeping the speed low enough not to cause damage to the machinery inside.

"Miss Van Etten, I am exceedingly honored that you chose to visit my mill." David's round, red face was stretched into a wide smile as he fairly bounced up and down on his feet. He was a big man, and the sight of him acting like a peedie child over his great-great-grandfather's creation always warmed the heart.

"The pleasure is all mine." Miss Van Etten immediately turned her head upward toward the cap of the structure in patent admiration. "This is one of the finest ones I have ever seen, and I've even been to Holland."

David almost sprang into the air at the compliment, and Sinclair swore that his large frame actually vibrated. "Indeed! That is most wonderful to hear. I try my best to keep her in good repair. She's a grand old lady now—well over a hundred years old."

"I imagine it was some feat to import all of her wooden gears, especially the great spur wheel," Miss Van Etten said.

David looked as if he wanted to sink down on his knees and ask her to marry him, regardless of the fact he was still madly in love with his wife of forty years. "You know about the parts of a windmill, lass?"

Sinclair would be more shocked himself if Miss Van Etten weren't constantly surprising him. The lady was indeed a clever one.

"I've always been interested in mechanical things," she said with a shrug. "I am friends with a member of one of the old Dutch merchant families, and he took me on a tour of his estates, including some windmills that he had decided to preserve."

Miss Van Etten sounded like Reggie, talking about faraway places that Sinclair would never see. The both of them belonged to a different world than him. One of wealth and travel. For all the time Sinclair had spent in the sea, he'd never sailed farther than Hoy and the main island of Orkney.

"You must see the inner workings of mine!" David waved toward the entrance of the windmill like a medieval courtier presenting his queen—and a slice of panic slid through Sinclair. He had specifically told the miller to *only* show her the ground floor. If David was about to offer a grand tour, Sinclair would need to think quickly of how to prevent it.

"The Earl of Mar must have been very pleased that his crofters had access to a meal mill like yours," Miss Van Etten said.

David's open expression immediately closed up, just as Sinclair himself stiffened. None of the islanders liked talking about the old laird. They'd all done their best to avoid Mar's attention.

David cast his eyes in Sinclair's direction. Everyone knew that it was Sinclair's mother who had been the most hurt by the earl—not that Sinclair had escaped unscathed from living at Muckle Skaill.

"The earl wasn't interested in the mill."

"His loss," Miss Van Etten said lightly. "Was his son any brighter?"

David's gaze once again flew to Sinclair, clearly discomforted by the questions when standing in the presence of the toff's unacknowledged offspring. It didn't help matters that the half siblings had been publicly at odds before Reggie's death. No one ever talked about his older brother in Sinclair's presence. Miss Van Etten, though, seemed to be making a habit of bringing up Reggie.

"Did you know the late heir?" Sinclair asked, hoping to deflect her questions with one of his own. To his surprise, the inquiry made Miss Van Etten miss a step. Perhaps she had only tripped on the uneven ground, but then she seemed to intentionally pick up speed and duck through the open doorway. With her intelligence and previous experience with windmills, she must have realized that it would be too loud inside for any meaningful discussions.

Why *was* Miss Van Etten buying Hamarray and Frest? It was the kind of spur-of-the-moment decision Reggie would have made. Could she have had an ulterior motive for the purchase? It hardly made sense. He could not see how two small islands in the North Sea would have any value to an American oil, hotel, and railroad heiress . . . unless perhaps if she and Reggie had been lovers and this was her way of mourning him. There was a somberness that Miss Van Etten seemed to hide beneath her layers of outward frivolity.

But even that explanation did not make sense. Miss Van Etten didn't seem the type to pine away on windswept isles, and Reggie had always kept his relationships light and frivolous.

Or perhaps Sinclair just did not like the thought of the heiress and his half brother together—which was definitely a reaction he did *not* want to analyze too closely.

"I would love to see your millstone and the brake wheel and, well, everything!" Rose shouted to Mr. Craigie, who was enthusiastically both promising to bring bread to the upcoming ceilidh and showing her how fine the barley flour was as it poured out from the chutes above. As much as she really did find the windmill machinery fascinating, she had another reason for wanting to see the upper floors, especially where they loaded the grain into the hopper. The structure was the tallest one on the low-lying island of Frest and was situated on a small jut of land with clear views of Scapa Flow. Rose had noticed a window at the very top, where the windshaft entered the structure and attached to the large brake wheel inside. It would have been the perfect hidden spot to spy on the British Grand Fleet. If the people of Frest had been supplying the Imperial German Navy with grain, what better place to look for periscopes of U-boats and secret signals than from the very place where the bere barley was ground?

"Of course you wish to see those! And the friction wheel *and* the main driveshaft *and* the hopper—we can't forget those!" Mr. Craigie's palpable love for his mill was surprisingly endearing, and Rose found herself hoping that the jovial man was not involved in any spy ring. In fact, she did not wish for anyone on Frest to be entangled in espionage. She generally *liked* these people, even the grumpy Mr. Flett, who so clearly doted on his children.

"The ladder isn't stable enough for a visitor to climb." Mr. Sinclair's words came out in a rush as he physically positioned himself in front of a rather sturdy-looking set of rungs.

"I can assure you that I have faced worse dangers than that," Rose said as she poked her thumb in his direction. "Besides, I clearly weigh less than either of you. If it can hold your tall frames, it should not break under mine."

"No, Sinclair is right." Poor Mr. Craigie looked utterly deflated as his big shoulders slumped. "It is no place for a lady."

"Well, it is good that I don't consider myself a lady, then," Rose snapped. Either these men were hiding something from her or they thought her a delicate piece of porcelain, liable to break at the slightest peril. Either way, she was more determined than ever to climb to the top of the windmill.

She tried to dodge around Mr. Sinclair, but he was too quick. Every move she made, he countered. Mr. Craigie watched their strange dance from a few yards back as he scratched at his temple.

"Really, Mr. Sinclair, there is no need for this chivalry," Rose shouted as she swiveled to her right.

"I'm afraid that is not true. The climb is highly dangerous, especially with all of the gears in motion," Mr. Sinclair yelled back as he sidestepped to his left.

"I assure you that I will not be so foolish as to stick a finger or limb between them." She tried going low and sliding behind him this time, but Mr. Sinclair anticipated her move and blocked her.

"You could slip."

"I never slip." Which was a good thing considering Rose's face was somewhere near the level of Mr. Sinclair's crotch at the moment.

"Uncle David?"

Both Rose and Mr. Sinclair froze as they glanced up to the opening in the floor above them. A young man about the age of nineteen stared down at them with an expression torn between befuddlement and worry.

"Yes, Young Thomas?" Mr. Craigie asked as he moved to stand within the adolescent's line of sight.

"The mill is moving too fast. I think the wind's picked up. A storm might be blowing in."

Mr. Craigie let out a mild oath as he dashed outside to adjust the sails. Knowing that the wooden parts could break or even catch on fire if they spun too quickly, Rose stepped back to allow Thomas to clamber down the ladder to assist his uncle. Unfortunately, that allowed Mr. Sinclair to shepherd her out of the building . . . except now it *was* actually dangerous to be inside it.

While Mr. Craigie and Thomas pulled on the brake rope and folded back the canvas sails, Mr. Sinclair shut the door of the windmill. He positioned himself on the outside like a sentry. It was clear that the stubborn man wasn't about to allow her back inside.

Rats.

As much as she hadn't wanted to suspect the islanders, they *did* appear to be hiding something. Spying on them was making Rose more uncomfortable than she'd anticipated. It had been easier in London, where everyone simply expected each other to have ulterior motives. Here, she felt more dishonest, but she had no choice except to press on.

Even if she couldn't explore more of the windmill today, that didn't mean her investigation was entirely thwarted. Young Thomas might be a bit easier to pry information from than the adults. Rose watched as he finished helping his uncle, and then she intercepted him before he could join Mr. Sinclair at the door.

"I'm Miss Van Etten," Rose said. "I'm in the process of buying Muckle Skaill."

The youth's pale cheeks pinkened as he tugged on his flatcap in the way of a greeting. "Pleased to meet you, miss."

Rose caught her first good look at his face, and her heart lurched at the hollowness in his blue-green eyes. She knew that look. It still stalked her nightmares. French. British. Belgian. American. It didn't matter. This boy had spent time in the trenches, and it haunted him.

Rose almost backed away, to leave the fellow to his well-earned peace. But she didn't. After all, if she failed in her mission, then there would be no amity for any of them.

"Do you help your uncle run the mill?" Rose quietly asked.

Thomas's shy gaze didn't quite meet hers. "I am until his son gets back home from the Royal Navy."

"That's kind of you."

"He pays me well, and we need the money with Mum helping to take care of my other auntie—Widow Craigie—and Da losing his leg at the Somme."

Rose had been doing jitney work in Paris then, and she'd gone to the station to meet trainfuls of the wounded from that battle. Volunteers would divide up the patients according to the severity and type of injuries and instruct the ambulance drivers where to take them. Those had been long, endless days that would always blur in Rose's mind. But she couldn't think of the past now. She *had* to focus on her present mission.

"You seem to know a lot about the operation of the windmill for just pitching in." Flattery was always the best way to secure information.

"I helped Uncle during the war before I turned eighteen and signed up. There was a lot of work back then."

"Oh?" Rose said, trying to sound mildly intrigued but not too interested. It wasn't easy with her heart pounding. Had the mill been so busy because they were supplying flour and information to German U-boats?

"The navy had a standing order," Young Thomas explained, "and then we also needed—"

"Young Thomas!" Mr. Sinclair's voice boomed as he walked over and slung his arm around the slighter man's shoulders. "I meant to talk to you at the sheep count yesterday but never had the chance to properly welcome you home."

"Thank you, Sinclair." Thomas's face had now flushed with something that suspiciously looked like guilt. What *had* he been about to reveal to her, and why did Mr. Sinclair appear to be at the center of all the secrets? Was the Viking the brains of the spy operations? He certainly seemed clever enough, but Rose had trouble imagining the honest man being a traitor. It felt wrong to her and maybe even oddly disappointing.

"Your mum must be over the moon having you back. Is she keeping you well stocked in bannocks?" Mr. Sinclair asked the young man.

Thomas laughed and rubbed his stomach. "Aye. It'll make it hard to leave in July when herring season starts."

"But the sea beckons you?" Rose asked.

Thomas made a face and shook his head. "I've always preferred the land to the ocean, especially now that Auntie's a widow and needs my help on her croft too. But we can't do without the coin I make on the herring boats."

Emotion ripped through Rose as she thought about the horrors the nineteen-year-old had faced in the mud of war. He was barely out of childhood. He'd more than earned the right to stay home as long as he wanted instead of shipping out once again. But what choice did he have? Frest and Hamarray hardly offered much in the way of jobs. Just as the male islanders were returning from war to work the land, the sailors who'd provided a market for their produce were headed home.

"But it is only for a few months," Thomas added with forced brightness. "I'll be back home before I know it."

"And your mum will be all ready to spoil you again," Mr. Sinclair said.

"That she will be," Thomas agreed with a real smile.

Just then Rose felt a raindrop hit her cheek, and she involuntarily started at the unexpected sensation. Before the war, she never would have reacted to such a faint touch, but now . . . but now she felt a flutter of nervousness flare to life.

Mr. Sinclair glanced up toward the sky. "We'd better get moving if we don't want to get caught in the storm."

"You could stay here," Young Thomas said. "Uncle wouldn't mind opening his house up to Miss Van Etten."

"No need to keep you and your uncle from the mill. We should have time to get to Widow Flett's before it hits us in earnest," Mr. Sinclair said as he raised a parting hand toward the Craigies and gestured with his other for her to follow.

"A relative of yours?" Rose asked as she caught up to Mr. Sinclair and forced aside her jumpiness.

"Of my stepfather, aye. Mrs. Flett was the wife of his late brother. Her granddaughter, Astrid, who lives with her, is near to my age and is like a cousin to me. I'm almost afraid to introduce you."

"Why ever so?"

"Because I fear the two of you will join forces to provoke me, and I'll never get another moment's peace." Mr. Sinclair faked a dramatic shudder that triggered a laugh from Rose that reached all the way down into her belly.

"It sounds like she and I will get along famously."

She appreciated how Mr. Sinclair didn't slacken his pace like most men did, as if she *wanted* to prance along in a mincing walk.

When they approached a handful of stone buildings, an ominous thump-thump-thump filled the air. The wind had picked up, and the light had grown thinner and grayer. It seemed like the perfect setting for a ghost story, but Rose didn't shiver at the chill racing through her. No, she welcomed it. Something about the haunting beauty of Frest seemed to paradoxically fill her.

"The byre door has blown off its hinges again." Mr. Sinclair sighed and strode over to the small stone shed, which had a thatched roof and a delightfully ramshackle appearance. A heavy wooden door smacked against the outer wall, as it hung attached only at the bottom.

Curious, Rose followed Mr. Sinclair. He stopped in front of the structure. Grabbing the massive, heavy wood, he lifted it up and onto the hinges as if it were nothing but papier-mâché. The bulge of his muscles under his wool sweater was the only sign of the effort he made.

As Mr. Sinclair tested his work, swinging the door back and forth, Rose noticed a curious tool peeking out. Triangular in shape, it had a wicked curved blade on the end of it.

"What in thunderation is that?" Rose jabbed her thumb in the direction of the murderous-looking implement.

Seemingly satisfied by his handiwork with the door, Mr. Sinclair peered over her shoulder. He didn't touch her, but he'd moved so close she could feel the heat rising off his body. He smelled like sweat and dirt—a combination that really shouldn't entice her . . . but it did.

"It's a scythe," Mr. Sinclair announced.

"Huh?" She had completely forgotten that she'd even asked a question, let alone what it was.

"We use it to reap the bere and the oats," Mr. Sinclair continued.

"That?" Rose refocused her attention on the piece of farming equipment. Leaning closer, she examined it. "Isn't it cumbersome?"

"Much more efficient than the old heuk, which is what we call a sickle here on Orkney. That was just a curved blade held in the hand."

"Isn't there a machine that will accomplish the task?" Rose stepped back. She vaguely recalled seeing all sorts of mechanized monstrosities on the farms she'd spotted from her family's private railcar, especially when she'd traveled through the Midwest en route to Santa Monica, California. "How much efficiency is lost doing it by hand?"

"Much," Mr. Sinclair agreed. "There are threshers and such that would assist with the harvest. They have them on Mainland, Orkney, and some of the other isles, but not on Frest. The earl and the lairds before him did not see a need for such an investment when the crofters could just do it themselves."

Rose thought about Young Thomas, Ann Inkster, and Mr. Sinclair himself and the many jobs that they took on to support their families. She couldn't recall one thing that she'd done for others until she'd climbed behind the wheel of an ambulance. There she'd found herself helpless to stop the suffering. It had been like pressing a small bandage against a hemorrhage. But here . . . here she had some means to make an actual difference. "Why don't you write me a list of the modernizations you think would be useful for Frest, and I'll take a look over it with you. I probably won't know a jot about any of them, but you can explain their value to me."

Mr. Sinclair glanced at her, his expression slightly guarded. "Why are you being so generous?"

"I don't know," Rose said honestly. "Maybe it is from listening to my father conduct business all these years. If this were a factory, it would only make sense to update the machinery. If I'm to be the laird, it seems like it is my duty."

"You and your father are close?" Mr. Sinclair asked.

His question pricked a long-buried emotion as old memories of hiding in her father's office flooded back. How many times had she wished he'd notice her and pull her into his lap with a chuckle? When his study was empty, she would crawl into his chair and breathe in the scent of his cigar smoke and dream of him talking to her with the same attention he'd shown his business associates.

"I don't think one can get close to Daddy. He's too absorbed in his projects, but I couldn't help digesting things from all the comings and goings. He 'retired' early, but his hobby is investing and starting new enterprises. Since his office has always been in our residence, a lot of prominent industrialists are constantly dropping by."

"A child always sees and learns more than the adults suspect." Mr. Sinclair spoke the words gravely, and his profundity caused Rose to study him. Before she could discover what she was searching for in his countenance, a new, cheerful voice called out.

"Welcome!" A woman with a weatherworn face poked her head out from the low door of the blackhouse. Her bright smile gave her round face a girlish glow that contrasted with the lines bracketing her lips. "I've just put the kettle on."

"Tea sounds absolutely delightful," Rose called back.

"Be forewarned, she often puts a nip of whiskey in her pot," Mr. Sinclair told her in a quiet voice that wouldn't reach their hostess.

"My kind of beverage," Rose purred throatily, and she was rewarded with a grin from Mr. Sinclair.

"Mine too."

When they entered the old-fashioned building, they found Widow Flett bustling about the peat-fed stove. She waved to them. "Take a seat. Take a seat."

The only chairs in the tiny room were ancient-looking wooden ones by the table. On its scarred surface lay a half-finished sweater. Like the one Mr. Sinclair wore, it had the most intriguing geometric pattern.

"Your knitting is absolutely beautiful." Rose leaned forward to study it more closely. The woolwork managed to appear both home-spun and chic.

"Thank you." Mrs. Flett beamed as she settled into a chair across from Rose. "My mother was from Fair Isle in Shetland. She taught me everything I know about making patterns and dyeing wool."

"You add color to the yarn yourself?" Rose asked as she lightly traced one of the X designs.

Mrs. Flett chuckled. "I card it and spin it too. There isn't one step that I don't do myself, except for the shearing. In my younger years, I used to do that too."

"It must take ages." Rose glanced up. Although she always had cultivated close relationships with the designers who made her couture clothes—including the famous Paul Poiret—she had never thought about the work that went into the cloth itself.

"Aye." Mrs. Flett laughed. "But it is a chore I've always enjoyed."

"Where do you get the dyes?" Rose asked.

"Astrid or Sinclair bring me back indigo and madder from the stores in Kirkwall, and I gather lichens for the yellow."

"The colors are just so bright." Rose studied the work. "How do you manage it?"

"That's a question you probably don't want the answer to," Mr. Sinclair warned just as Mrs. Flett leaned forward conspiratorially and said in a stage whisper, "Urine."

"Urine!" Rose jerked her hand away from the yarn.

"Aye." Mrs. Flett was chuckling so hard tears had appeared in the corners of her eyes. "It's the ammonia in it, or so Mr. Sinclair tells me with all his book learning. Whatever it is, it sets the dyes nice and bright."

Feeling a bit like when she'd read Upton Sinclair's *The Jungle*, Rose stared down at the knitting. Yet even knowing how it had been dyed didn't distract from its beauty.

"Do you ever sell any of these? I could see them fetching a pretty penny back in the States—as long as the ammonia part isn't mentioned."

"Aye." Mrs. Flett bobbed her head proudly, causing the ends of the scarf tied about her head to flutter. "I often knit for the Frest lads when they lend Astrid and me a hand with this old place."

"Is that how you got yours?" This time, Rose twitched the cuff on Mr. Sinclair's sweater. She didn't miss the amused gleam in Widow Flett's light-green eyes at the gesture.

"No." Widow Flett patted Mr. Sinclair's other hand. "I did him a turn better with all the work he does around here. I taught him how to do it himself."

Mr. Sinclair ducked his head, much like an embarrassed schoolboy. "Now, Mrs. Flett, you said that would just be our secret."

"And I've kept it, haven't I?" Mrs. Flett winked at Rose. "Mostly. It wouldn't be right to hide things from the new Lady of Muckle Skaill, now, would it?"

"Oh, definitely not." Rose laughed, taking the woman's cheerful, teasing words in the spirit they were meant. Part of her, though, couldn't help but wish that the statement were true. However, she was certain now that the islanders were all concealing *something* from her.

"He was at his wit's end trying to keep the bairns clothed when his mum died and his stepda was laid up in bed. Little Freya was ten and had been learning how to properly use the needles from her mother. Astrid—that's my granddaughter—and I did our best to help out, but Mr. Sinclair insisted on learning how to knit himself. Said he needed something to occupy his hands when he was up with the colicky babe. Alexander, now he was a fair crotchety infant. You wouldn't know it now, as he's the sweetest bairn you'd ever meet. I think his temperament was on account of him losing his mum in childbirth and his da taking to his bed only a few weeks later from an apoplexy. People don't believe newborns know what is going on around them, but those peedie ones, they sense things all right."

Rose stole a glance at Mr. Sinclair, who appeared to be trying to scrunch himself into a ball and disappear through the hard-packed dirt floor. Given his large frame and abundance of muscles, it did not work in the slightest. He just appeared vastly uncomfortable.

An odd, soft emotion crept through Rose.

She yearned to learn more about Mr. Sinclair's past—this man who had apparently single-handedly taken care of six children and a bedridden stepparent on a tiny windswept croft through a great, terrible war. It was odd for her—this need to uncover a man's life story instead of simply his body. But given how uneasy poor Mr. Sinclair appeared, Rose wouldn't press Widow Flett for more fascinating gems.

"Have you ever sold one of your knit creations to someone outside of Frest?" Rose asked, hoping to steer the conversation away from Mr. Sinclair.

"Aye. To some of the sailors who are stationed here. It gives them something to send back to their sweethearts. I've made good coin from those sales. Having the Grand Fleet here has been a big boon to Frest, a big boon."

A sentiment Rose kept hearing, from Mr. Sinclair and Janet Inkster to Young Thomas and now Mrs. Flett. But what would happen when the Allied powers decided the fate of the interned German fleet and the British guardships went home to other ports? What would replace this miniature boom for Frest? Would they all be like Young Thomas and be forced to make a living elsewhere? The thought caused a surprising raw pain to slice through Rose.

Before she could fully consider the questions rising in her mind like signal flares, the door behind her creaked open. Spinning, she found a young woman about her age untying a scarf from around her head. She wore a simple wool dress of dark blue and a tweed coat. When she spied Rose and Mr. Sinclair, her moss-green eyes widened. She looked like an older version of Freya and more like a sibling to the Flett children than a first cousin once removed. Mr. Sinclair, in fact, shared fewer similarities with his half sisters and brother than Astrid did.

"You must be the new Lady of Muckle Skaill—or whatever you're planning to call the grand house on Hamarray."

"Muckle Skaill." Rose grinned. "I don't think any other name would suit."

"Enough of the previous lairds thought so," Widow Flett observed wryly.

"Oh, indeed, and they all gave the house such silly, grand, romantic titles," Mrs. Flett's granddaughter said as she joined them at the table. "I am Astrid, by the by."

"What did the Earl of Mar call it?" Rose asked.

Like every other time she mentioned the nobleman's name, a cold silence descended, making Rose think of the air sealed in a frigid underground tomb. She didn't even need to follow the path of Astrid's and her grandmother's eyes to know their gazes had slid in the direction of Mr. Sinclair.

"Valhalla." A strange bitter undertone had crept into Mr. Sinclair's voice, and he spat out the single word as if it were a foul-tasting poison.

"The Norse heaven?" Rose wrinkled her nose. "At least he paid homage to Hamarray's Scandinavian past."

A harsh sound exploded from Mr. Sinclair. "He never paid homage to anything but his own . . . vanity."

The way Mr. Sinclair's gaze had flitted over the female occupants of the room made Rose suspect that he'd meant to say something much cruder.

"He fancied himself a god and the ruler of a drunken pleasure hall." Mr. Sinclair's harsh words pricked Rose's conscience. Had she not often compared herself to a female Dionysus? Why, she'd done just that during her party celebrating the Armistice—the night that had led her here. Mr. Sinclair would not have known about her claims, but she felt chastised by his words all the same.

The already pregnant silence grew even fuller.

Mrs. Flett gestured toward the teacups. "Drink up. It will do you all some good, and it's just the thing to warm us."

Rose obliged her and almost sputtered when the brew hit her tongue. There was more than just a "peedie" splash of whiskey in it. There was enough for a good burn.

Ignoring Rose's reaction, Mrs. Flett shifted her attention to regard Astrid. "Did your business on Mainland go well?"

If Rose was not mistaken, the young woman's eyes shifted ever so slightly in Rose's direction. Rose's finger tightened around her teacup. Astrid clearly seemed reluctant to talk in front of her.

Finally, Astrid answered her grandmother with a rather short "Aye."

"Kirkwall is a lovely town, isn't it?" Rose asked, keeping her voice perfectly casual. "Saint Magnus Cathedral with its red and yellow sandstones looks so different than the other grand churches that I've seen in Europe. There is just something warm and inviting about it."

Astrid gave a curt nod. Rose sensed that the woman wished for a topic change, which of course meant Rose *had* to pry further.

"Did your business take you near the cathedral?"

"Oh no," Astrid said, her voice as light as Rose's. "I was actually in Stromness."

Where the ferries from mainland Scotland docked. Interesting. *Very* interesting. It would be a perfect place for a spy to exchange information with her superiors.

"That is where my cars originally arrived before I arranged for the navy to bring them to Hamarray." Rose smiled. "I imagine it must be very exciting when a ship docks. I've spent time in Key West, Florida, and it always is a grand adventure when a big cargo boat is unloaded. Do you often see any?"

Astrid smiled. On the surface it seemed like a polite grin, but the corners were pulled just a little too tight.

Yes, Astrid Flett was hiding something. Whether it was a significant something remained to be seen. Rose's plan to learn more from the islanders was only inspiring more questions. She would just need to figure out how to dig further.

"I really did not see much while I was there. It was just a peedie errand, and I wasn't on Mainland for long." Astrid's mouth tensed a little bit more, and Rose knew she would not extract any more information today. If she kept probing, the islanders might realize that she herself was hiding something.

Settling back in her chair, Rose allowed the conversation to flow naturally among the four of them. Astrid gradually relaxed, but Rose remained on guard.

The residents of Frest most definitely possessed secrets, and it was obvious that Rose needed to find out exactly what they were concealing.

Chapter 6

"Would you please stop trying to jiggle the stones in my broch?" Myrtle asked as she looked up from her tape measure. "I've grown quite attached to it. I can't wait to see what treasures it might hold, but you don't see me ripping into it, do you?"

"Technically, it's *my* broch," Rose grumbled. Yesterday's storm had prevented her from visiting any of the other crofters, and she'd spent the evening knocking about Muckle Skaill in a futile attempt to discover where Viscount Barbury had locked away his records about the spy ring.

Myrtle raised a blonde eyebrow. "I called dibs, remember? You get the Viking, and I get my stone heap."

"Okay, fine. It's yours," Rose huffed out. Since she was giving Myrtle permission and the funds to excavate when Rose was officially the recorded owner of Hamarray, she supposed that the broch *was* more Myrtle's than hers.

Myrtle had been trying for ages to lead her own dig—even a small one—but as a woman, she was finding it frustratingly difficult to convince her college or even a landowner to allow her to oversee one. Any discovery she'd made in the field had been claimed by male archaeologists in the press and, even worse in Myrtle's viewpoint, archaeological circles. Rose was glad to give her friend this opportunity, but that didn't mean that she wasn't frustrated that her main reason for buying the islands remained irritatingly stalled.

Rose stubbornly poked at another stone. It scraped slightly but did not give. "What if the keyhole is hidden within this wall?"

Myrtle did not attempt to hide her eye roll. "This island is full of rocks. You can't possibly overturn each one."

"I can try." Rose sighed and sank against the ancient wall. The top of the structure had long since rotted or fallen away, leaving an almost perfectly round opening. Despite the drystone construction, the building was remarkably geometric and snug. The sun had just begun to peek over the horizon, and the circle of sky had a golden glow. It felt otherworldly, as if Rose were trapped in a magical place of ancient myth where time both crept and rushed by.

"Perhaps you need to confide in one of the islanders." Myrtle eased back on her haunches as she scribbled down measurements in her notebook. "Your Viking, perhaps?"

"He's really not *my* Viking. Besides, he *is* hiding something from me, maybe even several somethings. Everyone on Frest is. They all know more about the viscount and the earl than they want to admit. What if it has something to do with the spy ring?"

Myrtle adjusted a knob on the side of her tripod-mounted theodolite surveying tool, gazed carefully through the eyepiece for several seconds, and then, with a satisfied nod, made a note on the pad sitting on the wall next to her. Her friend's obsession with minuscule details had always seemed odd to Rose, but now that she was so desperate to gather any clues, she better understood Myrtle's desire for precision.

"You just don't seem to be getting anywhere with that key of yours. I heard several of the servants gossiping this morning about how you keep wandering the halls at night like a madwoman."

Rose gradually slipped down the rough rocks until her bottom touched the springy ground. "Perhaps I *am* mad—chasing after ghosts and half-baked memories and suspecting decent, hardworking people of undermining a war that their loved ones were fighting."

Maybe she was trying too hard to find meaning, any meaning, in all the tragedy she'd witnessed when she'd sped across France in an ambulance that often seemed more like a hearse.

"Specters and undercooked recollections do not sabotage automobiles and try to kidnap you," Myrtle reminded her.

"True." Rose massaged her temples, wishing she hadn't forgotten to bring her satchel. She really *did* want to play with a cig right now. "I need to figure out a way to break into David Craigie's windmill and have a poke around. I'm certain Mr. Sinclair didn't want me going beyond the first floor."

"You said that this David fellow lives adjacent to the mill," Myrtle pointed out crisply. "We are not exactly cat burglars who can sneak inside undetected."

"I—" Suddenly Rose broke off as she thought she heard something. Voices. Which generally would not be an unusual thing, but this was Hamarray. True, there was the skeletal staff at Muckle Skaill, but they had no reason to be on this end of the cliffs. Although Rose certainly would not begrudge her servants a stroll along the dramatic seascape, she somehow instinctively knew that someone else had invaded her little island. This warning sensation inside her didn't feel like her normal postwar skittishness but something more concrete.

"What—" Myrtle began to ask, but Rose shushed her with a slice of her left hand. With her right, she pulled her Bull Dog revolver from her pocket.

Slowly, Rose crept to the entrance of the broch. Staying hidden in the shadows, she stared out at the hills leading from the southern side of the isle—the side that faced Frest. The ground around the broch was bumpy with crumbling ancient rock walls. At one time, smaller round buildings had fanned out from the main tower, leaving a honeycomb-like patchwork of stone behind. Meticulous Myrtle planned on recording each structure's dimensions before removing even one handful of dirt.

Nothing moved on the landscape but a few mottled brown-and-white birds who hopped about as they swept their long curved beaks through the grasses in search of worms and insects. Amid the howl of the wind, Rose could detect only the haunting calls of the seabirds. They lived in huge colonies by the cliffs, and a large, rather angry group of white ones roosted in the broch itself.

Then she heard it—the deep rumble of male voices and the lighter tones of a woman's. Between the blasts of sea air and the avian chatter greeting the sunrise, Rose could not make out a single word, but she had no doubt that people were talking.

Waving at Myrtle to stay behind, Rose grabbed her friend's binoculars with her free hand and then slunk out of the tumbledown tower. Using the rabbit warren of stone walls as shields, she crouched practically on her hands and knees. The earthy scent of the damp loam filled her nostrils as she scuttled like a crab over the bumpy slope. Every now and then, she poked her head up for a better view.

She spied nothing but more feathered sentries until she reached the other side of the broch. A flicker of movement near the cliffs caught her eye. Scooching against one of the taller piles of stonework, Rose peered over the lichen-covered edifice.

The golden light caused the woman's strawberry-blonde hair to glint as she pointed off into the horizon. The white geometric designs of her sweater also reflected in the morning sun, making her easy for Rose to identify. Miss Astrid Flett.

She was flanked on either side by men wearing deerstalkers and plaid mackinaw jackets—not the kind worn by loggers in North America but the sporty version donned by wealthy hunters. Each fellow had binoculars pressed against his eyes as they studied Scapa Flow. Their attention seemed riveted to the German dreadnoughts and cruisers and also the British guardships. The masts and smokestacks of the vessels had transformed the harbor into something resembling a burned-out forest made of metal and vestiges of wood.

Every day that treaty discussions continue in Versailles is a day closer to the end of hope. The spy's words on Daytona Beach flooded back into Rose's mind. Could the plan truly center on the German Imperial Fleet, as she and Myrtle had conjectured? Had Rose just found the secret agents?

Yet instead of feeling a flush of success, she felt . . . oddly bereft. Even though she'd suspected the crofters were hiding *something*, she hadn't really believed them capable of spying—or at least she hadn't *wanted* them to be. She liked them all—these tough people who worked together to make a harsh life possible.

But Rose couldn't allow her nascent feelings for the islanders to interfere with her mission. Peace was too important.

Her body tensed like it did before a motor trial . . . or before a mad dash over a bomb-pitted road. Moving even more stealthily than before, Rose inched toward Astrid and the strangers. She crept on her belly now, heedless of how she was likely ruining her red wool jacket. She wished only that she'd worn her beaver coat instead of the vibrant hue.

The trio did not notice her approach. They were too focused on the Flow. The cries of the birds, the crash of the waves, and the rush of the wind all helped to obscure Rose's steady advance. She doubted that she made for a good scout—she was much more suited to being the getaway driver. But the environment of Hamarray was ideal for lurking.

"They're still south." Astrid's higher-pitched voice floated to Rose first.

South? Who was south? Other spies? Germany lay in that direction, and so did the Netherlands, where the kaiser was holed up in exile.

"I swear I saw one." An American accent, crisp and clear. Was *it* familiar? Rose had thought the voices of her attackers would be emblazoned upon her memory. But she strained now to recall the exact pitch, the right tone. She detected no hint of an underlying German inflection.

"It was diving down." The second man's voice sounded like he was from the States, too, but Rose couldn't quite place the region. And what was diving down? Could there be a U-boat still out there that the Allies knew nothing about? It wouldn't be that hard to hide something that could slink through the water undetected. Or would it? She really should study naval maneuvers more.

"I saw its very distinctive markings." The first man sounded like a stubborn child.

Was that in reference to a submarine paint scheme? Did they even have unique identifiers? Rose thought she'd read an article about one of them having an Iron Cross on its conning tower, but she couldn't be certain.

"The tirricks haven't returned yet, Mr. Herman." Astrid's voice sounded a bit too chipper, as if the men were straining her patience but she didn't wish to show it. What did Astrid mean by *tirricks*? Could it be a code word?

"I am *very* familiar with them." Mr. Herman puffed out his cheeks, causing the flaps on his hat to bulge out. "They are common enough, and I've seen plenty of them in the skies."

Were they talking about airships? Airplanes? That made less sense than a U-boat. Surely the Allies would know the whereabouts of those, especially the massive dirigibles.

"It was most likely a fulmar, who stay here year round."

"I doubt that. My knowledge of gulls is unparalleled. We have arctic terns in North America too."

Wait. Were they talking about *birds*? Birds!

"What's that?" The second man pointed to the sea. "Is it a great skua floating in the water?"

"That is the head of a seal, Mr. Miller," Astrid explained brightly.

"I really think it could be a great skua. I must spot one on this trip. I *need* that bird for my life list."

Thunderation! They *were* talking about feathered creatures. Feeling rather silly and more than a little relieved, Rose climbed to her feet. She needed to stop seeing spies behind every clump of vegetation.

"It could be a great skua." Mr. Herman championed his comrade bird-watcher.

"Great skuas do not typically float about in the water in that manner." Astrid's voice kept getting lighter and lighter. Pretty soon it would just float away.

Curious now about the debate, Rose stowed her pistol in her coat and lifted Myrtle's binoculars toward the brownish blob bobbing like a cork in the blue water below. "I don't think a bird—even a *great* one—would possess eyes that size either."

All three bird-watchers swung in her direction. Astrid, who already had pale-white skin, lost what little color she possessed. The men appeared even more startled by Rose's appearance.

"Who are you?" Mr. Herman asked. His rather prodigious mustache seemed to bristle in irritation.

"My word, if it isn't Miss Rose Van Etten." Mr. Miller adjusted his hat and smoothed his coat like a soldier at muster.

Alarm crackled back to life within Rose. The spies on Daytona Beach had known her name too. Had this man been following her? Why hadn't she listened to her original instinct that these fellows were dangerous?

"Miss Van Etten?" Mr. Herman's eyebrows, which matched his thick whiskers, shot so high that the tips disappeared under the brim of his deerstalker. "George Van Etten's daughter?"

Rose drew in a breath, trying to control the tension that seemed ready to pull her apart. She *was* recognizable. It didn't matter whether she was in the States, in England, or on the Continent. Someone *always* connected her with her father. But even as Rose fought for calm, she slipped her hand back inside her coat pocket as she grasped for the handle of her gun.

Mr. Miller ignored his friend and marched forward, a genial smile on his face. He looked to be in his late thirties and a decade or two younger than Mr. Herman.

"I saw you race in France before the war when I was touring the Continent. You're quite the gal! I shall never forget watching you win that motor trial!"

Rose's shoulders unhunched, and the downward trajectory of her fingers stopped. When people had first begun to associate Rose with racing instead of immediately with her father, she'd been elated. But now . . . well, it had been refreshing these last few days in Orkney, just to be . . . *her* with no preconceived notions about who she should be.

"Why, thank you! It is forever my aim to be memorable," Rose lied and winked at the man as she once again donned the blithe persona that everyone expected.

"But do you know anything about birds?" Mr. Herman demanded.

"Well, no," Rose admitted.

"Are you aware of any of the defining characteristics of a great skua or the sound of its call?" Mr. Herman's facial hair seemed to expand outward.

"I am not, but I am sure Miss Flett *is*." Rose flashed a smile in the direction of Astrid, who stood rather like a piece of statuary overlooking the cliff.

Mr. Miller waved his hand. "She is only a local Frest lass who Mr. Herman hires to bring him to the nesting grounds. It is Mr. Herman and I who are the *avid* bird-watchers."

"I would assume that the residents of these isles have seen more than their share of feathered creatures and are quite competent to distinguish a seal from a skua." Rose was feeling particularly protective of the islanders after having her own suspicions about them dashed, and she didn't like how these men were so cavalierly dismissing Astrid. She thought an amused sound might have escaped from Mr. Sinclair's cousin, who was finally looking slightly less stiff.

Mr. Herman patted his binoculars as if they were a talisman of knowledge. "One cannot expect a woman to understand the finer details required to truly comprehend the natural world."

Mr. Miller nodded solemnly. "The study of avian life is complex indeed."

"Well, I suppose it only makes sense that the birdbrained would understand all that is feathered and fowl," Rose said.

A sputtery cough definitely came from Astrid's direction. Mr. Herman's mustache stiffened with offense, while Mr. Miller's face flushed a most florid magenta.

"As you two gentlemen seem perfectly equipped to confuse seal for skua by yourselves, I would like to borrow your guide. I promise it will just take a jiffy."

Before either of the two men could object, Rose lightly grabbed Astrid's arm and steered her toward the broch. Astrid kept stealing wary glances at her. Despite her earlier humor, the island lass seemed nervous again.

"Please tell me that you are at least making a killing leading those two buffoons about," Rose said as soon as they were out of earshot.

"Making a killing?" Astrid asked.

Rose didn't know if Astrid was actually confused by the Americanism or still trying to be evasive. Clearly, she was not comfortable with Rose knowing about her apparent enterprise as a nature guide.

"Earning heaps of money," Rose explained.

Astrid made a sound that was as noncommittal as possible. It couldn't even be categorized as a sigh or a grunt.

It struck Rose that Astrid and her bird-watchers were technically trespassing upon Rose's land. "You do know that I don't give a fig that you're on Hamarray. You aren't causing any harm."

Astrid's lips tightened ever so slightly. "Are you certain? You don't mind Messrs. Miller and Herman traipsing about? This *is* your estate."

Rose tossed her hand into the air. "I'm okay with it within a degree of reason, but I'm sure it won't be difficult to work things out."

"Ah," Astrid said, her voice a little stiff. "How much compensation will you be wanting?"

"Oh, nothing like that. You're welcome to use the land. I just meant that I don't desire streams and *streams* of visitors. But since I've happily lived in hotels for months on end, I am not opposed to rubbing elbows with tourists."

"You won't be demanding a percentage of the proceeds? Or a small fee? Or something like that?" Astrid asked.

"No," Rose said. "Although I would like a list of all the people who visit." That would help her keep track of who was frequenting the island . . . perhaps for treasonous purposes.

"Will . . ." Astrid began to stiffen her shoulders, and then she paused, seeming to slump into herself, as if thinking better of what she was about to say.

"Will I what?" Rose asked. "If I learned anything from eavesdropping on my father's discussions with industrialists, it is that it's best to be up front and clear in the beginning of a transaction. It avoids so much unnecessary nastiness down the line."

"Will you put that in writing?" A thread of hesitancy laced Astrid's tone, but her voice never wavered.

"Of course. It is the best way to do business."

Astrid's tension eased a bit. "I was afraid you were going to say I should just rely on your word, you being a fine lady and all, or some tosh like that."

"Ah. Did Mar expect you to accept whatever he said at face value because he was a gentleman?"

"Aye, but his word is bruck. All the other lairds were the same—claiming rents, making us harvest seaweed for their profit, not ours—but the old earl, he was the worst of them all. Thought himself a feudal lord, he did. He certainly treated us all like serfs ready to do his bidding. Those who worked and lived at Muckle Skaill suffered the most. I don't know—"

Astrid broke off suddenly. Her expression once again became guarded as she slid Rose a look. "I have said too much. I didn't mean to offend you."

Rose shrugged off the apology, glad that one of the islanders was finally talking without restraint. "I'm not easily upset, and I don't see myself as a lady. Feel free to continue."

"Oh, it's not important." Astrid's voice was high and cavalier—*too* cavalier. Familiar frustration roared through Rose. It was clear that she wouldn't be unraveling any secrets of the crofters beyond Astrid's bird-watching venture.

Myrtle poked her head out of the broch. "A friend, then?"

"Oh yes," Rose said. "This is Miss Astrid Flett—stepcousin to Mr. Thorfinn Sinclair."

"Ah, another of the Viking's relations." Myrtle stepped from the ruined tower, wiping her hands on her skirt before extending her hand to Astrid.

"The Viking's?" Astrid arched a red eyebrow as her fingers closed around Myrtle's.

"We nicknamed your cousin that after we spotted him rowing toward Hamarray, looking extremely muscly and preternaturally intense," Myrtle explained.

This time Astrid's laugh was entirely free and filled with nothing but mirth. "Oh, please tell me he knows of this."

"Oh, he does." Rose smiled, remembering when she'd first encountered Mr. Sinclair. "He did not exactly blush, but his expression was even more priceless."

"Sinclair needs a bit more levity in his life," Astrid said.

"Is he the serious sort?" Myrtle asked, sounding intrigued as she shot Rose a speaking look. Rose had always preferred carefree men.

"Sinclair has always had to be. He's faced more than his share of responsibility," Astrid said. "Not that you'd ever hear him whinge about it."

An odd feeling stole over Rose as she thought about how Mr. Sinclair had taken on the responsibility of raising his siblings. He had a deep capacity to care—an emotion she'd rarely witnessed until her time driving ambulances in Belgium and France. Mr. Sinclair's was a quiet kind of passion but no less steadfast.

"He cares a lot about the folks of Frest," Rose said, surprised by the softness of her own tone. She could feel Myrtle's gaze sharpening on her.

"Aye." Astrid nodded. "He feels it is his duty to save the lot of us."

Rose rubbed her temples as a thought that had been pestering her bubbled to the surface. "When I met the crofters, everyone was saying how things had improved when the Grand Fleet was stationed here. That even with the young men off to the Front, they were selling more and making high profits on everything from wool to fish to finished goods."

Astrid nodded, her delicate features as stern as the cliffs of Hamarray. "That is right."

"But what will happen when the German internment ends and the British Navy's presence is even further reduced?" Rose asked.

Astrid jerked her head toward the sea, where the massive ships dotted the horizon—powerful remnants of a brutal war. "I do not know. But we are resilient on Frest. We have survived storms, raids, the transfer from one kingdom to another and then to a third, the Enclosures, U-boat attacks, and more. We will weather this as well. Somehow, we manage to make the sea and the land give up what we need from it."

While the islander focused on the water, Rose glanced back toward the turf, looking over Hamarray and out across the sandspit to the rest of her tiny domain. From this vantage point, she could see the entirety of Frest—spread out before her in a grassy mound. True, it looked as green and fertile as the famed Emerald Isle. Yet it was home to so many people—crowded into a space too small to support a living from the earth. But these people still managed it, using every resource they could—even the seaweed they turned into fertilizer.

Rose had come here to locate the notes that Lord Barbury had left and to help root out a spy ring. She hadn't planned on the people of Frest tugging on her soul, but they did. Their problems were beginning to haunt her as much as her mission.

As Rose started to turn back to Astrid's companions, her eyes fell on Muckle Skaill. The run-down, gray monstrosity stretched before her—all empty rooms and dust in what should be a grand seaside mansion.

Suddenly flickers of old memories stirred in Rose's mind.

I've always thought you smart as a whip, George, but building a hotel in a swamp? That's lunacy.

Instead of taking insult, Rose's daddy had just puffed out a ring of smoke as he'd pulled his cigar from his mouth. *You just watch. I'll turn Florida into a paradise. People will flock here.*

Her father had been true to his word. Rose had watched as a land of mud and mosquitoes had suddenly sprouted hotels, railroads, restaurants, theaters, and racetracks. She'd witnessed firsthand how tourism could build an economy. Astrid's bird-watching enterprise proved the possibility of attracting folks to these distant isles.

But would the people of Frest want such activity on their doorstep?

As Astrid returned to the naturalists, Rose's fingers brushed against a stray cigarette in her pocket. She withdrew it and raised it to her lips.

Slowly she pivoted, taking in the views of both Frest and Hamarray. In her mind, she saw new structures appear from the peat and gorse— ones that would not destroy the landscape but harmonize with it. When her gaze fell on Muckle Skaill again, she reimagined it as a grand hotel.

But was she capable of overseeing such a transformation if the islanders even wished it? It would require a commitment to Hamarray and to Frest that Rose did not know if she was capable of giving. Her whole adult life, she had never stayed in one place more than a month or two.

But the crofters were smart and hardworking. If she helped them put plans for a luxury retreat into motion, perhaps they could keep it going after her wanderlust hit again.

"I do believe you've already tried tugging on that book." Myrtle's voice was laced with amusement while she lounged on the settee in the library as Rose teetered on the top of a ladder. Like every evening since her arrival, Rose was focused on pursuing the third prong of her plan—trying to discover whether the viscount's key unlocked *anything* in the house. On the surface, searching for Barbury's papers seemed a much easier task than tracking down the mysterious *him* or unraveling the islanders' myriad of secrets. At this point, however, Rose had probably jammed his key into every receptacle where it could possibly fit but to no avail.

"You know, this process would go much faster if you'd lend a hand," Rose huffed as she reached for another tome.

Myrtle flipped the page of the bound pamphlet she'd found written by a resident of Orkney about the region's ancient mounds. "I'm busy researching. It is much more entertaining watching you than actually facing the tedium of tugging on book after book in the faint hope of discovering a secret compartment or safe."

"You are an archaeologist. You'll dig in the earth for hours overturning an inordinate amount of rocks, but you won't assist in a moderately dusty library?"

Myrtle laughed as she turned another page. "It is more than 'moderately dusty.'"

"At least there aren't any worms involved."

"But cobwebs and spiders are."

"I only disturbed that one giant nest." Rose feigned a shudder as she moved the wheeled ladder a little farther to the left.

The library was not as grand as the ones in either of her parents' massive homes. In fact, if it weren't for the chilly, damp draftiness, she'd even call it snug. Or perhaps not even then. The theatrically stunning views from the large mullioned windows imbued the room with drama, especially at twilight. Only mere yards from one of them, the world seemed to abruptly end with nothing but the churning blue sea below. Another perfectly framed a jutting peninsula of red cliff face as it plunged toward the white surf. Out of the third, one could see a vibrantly colored sea stack rising like a great column from the water. Turf grew on top, while streaks of white guano from the seabirds decorated the rest of the vermilion pillar.

It struck Rose with a sudden, almost physical force that this awe-striking beauty was about to be *hers*. It seemed nonsensical, though, to claim dominion over such wildness. A land like this would refuse any attempt at taming . . . yet people had inhabited Hamarray and Frest for millennia. Their descendants, folks like the Fletts, still eked out a living from the windswept loam and the rough waters. Somehow, Rose was becoming their landlady, and now the isles seemed to demand something from *her* almost as if *it*, not she, held title to the other.

"What does it mean to be a landowner of a British estate?" Rose asked as she turned away from the windows and tested another heavy volume.

Myrtle raised a single flaxen eyebrow. "Shouldn't you be the one telling me, seeing that you are about to become one as soon as the paperwork is signed?"

"I may have gotten myself involved in something I don't fully comprehend." The words came out with such dreadful solemnity that even Rose felt shocked. She *was* the queen of blithe . . . or at least she had been until the war had left her irritable and jumpy. Rose really didn't know who she was anymore, and it was becoming more and more apparent that she hadn't known for quite some time.

Myrtle straightened her back and faced Rose. "How so?"

"I appear to be acquiring tenants—a small village of them, in fact."

"You are purchasing two islands," Myrtle pointed out.

"But I'm only doing so to discover where this blasted *thing* goes and to see if the locals know anything of use to aid my poor attempts at sleuthing!" While clinging one handed to the ladder, Rose yanked the key out from under her blouse. She shook it at Myrtle, as if the gesture would finally produce successful results. "I didn't realize I'd be buying a *business*."

"You are the one who hobnobs with Europeans." Myrtle rose from the settee to move closer to Rose. "Before the war, you were constantly staying at grand estates."

"But I was there for the racing and the parties. I wasn't mucking about the agricultural parts of my friends' holdings or sticking my nose into their ancient ledgers. You, on the other hand, study societies and how they work."

"Long-dead ones!" Myrtle protested.

"But you took all those dreadfully dull history courses at college. Certainly one of them dealt with *something* about English land management."

Myrtle shook her head in affectionate exasperation as she stared up at Rose. "What precisely *did* you pay attention to at university?"

"Our brother school's football team," Rose ground out in frustration.

Finally, Myrtle took pity on Rose. She sat straight up, and her voice sharpened as she descended into professorial mode. Never before had Rose been so happy to hear her friend's crisp intonation. She felt like she needed to be back in the classroom, focusing on details that she'd foolishly dismissed as too boring.

"There is a sense of noblesse oblige," Myrtle explained. "This idea that the gentry should use their position and wealth in the society to improve the conditions of those who depend on the estate, including the surrounding community."

"Like Andrew Carnegie's 'Gospel of Wealth'? He and Daddy were always talking about it when he came for visits."

"I think the notions are akin to each other, but I feel like the former involves a more personal relationship and is not limited to grand charitable works. There is a connection to the land, too, to the particular cultural fabric of the area. Noblesse oblige is more agrarian than industrial at its root, perhaps? Folks from Pittsburgh to Puducherry can apply for Carnegie's funds. The industrial philanthropist tries to change the whole world. The laird, though, is responsible to those on his or her lands. If their duty does extend in any direction, it is through time. It is their job not only to protect and manage their estates today but for their children and the children of their tenants in the future."

Rose let out a frustrated sound that almost, *almost* could have competed with one of Mr. Flett's. "It all sounds so desperately esoteric. I am not sure what to make of it—any of this, really."

"You've basically got a deeper responsibility to and a relationship with the crofters than you would if you were a landowner in America." Myrtle gave a little shrug, as if her words resolved the matter.

They did not.

"Two other things that I've worked studiously to avoid in the past," Rose said softly as she climbed down the ladder. Before she'd joined the war, she'd wanted an unfettered life where she could flit from hotels to ocean liners to motor trials to hot-air balloon rides to rented villas to speedboat races. Now she didn't know *what* she desired, and her search for Barbury's report on the spy ring seemed even more futile than before.

Myrtle regarded her curiously. "Why are you so concerned with the duties of a British landlord? It is not as if you plan on staying on Hamarray and Frest after you've found Barbury's journal—or whatever he secreted away. Aren't you just going to sell your interest after I'm done excavating the broch?"

"That's what I was initially planning—and probably still am." Rose strutted toward a window and tapped her finger against it before turning again. "But I seem to possess this odd . . . I don't know . . . compulsion to become involved. I've even toyed with the idea of turning Muckle Skaill into a hotel and Hamarray into a seaside retreat." Perhaps because Rose could actually *do* something about the difficulties the islanders faced.

In the war, she'd been powerless to save so many of the wounded. Yes, she'd carted them to the hospitals, but she could not really *save* them. Not from the pain. Not from their wounds. Not from the gas. It was only Providence who had dictated who died and who survived. She'd merely been the driver, not even a nurse or a doctor. Yes, she had assisted, but in a way, she'd been helpless too. Who was not helpless in the face of war?

"A hotel?" Myrtle asked, arching her blonde eyebrow again. "Like one of your father's?"

Rose thought about the efficiently run lobbies with their gorgeous, gleaming interiors. They were stunning but not precisely welcoming. "Not exactly. More of a place one immediately feels at home in, comfortable in."

Myrtle's eyebrow climbed even higher. "That seems a change of pace for you."

Rose reached for a Lucky Strike. "You don't think I can make a success of it?"

Myrtle set aside her book, signaling that she was now fully engaged in the conversation. "Rose, you are the type of person who always accomplishes what she wants. In fact, if you are planning to convert this mansion into accommodations, I'd recommend also building a small rustic lodge. The less wealthy bird-watchers could stay in the cheaper rooms, along with the archaeologists who come to excavate the broch. Is being a hotelier what *you* want, though?"

"Hell, I don't know what I want, M. I feel like I've been standing at the crossroads for ages, and just when I finally started down one path, something has come along and is yanking me onto another." Rose sucked on the roll of tobacco and strongly considered lighting it.

Myrtle must have sensed Rose's frustration and almost rising panic, because she tried lightening the mood with a wink. "Could that *something* be a certain somebody—a sinfully handsome Viking, perhaps?"

To Rose's surprise, she found it difficult to assume her normal flirty, cavalier nonchalance. "Mr. Sinclair is very passionate about Frest and its people."

Myrtle dropped her attempt at forced joviality instantly. "I was *not* expecting that response."

Rose sped up her pacing. "Neither was I. It is not normally the type of intensity that I pay attention to in a man."

"He isn't your typical Casanova-style swashbuckling adventurer."

"Not at all." Rose rolled her shoulders.

"I still cannot believe you had dinner with his family. Have you ever dined with children before?"

"Not since I was one, but they are delightful. I can't seem to stop thinking about them and the other crofters. Did I tell you about Young Thomas? The poor lad fought in the trenches, and all he wants to do is stay home and work his parents' and aunt's land. Yet he's about to go to sea on a herring boat because there's no other employment to be had. It's just like how shy Ann Inkster works here at Muckle Skaill as a maid to help support her family even though this mansion practically scares her to death. Then there's Astrid, who leads moronic men to bird nests to make a bit of coin, and her grandmother, who slips whiskey into tea, which is exactly what I am now planning to do when I am her age. And David Craigie might look like an absolute bruiser and may be hiding a secret in his windmill, but he is the sweetest fellow who is just brimming with pride over grindstones and gears, of all things. I find myself hoping to high heaven that none of the islanders are involved in spying because I just like them all so damn much."

"Are you falling in love with Orkney?" Myrtle sounded flabbergasted.

Rose didn't blame her. *She* was more than a little discombobulated herself. Not particularly wanting to know the answer to the question her friend had just posed, Rose resumed pacing. Walking the cigarette through her fingers, she decided to focus instead on her plans. Strategy was so much easier to deal with than emotion.

"I will contact my attorneys in Edinburgh to make sure that the sale of the property is concluded soon," Rose said. "Being the true owner will only give me a greater excuse to poke around, and if I do decide to build a hotel here, it is a good first step."

"Is the Earl of Mar in Edinburgh?" Myrtle asked. "If not, there might be a delay in getting him to sign the papers."

"I believe he is, but his land agent is handling all of the details."

"Perhaps that is who you need if you decide to keep the islands," Myrtle suggested as she picked up her book again.

"An estate manager?" Rose said, considering the idea. She recalled some of her British lovers complaining of the need to meet with their land agent about some matter or another when they just wished to stay abed. It suddenly struck Rose that estate managers could form very close relationships with their employers through the years. Land agents also possessed great access to the holdings. Such a man could easily be the *him* that Barbury had referred to . . . or, just as plausible in the other direction, the spy.

"Yes, one of those," Myrtle said absently as she became reabsorbed in her reading.

"That's it!" Rose said excitedly as a welcome sense of clarity struck.

"What's it?" Myrtle sounded slightly annoyed as she lowered the small tome once again.

"I need to meet this land agent of Mar's. I'll make some excuse— maybe that I want him to bring me the papers to sign. It will be an excellent opportunity to gauge whether he could be connected to the viscount's mission! I can also ask him about the running of the estate."

"So you *are* planning to keep it?" Myrtle asked. "If so, can I excavate the mounds on Frest? They honestly intrigue me even more than my broch. I keep feeling that there is something under them that I need to discover."

Once again, Rose didn't answer Myrtle's first question because, thunderation, she still didn't *know* her ultimate goal. Rose had always been one to let life sweep her up into one adventure and deposit her in the next. That was how she'd ended up in the middle of a war and now with the responsibility for two islands on her shoulders. She wasn't someone who stuck around, and the people of Frest deserved better.

"If I don't sell off, you can excavate what you want so long as we get full permission from the crofters. But the only thing that I'm certain of right now is that I am going to bring Mr. Sinclair with me when I meet this estate manager."

"Your Viking?" Myrtle asked.

"How many times do I have to say that he's not *my* Viking?" Rose crushed her damp cigarette in her hand.

"You seem awfully attached to him, considering the short span of time that you've known each other."

Rose snorted, the idea of needing anyone but herself more unsettling than she wanted to admit. "If I am to hire a land agent, he would be my first choice, since he clearly knows the islands and is already a de facto leader of the crofters. It will be interesting to see how he interacts with Mar's old estate manager."

"Rose, you do realize that you barely know the man," Myrtle pointed out. "What makes you think he is ready for such responsibility?"

Rose laughed—the sound rather bitter. "Because he certainly understands more about duty than I do. Besides, I have other reasons for considering him for the position. He's hiding something from me, and it will give me a chance to watch him."

"Keep your friends close and your enemies even closer?" Myrtle repeated the old adage archly.

"Yep."

"Are you sure it's because you think he's the enemy that you want him near?" Myrtle asked, this time her voice softly serious instead of teasing.

And for the third time that night Rose ignored her friend's inquiry. And the reason for it was simple.

The potential answer frightened the dickens out of her.

Chapter 7

The sound of the motorboat caused Sinclair to lift his head from the crab pot he'd been fixing. Normally he did such things after sunset by the peat fire, but he was currently waiting on the ancient stone jetty for Miss Van Etten's arrival. She'd sent one of her servants over to his croft yesterday with an invitation for him to accompany her to Stromness to meet Mar's former estate agent, Mr. John White, and her solicitor, Mr. Lewis. Although Sinclair had little time to spare, he did not want to turn down the opportunity to be involved in the transfer of title to Frest, no matter how tangentially. Miss Van Etten had also promised to tell him about her plans for improving both islands.

A strange anticipation had swirled through Sinclair since he'd received the missive. He told himself that it was because he was looking forward to skimming through the waves in *The Briar*. After his experience in Miss Van Etten's automobile, he really shouldn't have been so eager to climb into any machine navigated by the heiress. Sinclair was supposed to be the steady one, the reliable one, the *boring* one. He wasn't the Earl of Mar seeking pleasure over all else. He had no time for frivolity or even adventure. Such distractions could come at a cost to his siblings' welfare—and that was a price he would never be willing to pay. But still, Sinclair couldn't stop his thrill when he spied the sleek vessel slicing through the water at a speed he could never achieve in his craft, no matter how strong the wind or how much time he put into maintaining the motor.

"Are you ready?" Miss Van Etten shouted over the burble of her engine, slowing her vessel as she approached the collection of old stones jutting into the North Sea that composed the pier of Frest.

"Aye," Sinclair said as he once again unsuccessfully tried to push down the swell of excitement rising through him like a dangerous gale.

Hoisting a crate of cheeses with its false bottom, Sinclair hopped into the vessel. As long as he was going to Mainland, Orkney, he might as well engage in business—both licit and illicit.

After Miss Van Etten reversed and brought the speedboat around, she winked one of her topaz eyes. That was his only warning before she jammed the throttle forward, and they shot through the water like a merry porpoise. The force slammed Sinclair back against the padded leather seat. Although the sea was relatively calm today, freezing spray shot into his face. Luckily, he was accustomed to icy showers and knew how to resolutely stare into the biting deluge.

Miss Van Etten did not display such stoicism.

She laughed into the frigid mist, her brightly painted lips parted in delight. Water clung to her long black eyelashes, making her appear even more like a bonny mermaid intent on seducing mortal men. Her mirth exploded into a long battle cry worthy of a Valkyrie that seemed to call to something long forgotten inside Sinclair.

He was no stranger to the waters around Frest. He often spent the lengthy summer days on his boat trying to bring in a good catch that would not only feed his siblings but bring in some money. He would bob along, carried up and down by the swells, propelled by either the wind or the slow put-put of his boat's motor. As the hours slipped away, he would become part of the North Sea, like a piece of driftwood carried along.

Miss Van Etten was *not*.

She skimmed along the surface, bursting through the waves, momentarily breaking them to her will. It was not just her machine that was marvelous; it was the woman herself. She remained in a state of constant vigilance like that of a great skua on the lookout for fish to snatch. Her eyes flicked over the waters, reading the way the current flowed. Without slacking her speed, she adroitly avoided skerries and shoals. The waters around the isles could be difficult to navigate, but despite being a newcomer, Miss Van Etten charged through them like a longtime resident. She showed no hesitation even as the rusting German dreadnoughts towered above them. She skirted through the monstrous vessels and their smaller brethren as if they were just part of a course set up for her pleasure.

The smaller German destroyers were in better repair than their larger ships, which matched the rumors Sinclair had heard about the massive vessels facing near mutiny and the sailors refusing most commands, including the orders meant to maintain the dreadnoughts. As Miss Van Etten and Sinclair sped along like a hornet among giants, he caught glimpses of wan faces staring down at him. Some looked envious. Some seemed enraged. But all had the stark hollowness of men worn down by a war they no longer wished to fight yet were now endless prisoners of.

"It's spooky, isn't it?" Miss Van Etten called over the roar of her motor. "Like a scene from a ghost story or a set from a scary film."

The sky was a dull gray, the light low. The moored ships, operating with skeleton crews, did seem like empty hulks in a misty landscape— the last remnants of a terrible, bloody conflict and of a fleet, built at great expense, meant to challenge and defeat the might of the British Empire in one great Wagnerian Götterdämmerung at sea. Their failure to find that climactic battle had left the war to be mostly contested in the muck on land.

"It does send a chill up one's spine," Sinclair agreed.

They popped out from the maze of the defeated fleet and sped straight toward a British cruiser. The red ensign stood out boldly against the monochromatic sky. The figures on board bustled about their duties. The vessel's guns were visible and clearly readied for any sudden movement by the interned Germans. Even the hull seemed to shine, the entire vessel bristling with life and action. Sinclair shielded his left eye as he stared up at the ship. He had grown accustomed to seeing these powerful boats inhabiting the water around his home. Although the war had brought hardship to so many, it had meant a degree of prosperity for Frest.

"Will you miss them when they're gone?" Once again, Miss Van Etten surprised Sinclair with her astuteness. The woman missed little, whether on the water, over the land, or in the soul.

"I won't mind seeing the last of the Germans, but it'll be strange not to see a fleet on the horizon anymore. A lot of folks will feel their absence."

"They brought you all plenty of customers." Miss Van Etten somehow managed to make her voice soft despite the need to project it over the thunder of the speedboat's engine.

"And a bit of the world to Orkney," Sinclair added as he glanced over his shoulder in the direction of Flotta. "They even built a movie theater on one of the naval bases. There were boxing matches that ten thousand would attend."

"How would you feel about a plan that would continue to attract visitors, ones flush with cash and eager to spend it?"

Sinclair stiffened as a foreboding tingle slipped through his veins. Echoes of drunken guffaws followed, harbingers of memories best forgotten. Even out in the sea with the cool wind and spray slapping his cheeks, Sinclair felt a suffocating heat bearing down upon him.

Firmly, he forced the demons back in the recesses where they properly belonged. Miss Van Etten was *not* the earl.

"What exactly are you thinking, Miss Van Etten?" Sinclair chose his words carefully, keeping his tone neutral.

"Your cousin Astrid inspired the idea, actually."

"Astrid?" Sinclair had seen her briefly yesterday, and she *had* seemed curiously pleased. But he hadn't paid it much attention. Astrid was always good at keeping secrets.

"Yep. I ran into her and her bird-watchers—annoying fellows but with deep pockets."

"Are you thinking about attracting more of them?" Sinclair asked, trying not to sound as dubious as he felt. Although Astrid had managed to collect a surprising number of clients over the years—even during the war—there were more convenient places in Scotland, including more populated Orcadian isles, for avian viewing.

"Not just them but all sorts of adventurers."

Adventurers. The word reverberated through him like the haunting call of a calloo. More snide laughter whispered along the edges of his consciousness, demanding an entrance he did not wish to give. A gunshot. More pops. The cry of a wounded animal.

"Sportsmen." He had no idea how he managed not to spit out the word.

"Perhaps," Miss Van Etten said lightly, and her casual response landed upon his heart with a giant painful thud as he recalled other blithe, cavalier grins and the acrid smell of gunpowder.

"What about the sheep?" This time the bitterness soaked into his tone.

Miss Van Etten sent him a curious look before she glanced back at the waters before them. "Well, they might be an issue with increased traffic on the island, but I doubt it will interfere with any husbandry or crops," Miss Van Etten said.

"What type of hunting are you considering?" Sinclair demanded.

"Hunting?" Miss Van Etten yanked on the wheel to avoid a fishing trawler making its way out to sea and clearly not used to such a swift boat cutting across the Flow. "Is that what you think I've been talking about? I have no desire to have people traipsing about shooting things. I've never had much fondness for the sound of guns. Especially not now."

Some relief trickled through Sinclair, but he didn't allow his body to relax. Perhaps Miss Van Etten did not mean to turn Hamarray into a hunting estate, but he was still not fond of rich, self-entitled "outdoor enthusiasts" traipsing all over the connected isles. Their definition of *sporting* and his own had never matched.

"I was thinking of perhaps turning Muckle Skaill into a hotel and the whole of Hamarray into a resort where visitors could go on a proper British ramble or sail in the Flow if they wanted. We could stock the pond near the mansion with fish, and of course the seashore would be an attraction in and of itself. This could be the perfect escape."

For the wealthy, entitled nobs who think they own and control every-thing in their purview. For the crofters, it was their way of life, one that they could never retreat from, even when rich visitors stalked through their lands.

"The hotel would provide jobs for the crofters—"

"You want us all working at the big house!" Sinclair interrupted, trying and failing to keep his tone measured. He was known for his lack of temper, yet Miss Van Etten had a singular ability for trying his latent one.

"Well, no, not everyone, of course, but the younger folks looking for jobs—like Young Thomas Craigie," Miss Van Etten said, speaking even more rapidly than normal. It seemed as if she'd entirely missed his concern in her excitement. "I haven't thought all the details through, but I have some ideas of how it could work. The dining room is big enough to set up a small restaurant that would feature dishes produced on Hamarray and Frest—lots of lamb, mutton, fish, handmade cheeses—basically the same as the menu that the children and I are organizing with the crofters for the ceilidh. Maybe a local woman could run the place. And then there would be sales of knit woolen goods to the visitors like there was to the Royal Navy—"

"You're expecting a bunch of toffs to eat a plain Orkney dinner and wear our simple clothes?" Sinclair probably should have used a less derogative term than *toff*, but old and new concerns had forced out all his carefully cultivated niceties.

His rather salient point did not seem to even prick Miss Van Etten's enthusiasm. "We're selling a concept—a state of mind. People are tired after years of bloodshed and now an outbreak of a virulent strain of influenza. They've seen or read about the horrors of industrial war. Here they can get away from it all."

"We're not some bucolic paradise found between the pages of sentimental drivel about an agricultural Eden that never existed." Sinclair also forgot all about plain speaking. As the past reared up, so did his old purloined education garnered from books his brother would secrete to him.

"Of course not." A cynical tone suddenly grounded Miss Van Etten's previous breathy excitement. She no longer sounded like a wealthy heiress about to embark on some grand lark but a businesswoman. She yanked back the throttle of her speedboat, causing the vessel to jerk to a halt as she turned to really look at him. "But *they* won't know that."

"So these adventurers will come here to seek their pleasure, and we crofters will dance to their whims." The words burned in his mouth like a rotgut whiskey. He'd already witnessed the suffering the cavorting toffs had wreaked on the island before. They'd replaced the sheep with hares, fallow deer, and other nonnative nuisance beasts. While the interlopers had feasted on the game the nobs had "stalked" on a tiny, treeless isle, the crofters had struggled to exist with the bulk of the grazing grounds gone and the new critters eating their remaining crops. The islanders had been forced to send their sons and daughters to work at Muckle Skaill, where they'd served the demands of the bacchanalian earl and his less-than-moral companions.

"You make it sound positively feudal." Miss Van Etten lifted one hand briefly from the steering wheel to wave it dismissively.

It had been.

"And how do you regard it, Miss Van Etten?"

"As a business venture run by the crofters. It is a moneymaking scheme. Daddy's hobby is being a hotelier. I know it can be lucrative."

Sinclair couldn't imagine being so wealthy as to consider hotel ownership as a mere diversion. "For the owner, perhaps."

"It will bring paying customers to Frest," Miss Van Etten contradicted.

"Toffs only take what they want. They don't give back—at least not in these parts. They expect to get whatever and whomever they want." Sinclair had seen only too well the price his mother had paid for the presence of the earl on the isle. She'd started working at Muckle Skaill as a girl on the cusp of adulthood dreaming of romance and a happy, contented life as a crofter's wife. A decade later, she'd escaped the mansion in the middle of the night with only the torn clothes on her back and her injured, fatherless son bleeding in her arms.

"Well, I simply won't stand for that," Miss Van Etten said, as if she could magically wave away inequity. "I'll make sure the dealings are fair. I may not know much about running crofts, but I am a student of hospitality."

Sinclair did not doubt that Miss Van Etten knew a great deal about hotels and opulence. He had much less faith in her commitment to protect the people of Frest.

"Besides," Miss Van Etten continued as she pushed the throttle forward again, "I've been toying with the idea that maybe we could expand beyond just catering to the wealthy. Myrtle suggested that I build a rustic lodge for middle-class nature enthusiasts and archaeologists. She is planning on excavating the broch and is hoping to convince her university to allow her to bring students here next summer. Who knows what she may uncover? We could bill Hamarray and Frest as the little Pompeii of the Northern Isles."

"We're not sitting on the perfect remains of an intact Roman city." Sinclair rubbed at his scar on his cheek again. The last thing the folks of

Frest needed was a bunch of university lads poking around Fornhowe and the center of their operations. It was dangerous enough with Miss Van Etten's unholy interest in David Craigie's windmill.

"Again, it's all in how we present it. You should have seen how excited Myrtle is about visiting Skara Brae on Mainland, Orkney. Wouldn't it be wonderful if you had houses so well preserved on Frest? Just think of what could be under the mounds on your croft and the one in the center of the island!"

He knew exactly what was under one of them, and he didn't want Miss Van Etten knowing. "Nothing but dirt and old folktales meant to thrill the bairns. Although perhaps we'll get lucky, and one of the creatures who supposedly live in them will spirit the university students away. That would be one way to deal with nosy visitors."

Stromness Harbor was in sight now and dotted with sea traffic, so Miss Van Etten could only shoot him a very short half-amused, half-frustrated expression. Somehow, she managed to both frown and smile at once.

"You *do* realize that people are a requirement for an economy."

"Aye, but must it be those types of people?" he muttered. At that very same moment, Miss Van Etten began to cut the engine, making his words unfortunately clear.

"You do realize that I am one of *those* types of people." Miss Van Etten thankfully sounded more amused than miffed, but Sinclair thought for a minute that he detected an off note in her voice, as if he'd *hurt* but not angered her.

"You're not." The words flowed from his mouth before he thought better. But as he spoke, he realized the startling truth. He *didn't* regard her as one of the earl's ilk. But was he just allowing himself to be duped by her allure? His mother had found the earl charming before she'd discovered she was meant only as a plaything—easily shelved, easily retrieved, easily broken, easily replaced.

Yet Sinclair wasn't handing over just his trust and future to Miss Van Etten but that of all the Frest crofters. He could not, *must* not, permit himself to be swayed by the reactions she seemed to elicit from the realm of his subconscious.

⬥

Rose had planned their arrival at Stromness to give her time to surreptitiously follow Mr. Sinclair before Mr. White and Mr. Lewis's ferry pulled into harbor. She was certainly no expert in shadowing a fellow, but Mr. Sinclair wasn't acting like a man with something to hide. He whistled cheerfully as he boldly strode through the main street that lined the water. Holding a rather massive crate of what she supposed contained produce, he did not spare a glance behind him. It was a good thing that he didn't, for Stromness was not exactly New York City with its teeming crowds and endless streams of wagons and vehicles. Aside from ducking down a narrow lane or inside the entrance to a house or storefront, she really had no place to hide.

Perhaps she was wrong about her suspicions. Maybe Mr. Sinclair was exactly who he seemed—an honest crofter with no secrets.

Or did Rose just *want* him to be?

Just as if her doubts had manifested into reality, Mr. Sinclair slipped inside a narrow passage between an inn and a grocer's. She hesitated a beat or two before following. By the time she peered down the shadowy alley, Mr. Sinclair was already disappearing behind a corner. She slid her hand into her reticule and touched the cool steel of her snub-nose revolver. Her weapon now in reach, she slunk into the tight space. The buildings were so close that they blocked most of the sun, and a chill leached through Rose.

Quietly, she tiptoed down the path and peeked around the side of the public house. Mr. Sinclair stood patiently at the back door, his arm muscles bulging under the weight of the case he held. Rose released a noiseless sigh. Of course he'd go to the back to deliver foodstuff. She really was painting everything with undeserved suspicion.

Just as she was about to back away, the door swung open, and a heavyset man with a thatch of red hair emerged. "Bit early in the week for a delivery, isn't it?"

"I had to make an unexpected trip to Stromness," Mr. Sinclair said.

The man eyed the bottom of the crate. "Did you bring more than just cheese?"

"I wouldn't come without your other order," Mr. Sinclair said. Something about the careful, circumspect way the men were talking caused Rose's suspicions to reignite, and she found that she'd begun to resent those doubts. She didn't want Mr. Sinclair to be the villain.

"The package is safe where it always is?" the man said.

Package? What was this mysterious second delivery? Could it be intelligence about the British guard ships or the state of the German Imperial Fleet? A pub near a busy port would be the perfect place to exchange information. No one would think it amiss for a passenger to head straight to the local watering hole after stepping off the ferry. In fact, it was at this very establishment that Rose planned on meeting Mr. White and Mr. Lewis. At each thought, Rose's spirits plummeted even further, and her stomach sloshed uncomfortably.

"Under the cheese?" the publican asked.

"Aye. Under the cheese," Mr. Sinclair confirmed.

The innkeeper finally accepted the crate. Grunting when the weight transferred to him, he disappeared into the house. He returned later with a sack of money. Judging by how it bulged, the Orcadian wasn't just buying wheels of cheese, and the exchange of forbidden secrets always paid well. Rose should have been elated to discover another potential clue, but instead she felt a peculiar sense of defeat that slipped through her muscles, weakening them.

As Mr. Sinclair hid the money in an inner pocket of his oilskin jacket, Rose backed away, her limbs still feeling shaky. It wouldn't do for him to discover her in the alley, especially when she had no idea how to process this new discovery. It was certainly not enough to go to the authorities with, but she did not know exactly how to proceed. Part of her didn't even *want* to know more, but she had no choice but to keep digging—not when peace was at stake. Perhaps she and Myrtle should start coming to this particular establishment for dinner, especially when the ferry from mainland Scotland was due in. She certainly would not want to cast suspicion on the islanders unless she was absolutely certain of their involvement. The only way forward seemed to be gathering more intelligence, even if she had begun to dislike where or rather *whom* she had to search.

Walking briskly back to the main street and fighting back an unexpectedly strong bubble of pain inside her chest, Rose headed straight for the front entrance of the pub. Although she would have strategically preferred to stay in the bar area where the gossip flowed the best, it tended to still be the domain of men. Normally Rose didn't mind ruffling the feathers of puffed-up peacocks, but creating a stir wouldn't help her investigation, and she wasn't in the mood to attract attention. Instead of grabbing a stool for herself, she asked for a table in the back snug.

The inn served a light lunch, and a few patrons were gathered in the homey room, where a fire crackled in the hearth. Unfortunately, the conversations that Rose overheard were as wholesome as the stone room with its polished wood furniture. Discussions about the weather, shoals of fish, and ferry passages weren't particularly helpful, but they were oddly soothing. Normal even. Breathing in and out, she let the pain inside of her fade away, and she quieted her thoughts. She couldn't have questions skittering around her brain when the former land agent of Muckle Skaill arrived. She needed to be focused.

Mr. White soon appeared in a black wool overcoat and top hat. He was of a middling age with a passing claim to handsomeness, if one liked their men winsomely earnest, well groomed, and a tad pale. Rose supposed that the solicitor with his half smile framed by a fashionable mustache exuded a sense of nonthreatening charm, which she'd always found both disingenuous and dull. Nobody was ever naturally this consistently pleasant.

"You must be Mr. White!" Rose said, imbuing her own voice with false enthusiasm as she stood up to greet the man and her own lawyer, Mr. Lewis, who was a tall, uncompromising gentleman in his sixties. The former land agent of Muckle Skaill, however, did not detect her facade, and his grin grew warm, but not, of course, *too* warm.

"And you must be Miss Van Etten," Mr. White said, his voice as kind and solicitous as his face. "It is a pleasure to meet you. I was so pleased when you requested that I bring you the papers. It is an honor indeed."

"Oh, the pleasure and honor are all mine." Rose gave a magnanimous sweep of her hand to the chair across from her as she began to resume her own seat. She could play the lady bountiful when needed, as she next indicated for Mr. Lewis to take the seat kitty corner to her. That left one chair open for her surprise guest.

"Here is the paperwork you need to sign," Mr. Lewis said, handing her a folio. "You shall find it all in order."

Rose nodded and removed the documents. As she began to scan them, Mr. White cleared his throat, the sound light and ever so polite. Rose lifted her eyes to his. "Yes, Mr. White?"

"Miss Van Etten, I assure you that there is no need for you to trouble yourself with reading the material. You have employed an exceedingly good solicitor, and I am an honest man who would never seek to mislead a lady."

"That may all be true, but I am still going to review it myself." Rose didn't attempt to hide the brittleness of her smile. She had been looking over contracts since shortly after she could read. As a child, she had nurtured the vain hope that if she could converse with her father about matters of business like his industrialist friends, then he might pay her some attention. In later years, she'd discovered that it was much easier to cause a scandal to attract notice.

"But it is quite weighty phrasing—" Mr. White continued, concern dripping from each word.

"Miss Van Etten is about to become laird of two isles." Mr. Sinclair's low voice broke into the conversation. "I don't think mere pieces of paper will intimidate her."

The two attorneys turned at the same time Rose did toward the Viking who stood before them. His rough oilskin coat was unbuttoned to reveal his sweater below—the one he'd knit himself. He didn't have the city polish of the men seated beside Rose, but he didn't need a suit to profess his competence. He simply radiated it.

"Please join us, Mr. Sinclair." Rose pointed toward the empty chair with as much flourish as she'd done when offering Mr. White a seat. "Mr. White and Mr. Lewis, this is Mr. Sinclair of Frest. I have invited him, as this is also a matter of import to the crofters on that island, and he serves as their representative."

Mr. Lewis, who was well accustomed to Rose's unconventional behavior, greeted Mr. Sinclair politely. Her lawyer's gravitas in the face of Rose's unpredictability was one of the reasons that she continued to engage him.

Mr. White, however, was not nearly so sanguine at suddenly having a tenant farmer at their table. Even his ever-present pleasant mien couldn't quite obscure his sourness as he observed in a rather clipped tone, "We have met before."

"Oh yes," Rose said, seeing her opening to pry into Mr. White's connection with the isles and his opportunities to spy. "You must have been a regular visitor to Frest and Hamarray as estate manager."

Mr. Sinclair snorted while Mr. White's cheerful demeanor slipped a bit more. "I made sure that the estate was to Lord Mar's standards."

Which by all appearances weren't that high. But Rose didn't make that observation . . . *yet.* She still wanted to discover more from this man, even if it sounded as if he might not have traveled to Hamarray and Frest as much as he should have.

"Did you stay often at Muckle Skaill?"

"I kept things running efficiently." Mr. White's carefully chosen words did not inspire confidence in Rose. But he *was* certainly good at manipulating the truth to his favor, which would be beneficial to a spy.

"Are you a particular friend of the earl?" Rose asked.

"I would never be so bold as to claim the esteem of a man in his position." Mr. White gave a mincing smile worthy of Jane Austen's Mr. Collins. Rose had no difficulty surmising that Mar and Mr. White had cultivated only a distant employee-employer relationship at best.

"Were you close at all with his late son?"

A particularly well-timed cough arose from Mr. Sinclair, and Mr. White's congeniality cracked again. Now that was interesting. Unfortunately, neither man seemed willing to elaborate on their response to her query. Mr. White only said in a rather somber voice, "I did not know the viscount terribly well. It is a tragic shame about his loss. So many young men cut down before their time. They did not have the fortune to avoid the war like some."

He shot a rather smug look in Mr. Sinclair's direction that made hot rage surge through Rose. How *dared* he! How *dared* he turn the sacrifice of so many into not just a platitude but a snide *insult* at that.

Rose didn't show her anger. Not yet. Mr. White would receive his comeuppance in due course.

"I only ask because I am curious about the relationship between a landowner and an estate agent. I am, of course, on the hunt for one of my own, and I thought you three gentlemen would be the best to guide me."

Mr. White looked torn between puffing up his chest and shooting deadly daggers in the direction of Mr. Sinclair. For his part, the crofter seemed rather stunned at being included in her statement. Mr. Lewis's patrician face remained as unreadable as always.

Rose turned to her attorney first. "Mr. Lewis, would you be so kind as to explain to me exactly what a British land agent's duties are and what his education tends to be?"

"An estate manager is charged with being the landowner's representative. He takes care of legal matters, tenant relations, buildings, duties to the community, forestry, a whole host of matters. Some are solicitors, some are graduates of the Royal Agricultural College in Cirencester, and some are members of the Land Agents' Society. There are even rumors about the founding of a new estate-management college, since it is currently difficult to find suitable agents." Mr. Lewis's normally impassive face showed a flicker of sadness, and Rose instantly knew that he was thinking of his grandson who had died at the Dardanelles. The war and its terrible casualties were the reason that it was difficult to find young men to fill positions. Instead of beginning their careers upon departing from university, they'd met their deaths instead.

Images of the blessés Rose had transported crowded her mind— men unable to breathe with lungs damaged from mustard gas or others with faces so torn by shrapnel they had barely looked human anymore. But each of them had been *somebody*, each of them once a hale, hearty young man with ambitions for the future. But the war hadn't cared about those hopes, hadn't seen them as individuals. They were numbers thrust against the numbers on the other side of the barbed wire.

But Rose had a chance to carry on a mission of one of the lost— Viscount Barbury. She couldn't allow the memories of the past to distract her. She needed to stay focused on the conversation to pick up any nuances that either Mr. White or Mr. Sinclair might display. As Myrtle had said, Rose needed to keep her enemies close.

"What are some qualities of a good land agent?" Rose asked as she turned to Mr. White, her voice unusually sharp as she tried to distract herself from the memories bearing down on her.

"Honesty, of course," Mr. White said, his obsequious smile back in place. "Loyalty to you and the estate. Knowledge of the applicable law and understanding of land valuation. A thorough understanding of accounting. Steadfast. Even tempered. An understanding of agriculture—crops, farm machinery, animal husbandry. A good grasp on local politics would be handy, although not strictly necessary, as the land agent could make it his duty to learn. He would also ideally have an understanding of the estate itself—perhaps even a past history with it."

"And what attributes would you add, seeing you've dealt with land agents from the other side of the coin?" Rose pivoted toward Mr. Sinclair.

He rubbed his scar—a sign that seemed to indicate his discomfort. Mr. White shifted, obviously not approving of Rose including one of her own tenants in the conversation about whom to hire.

"All the points Mr. Lewis and Mr. White said were good ones, but I would add that the man must be capable of forming a good relationship with the crofters as well. He must keep his word to them too. Trustworthiness breeds efficiency in my mind. We crofters always work hard, and we are more willing to make improvements when we know we shall be compensated for them, whether that be through direct payment or a better quality of life. A land agent should understand island existence—not how to manage a big sprawling estate in Devon or Hampshire. He should know how to dig drainage ditches to reclaim land and how to gather seaweed for fertilizer or how the fishing season affects the crofters and when the best time for dipping the sheep . . ."

"Sheep are dipped?" Rose asked in confusion. "What in heaven's name does *that* entail?"

"Rounding them up and placing them quickly in a bath to protect them against fungus and insects. We have a special chute that we built just for that purpose," Mr. Sinclair explained.

"Did you know about sheep dipping?" Rose asked Mr. Lewis, fascinated by this tidbit of crofting life.

He shook his head.

"Mr. White?"

"Uh . . . no," Mr. White said, "but it is a matter of small import. My concerns have mostly been focused on maintaining Lord Mar's Valhalla, the hunting grounds, and the live game."

Rose was beginning to wonder if the former land agent had visited the estate much at all. He sounded more like an absentminded gamekeeper.

Rose tapped her chin as she considered all the information. It wasn't difficult for her to realize exactly *who* was the most capable of managing Frest . . . or of organizing a spy ring. In this case, both were the same individual: Mr. Sinclair. He was at once the person connected to Hamarray that she trusted the most . . . and the least. For both those reasons, she wanted him by her side, even after, or maybe because of, what she'd witnessed in the alley behind the pub. It would make it so much easier to track his activities if he was on her payroll.

"I have the perfect candidate in mind," Rose announced. "I just need to ask him a few preliminary questions."

"Who?" Mr. White asked with a benevolent grin.

Rose turned to Mr. Sinclair. "Do you have any experience with keeping accounts?"

※

Sinclair froze as Miss Van Etten cast her brilliant golden-brown eyes in *his* direction. His heart sputtered like the old motor on his fishing boat when he demanded too much from it. Yet at the same time, energy flooded him, making him feel like he was rising on a swell of water. Whether the seas were in his favor, though, was yet to be ascertained.

"It may be prudent to consider someone *not* of Frest," Mr. White said quickly. As always, the damnable man's words were polite enough on the surface, but it was clear he thought that Sinclair lacked the requisite education and social standing. Which was rich considering that Mr. White was the city-bred fool who wouldn't know a ram's hindquarters from a ewe's.

Miss Van Etten literally waved away the old land agent's concerns with one sweep of her kid-gloved hand. "Nonsense. Mr. Sinclair is right that the island is unique and requires someone deeply familiar with it.

176

Every quality the three of you have listed, Mr. Sinclair has exhibited in the time I've known him, with the exception of knowledge of accounting and law. And I can always consult Mr. Lewis and his associates on the latter."

Emotions rushed through Sinclair like a winter gale sweeping over the strand, stirring up dreams long buried and feelings he hadn't quite encountered before. He'd forgotten what it felt like to have someone see *something* in him—to imagine a future for him.

"I can keep accounts." Sinclair almost winced at the sound of his voice. It had a choked quality to it, but luckily the toffs didn't seem to notice. Reggie had always thought Mr. White a preening idiot, and he'd planned for Sinclair to help run Hamarray and Frest when he came into his inheritance. It was one of the reasons Reggie had smuggled books to Sinclair and taught him what he'd learned about estate management. But their estrangement had decimated that boyhood plan. Then his sibling's death in faraway France had snuffed it out completely. Now it seemed to emerge from the ashes, conjured by the most unlikely source.

"As I said before," Mr. Lewis added carefully, "there are colleges that provide—"

"Bah!" Miss Van Etten's hand popped into the air again as she waggled her fingers. "My father only had an education in a one-room schoolhouse until the age of twelve. He managed to rise from being a shopkeeper's assistant to one of the richest men in the world and head of several business empires. Mr. Sinclair clearly has a fine mind. He'll do splendidly if he wants the position."

Did he *want* the position?

Miss Van Etten focused on him again. "I shall pay the going rate—whatever that is. I'll have Mr. Lewis research that and draw up the paperwork for your employment."

Land agents made an extremely good living. Sinclair would have no trouble supporting his siblings. He would not have as much time for fishing and the odd jobs he did for extra money, but he wouldn't have a need for them. While it would be difficult maintaining both the croft and the estate, he was used to long work-filled days.

"This is—" Mr. White's normally pleasant-pitched voice had turned downright blustery, revealing the persona that he normally showed only to the crofters.

"Rather sudden," Miss Van Etten's attorney broke in, his voice calm but laden with meaning. He, too, did not approve of his client's choice in land agent, not that his reaction surprised Sinclair. In the eyes of these men, he was a mere laborer who'd spent his entire life on a small insular island in the middle of the North Sea.

"Not really. Mr. Sinclair has actually been working as a de facto land agent already. If it wasn't for him, I wouldn't even be trying to improve Frest and Hamarray."

"I'll be happy to fulfill the position." Sinclair spoke quickly before the solicitors could interject with more objections. The islanders would need to select a new representative, since he would have divided loyalties, but he would have more power to improve life on Frest as their land agent.

"It's settled, then." Miss Van Etten clasped her hands together in a sweeping gesture of finality. "Now, let me read these documents and get them signed. Then, Mr. Lewis, you can see that the land transfer is properly registered, and I can officially become the owner of Hamarray and Frest."

To Sinclair's surprise, a sense of relief slipped through him. Mar was really, truly going to be gone from Orkney and his life. But what would the future be like under the new Lady of Muckle Skaill? She might have chosen him now as her land agent, but he didn't agree with her idea of turning Muckle Skaill into a hotel or erecting a rustic lodge. Other than that, he knew little of her plans for the islands . . . or even why she wanted to purchase them so badly. Had he just agreed to dance to the whims of another nob who couldn't even decide upon the tune that she wanted to play?

As *The Briar* approached Frest, Miss Van Etten slowed the speedboat and turned off the motor. As they bobbed, she turned toward Sinclair with a serious expression on her face. The winds weren't whipping today, and they were alone in this stretch of the water. Although they could spy the Flett croft, it was as if they were the only two in a sea of turquoise.

"I'm sorry I sprang my offer to be land agent so abruptly. I probably should have asked you in private, but I couldn't help myself. I wanted to do it in front of that smug Mr. White."

Sinclair grinned as he thought of the man's slack-jawed response. "After years of him demanding rents and dismissing any of our requests for improvements, I rather enjoyed it myself."

"I truly do wish for you to be the estate manager, but I don't want you to feel forced into accepting it. I promise I won't hire a 'toff' from London or America if you're only agreeing to be land agent to avoid that."

"I desire the position," he admitted and then paused to ask the question that had been pestering him. "But why are you so certain I'll be good at it?"

"Simple," Miss Van Etten said with a conviction that stunned Sinclair. "You clearly love the land, and you understand the crofters. When we toured the farms, you knew exactly who was doing what improvements and what more could be done."

It took Sinclair three swallows to clear the ache in his throat. Ever since his mum had died, he wasn't accustomed to receiving praise. "You don't have any worries about me being more loyal to the islanders than to the estate?"

Miss Van Etten laughed, the sound not snide but amused. "Mr. Sinclair, I am improving this land *for* the people of Frest. I trust you to be honest—perhaps even too honest—at least when it comes to the management of the crofts and Hamarray. You won't sugarcoat anything, and I like that in a person, especially in a manager. I don't sweeten things either, and I find life more refreshing that way. Don't you?"

"Aye," he admitted, then paused, thinking over her words. "What did you mean by 'at least when it comes to the management of the crofts'?"

She turned then suddenly toward him, the gold flecks in her eyes shining with clear challenge. If she'd meant to unsettle him, it was working. "There are things you are keeping from me. I don't believe they will interfere with your duties as an estate manager, but there's something mysterious about Frest and your past that you're determined to keep hidden."

"It is just the endless howl of the wind that makes you think that. Orkney's gales can make everything appear a bit gothic to the imagination." Sinclair chose his words carefully. The crofters didn't need her digging into their secrets.

"Hmmm, I still think there are things about you that I don't know." Miss Van Etten tapped her fingers lightly against his arm, as if to punctuate her words. Even with the oilskin jacket separating his flesh from hers, heat swirled into him. Although the waters remained still around them, *he* churned.

"Ah, well, I'm sure we all have some secrets, no matter how inconsequential or mostly forgotten," he managed, hoping he sounded clever instead of trapped.

"Oh no, not me. What you see is what you get," Miss Van Etten said airily.

Sinclair didn't believe her, and he doubted that even she thought that her statement was true. He'd begun to notice that she used blitheness to keep people at bay. It was as if she paradoxically used charm to pull people toward her while at the same time retreating herself.

As if confirming his suspicions, Miss Van Etten pushed on *The Briar*'s throttle, and the speedboat's nose pointed directly toward Frest.

"Humph." He practically shouted out the sound to avoid it being drowned by the motor.

"I am an open book," she returned gaily—too gaily. "I hide nothing."

That was certainly *not* true, but before he could decide whether he wanted to press her further, Freya appeared on the bank. His half sister waved enthusiastically and then cupped her hands to shout something. Once again, Miss Van Etten turned off the engine of *The Briar*, and Freya's words became comprehensible.

"Would you like to come to supper to celebrate officially becoming Lady of Muckle Skaill? Hannah is running over to Hamarray to invite your friend, Miss Morningstar, too," Freya hollered. "I made a tablet, which is sort of a fudge!"

"It's not quite official until the deed is registered, but I would be delighted to come!" Miss Van Etten hollered back. "Your cooking is always a treat!"

Freya clapped her hands together just as the twins appeared near the beach. Freya turned to her sisters and yelled, "She's coming."

The ten-year-olds immediately let out cheers and hurried back into the house, presumably to set the table and tell the others. Freya gave one last wave before she gathered up her skirts and tore up the hill toward home.

"It was kind of you to agree to come," Sinclair said softly so there was no chance of his siblings overhearing. "I am sure you had plans of your own to mark the occasion."

"Actually, I didn't." Miss Van Etten surprised him.

It would be easy to dismiss her response as a product of having so much wealth that the purchase of two islands was not a momentous occasion for her, but he thought he heard an odd, underlying note to her voice that sounded suspiciously like wistfulness.

"I suppose I might have had a bit of champagne with Myrtle, but this is much better," Miss Van Etten said without a trace of charming blitheness. "It was very thoughtful of your siblings to think of me."

"They have talked about nothing but you since your arrival," Sinclair found himself admitting. "Hannah is still all agog over your racing career, and you have very much impressed Margaret—which is no easy task. The twins, of course, cannot stop talking about your clothes."

"I never realized how wonderful children can be." Miss Van Etten glanced toward the Flett croft, that hint of yearning in her topaz eyes now. "To be honest, I haven't spent much time around young folks, which I am now beginning to think is my loss. They don't have the airs of adults, and their welcome seems so sincere."

Sinclair thought about the fakeness of the Earl of Mar's world. In England, the monster was seen as a gentleman, as he followed the ridiculous social protocols of upper society. But all that mincing just hid his depravity, which he'd unleashed on Hamarray. The same toff who would not approach a woman without a proper introduction in a ballroom ordered his female servants—women he had the responsibility to protect—not only into his bedchamber but also into those of his cronies. Mar had been the doting father to his legitimate offspring, taking Reggie with him on holidays instead of banishing him to the care of a nanny or a governess on one of his other estates. Yet Mar had forced his illegitimate son to fight with his other young servants as his drunken cohorts placed bets on the outcomes.

Even Reggie—the cosseted heir—had been affected by his father's gilt-covered dissoluteness. He could never quite reconcile the man who'd taught him to ride and shoot with the villain Mar had become when Reggie had been safely ensconced in a different wing of the house. Reggie had dealt with the conflict by doing his best to ignore Mar's darkness. He'd created fantasies of grand adventures in his mind to distract himself from what he could not help but witness. His drive for heroism had been, in part, compensation for Mar's misdeeds—a cosmic balance of sorts. Going to war had been Reggie's chance to prove his goodness once and for all.

Although not all toffs practiced the kind of despicableness that Mar hid, there was a false glitter about many of their lives. For the first time, Sinclair wondered what it would be like for a young woman with Miss Van Etten's spirit and intelligence to grow up in a society that especially prized demureness in girls. Would it have been hard to find her place in it? Had she, like Reggie, noticed its fakeness? Was blitheness her way of dealing with it like heroism had been Reggie's?

"The children are truly excited for you," Sinclair told her quietly. "Freya wouldn't have baked the tablet otherwise. It is a treat that my mother used to make us only on very special occasions. It takes a great deal of sugar, so she wasn't able to afford it for all our birthdays. The last batch she put in the oven was when she found out that little Alexander was on his way. And before that, she cooked it when Freya knit her first stocking by herself."

"And Freya made the tablet for me!" Clearly astonished, Miss Van Etten swung toward him. The fact that she'd instantly recognized how much the dessert meant to his family touched Sinclair. Reggie—who'd grown up having his every demand immediately met—would have never fully realized the significance of the fudge. But Miss Van Etten—whose parents were even wealthier than Mar—understood.

"Aye, Freya did," Sinclair said, "and I'm sure the bairns clamored to help her."

To Sinclair's shock, Miss Van Etten's eyes misted. The sight knocked the wind straight out of him like a heavy strike to the chest. Emotions rushed to fill the sudden void—emotions he didn't want to try to identify.

Miss Van Etten blinked and jerked her head toward the bow of *The Briar*. He thought her hand might have trembled just a bit as she reached for the throttle.

"Well then," she said in a cheery, chipper tone, "we mustn't delay in getting to shore."

She shot *The Briar* forward at breakneck speed, as if she could out-run her reaction to his words. But Sinclair was beginning to worry that it wasn't possible for *either* of them to escape the emotions gathering around them like dangerous storm clouds.

"I wanted to give you this, Miss Van Etten." Little Alexander had left his seat at the dinner table to hand Rose a chipped cup filled with water. In the center, a single delicate purple flower floated. Bending close to it, she noticed it had five heart-shaped leaves and a bright-yellow center.

"Oh, it is lovely, Alexander!" Rose said, afraid to even touch it with her finger—it looked so fragile. Instead, she lifted the porcelain toward her nose and sniffed. A faint but sweet perfume teased her senses.

"What is it?" Rose asked as she handed the cup to Myrtle, who was sitting next to her.

"A Scottish primrose." The boy rocked back on his feet and puffed out his chest proudly. "They are very rare."

"Especially this time of the year," Margaret said solemnly. "It is fairly early to spot one."

"It is beautiful," Myrtle said.

"We think it grew just for you, Miss Van Etten," Barbara said excitedly.

The girl's twin nodded emphatically and added sagely, "Being that today you became laird and that Rose is your first name."

"We just had to give it to you when Alexander found it," Hannah added.

"Thank you," Rose said, wishing that she didn't feel that dreadful burning in the backs of her eyes again. What was it about these earnest children that turned her into a watering pot? Of all the hothouse flowers that she'd received through the years, none of them had moved her like this one tiny bud. An alien sense of belonging drifted through Rose.

It had been so long since she'd felt it that she almost didn't recognize the elusive emotion. And when she did identify it, worry immediately stabbed her . . . for belonging was a fickle feeling whose absence lingered longer than its presence ever did.

And worse, she was experiencing a connection with the very family she might tear apart with her investigation. What would become of them if Mr. Sinclair was indeed the spy? What pain would she deliver upon them all?

"Freya," Mr. Sinclair said suddenly, as if he sensed Rose's growing discomfort, "I do think it is time for your tablet."

"Waste of sugar, if you ask me," Mr. Flett grumped from the head of the table.

Freya merely stopped to give him a swift kiss on his weathered cheek before she bustled over to where the fudge sat. "We all know it's your favorite too, Da."

The older man snorted, but his disapproval had turned into fondness. Freya beamed from ear to ear as she brought over her late mother's special dessert. She made a production of cutting it at the table, and all the children leaned forward in their seats to watch, as if at a picture show. Their excitement seemed to slip inside Rose, and she felt a crackle of energy that had long eluded her.

Happiness.

She felt *happy* over *fudge*? But then again, it wasn't just any treacle. It was a gift, a celebration, a tradition that the Fletts were sharing with her. And that . . . that humbled Rose.

Mr. Sinclair, Myrtle, and the Fletts did not touch their dessert as they waited for Rose's first bite. Conscious of their eyes upon her, she took a healthy chunk. Sweetness exploded on her tongue, and she didn't stop the enjoyment from showing on her face. Allowing her eyelids to flutter closed, she let out an appreciative "Mmmmm." When Rose opened her eyes, she saw that Freya's cheeks were pink with pride.

Myrtle took a taste and smiled broadly. "This *is* delicious. You should make it for the ceilidh. I am happy to purchase all the ingredients you need for a massive batch."

Little Alexander bounced up and down in his seat. "They liked it! They liked it!"

"I knew they would," Hannah said crisply. "They are ladies of adventure, after all, and it is a sweet for the bold."

Rose laughed at the twelve-year-old's pronouncement, but the mirth seemed to catch in her throat for just a second when she caught sight of Mr. Sinclair. The man's blue gaze *burned* with warm, wonderful heat.

Looking away before she shivered, Rose focused on the dessert. "This is the most delightful thing I have ever eaten. It is even better than fairy floss. Your cooking is truly a marvel, Freya."

"What's fairy floss?" Alexander asked.

"Spun sugar," Rose said, surprised the children hadn't tasted the confection before realizing that sweets were probably hard to get on Frest, where everything had to come in by boat.

"It sounds divine." Mary sighed.

"I'll bring some back with me the next time I travel to a place with a store that sells it," Rose said unthinkingly. But as soon as the words fell from her lips, she almost started in surprise. Goodness, was she making plans? She needed to be careful about giving promises she couldn't keep, especially to children. She'd sworn as a small girl that she'd never make a habit of causing disappointment like her parents had.

"What treat did your mother make for you when there was something to celebrate, Miss Van Etten?" Margaret asked as she neatly folded her hands on her lap after finishing her last bite of the tablet.

The question—the innocent, sweet question—seemed to fly through the air like a dart and hit Rose dead center in the heart. Old memories crowded her mind: celebrating birthdays alone in the nursery with her latest nanny, dressing for her debutante ball under the watchful eye of a distant aunt while her mother was away in Europe and her father distracted by business, winning her first race only to be scolded about it by her father as her mother sobbed into her handkerchief . . .

"I . . . uh . . . well, my mother doesn't bake," Rose said rather dully. She tripped over her words—something that she rarely did.

"Women of their class do not bother themselves with kitchen duties," Mr. Flett waspishly said at the same time that Myrtle quickly added, "Mrs. Van Etten is not precisely what one would call a chef."

"Did she buy you a special dessert, then?" Alexander asked. "Like the fairy floss? Or did your father pick up something like Thorfinn does sometimes when he brings us home treats from the market?"

Her parents hadn't even expended that effort. Oh, they'd showered her with gifts but in an offhand, unthinking way—like the rocking horse her father had purchased for her when she was twelve and much too big for it. She'd gotten whatever toy that she'd wanted . . . but she'd always had to ask for it.

"Well, my parents . . . well, they were very busy . . ."

Tarnation. Had her voice just *quavered*? In *public*? What was wrong with her today?

"You know, Miss Van Etten, we really should start on that walk we talked about before we lose the light." Mr. Sinclair suddenly pushed back his chair with a loud scraping sound and rose to his feet.

"Walk?" Rose said rather dazedly as she tried to collect her suddenly scattered emotions.

"To take a stroll among your new holdings." Mr. Sinclair headed over to her chair and crooked his elbow. He had *never* offered her his arm before. She had always been the one to take it.

"Oh, the amble we were going to take!" Rose said too brightly as she realized Mr. Sinclair was providing her an escape. It seemed like the Viking might have a suit of shining armor too.

As she placed her hand about his arm, she heard a rather scornful sound from Mr. Flett. Clearly, he did not approve of his stepson escorting her about like a gentleman. Whether that was a reflection on her, Mr. Sinclair, or both of them, Rose did not know, nor did she particularly care. She just wanted outside in the cool spring air—away from the crackling peat fire and the adorable Fletts with their heartfelt questions.

"Do you wish to join us, Miss Morningstar?" Mr. Sinclair asked.

Her friend studied Rose, and it wasn't hard to detect her concern. To Rose's surprise, though, Myrtle shook her head at Mr. Sinclair's offer. "I think perhaps this is a walk best taken just by the two of you. The children and I can have a poke around the howe on your property until you return. I've been itching to take another look at it, and I brought my notebook just in case I had the opportunity to record its dimensions."

Myrtle gave Rose a meaningful nod, and Rose realized that her best friend wanted her to have this moment with Mr. Sinclair, and that shook something else loose inside her. Unfortunately, it was just one more feeling that Rose did not quite know what to do with.

Rose let Mr. Sinclair guide her over the threshold into the still night. The wind was abnormally quiet, which made conversation possible. Thankfully, though, Mr. Sinclair did not mention her emotional reaction.

"So what shall be your first step as Lady of Muckle Skaill?" Mr. Sinclair asked as he led her away from his house and farther inland.

"Don't you mean *our* first one?" Rose squeezed his arm lightly and tried to lose herself in planning the future that she had rather blundered into. Yet even that didn't provide a total escape from the conflicting emotions churning inside her. After all, she was purposely partnering herself with a man who could be a spy—a man she might destroy or who might destroy her. "As estate manager, you shall be playing an intrinsic role in many of the decisions. I know nothing of agriculture."

Mr. Sinclair glanced at her, his gaze searching. "But surely you have some ideas of your own other than the hotel and the lodge. After all, you are the one who decided to purchase the isles."

Ah, yes, she *should* have some dreams for the place, shouldn't she? It wasn't as if she could very well tell Mr. Sinclair that her only concrete goal regarding the physical property was to search for secret compartments or passages that might hide Lord Barbury's paperwork. And even that plan was turning more and more into an ill-conceived whim. She had unearthed nothing but poorly defined suspicions of a people whom she would much rather trust instead.

"Muckle Skaill needs to be repaired," Rose said finally. "Even if it is not turned into a hotel, it is in terrible condition."

"I have heard that it is falling down." Mr. Sinclair's voice was curiously neutral, just as it always was when talking about the old mansion. Was there something in the building that he didn't want her to find?

"Are any of the locals good handymen?" Rose asked, determined more than ever to discover what lay in the walls of her new home.

Mr. Sinclair chuckled. "You will find that every single one of us is a jack-of-all-trades. We have to be, living out here like we do."

"Would Young Thomas be suitable?" The nineteen-year-old had already been a font of information . . . and his story had been weighing on Rose for several days now.

"Aye," Mr. Sinclair said, sounding pleased and a bit excited, "and he needs the work too. What made you think of him, lass?"

"When I met him at his uncle's windmill, he mentioned that he'd have to go to sea in the summer to earn enough coin. He didn't seem particularly thrilled to be going but resigned."

"The lad has always been a landlubber, and he enjoys working with his hands. He'd appreciate the offer," Mr. Sinclair said.

"If the going wage isn't what he'd earn on a herring boat, I want you to make sure that we pay him what he would've gotten during the fishing season." Rose increased their pace even though the climb had become steeper. It felt good to feel her heart pumping a bit. "I'm sure you can handle hiring him."

"Yes, miss." Mr. Sinclair seemed to practically spring over a clump of bright sea pinks, and Rose's own heart lifted just a little. After floundering in so many doubts, it felt good to discuss at least one tangible plan with a clear execution and result—even if the contentment was just for a whisper of a moment.

Rose filled her lungs with the salty air and stared at the rising land in front of her. Her gaze landed on the mysterious hump of sod at the very center of Frest with a ramshackle shed on top. Even without having Myrtle's fascination for old tumbledown things, Rose had to admit that the curiously shaped grassy lump intrigued her. There was something compelling about this bumpy mound at the top of the gently sloping hill with nothing else around it save that one narrow building and some scruffy, disgruntled sheep. With the sun already dipping toward the horizon, casting long shadows over Frest, Rose could almost imagine one of the ancients appearing out of the purplish haze and performing some long-forgotten ritual.

"Do you honestly think that there is nothing but dirt in that particular mound?" Rose jabbed her thumb toward it, recalling her earlier conversation with Mr. Sinclair about the huge piles on Frest.

Mr. Sinclair's body went even more taut than when she'd first met him. She wondered how he even managed to lift a shoulder into a shrug. He clearly meant the gesture to appear nonchalant, but it exhibited only his tension. Rose's heart squeezed almost painfully before it kicked into a gallop. Was this odd formation in the ground somehow connected to the secrets that Mr. Sinclair and the islanders were keeping?

"It is only the trick of light that makes you think it is more than just an impressive dome of sod," Mr. Sinclair said quickly, raising Rose's suspicion even higher.

"Whose croft is it on?" Rose asked.

"This is the common grazing ground on Frest." Mr. Sinclair spun his arm around, indicating an oval grassy plot encircled by a drystone fence.

Rose had seen courtyards bigger than this, but she did not want to insult him by saying so. No wonder he had been so concerned about ensuring that she extend their grazing rights on Hamarray. But the revelation didn't explain his current caginess or why a premonition kept skittering up and down her spine like an overindustrious spider.

"If the lump of earth is on common land, then I cannot imagine that no one has explored it." Rose tried pushing Mr. Sinclair just a bit more. "It's just too tempting sitting there, all hauntingly mysterious. It is practically shouting, 'Come. Look at me! See what treasures I hold!'"

Mr. Sinclair chuckled, a deep rumbling sound. It seemed to roll through her, first lifting her and then sending her crashing down. She wanted to joke with him, truly and fully—to *feel* the laughter. She was tired of this game, tired of not knowing whether she could trust him. But she couldn't allow herself to relax, not with this man who held so many secrets.

"If you are hearing voices from that howe, it is likely trows."

"Howe? Trow?" Rose asked and then allowed a faint smile. She mustn't let Mr. Sinclair see her internal strain. "I sound like I am reciting a child's nursery rhyme."

"A *howe* is Orcadian for a mound like that. That particular one is called Fornhowe. And a trow is a short misshapen creature who looks like a peedie little man. They are known to steal away fair maidens, so you might want to be careful around that particular mound, especially if they're already calling to you."

"A trow would probably throw me back. I can be rather trying at times. In fact, I take perverse enjoyment in being difficult."

"I don't think you're as demanding as you think you are." Mr. Sinclair's simple observation, spoken with no artifice, had her reaching into her satchel for a cig to play with. This man's ability to see past all her facades left her shaken, and not just because he could be a German agent. Spy or no, he was a danger to the parts of her that she kept hidden . . . even from herself.

"What makes you say that?" Rose didn't know why she spoke. It was a question that shouldn't matter and might prompt answers she didn't want to hear.

"Because you're the first laird in over a century who's seemed to give a shite about us crofters."

She tapped her cigarette against the case, as if she had ash to knock off. She felt raw—like a piece of skin after a blister was popped. "Who says I give a shite?"

"You do," he answered, his deep-blue gaze holding hers fast, "by standing here listening to me, by visiting the people of Frest, by agreeing to resolve the Sheep Problem . . . and by saying *shite* instead of *shit*."

She lifted the roll of tobacco to her mouth and sucked on it, wishing she could light up. She wanted to smoke her buzzing emotions into submission. She was here to uncover a spy ring, not secrets about herself—especially when the man unearthing them could be the enemy.

"Trows won't scare off Myrtle either—not when there's a mound to be explored." Rose turned the conversation back to slightly more comfortable ground—for her at least.

"Like I have said afore, Fornhowe is naught but a dirt heap. Miss Morningstar is right to concentrate on the howe on the Flett croft. I try not to disturb the land around it, but a few times I have turned up odd objects with the plow. Your friend is welcome to take a spade to that mound if she wishes."

Mr. Sinclair definitely *was* desperate to keep her away from Fornhowe, which made it all the more necessary for Rose to explore it. A nervous energy seeped into her, and her stomach soured as she thought of the secrets that she might discover. She did not want this man, these *people*, to be guilty. But she could not ignore these clues— clues that would have made her excited just weeks before. Now she almost dreaded the duty she had so willingly assumed in the beginning, before the potential spies had possessed faces, identities.

"Wouldn't your stepfather object to Myrtle digging around on your croft?" Rose asked.

"I can persuade him," Mr. Sinclair said. "After all, it might be a chance for him to learn about the ancestors of his that he's so proud of. He believes his father's line has lived on Frest since time immemorial."

Rose did not believe that the crotchety Mr. Flett would approve of anyone disturbing his forebears, especially rich American women. No, the only way the elderly man would agree to sacrificing the howe on his croft was if there was something more valuable worth protecting in Fornhowe. The so-called dirt heap definitely held the key to the islanders' secrets, but the idea of uncovering them made Rose queasy.

She sorely hoped that whatever she discovered at Fornhowe wouldn't point toward espionage but rather away from it.

Chapter 8

"Do we really need to explore this mound in the darkness? Maybe we should try our luck at being cat burglars and break into the windmill instead," Myrtle whispered as they carefully picked their way up the hillside leading to Fornhowe. Stars dotted the sky, and a chill wind swept over Frest, causing the grasses to brush against their skirts. The full moon cast a pale, wan glow over the treeless landscape. Without the sun illuminating the powerful seas and white sands, the outline of landscape took even more precedence, rendering each odd bump even more mysterious. The white-gray standing stone near Fornhowe seemed to capture the light, throwing it back toward Rose and Myrtle. It was not hard to imagine fairy folk flitting about on an evening like this—or specters of the ancient human inhabitants drifting above the isle over which they'd once held complete dominion.

"Don't tell me you've suddenly become superstitious," Rose teased in hopes of lightening the mood—or at least uncoiling the dreadful tension twisting her gut. Her skittishness since the war seemed particularly inflamed tonight.

"Heavens, don't bandy it about that I believe in the supernatural," Myrtle said. "The males in my field will take it as more evidence that women do not have the proper scientific temperament to draw rational conclusions from the past."

Even amid all of Rose's other emotions, familiar rage burned through her at the unnecessary adversity that Myrtle had to face in her career simply for being born a woman. "I shouldn't have teased. I'm .sorry. I'm just anxious. No matter what we find under Fornhowe, I hope we will also unearth a finding of great archaeological import. Then you can show those stuffy professors how truly brilliant you are!"

Myrtle's voice was laced with both amusement and frustration. "More likely they'll accuse me of being little better than a grave robber when they find out that I crept through the countryside like a thief to make the discovery."

"Technically, I do own this land," Rose pointed out at the same time she stepped in a divot. Her foot twisted but not enough to injure it.

"Then why are we bumbling around with shuttered lanterns?" Myrtle asked.

"Because we are trying to catch *spies*."

"Oh yes, that. How dandy!" Myrtle said. "And to think you wondered why I initially tried to decline your invitation in favor of a good book in front of a crackling fire."

"Oh, admit it." Rose poked her friend's arm with her elbow. "You want to see what is inside this mound as much as I do."

Myrtle sighed. "The timing is devilishly inconvenient, though."

"I prefer *atmospheric*."

"Tonight *does* possess a rather primordial feel," Myrtle added as they climbed the last rise and stood before the mound. The moon rose directly above the howe, and the edges of the earthen structure seemed to shimmer against the star-carpeted sky.

"Should we start with the fish-drying shed?" Rose pointed to the stone structure on top of Fornhowe as she battled back her own anxiousness.

"Well, that obliterated the haunting romance," Myrtle said as she tilted her head back. "I'd rather not start with the smelliest task. Besides, I'm interested in what's inside the mound, not what's on top of it."

"You can investigate the perimeter, and I'll peek into the drying shed. It doesn't make sense to put it there. Why didn't the islanders build it closer to the jetty? Why cart their catches all the way up here?" Saying the question squeezed Rose's stomach like a vise, but she could not ignore her suspicions.

"More statements like that, and I'd say you're well on your way to thinking like an archaeologist."

"I was rather hoping that I was adopting the thinking of a spymaster rather than a professor," Rose said with a lightness she certainly did not feel as she started up the side of Fornhowe. Her feet pressed deep into the springy ground—a perfect metaphor for the absolute bog forming inside her.

"Both involve the study of human nature and patterns, do they not?"

"I suppose." Rose grunted as she stopped trying to stride up the surprisingly steep incline in any dignified manner. Using her hands as leverage, she scrambled up the uneven surface. "This is not an easy climb." The uncomfortable sensation in her belly worsened. She still wanted answers, but she feared what they would cost her . . . and the crofters. She hated how each detail of Fornhowe was making the islanders appear more and more guilty of hiding something.

Pushing her emotions aside along with her nervousness, Rose scurried up the rest of the hill. Mud squelched against her knees, and at times, it felt like she was sinking into the very earth. The island of Frest, it appeared, wouldn't give up its secrets any more easily than would its inhabitants.

Slightly out of breath and dirty from waist to foot, Rose finally clambered to the side of the windowless structure. In America, it probably would have been a timber-built shack. Here, with wood so rare, even an outbuilding was built of expertly laid dry stone and as sturdy as a fortress . . . or perhaps there was a more sinister reason for the seemingly innocuous structure to have such thick walls. An involuntary shiver raked up Rose's spine.

She slowly stalked around the outside, but she could see no light escaping from any crack. Her heart fluttering like the wings of a sparrow in anticipation and dread, she pushed on the door and found it unsecured. She nudged it open, and each exposed inch tormented her. Darkness greeted her along with the pungent mix of fish, salt, and peat smoke. Slipping inside, she lifted the lantern's shutter in one swift move, and a scream caught in her throat.

Hundreds of glistening orbs stared at her.

Fish eyes, Rose told herself. Trying to steady her bouncing nerves, she studied the harmless rows of dried fillets.

Her shoulders slumped. She did not know what she had expected to find, but she had feared what the people of Frest were hiding.

After shutting the door to avoid light spilling out of the building, she lifted her lantern high. It was hard to take a good inventory of the place with scales and fins hanging everywhere. Fishy eyes bored into her, each glistening like a grotesque sequin. Rose did not generally consider herself squeamish—even before her days as an ambulance driver—but another shiver skittered up and down her spine. Resolutely, she forced herself to scan for anything that would indicate clandestine activity, perhaps a hiding place to pass messages or tools like expensive binoculars that the crofters could not afford themselves.

There was a pit in the center of the floor, and Rose swung her lantern above it. She could see nothing but a deep, narrow shaft straight down. She lowered the lantern into the hole but could spy only rock reinforcements that created a chimney. The crofters must build a fire underground in the howe.

Renewed tension twisted Rose's stomach into even tighter knots. There had to be an open space directly *under* her. A concealed one. In the center of an ancient mound. But how did they get to it?

This time Rose's shudder shook her whole body. What covert deeds were the islanders going to such lengths to hide? Could they even be doing it now—concealed by both the night and centuries and centuries of dirt?

Sitting back on her haunches, Rose considered her next step as her swollen heart pounded in an almost brutal rhythm. She needed to get inside the mound, but the entrance was likely hidden. Searching the small shed again, she noticed a ball of twine that the crofters must have used to tie up the fish. After tying one end around her lantern, she slowly lowered it until it rested on the ground below. She peered inside, but she could not see anything below.

Losing no time, she hurried back into the night and skittered down the hill. This time dirt flew into her face, but she'd been covered with grime before. Even one long slip didn't cause her to slacken her pace.

"Land sakes," Myrtle hissed as she raised her half-shuttered lantern in Rose's direction for a brief second. "You sound like a herd of angry ostriches. If this is your idea of subterfuge, I suggest you give up spy craft immediately."

"There must be an entrance to Fornhowe on the ground." Rose grasped her friend's forearm. "Come on. Hopefully I've literally shined a light on it. Either that or I've already announced our presence."

"You're not making sense," Myrtle hissed, but Rose ignored her friend as she dragged her along. They'd gone only about a quarter of the way around the howe when Rose spied a soft glow in the cracks of a jumble of rocks.

"There," Rose said, still huffing and puffing. "That's the way inside."

Myrtle crouched down and used her own lantern for more illumination. "It looks like someone has either dug their way into the mound or cleaned out the original entrance."

They worked quickly to clear away the small stones, both realizing that they could be discovered at any time. When all had been moved away but one giant rock, they stopped, staring. The final obstacle was a rather intimidating lump, but both she and Myrtle were stronger than most people expected of women. Rose had earned her muscles working on her automobiles, while Myrtle was accustomed to the physical labor of an archaeological dig.

"It's going to take the two of us to move that one," Rose said as she assumed a better position for lifting.

"Are you sure you won't be overtaxing yourself?" Myrtle asked.

"It's been months now since my illness. I still can't bring a lit cig to my lips, but I can roll a pebble or two." Rose gave the boulder a push and managed to wriggle it in the right direction.

"Easy now, Samson," Myrtle said as she moved to assist. "No need to perform the feat all by yourself."

"Since we're opening a potential tomb, wouldn't it make more sense to reference angels? As I recall, Samson brought the roof down on himself," Rose grunted out.

It took Myrtle a moment to respond as they both struggled under the weight of the rock. When she did finally speak, her voice sounded more than a little strained. "Since neither of us is the least bit angelic, I decided to use the proverbial strongman."

"Ah," Rose breathed out, a little winded herself as they finished removing the huge stone. They were now staring down a flat passage, not even big enough to crawl through on hands and knees.

"I cannot believe that the crofters would exert all this effort just to light a fire to smoke fish." Rose pushed her fingers into her hips, loosening some of the strain she felt there. She wished it would be so easy to relieve the pressure bearing down on her heart and the nervousness crowding her soul. She dreaded the shadowy passage and the dark answers it might hold. If the islanders were indeed involved in the spying, she would feel no triumph—just a burdensome sense of duty.

"Neither can I," Myrtle agreed, her voice solemn, without a trace of her normal irony. Sinking to her haunches, she used her lantern to study the dirt at the beginning of the slim passage. "I see skid marks, like they've pulled a sort of sled through here. Someone has definitely been using this place recently."

Rose knelt and looked as far as she could into the tunnel. It did not broaden inside. If anything, it grew even more narrow. The sight made her jumpier than one of the jackrabbits on Myrtle's ancestral ranch, but Rose had never allowed anxiousness to stop her. "There is no sled now that I can see. We'll have to crawl on our bellies."

Myrtle stuck her head beside Rose's. "Slither is more like it."

"I'll go first." Rose flopped on her stomach and began to wiggle through the tight space. Since she could not hold Myrtle's lantern in her hand while she moved, she had to push it ahead of her a foot or two, jiggle her body after it, and then repeat.

Unlike on Daytona Beach, if she encountered spies in this coffin-like space, there would be no running. Her breathing grew uneven, and she willed her thoughts away from capture. It was slow progress as she slipped deeper into the bowels of the prehistoric structure. The entire way was lined with stones, neatly arranged with almost haunting artistry. But Rose didn't stop to admire the work of the ancients. Instead, she focused on the yards, one after another, leading her closer to answers she now dreaded.

Suddenly, the hellish squeeze opened into a surprisingly large vaulted space. The light from both her lantern on the ground and Myrtle's in her hand illuminated the layers and layers of horizontal rocks shoring up the tunnellike chamber. Thin vertical flagstones were spaced evenly along the wall, reminding Rose of standing stones. They appeared too brittle and skinny to serve as true pillars. Instead, they seemed to be more for visual effect. Inside each of the sections were openings that looked a bit like hearths. At one end, Rose caught a glimpse of an additional passage. The view of the other was incongruously blocked by—

Giddy relief caused a bubble of mirth to rise up inside Rose, and she didn't try to stop it from fizzing out into a chuckle. The people of Frest were keeping a secret indeed—but a delicious, not treasonous one.

"It's a *still*."

It all fell into place now—Mr. Sinclair's conversation with the publican in the back alley, the abrupt changes in conversation, the need to mill more grain. Rose laughed again as she realized why Mr. Sinclair had been so intent on keeping her from climbing the ladder in the windmill. She would have known by the rollers that they weren't just grinding grain into flour but crushing it for whiskey.

"Did you say *still*?" Myrtle asked as her head popped out of the passage.

"Yep. A rather large one," Rose said, handing her friend back her lantern. Rose untied her own from the twine she'd used to lower it and then lifted it to illuminate more of the copper behemoth stuffed into one end of the ancient structure. Light reflected off the shiny surface, giving the contraption with its rounded belly and thinner neck an almost jolly appearance.

"I'd say." Myrtle's chin moved up and down as she followed the twisty copper piping that led to a barrel.

"This must be the source of the whiskey I had at Widow Flett's cottage." Feeling lighter than she had in years, Rose walked forward and tapped on one of the sealed wooden casks lining the stone-hewed walls. "I can't believe moonshine tastes so good."

"This looks a lot more sophisticated than your average illicit still." Myrtle swept the light of her own lantern around the inner sanctum of the tomb.

"No wonder Mr. Sinclair didn't want me sniffing around Fornhowe. It's the perfect hiding place, especially with the drying shed to explain away the smoke."

"I wouldn't say *perfect*." Myrtle clicked her tongue against the roof of her mouth. "Who knows what archaeological treasures are hidden in here that the soot could be damaging!"

Rose stood on tiptoe and peered into one of the hearth-like openings in the wall. Her light flickered over something that looked like wood at first. Bringing the lantern up higher, she sucked in her breath.

"Is that . . . ?"

"A pile of bones?" Myrtle asked matter-of-factly. "Yes. Human femurs by the look of them."

"Just femurs?" Rose inquired as a cold sensation slithered over her skin. She'd seen exposed human bone before—in the living and in the dead. But still, a collection of a single type of them unnerved her. Perhaps she had been too hasty in exonerating the crofters.

"Most likely. It is not uncommon for body parts to be organized by type in these old cairn tombs."

"They *are* ancient, though?"

"There's no way to actually date them, but they look old and discolored. You don't have to worry about your spy ring chopping up witnesses and sticking them in here as they distill whiskey."

"A balm for my nerves." Rose said the words flippantly enough, but part of her meant it. Her emotions were bouncing around like an uncontrolled rubber ball, and she was thankful for Myrtle's reassurance.

"It is simply a marvelous find." Myrtle gazed at the mass of femurs with an adoration that a miner would give to a vein of gold. "Thankfully, the crofters haven't disturbed them."

"They are the remains of their forebears," Rose pointed out.

"Oooh. I think I spy pottery behind them—complete bowls and not just shards. And there to the right? Could those be beads? This *is* a treasure trove."

Most people wanted to find objects that glittered, but not Rose's best friend. Even a fragment of dried clay could send Myrtle into a state of euphoria.

"I shouldn't have left all of my supplies back at Muckle Skaill." Myrtle bounced impatiently on her heels. "I can't touch anything until I've properly recorded it."

"The tide should still be out, and I can wait here while you walk back to Hamarray. I promise I won't disturb any pieces of antiquity, but just because the villagers are hiding one secret in this cairn doesn't mean that someone else might not have had the same idea."

"Still looking for where the viscount hid his report about the spy ring?"

"I'm afraid that will be written on my tombstone, but yes." Rose sighed.

"You do comprehend that if I return with all of my tools, I shall be here until at least sunrise or even after."

"It wouldn't be the first time we stayed awake all night. This might not be one of the parties we used to attend, but I don't mind keeping you and a pile of femurs company."

Myrtle bobbed her head excitedly before she disappeared, wiggling down the long dark tunnel leading back into the world. Rose resolutely marched to the next shelf, ignoring the sense of discomfort that came with her friend's departure. A new assemblage of disarticulated remains greeted Rose, and old memories of broken bodies danced at the edges of her mind. She forcefully held them at bay, telling herself that this was different. This was an ancient tomb where the dead had been laid respectfully. It wasn't a battlefield. Yet it became harder and harder to focus on the difference when each cavity revealed a similar collection.

Squaring her shoulders and trying to ignore the increasingly brutal pounding of her heart, Rose held her lantern aloft as she headed toward the back chamber that she'd noticed upon entering the cairn.

"Let's see what new macabre discovery is awaiting me now," she said, her voice echoing through the empty rock structure.

Just as the golden light from the lantern illuminated a wall of skulls, a boom rocked the chamber.

Rose heard only an exploding shell on the Front. Pebbles and dirt fell on her head, bringing with them both pain and panic. Perspiration drenched her, and her lantern slipped from her sweaty palm. Rose's frozen limbs ceased cooperating, and she could not coax her muscles to dive after the glass-encased light. When it crashed to the floor, the skulls seemed to grin before the bulb broke.

Instead of being plunged into darkness, Rose was dropped back into the war. The bones she saw now had been ripped apart by shrapnel as the sounds of shelling filled the air.

Sinclair awoke from a deep sleep with a start. He'd been a boy again, fishing with his older half brother for the trout the earl stocked in the loch on Hamarray. But their laughter had been interrupted by the sound of a nearby hunting rifle, and Sinclair had tried to scramble into a hiding place. Although the earl approved of his heir engaging in all sportsmen's activities, Mar did not wish for his bastard son to despoil his fishing grounds. And the earl had a way of displaying his displeasure with his fists.

Scrubbing his face, Sinclair knew he wouldn't easily fall back asleep. After grabbing the patch he used to hide the mess Mar had made of his face, he tied it securely. Next, he pulled on his boots. There was always a chore around that needed doing. He'd just finished donning his sweater when someone began pounding on his door.

Sinclair, who slept in the loft, quickly climbed down the ladder. In the back room, he could hear the children's sleepy, confused voices. He didn't take time to soothe them—not when he didn't know the problem himself. When he raced through the front room, where his stepfather slept, Sigurd lifted his head and grumpily asked, "What is that muckle noise?"

Sinclair didn't answer as he pulled back the front door to reveal a very rumpled, very muddy friend of Miss Van Etten's. "Miss . . . Miss Morningstar?"

"There's been an accident," she gasped out. "Up at the mound in the middle of Frest."

"Fornhowe?" Sinclair asked. Why in bloody hell would Miss Morningstar be at the ancient structure when any sane person was abed? Shite, had she discovered the still? If the exciseman found out about it . . .

"Yes! The central earthen mound." Miss Morningstar unceremoniously grabbed his arm and dragged him into the moonlit night. "The entrance caved in, and Rose is inside. I can't move the rubble myself, and you were the closest person I could think of who could help."

Miss Van Etten.

All questions about why the women were poking around the illicit distillery fled, replaced by sharp, clawing concern. "Is she hurt?" *Alive?*

"I . . . I don't know." Miss Morningstar's panicked voice broke, and the brief pause reverberated in Sinclair's own heart. "I went to gather my tools from Muckle Skaill. I'd just recrossed the strand when I heard the awful sound. I thought I saw . . ."

"Saw what?" Sinclair asked, scanning the darkness for more trouble as they began to race to Fornhowe.

"Oh, it's not . . . not important. Just my imagination," Miss Morningstar said hurriedly. She stumbled a little then, and Sinclair wondered if she'd done it on purpose to distract him. Her next words, though, drove those thoughts straight from him with the force of a sledgehammer.

"I heard Rose moan and cry out, but I couldn't get through all the debris."

"How badly do you think she's injured?" Panic, sharp and metallic, ripped through him.

"I . . ." Miss Morningstar glanced in his direction. He did not know what she saw in his expression, especially given that the only illumination came from the pale moonlight and her lantern, but whatever it was, she decided to continue. "I believe it is one of her attacks."

An attack? New fear scorched Sinclair. "Is someone in there with her? Are they dangerous?"

"No—nothing like that. She has experienced these . . . episodes since her return from the Western Front. In soldiers, they call it shell shock."

"She was in France during the war?"

"Yes. As a volunteer ambulance driver. Toward the end, her unit was assigned to pick up blessés from a poste de secours near some of the most intense fighting. She drove under heavy shelling and was gassed several times—once fairly badly."

Respect roared through Sinclair along with the familiar guilt. So many people—good men and women—had risked and sacrificed so much while he had remained safe and sound in Orkney. Duty had kept him far away from the trenches, and he would make the same choice again. But that did nothing to dull the pervasive sense that he should have fought.

Miss Van Etten had. Not with a weapon but with a vehicle. She'd driven men to safety, putting her own life at risk. He'd always known she'd raced automobiles and speedboats, but this . . . this explained so much. Her intensity. Her agility. Her focus. All had been hardened on war-torn roads with deadly bombs and toxins dropping from the skies.

"Are her lungs damaged from the mustard gas?" Sinclair asked, the words hard for him to even say.

"We believe so. She also had a bout of camp fever—perhaps even the Spanish flu. Ever since then, she's found it difficult to smoke. But she hasn't had any other issues—not that she's told me at least. Rose doesn't like admitting any weakness, and she won't be too happy that I told you about her shell shock. But you were bound to learn about it if this particular attack is as bad as I fear it is. The cave-in must have triggered her old memories, and she can get lost in them."

"How does she find her way out?" Sinclair asked. His throat had tightened so much he did not know how the question made it through his corded muscles.

"She's always been a spitfire, and she manages to battle through it."

But that fight would come with its own costs. Sinclair had punched down enough of his own demons to understand that. He knew the internal injuries they left in their wake—the wounds scabbed over, some of them even scarred, but others kept breaking anew.

A memory of Miss Van Etten's laughter as she sped through the water on *The Briar* or over the sand in her Raceabout drifted through his mind. He'd thought it alluringly carefree, but now . . . now he realized the underlying strength.

The urgency inside Sinclair increased—hot and fierce. They'd reached the entrance to the cairn now. The rocks he'd placed to obscure the entrance from the exciseman had been moved aside—most likely the efforts of Miss Van Etten and Miss Morningstar. It didn't matter right now that the two lasses had almost certainly discovered the illicit still. The only thing that Sinclair was focused upon was saving Miss Van Etten.

"Rose? Rose?" Miss Morningstar called into the rubble. "Can you hear me?"

No response.

"Step back, lass," Sinclair told Miss Morningstar gently. "I'll start digging."

He quickly surveyed the jumble before hefting the first rock. It wouldn't do to cause more of the entrance to collapse, especially when he didn't know what had caused the cave-in in the first place. Thankfully, it took only a second for him to devise his strategy. Then he set about methodically moving each one.

"Can I help? I am more able than I look." Miss Morningstar hovered behind him, her nervousness a palpable force. "I do a lot of excavating in my profession."

Sinclair wasn't one to underestimate the power of a lass. He'd witnessed too many widows and their female offspring eking out a living from this windswept isle. But the entrance was narrow, and it would be faster for him to work alone.

"We'd just be stepping over each other, Miss Morningstar." Sinclair hefted one of the bigger rocks and set it to the side.

"Is there someone else I can call upon to assist or at least give you relief?"

"There's no need." Sinclair shook his head. "Only one person can work at a time, and I'll be fine. I've spent more than one day doing nothing but building stone walls or digging drainage ditches. I can clear this tunnel."

And if the damn thing was going to collapse on anyone, he didn't want it to be any of the other islanders.

"Okay." Miss Morningstar breathed out the Americanism as she fidgeted behind him. He didn't blame her for anxious impatience. Not when he felt it so keenly himself.

"You can head back for a shovel, though," Sinclair said. "You'll find one in my byre."

He did not know if he could even risk using the implement, but it at least gave Miss Morningstar something to do other than fret. As she dashed into the darkness, he kept heaving away stones and scraping dirt. His fingers started to bleed, but he paid them no mind. That pain he could deal with; thinking of Miss Van Etten trapped in the dark with only the nightmares of war for company he could *not* tolerate.

Every time he heard even a pebble shift, fresh terror scoured him. Yet by some miracle, he did not trigger another cave-in.

Miss Morningstar returned, and he barely glanced up to acknowledge her. He was like a machine now. Aye, his muscles ached and burned to prove he was still human, but he'd become a single-minded, rhythmic flurry of repetitive motion. He used the shovel when it was safe and his bare hands when it wasn't.

Finally, he broke through the last of the mess. He would have fallen to his knees with relief if he hadn't been already on them. The bulk of the passageway still remained intact. The ancients had a knack for building sturdy structures—fitting dry stones together in a manner that defied not just the elements but time itself. But it seemed like tonight age had won the battle—at least at the tunnel entrance.

"I'll go first," Miss Morningstar said, "as mine is the more familiar face."

"The tomb could collapse. I'm not sure how much damage the tunnel and vault have sustained."

"She's my best friend." Miss Morningstar resolutely slipped into the tunnel and disappeared as quickly as an Orkney vole scampering through its own burrow.

Sinclair followed at a much slower pace. As a lad, when he and Reggie had first explored it, he'd had no difficulty scrambling through. Now his broad shoulders gave him a devil of a time. But he managed, as did the other men who helped to distill the bere whiskey.

When he struggled into the main chamber, he found it untouched by the cave-in. The copper still stood at one end, looking like a chubby sentry. None of the walls had crumbled. The shelves that held the ancestral bone looked as stable as ever. Relief and horror warred inside Sinclair. The distillery was safe, but there was no sign of Miss Van Etten.

"Shite! She's trapped in the skull room." Sinclair immediately headed toward it.

"The skull room?" Miss Morningstar asked, her voice clearly torn between concern for her friend and professional curiosity.

"Aye," Sinclair said as he ducked into the alcove with Miss Morningstar on his heels.

At the sight of a physically unscathed Miss Van Etten, Sinclair started to take his first good gulp of air since Miss Morningstar had told him about the cave-in at Fornhowe. But before he could finish the breath, his lungs seemed to collapse on themselves. Miss Van Etten was frozen in a corner, her topaz eyes large and unseeing. A painful fissure burned through Sinclair's heart. The normally indomitable woman clutched at the fabric of her coat, clenching something that hung around her neck. She made no movement except an occasional blink. Terror marred her face, her pale skin taut and almost translucent.

Every fiber of Sinclair yearned to go to Miss Van Etten—to gather her into his arms like he did one of the bairns after a nightmare. He wanted with an almost physical need to be the one to soothe her, to hold her until her vivacious spirit returned, her cheeks pinkened, and her eyes flashed back to life.

But that was not his place.

Miss Van Etten needed the security of a well-known companion—not a recent stranger turned employee.

Miss Morningstar paid no attention to what, to her, must be a marvelous archaeological discovery. Instead, she focused solely on her friend. Crouching down, she moved close to Miss Van Etten but did not touch her.

"Rose? Rosie? It's me, Myrtle."

Miss Van Etten did not respond.

Miss Morningstar reached into her pocket and withdrew a peppermint. The sharp, pungent smell of the candy filled the small alcove. Miss Van Etten seemed to inhale a little more deeply, perhaps detecting the scent.

"We're in the mound, Rose." Miss Morningstar kept talking, her voice pleasantly conversational. "Remember? There was the still, and then we found evidence of the peoples who first built this cairn. I went back to Muckle Skaill for my tools. There was a cave-in before I returned, but Mr. Sinclair dug out the passageway. Everything is fine. We're all safe.

"You remember Mr. Sinclair. Your Viking?"

Her Viking? A fiery warmth blazed a path through the miasma of worry and fear thundering inside Sinclair. He did not know why the notion of belonging to someone, belonging to *Rose*, pleased him, but for the moment, he simply accepted that it did. He had no time to be analyzing his feelings with Miss Van Etten suffering from shell shock.

A spark flickered in the heiress's eyes that did not appear to be generated by her friend's lantern. She shifted her head ever so slightly, her gaze first falling on Miss Morningstar and then him.

Miss Morningstar touched Miss Van Etten's gloved hand. The heiress slowly shifted to glance down at her friend's fingers, as if emerging from slumber—or, more accurately, a nightmare.

"Here's a peppermint," Miss Morningstar said gently, dropping the candy onto Miss Van Etten's palm.

"Thank you." Miss Van Etten's voice sounded a bit distant still but not weak—*not weak*. Sinclair's knees went soft, and he briefly rested his hand against the rock wall. It seemed Miss Van Etten's spirit was indeed made of stern stuff.

As she sucked on the candy, Miss Van Etten still gripped her friend's hand. Now that the lady seemed to be on her way to recovery, Sinclair wondered for a moment if he should retreat to the main chamber. He did not really belong here, encroaching on his employer's private moment as if he were part of her intimate circle.

Before Sinclair could step back, Miss Van Etten began to rise from the ground. Her movements were a bit jerky, but she shook her head when he stepped forward to assist her and also refused Miss Morningstar's other hand. Sinclair watched in amazement as Miss Van Etten both physically and mentally gathered herself. As she made a production of dusting off her skirts with her trembling fingers, her expression shifted from flat and hollow to determined, which then promptly morphed into a facade of cheer. The woman wielded her joie de vivre like a claymore, and her sheer strength humbled Sinclair. He'd been a fool to ever think that her blitheness came from cavalier privilege. Her good nature was a hard-won battle.

"Well, I believe I've had enough of dark holes and human bones for one night," Miss Van Etten said, her voice strengthening with each word. "I am afraid you might have to record your findings alone tonight, Myrtle."

"I am no longer in the mood for archaeology," Miss Morningstar said. "Let's walk back to Muckle Skaill. It will be nice strolling under the stars, getting our bearings again."

"The tide will be in by now," Sinclair pointed out softly as he stepped back to allow the women to pass into the main chamber.

"So we're marooned on Frest?" Miss Morningstar spoke calmly enough, but he didn't miss the worry in her voice. After all, he felt it too.

"You're welcome to stay in my family's cottage until morning," Sinclair offered. "I'm afraid I can only offer you the loft, as it is the single private room. It isn't luxurious, but it's comfortable enough to lay your heads. Or I can take you over to Hamarray on my boat. I know the waters well enough, and there is some light from the moon."

"No need to risk navigating at night, especially with the tricky currents around here," Miss Van Etten said with an almost airy tone before she ducked under the passage. Sinclair, though, didn't miss her slightly shaky intake of breath. The tight corridor unsettled her, but she had plunged ahead without hesitation. The new Lady of Muckle Skaill was indeed admirably tough.

Miss Morningstar shrugged before she, too, disappeared into the tunnel. When Sinclair wriggled through and clambered to his feet, he found Miss Van Etten only a yard from the entrance, her chin tilted toward the sky. Her hat must have fallen off somewhere, and her short black curls were in wild disarray, but she still managed a fierce, upper-crust elegance. And for once, he didn't feel pushed away by it. This was not unearned arrogance but true strength.

Miss Van Etten turned then, and he watched as she purposely arranged her face into a pleasant mien. But when she linked one of her arms with his and the other with her friend's, he could feel the tremble that she otherwise hid so efficiently. Her back straight, she led them down the uneven hillock like a Roman general advancing over Hadrian's Wall.

When they reached Sinclair's front door, Miss Van Etten stepped back. "You two can go inside. I'd rather sit and watch the stars."

"Are you certain that you wish to stay out here, lass?" Sinclair asked. "It's dreich tonight."

"The chill feels good." Miss Van Etten gave what Sinclair now realized was a practiced smile. "I got used to the damp in France."

Apparently, blitheness made just as good a shield as it did a blade. "Could I at least bring you blankets?"

Miss Van Etten tilted her head. With the moonlight bestowing her white skin with a pearly glow, the result was stunning. Sinclair sucked in his breath as she studied him from beneath her long black lashes.

"As long as it comes with a flask of the whiskey that I tasted at Widow Flett's."

There was no doubt that the heiress now realized the liquor had been distilled at Fornhowe, but neither of them mentioned it. It relieved him somewhat that she didn't seem angry, but he was just learning how well Miss Van Etten could obscure her true emotions. Even if she didn't intend to turn them in to the exciseman, she could always insist on a share of the proceeds. Other lairds would see it as their right, and so might she. But it wasn't a fight to have now.

"I can arrange a wee dram or two," he promised, keeping his tone as light as hers as he opened the door for her friend.

"I am happy to stay outside with you, Rose." Miss Morningstar paused at the threshold, her lips pursed with concern.

"There's no need for both of us to spend a sleepless night. I shall be fine."

The archaeologist shook her head. "You should not be alone, Rose. Not in the dark."

Miss Van Etten sighed wearily. "If you insist on staying with me, I shall have no choice but to go inside. You have never handled sitting still in the cold. You'll be a frightful, shivery mess within minutes. I will be fine, M."

Miss Morningstar's expression grew as mulish as Miss Van Etten's, and it was clear that the women were about to meet a stalemate.

"I can stay with Miss Van Etten," Sinclair said. "I won't be getting more sleep tonight anyway." After all, he was giving up his bed.

"Would that work for you?" Miss Morningstar asked her friend.

"Fine," Miss Van Etten said crisply before she marched in the direction of the sea.

Miss Morningstar sighed heavily. "Let's be quick about getting me settled. I don't want her alone too long."

"Aye," Sinclair agreed, thinking about the hollowness in Miss Van Etten's eyes when they'd discovered her in the skull room and the way her hands had briefly shaken.

Together, he and Miss Morningstar hurried into the cottage. Thankfully, Sigurd was sleeping soundly. Freya had already gotten the children back to sleep, and it took Sinclair only a few moments to explain to her what had happened. While Freya helped prepare Miss Morningstar a pallet in the loft, Sinclair grabbed three of the heaviest wool blankets woven by his mother and a bottle of whiskey. As he headed back into the air, a chill stole through him that had nothing to do with the dreich and everything to do with the fact that the recent events in Fornhowe had left him upended.

He could not escape the sense that his already conflicted relationship with Miss Van Etten was about to get even more in a tangle.

Chapter 9

Sinclair found Miss Van Etten on the beach staring out at the inky sea.

People generally looked small and lonely against the backdrop of the Flow. Not Miss Van Etten. She appeared fierce, indomitable—as if she could stare the sea into submission. Perhaps it was the set of her shoulders or the way her short hair danced in the wind. But most likely it was her undeniable spirit.

But her strength didn't mean that she wasn't in need of a companion to help ward off the darkness not born of the night. Even if he wasn't the gallant knight to her lady, it didn't mean that he couldn't sit with her a spell or two.

"Would you care for some company, lass?" Sinclair asked as he handed over the pile of blankets and the whiskey. "Or would you rather me find a spot a peedie further down the strand?"

Miss Van Etten patted the ground next to her, and he sank to the sand. She threw one blanket over her shoulder, adjusting it. Then to his utter shock, she lifted one end of the material to make an opening for him.

"You don't need to worry about me, Miss Van Etten. I'm accustomed to the dreich."

Ignoring his protest, she scooted toward him and raised her arm to make an even more inviting cave. Sinclair cleared his throat. She merely raised a challenging eyebrow.

Devil take him. Against all bloody reason, he *was* going to give in.

Slipping under the wool, he allowed her to stretch the corner over his back. He reached up; then his hand brushed against hers as he pulled down on the blanket, bringing it closer . . . bringing *them* closer. It made no sense—an heiress and a poor crofter like him acting like young, foolish sweethearts. But he couldn't stop himself. He didn't *want* to stop himself. He'd been fighting the tug toward her for too long, and tonight . . . tonight his resistance had been ground to sand.

Their shoulders were flush against each other now, heat transferring between them. He didn't need the blanket for warmth. Mere contact with her was enough to heat him for weeks, perhaps even months. It seemed the lass was so good at holding darkness at bay with her light that she was even chasing away his.

Miss Van Etten spread the other blankets over their legs, cocooning them together. She opened the whiskey bottle and drank a dram straight down. Then she handed it to him. He accepted and took a swig. He'd never imagined drinking with an upper-class lady—let alone sharing the same container of moonshine. It should have felt all wrong. But it didn't. It felt all right . . . at least it did tonight.

"I cannot believe that home-distilled liquor tastes so complex and smooth," Miss Van Etten said. "Although your operation *is* bigger than most illegal stills."

Sinclair rubbed his thumb against his scar as her words reminded him exactly why he shouldn't be allowing himself to feel so comfortable. "What are your intentions?"

She laughed then, the sound short and a bit self-deprecating but no less real. "Rarely honorable."

Sinclair gave a slow half grin and lifted the whiskey to his lips again. "I meant about the hidden distillery."

After reaching for the bottle, she sipped a little more. "I was planning to talk to my new land agent about it. He seems a clever sort of fellow."

Sinclair froze, allowing the whiskey to burn a path through him. He wasn't sure what her flattery portended. He hoped she meant only to set him at ease with the compliment, but he feared she might be trying to coax him to take her side in the matter over the islanders. When he spoke, he chose his words cautiously.

"Does he now? And why would you be needing a bright chap?"

"I would think that setting up a legitimate distillery will be a bit of a challenge. Getting licenses, negotiating with the locals, those types of things."

"It is the crofters' recipe and our bere barley that David Craigie rolls for us," Sinclair pointed out carefully before he could even allow himself to consider her words. The earl would have automatically demanded the lion's share of all proceeds, but Mar never would have helped herd sheep or had a fascination with windmills. Sinclair never knew what to expect from Miss Van Etten, but he was beginning to suspect that she might be more principled than she let on. But that didn't mean he fully trusted her. Not yet, at least.

"I'm looking to be an investor—a silent partner. We can consult with Mr. Lewis about the best way to proceed legally. I have enough connections in Britain that I'm sure we can sail through the process. Once it is certain that we can abide by the applicable regulations, I'll provide the people of Frest with whatever you need to build a proper distillery on Hamarray."

Sinclair tried battling down the excitement flickering inside him. It would not do to become overly enthused. Steadiness was always the best course, and Miss Van Etten had not mentioned what share she would demand.

"What percentage of the profits will you be taking?" Sinclair tried not to make the question a sharp demand despite the way his heart was squeezing so forcefully.

"How is it currently divided?"

"Every family gets an equal portion."

Miss Van Etten was silent as she considered this, and sickly sweet nervousness filled Sinclair. Finally, she spoke, her voice thoughtful. "I wouldn't want any proceeds until the new distillery is making more money than you currently net now. Once it hits that margin, I shall take just fifty percent of what a single crofter's share is. And I also want to receive permission for Miss Morningstar to excavate Fornhowe."

Although Miss Van Etten's financial offer was exceedingly generous, the last bit caused Sinclair some pause. He did not want the islanders' heritage carted off to New York or London. "What would her plans be?"

"Meticulous," Miss Van Etten said. "She is not a treasure hunter but a fact seeker. We can work out with her what she will do with her physical finds, but provided the law allows, we can see that they stay in Orkney. She will work in concert with the desires of the people of Frest. If you cannot come to an agreement with her, then there shall be no dig."

"That will be in writing?" Sinclair asked, remembering all the earl's broken promises.

Miss Van Etten grinned. "I wouldn't have it any other way."

"Then I believe a whiskey-distilling partnership may be arranged, Miss Van Etten."

"Rose."

That one word caused something to take root and blossom in his chest. Not milady, not ma'am, not Miss Van Etten, but *Rose*.

"Are you certain, miss?"

She waved her gloved hand in the air. "We are currently cuddled under the same blankets, and you now know about my shell shock. I think Christian names are in order, but I shall still call you Mr. Sinclair if that is what you desire."

"Sinclair." He swallowed. "Just Sinclair."

"Do you prefer that to Thorfinn?"

Did he? A sneering, cultured voice from Sinclair's memory ripped through the fragile sense of contentment that had been building inside him.

No one should call the boy Thorfinn. Naming a bastard after gods and legends? Tell the servants to cease this nonsense. It has persisted too long. I am tired of hearing it. Just use the whelp's mother's surname.

"Other than the bairns, only my mother called me that." *When she could.*

"Then Sinclair it is," she said. "Although I shall likely always think of you privately as Thorfinn. It just suits you so."

"Because I'm a Viking?" he asked, his voice thickening as he remembered Miss Morningstar calling him Rose's. He wasn't sure what answer he wanted to hear, but the question had slipped out all the same.

"Well, there's that." Rose grinned and then sobered. "But mostly because it is a powerful name, and from what I have seen, you are a man of great strength."

Sinclair's entire body stiffened as fissures of energy seemed to flow over his flesh. "You do not find it a presumptuous appellation for a mere crofter?"

Rose's lips tilted upward at the corners, and she looked like a fae selkie come to tempt a mortal man. Sinclair knew the tales never ended well for the human, but he'd already sunk too deep tonight.

"There's nothing mere about you, Thorfinn Sinclair."

Thorfinn. Something about how Rose said his name made it roar through him. She'd called him powerful, strong. Attributes he'd never ascribe to himself. Aye, he could heft rocks, single-handedly haul up a full net of fish, and spend the entire day cutting peat with nary a break. But they both knew that wasn't the kind of stoutness Rose meant.

"I am no hero, Rose. I've never been farther than Kirkwall, not even to visit mainland Scotland. Some may even call me a coward. I had a chance to be a batman in the war. I turned it down." The confession spewed out of him before he could stop it. But he couldn't have her thinking him some sort of a paragon. Not when he knew better.

Rose leaned forward to study him. Unconsciously, he moved to rub his scar, but she stayed his hand. Despite her gloves, he could feel the warmth of her fingers against the inner skin of his wrist.

"It does not take courage to rush to war. I should know. I was one of the adventurers who did." A note almost like self-recrimination had crept into Rose's voice.

"You saved soldiers' lives."

"And *you* kept an entire island from starving," she countered.

"That's a peedie overdramatic," Sinclair protested.

"It hasn't escaped my notice how many farms are run only by widows. During the war, even more were operated by the wives of soldiers and sailors. True, there were other able-bodied men on Frest during the fighting, but they are all older and would have had enough trouble maintaining their own croft without the aid of their sons. Everyone we visited mentioned how you've pitched in whenever there was a shortage of hands."

Sinclair shrugged, struggling to accept the praise she offered. It felt like when his brother had convinced him to try on an elegant evening jacket as a lark. Even with Reggie being older by two years, the seams had felt so tight that Sinclair had worried that he'd cause them to burst if he moved his arms a scant inch. "I did what needed doing."

"I don't know why I went overseas." Rose's voice grew rough and dark—so different from her blithe, carefree tone. Her melancholy scraped against Sinclair's own as Rose shifted her body toward the ocean. "So many of us rushed to the war not knowing why, looking for some sort of adventure, maybe validation even, and all we found was mud, deprivation, and death."

Validation. Something Sinclair had been seeking his entire existence. He hadn't expected that an infamous adventuress would be searching for the same thing.

"But you stayed," Sinclair pointed out.

"We all did," Rose said, "an entire generation of us. And now it's over. And those who are left are supposed to return home."

"What's home to you?" Sinclair asked, wondering again why she was here on this windy, remote isle instead of back in the gilt of industrialized America's high society.

"Now, *that* is the difficult question." Rose twisted her head so she was staring up at him, her lips just inches below his. "But I wager you know exactly where home is for you."

"Right here," he said without hesitation.

"Is it okay if I kiss you, Thorfinn Sinclair?" Her words were low and earnest. "I need to taste some of the goodness in the world right now. Will you help me banish the memories, even if it is just for tonight?"

"Aye." He had to push the single word through a suddenly stiff throat, and his heart fluttered in his chest like an oystercatcher's wings as it took flight. He understood only too well her need to push away the pain and try to replace it with something that, for once, didn't hurt.

Rose's mouth tilted upward, and Sinclair's moved down. The position wasn't the most comfortable, but it didn't matter. He'd contort his body in any manner if it meant holding Rose. Her lips were warm and pliant under his, welcoming.

Despite his having the advantage of a superior angle, Rose drove the kiss. Her mouth rubbed slowly against his, drawing out the sensation pumping through him. Pinpricks of delight filled him, like starlight dotting the firmament. The small flashes turned into a million small explosions, driving him nearly mad with want.

Yet Rose did not increase the sweet, torturous tempo. Sinclair gasped against the glorious pressure building inside him. Taking advantage, Rose deepened the kiss, and the light inside him threatened to blind him. Yet still she measured their pace, intensifying the craving.

Then without warning, she broke away and stared skyward. In Rose's pupils, Sinclair could see flashes of green, blue, and pink. Glancing up as well, he beheld the shimmering, ever-changing glow that held her in a trance. Warm surprise shot through him at the sight and mixed with the heat already radiating inside him.

"It seems the merry dancers have returned just for us," Sinclair said softly. "It is very late in the year to spy them."

"I'd only heard about the northern lights being green." Rose's swollen lips parted as she placed the back of her head against his chest, clearly angling for a better view. Gathering her in his arms, Sinclair laid them both down on the sand. The sky stretched above them, the bright, silvery moon an intriguing contrast to the kaleidoscope of undulating colors.

"'Tis the most common hue, but on occasion the fae lights decide to put on an even grander show for us mortals. On extremely rare occasions, they glow red."

They'd been that color the first anniversary of his mother's death, and Sinclair had always thought they'd been a message from her. When they'd resided in the servants' quarters at Muckle Skaill, she used to sneak him onto the roof to watch the merry dancers. It had been one of the few pleasures of living there—just the two of them on top of the world, free from the confines of the ghastly mansion. She'd cuddle him tight and tell him stories of a world where evil didn't prevail and where kings were good and kind. Under the magical sky, Sinclair could pretend that he wasn't tired from mucking out the stables or cleaning the chamber pots . . . or, if the earl was in residence, that he wasn't still smarting from the latest blow he'd received for some perceived insolence.

Sigurd had never understood his wife's fascination with the aurora borealis, but he'd never stopped her from racing out of their home with Sinclair and then the other children whenever the lights had appeared. Sinclair had carried on the tradition after his mother's death, and he'd tell his siblings his mother's old wonderful tales—so they could know her as he had. And during those nights, he swore she smiled down on all of them.

"I don't think I've ever seen anything so beautiful—even the stained glass windows in Sainte-Chapelle cannot compare, and I've always thought the Parisian church one of the most magnificent places in the world."

The awe in Rose's voice transfixed Sinclair. Fierce pleasure swept through him that she'd found so much joy in one of *his* favorite marvels. Rose had traveled to places he'd only read about, and some he had never heard of, yet his little corner of the earth could still astound this woman.

"There's a beauty here that runs so deep it sometimes hurts your soul," Sinclair admitted.

"Thank you for sharing it with me, Thorf . . . I mean Sinclair."

"Call me Thorfinn." The words burst from him, and he realized how *right* it felt.

"Thorfinn." She said his name with a smile he could hear, even though both their gazes were pointed skyward.

Unable to stop himself, he reached out and gently grabbed Rose's hand. She threaded her fingers with his as they watched the living rainbow of light arc and shrink, then grow again. The glow seemed to reach down and swirl around them, making them part of the splendor.

But even as they lay together, the crofter and the heiress lost in a fairy-tale world, Sinclair knew that just like his mum's stories, the fantasy would come to an end, and reality with all its brutal harshness would return.

"You shouldn't be out here alone!" Myrtle scolded as she flew from the Flett cottage and stomped her way over the sandy beach.

Rose jumped at her friend's cry. Turning away from where she'd been watching two otters frolic along the shoreline, Rose greeted Myrtle with a scowl. "Heavens to Betsy, I don't need to be watched like a baby. I'm perfectly fine now."

Myrtle stopped, her wide blue eyes looking almost purple in the pink dawn light. "You don't know. Do you?"

"Know what?" Rose asked, reaching for her reticule before remembering that she'd left it and her hat at Fornhowe. Without a cigarette to play with, she bent down and plucked a cockle from the sand.

Myrtle thoroughly scanned the empty beach and moved closer to Rose. When she spoke, her voice was barely above a whisper. "The cave-in wasn't accidental."

Rose, who was in the process of walking the shell between her fingers, bobbled it as a spike of fear stabbed her. "What do you mean?"

"I saw two figures running from Fornhowe last night," Myrtle hissed.

The horror that Rose had managed to push away reared back into her soul. "Spies?"

"I believe so," Myrtle said. "When I was crossing the strand, the sound seemed more like an explosion than a simple collapse of the entrance. Didn't you think so? You were inside the chambered tomb. I thought you *realized*. No wonder you were so unconcerned about being alone on the beach. I thought it was just your habitual bravado."

Rose rubbed the cockle between both her hands. Its ridges scraped against her palms, helping ground her in the present even as the darkness seemed to cluster around her and her limbs grew shaky. "I heard something detonate, but I dismissed it as part of my hallucinations. I should have considered that it was real, given what happened in Daytona. But it's been so long. Nothing happened when I was in London."

"Somehow the spy ring must have learned you were here, and it spooked them," Myrtle said.

Rose's stomach flopped over, and she dropped one hand to rub it. But it didn't help the queasiness or the pain. "I hoped I could be done with suspecting the islanders when I found the still, but I can't, can I?"

Myrtle slowly shook her head as she wrapped her arm around Rose's shoulder. "No, you can't. I'm sorry, Rose. I know you like all of them."

"Would you be able to identify the people who you saw running? Was one of them a particularly massive man?" Rose asked.

"I can't say." Myrtle shook her head. "They were just shadows moving through the dark. If I hadn't heard their footsteps, I would have thought it my imagination. I do not even know if they were short or tall, male or female."

"So it could be anyone," Rose said glumly as she hurled the shell into the ocean just as she had done on that faraway November night in Florida. This time she reached for a piece of green sea glass.

"I do not believe it was your Viking. The figures were headed away from his croft, and I doubt he would have had time to double back and clean the mud off before I knocked on his door. That, and he clearly was intent on saving you."

Rose's heart ached as she realized that even with all the information Myrtle had just given her, she could not completely dismiss Thorfinn as a suspect. He might not have been involved in the plot to literally bury her alive, but if there were agents on the island, he could be one of their contacts. But after last night . . . the kiss that they'd shared . . . the words that had passed between them. The thought of having to turn him in as a traitor nearly sliced Rose in half.

When her lips had touched his, she'd *felt* something powerful. She hadn't had a pleasurable sensation that strong since long before the war. And she wanted more of it . . . more of *Thorfinn*. And that had frightened her even before Myrtle's revelation about hearing an explosion. Since childhood, Rose had made it a point never to need anybody, and she certainly didn't like to long for a man. Attraction was one thing; yearning was another—an *unwanted* other.

"But we cannot be certain about anything, including Mr. Sinclair," Rose said softly, careful not to use his first name. She did *not* want to discuss what had happened last night on the beach with Myrtle right now, not when they had spies to contend with.

"I suppose we can't," Myrtle said softly before her voice firmed. "We need assistance, Rose. There've been two attempts on your life now. It's time we contact the authorities."

"But we still have the same problem as before." Rose squeezed the smooth glass so hard that it popped from her hand like a slippery fish.

"We don't know who to tell, and we have no proof. No one will take your observations any more seriously than mine."

"But there was an explosion!" Myrtle practically shouted the words, and Rose quickly waved for her friend to lower her voice. No one appeared to be around, but they needed to be careful.

"Which everyone thinks was just the sound of a cave-in that they'll attribute to the clumsiness of two female outsiders and the instability of an old structure," Rose countered.

"That's stood for over a thousand years!"

"I was ambushed before, and the authorities dismissed it as an accident and feminine nerves." Rose crossed her arms over her chest and began to pace in a tight circle. "We are getting close now, but we need something more concrete. All we will accomplish if we tell the British government now is to bring the excisemen down on the islanders' heads for the illegal distillery."

"Do you really think it is safe for you here?" Myrtle asked.

"I don't know where *would* be safe, especially since they know I've unraveled this much of the mystery. They've already attacked me on both sides of the Atlantic!" Rose pivoted sharply. "We don't even know for certain it is an islander who is involved. The earl could have sent the men or even his land agent. I thought Mr. White did not seem the sort to be a spy, but it is rather suspicious that the attack comes only a few days after I met him. Perhaps I was hasty to discount him."

"I don't like the current plan. It's getting too dangerous." Myrtle shook her head worriedly.

Rose tamped down on her own concerns. "It's the only viable one we have short of giving up, and I'm *not* doing that. I will see that the viscount's mission is completed."

"And what then, Rose?"

Myrtle's question shredded through Rose like sharp steel shrapnel. She knew her friend wasn't referring to the logistics of informing the proper officials about the spy ring but what Rose herself would do.

She'd been devoted to fulfilling the goals of a dead man. And when that purpose had dried up, what would Rose have?

It was something she did not wish to consider. But one day she would have no choice. Fortunately, this was not that moment of reckoning.

"Rose! Myrtle!" Astrid's voice carried over the sound of the surf.

Rose, along with her best friend, glanced in the direction of the friendly call. Sure enough, Astrid was strolling up the beach with her grandmother beside her. Little Alexander ran in loops in front of them, his round cheeks red with excitement.

"I hope you don't mind us popping in for breakfast," Astrid added when she was in closer range for a conversation. "Freya sent Alexander over to our croft to invite us. His explanation of how you two came to spend the night was a bit jumbled, but it sounds like you had an adventure."

"Of course they are glad to see us." Mrs. Flett fairly stabbed her cane into the sand. "I brought some of my whiskey for the tea."

Exceedingly glad for the distraction, Rose laughed as she headed over to offer the older woman her arm. "An addition that is always welcome, Mrs. Flett, and I do believe I now know the source of your wonderful drink. And before you fret, neither I nor Myrtle will be turning any of the islanders over to the excisemen."

"So you were at Fornhowe last night?" Astrid asked, her green eyes wide.

"I told you so!" Alexander dashed up to say the words before he flitted away again. "And it collapsed too!"

"Is that true? I did wake up in the middle of the night thinking I heard something."

"Pfft. That howe has been there for years." Mrs. Flett sniffed. "It isn't just going to fold up like a fan."

"I am afraid to say that the beginning of the entrance did fall down, but no other part was damaged. The still is fine, along with all of the prehistoric artifacts," Rose said, choosing her words carefully. Astrid, after all, did have connections beyond Frest, and she could easily be passing along information when she visited Stromness. It might be dangerous to let this woman know that Rose and Myrtle realized that the cave-in wasn't accidental.

"It's mighty strange." Mrs. Flett shook her head. "Mighty strange it would just give way like that, especially with you inside."

"Oh, Nana, it is a miracle that it hasn't done so before. The cairn is so ancient no one knows when it was built. Some dirt must have shifted the wrong way—that's all." Astrid patted her grandmother's hand reassuringly, and Rose wondered why the young woman seemed so eager to accept that the entrance had naturally fallen. Did she just want to stop Mrs. Flett from worrying? Did she think that Rose and Myrtle would be insulted by the insinuation that they had triggered the incident? Or was it because Astrid *knew* about the explosion and wanted the truth to remain hidden?

"I'm so glad you could make it!" Freya called out excitedly from the doorway, preventing Rose from asking any probing questions. All the Flett children crowded around them as they entered the small house. Rose had no idea how they were all going to fit around a single table, but somehow they managed. Rose found herself wedged between Myrtle and Thorfinn as the conversation bounced around her, as chaotic as the cramped seating.

"Miss Van Etten!" Widow Flett craned her neck to call around the twins, Mary and Barbara. "Now that you are indeed Lady of Frest and Hamarray, what are your first plans?"

The question spoken with such matter-of-fact directness not only miraculously silenced the roar of conversation, but it sharply reminded Rose of duties that she had assumed. As she stared down the table at Widow Flett's clear light-green eyes, the enormity of her role crashed down upon her. Swallowing, she glanced toward Thorfinn. "That is something that I need to discuss with my estate manager in more detail."

Mr. Flett's thin frame stiffened like a boxing champion called into the ring. "Who is this land agent?"

Startled that Thorfinn had yet to reveal his new position to his family, Rose sent him a questioning look. He hesitated for a moment and then slowly inclined his chin.

Rose turned back to the older islander. "Only the most suitable man for the position. I think even you will approve. He's hardworking, knows the land, and is smart as a whip."

Thorfinn shifted a bit uncomfortably in his chair at her praise, but when his gaze found hers again, his left eye glowed with a steady warmth. Memories of the previous night swept over Rose, filling her with a delicious heat. She'd never known that sweet moments could burn so intensely. Yet their honeyed kiss and even more innocent cuddling had heated her body and soul more than any previous bed sport. And damn it, but she still desired more, no matter how much the sheer force of that want troubled her.

"Who is the new estate manager?" Margaret asked, her petite features as serious as ever.

The right side of Mr. Flett's face had twisted into a mocking sneer. "Yes, indeed, tell us who this paragon is, Miss Van Etten."

Widow Flett sent her brother-in-law a rather exasperated look. "Isn't it obvious, Sigurd, even to old, crotchety folks like you and me?"

"Is it someone we know?" Alexander asked, bouncing in his seat.

"It's your brother, Mr. Sinclair." Rose couldn't help but shoot Thorfinn a fond look. A slow smile spread across his handsome features.

Mr. Flett glanced over at Thorfinn with an inscrutable expression on his weathered face. He didn't appear particularly unhappy, but neither did he seem overjoyed. He most definitely did *not* look proud. His only verbal response was a rather dubious *harrumph.*

Jammed so close to Thorfinn, Rose could feel the entire length of his body grow taut at his stepfather's less-than-enthusiastic response. Worried, she darted a glance at him and saw that his smile had dimmed.

He'd known Sigurd would react this way, Rose realized with a pang to her heart. That was why he hadn't told his family yet. He hadn't wanted to face the fact that his stepfather wouldn't be thrilled by the news. And the bitter old man should *be* ecstatic and brimming with joy. Why wasn't he? Why was Thorfinn's relationship with his stepfather so strained, especially when it was clear that Thorfinn provided for this man and his children?

"That is wonderful news!" Astrid clapped her hands together.

Widow Flett gave Rose an approving nod. "I knew you were a smart lass when I first met you."

"What's a land agent?" Alexander asked, pausing in buttering his bannock.

As Rose explained, she watched Mr. Flett surreptitiously. He was chewing with a deliberation that made her pity his food.

"It now makes sense why Young Thomas said that *you* asked him to start repairs at Muckle Skaill," Astrid told Thorfinn. "I thought you were just doing Miss Van Etten a good turn by helping her find someone to assist."

"Are you planning to make Muckle Skaill your year-round residence?" Barbara bounced in her seat.

"I, uh . . ." Rose stumbled on the words. She had no idea how long she would stay on the island, and she did not want to mention her plans for a hotel before she had a chance to discuss it more with Thorfinn. He did not seem at all in favor of it. Although she disagreed with him, she did not want or need to start out their business relationship with him thinking she was trying to undermine him.

"Ooooh," Mary added, "you have a secret plan, don't you! I can tell by the way you paused!"

"Oh, tell us! Please, do tell us! Nothing ever happened on Frest until you came. This is all so exciting!" Barbara begged. The pleading looks on the girls' faces almost made Rose crumble.

"Barbara, Mary," Freya hissed, "it is not polite to pry."

"Unless you are as old as I am," Widow Flett added sagely as she turned those soul-stripping pale-green eyes of hers in Rose's direction.

Feeling rather under attack, Rose glanced helplessly in Thorfinn's direction. Unfortunately—or rather fortunately for her—that caused all the women at the table to also send him beseeching looks. He groaned and laid his fork down on the table. "Before I tell you Miss Van Etten's plan, I want to be clear that nothing about it is certain—"

"He has concerns," Rose broke in, wanting Thorfinn to know that he was free to air his objections publicly, "which I take seriously."

"Oh, just tell us what the idea is," Widow Flett said, not even trying to hide her frustrated interest.

"She is considering whether or not to turn Muckle Skaill into a hotel," Thorfinn admitted with a weary sigh.

Mr. Flett slammed down his cup, causing everyone at the table to jump. Before speaking, the elderly crofter clenched his left fist, his tendons bulging beneath his paper-thin skin. "Hamarray does not need more outsiders traipsing around."

"Actually, that is precisely what it needs." Rose kept her tone measured and respectful, but she would not allow the curmudgeonly Mr. Flett to simply dismiss her idea. "The Grand Fleet has left, and the Royal Navy won't be guarding the German vessels forever. You will need markets for your goods and produce, and I hope to bring one to you."

"I think a hotel would be grand fun!" Barbara sighed. "I've only peeked into the lobbies of the ones in Kirkwall."

"Whatever gave you the idea to make Muckle Skaill into one?" Astrid asked, seemingly intrigued rather than disdainful.

"Well, you, actually," Rose said.

"Me?" Astrid asked, pressing her hand against her chest.

"Your bird-watchers," Rose explained. "It made me think of ways we can draw people to the island. I saw how my father transformed Florida with his grand retreats."

"But Orkney is not contiguous to Britain like Florida is to the United States," Thorfinn pointed out.

"But it was considered a swampy land unsuitable for easy travel." Rose pushed her chair back as she became more and more animated by the discussion.

"I don't mind the idea of a hotel myself," Widow Flett said carefully, tapping her fingers against the table, "but I agree with Sinclair. I cannot see people from cities traveling all the way here. Aye, some will come for the birds and the quiet, but they would not be enough to fill one wing of Muckle Skaill."

"Frest and Hamarray offer more than you realize," Rose said earnestly, leaning her entire body forward. "I am one of those city folks, and I have found myself quite content here."

As soon as she said the words, she realized how true they were. Orkney both gripped and soothed her in a way no other place ever had.

"We have the ceilidh coming up in a few weeks." Mary jumped excitedly, and her elbow hit her glass of milk. Thankfully, Thorfinn caught it before it crashed to the table.

"I'm afraid that I couldn't have a hotel ready by then," Rose said.

"But it could be a trial!" Barbara said. "You could invite a few of your friends and see how they like it. Then you'd know if a hotel would work! It will be grand fun!"

"There are enough rooms in the wing where we are staying that we could arrange to get presentable for a small party." Myrtle spoke for the first time. "I will be happy to help any way I can."

"I am not sure if this is a good idea." Thorfinn sounded more somber than the circumstances seemed to warrant, and Rose glanced curiously at him. He looked . . . stark.

"As much as I love our ceilidhs, I worry that it would not be enough to attract visitors." Widow Flett leaned back in her seat and reached for the cane she'd propped against the chair. Idly, she began to tap it against the floor.

"I do not know why we are talking about attracting them in the first place." Mr. Flett cut his bannock with such force the knife screeched against the plate.

Widow Flett rolled her eyes at her brother-in-law. "Because not all of us want to live in isolation. Some of us actually *like* people."

"A race!" Hannah suddenly shouted. "You could hold a motor race on the day of the ceilidh! You're Miss Rose Van Etten—the famous motoriste! People will come to see you—I bet more than Muckle Skaill can hold! If there isn't room for everyone, then they can stay in Kirkwall. I've heard you say how the beach around Frest is a perfect natural track!"

An odd emotion curled through Rose at the twelve-year-old's excited suggestion. As much as she loved to drive, racing was part of her old life. It was who she had been before the war but not now.

"It would be rather difficult to organize something that quickly," Rose said.

Myrtle leaned back in her chair to look directly at Rose. "I've seen you throw together shindigs in under a week."

"That was in America."

"You have just as many connections in Britain. I'm sure Percy will help us. Who knows who you might *flush* out." Myrtle not only stressed the word *flush*, but she also winked when she said it. With Rose sitting slightly behind her and the angle at which Myrtle held her head, no one else could possibly have seen it.

Rose paused for a moment, trying to decipher Myrtle's message. Then it struck her. If the spy was someone off the island, a big event would present the perfect cover for a return. But this time Rose and Myrtle would be prepared.

"I suppose you're right, Myrtle," Rose said slowly. "If Percy helped arrange things from his end in London, I probably could pull something together. After all, drivers in Europe are itching for the chance to race after four years of war, and it is excellent timing to attract competitors to a new event. Muckle Skaill won't possibly be completely up to snuff, but some guests could stay in Kirkwall like Hannah suggested."

"I think it is a perfect idea," Astrid said. "It would be a good way of testing both whether Frest and Hamarray can attract tourists and whether or not we islanders like having so many visitors."

"But do we really want vehicles roaring about our homes?" Thorfinn asked.

"I don't desire it at all." Mr. Flett harrumphed.

"You wouldn't," Widow Flett said dismissively before she turned to Thorfinn. "It is only a few days, Sinclair. If it is a failure, then we shall know not to proceed further. If it is a success, we can discuss it more. Let Miss Van Etten and Miss Morningstar hold this event, and in the meantime, we will talk to the other crofters if Miss Van Etten is willing to listen to their opinions. Then after the race, we can meet again and come to a decision. Miss Van Etten will decide what she makes of our request."

"That is a wonderful idea," Rose said. "And if the people of Frest ultimately do not wish to have a hotel on Hamarray, then I will stop all plans."

"Good." Widow Flett thumped her cane against the floor. "It is decided. Miss Van Etten shall hold the race near the day of the ceilidh."

"If this celebration does come to be," Mr. Flett said rather dourly, "perhaps I shall get on the stage and tell one of my tales."

The twins squealed as Hannah, Margaret, and Alexander bounced in their seats. Freya glanced over at Rose and Myrtle. "Da is the best storyteller in all of Orkney. He also spins yarns at the ceilidhs. So did our mother."

"Which story? Which story?" Alexander demanded, tugging on his father's arm.

Instead of addressing his son, the man focused on Thorfinn, his eyes the color of a bitterly cold sky. "It'll be a tale about a selkie."

Mr. Flett swiveled, slowly and deliberately, stopping when he faced Rose. The right side of his thin mouth lifted in clear challenge.

"Do you know what a selkie is, Miss Van Etten?"

"I'm afraid I don't, Mr. Flett—although I have become acquainted with trows."

"It is a seal who transforms into a human when it sheds its skin." Mr. Flett's voice and eyes were as sharp as one of the flint blades Myrtle was hoping to find at Fornhowe.

"That sounds like a rather painful process, Mr. Flett." Rose lifted a bit of cheese to her mouth and nibbled.

The children giggled. Their father remained unamused.

"I do not believe selkies suffer any discomfort—it is they who bring agony upon the poor mortals foolish enough to take them in."

"I do believe you are skipping the part where the human hides the poor creatures' pelts, preventing them from returning to sea," Myrtle interjected.

"Ah, but in my tale, the selkie princess is bored of her life at sea and is seeking to amuse herself on land. She tells the man who discovers her to hide her skin. Entranced by her beauty, he complies and falls in love with her. He gives her all that he owns and his heart. But when the selkie grows tired of living on the isle, she instructs one of her children to find her pelt. And then she dons it, leaving behind the brokenhearted gappus and her human bairns."

"I have always been partial to less melancholy tales myself." Rose shrugged despite the chill that washed through her. She'd always lived a carefree life with no one reliant upon her, not even a pet. Rose had spent her entire adult life transient—and even her adolescence had been nothing but a collection of boarding schools.

But suddenly Rose had begun to make promises. Hell, she'd even formulated future plans rooted to one physical spot. What if she was making guarantees, forming *connections*, that she could never keep?

Chapter 10

"Try picturing it in your mind." Rose slowed her speedboat to a stop near the cliffs of Hamarray. From the water, the crags appeared even more striking—great, sheer towers of sandstone rising from the turquoise water. It was as if a piece of the Grand Canyon had traveled to the North Sea and taken up residence among the waves.

"Imagining it is not the problem." Thorfinn had his arms crossed over his chest as he glowered at the gables of Muckle Skaill peeking above the grassy cap of the precipice. "I've seen revelers on Hamarray before. They only brought misery to us crofters."

Rose found herself momentarily distracted by Thorfinn's flexed muscles—something that had been happening with quite some regularity since she had picked him up this morning to travel to Kirkwall.

As she had promised Myrtle, she had not strayed from Thorfinn's side in case the spies decided to attack. Thorfinn might be a suspect still, but he clearly wasn't trying to *kill* Rose. After all, he could have easily ended her life on the beach. Myrtle had wanted Rose to stay inside Muckle Skaill, but Rose refused to be cowed—nor did she want to drag Myrtle away from exploring the broch or Fornhowe. After all the help Myrtle had given her, Rose was not about to ask her friend to delay her career dreams for even a day, especially not when Myrtle was finally on the cusp of realizing them.

Once Rose and Thorfinn had arrived in Kirkwall, they'd phoned Mr. Lewis to discuss what steps they needed to take to legitimize the distillery. He'd promised to draw up a partnership agreement between Rose and the crofters and to begin the process of attaining the appropriate license.

Rose had questioned Mr. Lewis about Mr. White's character. Although she had feigned concern about his previous management of Hamarray and Frest, she had really been digging to see if there was anything that would make it more likely that Mr. White could be a spy. She *did* learn that his firm had been shedding clients for the past few years, which could have given Mr. White an incentive to seek German coin.

After Rose had finished that conversation, she had contacted her friend Percy in London. As an obscenely wealthy newly minted duke, he had both the political and social power to help her throw the race together in an absurdly short period of time. Thankfully, he'd been bored out of his mind after leaving the Royal Air Force and itching to return to his racing days. He'd leaped at the chance.

Between mentally juggling duties of laird, race host, and spymaster and currently conning *The Briar*, Rose should *not* be indulging in fantasies about Thorfinn, but her mind . . . and body . . . simply did not wish to cooperate. Trying once more to redirect her thoughts toward business, she said, "Think of visitors lounging in a garden—a drink of Frest Whiskey in their hands, wearing Widow Flett's sweaters as they prepare to take a bird walk with Astrid before having a repast at the restaurant managed by Widow Craigie."

"Widow Craigie's cooking is the worst on the isle." Thorfinn's chest puffed out. Rose truly tried not to notice how the movement tightened the knit of his sweater even more, but she utterly failed to look away. It had been almost thirty-six hours since their kiss on the beach, and Rose still felt as primed as a well-tuned Mercer.

Rose forcibly dragged her gaze back to Thorfinn's face and struggled to hold on to the gist of the conversation. "Widow Craigie's skill in the kitchen is not the point."

"If you're wishing to start a pub, the quality of food *is* the point." Thorfinn couldn't quite manage to keep a straight face, revealing that even he realized the silliness of this particular objection. As his mouth curled at the edges, Rose's stomach flip-flopped . . . or maybe it was her heart. The man was as tempting as mulled wine on a frigid day. And maybe the best way to handle the distraction was to take a good long sip until she was satiated.

"What precisely don't you like about my brainchild?" Rose gently sank her finger into his chest, finally giving in to the need to touch him. She might not be certain that he wasn't a spy, but she had been planning on keeping her enemies close, after all.

"The fact that your idea involves toffs running amok."

Thorfinn's gaze seemed focused on her lips, and she wondered if he had difficulty concentrating too. Rose could hear her blood rushing through her ears, just like she did before the start of a big race. Entirely done with trying to suppress the surge, she leaned closer to him. "I'm a toff."

"Aye." He moved toward her, their gazes now intertwined.

She ran her fingers up his sweater. "Wouldn't you like to see *me* run amok?"

"Could be dangerous." He trapped her palm against his chest.

Rose sucked in her breath at the feel of him—hard, indomitable, but *not* entirely unyielding. "Good thing I don't mind peril."

Their lips met, and she felt like she'd depressed an accelerator connected to her heart. The darn organ nearly jumped from her body. This time she wasn't interested in keeping the necking gentle. She wanted it hard and rough and most of all powerful. She slipped her tongue into Thorfinn's mouth, tasting him. He groaned, and the guttural sound drove Rose to deepen the kiss. His fingers knocked off her beaver-fur cap and buried in her short hair. Slipping her palm from his chest, she gripped his back as she welded her body to his.

Frenetic energy pooled inside her. She'd never felt a need this strong, this *urgent*. If Rose gave in to it completely, perhaps she could dampen its fearsome power and purge some of the want from her—just like how a good, fast ride expelled her demons.

"Rose." Her name emerged from Thorfinn's lips as a half prayer, half moan as he tore his mouth away from hers.

"Mmmm." She nibbled at his neck, loving when his tendons went taut. She flicked her tongue against one, and his fingers pressed against the back of her skull.

"Rose." Her name sounded even more hoarse.

She pressed her mouth against the hollow of his neck, and his body quivered. She smiled against his flesh. Before she could properly explore the sensitive spot, she found herself gently but *unceremoniously* lifted from him.

His handsome facial muscles were strained, and red flags of color blazed over his sharp cheekbones. "Rose." Her name was still more moan than word. "Someone could see us. We're in full view of the cliff and Muckle Skaill."

Rose merely smiled and undid the top toggle on her beaver-fur coat. "Might as well give the bird-watchers something interesting to watch."

A choking sound emerged from Thorfinn, but Rose merely arched her brow. "I did warn you that I have a wicked reputation, dear heart."

"But I don't, lass," Thorfinn whispered.

Realizing that Thorfinn did have a point, Rose sank back into her seat and gave him a rueful smile. "Is there any chance you could be persuaded to continue this somewhere more private?"

He glanced at her out of the corner of his left eye, looking both wicked and perhaps a tad bashful. "There . . . there might be a sea cave nearby, lass, that's big enough and deep enough for *The Briar*."

"Oh, might there be!" she teased. "And *might* you also be able to direct me to it?"

"I could be convinced." He settled back in his seat.

She feigned a pout worthy of Mary Pickford. "But you've taken away my best means of persuasion due to the possible presence of *bird-watchers.*"

"Perhaps a *promise* of a reward will entice me."

"Oh, I can guarantee one." Rose winked and placed her hand on the throttle. "Where to, Captain Cook?"

"Head to that crevasse in the cliff. See it? It's to the right of the big sea stack," Thorfinn said as he pointed out the way.

Rose nodded and started the engine. When she reached for the throttle, he laid his hand over hers.

"I'd take it slow. There are a lot of shoals around here, and the currents can be unpredictable."

"My type of water." She sent him a grin, but she listened to his advice. Traveling at this pace, it wasn't hard for her to hear his further instruction as they navigated through the particularly tricky sections. As they neared the jagged cliffs, squawks filled the air . . . along with a particularly pungent odor of guano.

"My word, the birds are noisy today!" Rose said as they inched past the sea stack. Birds of all shapes and sizes nested among the cracks and clefts, while still more swooped in and out of the rock formations. Still others hopped along the edges while some squabbled and pecked at each other. It was at once oddly peaceful and utterly chaotic.

"Many of them are returning for the spring and summer." This time Thorfinn had to shout over the avian calls rather than her motor. "You might want to keep an eye out for the tammie norries—or puffins, as they're called outside Orkney. Most find them to be adorable, wee birds."

"They're not too happy about us being here, are they?" Rose asked.

"They never are." Thorfinn grinned, and then he jabbed his finger toward what looked like just a dark shadow in the recesses of the main cliff face. "That's the opening."

"It's well hidden," Rose said as she carefully steered through the gap in the rock.

"This precipice is riddled with alcoves and caves."

"Good for smuggling whiskey?" Rose teased.

"Aye. And for secret adventure." He raised his eyebrow ever so slightly, and the devilish angle ignited a windstorm of sensation inside her.

"So is this where you take all the lasses?" Rose asked as she cut the engine.

"Just you, Rose. Just you." He reached over and cupped her face. When his thumb brushed across her cheekbone, the extra friction from his calluses caused splinters of delight to sparkle through her. There was a raw honesty to this man that seemed to scrape through all the facades she'd ever built, leaving her vulnerable to him . . . and perhaps even to herself. She'd been wrong to think a dalliance with Thorfinn would dim this need inside her, but she'd plunged too deeply into the maelstrom to fight her way back out now. She was stuck in the eye of the hurricane, left without her blitheness to shield her from the emotions that she did not wish to feel.

A bird fluttered past them, and Rose lifted her head. High above, the red rock formed a nearly perfect vault. A ragged opening in the very center revealed a swath of bright-blue sky. Sunlight streamed into the center and reflected off the water below. Glowing patterns danced along the walls, reminding Rose of the northern lights. Gannets, their white bodies shining, nested above them.

Like a grand apse in a medieval church, the cavern demanded a certain reverence and solemnity. A call of *something* stirred deep within Rose. She felt small yet powerful all at the same time.

"It is stunning here."

"Aye."

Thorfinn's hoarse response slid over Rose's skin like a caress. Shivering, she returned her gaze to him. His warm palm still framed her cheek, his aquamarine gaze washing over her like sun-heated water. His mouth covered hers, and she allowed herself to be lost in his passion.

Thorfinn did not possess the practiced finesse of her previous paramours, but that made the kiss only more powerful. There was a forthrightness to his desire that stripped away all pretense—even hers. She met his rawness with her own.

Their heavy breathing and moans echoed off the thick sandstone until they were surrounded by a chorus of their own making. The world seemed condensed into this place, into this moment, into *them*.

Rose had spent her life searching for exhilaration, but she'd never found it so completely as she did right now. Sensation after sensation rippled through her, driving her nearly mad yet soothing a long-unsatisfied want.

She needed more of the almost painful exquisiteness, more of *him*. She broke away from Thorfinn to undo the other toggles on her coat. He followed each flick of her fingers with his green-blue gaze, his chest rising and falling as if he'd just rowed for miles over a stormy sea. Rose let the heavy fur fall from her shoulders, and the left side of Thorfinn's mouth quirked.

"Aren't you afraid of catching a chill, lass?" Thorfinn's voice sounded as rich and thick as honey straight from the comb.

She arched a challenging brow. "Aren't you going to keep me warm enough?"

A decidedly wolfish expression fell over his face, and he looked more like a storybook Viking than ever. If she'd thought his kiss powerful before, it was nothing compared to the hungry way he devoured her mouth.

She moaned as his lips moved from her mouth to trace along her jaw. He'd softened the pressure but somehow demanded more. Need pooled in her body. Desperate, she guided one of his work-worn hands to her breast. He instantly complied with her unspoken plea, massaging as he continued his devilish assault on the sensitive juncture between her chin and her ear. Yet it still wasn't enough. She brought his other hand to the brooch pinning the front of her white silk blouse together.

Unlike some of her previous lovers, Thorfinn couldn't manage the task one handed—nor did he simply tear the sheer fabric. Yet she found the sensation of his fingers working so diligently upon the clasp more erotic than any flourish of showmanship. Even with his focus on the pin, he still moved his mouth in tantalizing sweeps along her skin. A shiver racked her, causing his hands to slip slightly. He chuckled instead of grunting in frustration—the sound the very flame needed to ignite the bubble of joy inside her. She not only laughed, but she *felt* it too—happy and bright.

Finally, the brooch opened, and his hand slipped inside her blouse. Her eyes fluttered shut as his thumb traced her collarbone while his fingers began their dive through her undergarments to reach her bare flesh. First the slip, then the chemise, then . . .

The key.

She'd forgotten about Viscount Barbury's key. Horror struck through the bliss. Had she just made a fatal blunder?

Rose's eyes flew open, but they didn't meet Thorfinn's blue gaze. Instead, she saw the crown of his head as he bent over the key clasped in his hand. Another chill sliced through her as Thorfinn's hand appeared to shake.

Was it rage? Was he the spy? Pain and fear pummeled Rose with equal measure. Brutal irony struck at her soul as she realized that the very man who'd finally made her feel something might also be the one who actually was trying to kill her.

Slowly, carefully, she adjusted her head back, her heart aching with terrified pressure. She could sense Thorfinn's intensity as he fingered the key. Flipping it over, he rubbed one of the deep scratches near the teeth.

When Thorfinn's left eye lifted toward her face, Rose saw pained confusion, not murderous fury.

"Where did you get this?" His voice sounded as if it had been broken and then pressed back together.

"I, well, I . . ." Rose's entire body trembled.

"It was my brother's. Did you find it in his old room? Why do you wear it around your neck?"

Everything inside her froze now. "Viscount Barbury was *your* sibling?"

Thorfinn's expression shuttered as every muscle in his face seemed to contract. She'd seen that expression before during her first dinner with his family when she'd mentioned the earl and the viscount.

Thorfinn dropped the key and glanced away from her. "Not acknowledged."

Thorfinn was Mar's illegitimate son. The revelation blasted through Rose. Was this the secret he'd been hiding, or was there more? A lethal more? Had his abandonment by his noble family made him hate the British ruling class enough to spy for Germany?

Shit. Where had Rose put her reticule, which she'd retrieved from Fornhowe? She should be reaching for her gun, not sitting here in *The Briar* like a silly, frightened, brokenhearted maid.

"Were you close to Barbury?" Rose tentatively grabbed Thorfinn's shoulder, needing to see his face even as she searched for her purse with her other hand. Could Thorfinn actually be the *him* Barbury had mentioned? Or did Thorfinn know about the key only because he'd spied on the very family who'd rejected him? Her stomach roiled, but she forced it to settle. She had not flinched under shellfire, and she would *not* now, no matter how torn apart her innards.

"I do not talk about my connections to the earl and Muckle Skaill." Thorfinn still did not raise his head, but she could hear the scrape of teeth against teeth as he tightened his jaw even more.

"Please." Life with her parents had taught Rose to demand, not to ask and hope for a response, but she was pleading now. "Please, Thorfinn. This is important. Vitally important."

Thorfinn's head snapped back up—this time his expression had turned suspicious, fierce even. Fear serrated her, and she surreptitiously renewed her search for her revolver. Had she shown her hand by push-ing too hard to confirm that he wasn't a German agent? Was her heart overriding her head?

"Why is my relationship with my brother so crucial?" Thorfinn demanded.

"It just . . . is?" she offered weakly.

His left eye narrowed. "Did you know Reggie?"

Reggie—not Viscount Barbury or even Reginald but Reggie. That implied some sort of comradery, some sort of intimacy . . . did it not? Or was she simply a fool grasping at any explanation that did not make her intended lover a villain?

"Rose, you would have had entrance to the same vaunted circles as Reggie before the war. I remember my brother telling me about attending races at Brooklands and lavish parties on the French Riviera. He said the lasses there were . . ."

Thorfinn's left eye grew so wide it would have been comical under any other circumstances. He choked off his sentence. Horror and embarrassment flashed across his face. "You weren't . . . I mean, were you . . . did you and Reggie . . . well . . ."

"Were we lovers?" Rose forced her facial muscles to remain in a neutral, emotionless position, but a trickle of relief had finally started to flow through her. Thorfinn's questions were not those that a spy would ask but those of a brother horrified that he was dallying with his sibling's gal. And if Thorfinn and *Reggie* had indeed been friends, there was a good chance that Thorfinn *was* the *him* the viscount had told her to find. If she were dying and had to name someone to help unravel a spy ring, she could not select anyone more stalwart.

Thorfinn made an incoherent sound. Rose took that to mean yes.

"I promise I'll answer that question and explain everything, but first you must address mine." She was shaking now—not from fear but from the rebirth of a faith she hadn't known that she'd had.

Thorfinn looked torn, but she could see his curiosity winning out. "What do you wish to know, lass?"

"Just the nature of your relationship with Viscount Barbury. Were you chums?" Her words were as rushed as the emotions sweeping through her.

Thorfinn slumped against the leather seat of *The Briar*, and the pain that he'd been hiding became brutally apparent. "Aye. Very good ones—at least until I ordered Reggie to stop dallying with Astrid when I found him kissing her. We both knew that he'd never marry a lass from the isles. Things just grew worse between us when I refused to be Reggie's batman. He took it personally, as if I were questioning not just the validity of his cause but his own sense of honor. But I couldn't leave the children and my stepda to starve. After Reggie and I argued, he got drunk and told all of Kirkwall and Frest that I was a coward. It was the last I ever saw of him. He came to the island once after he was captured and had escaped from the Germans, but he didn't try to contact me. Astrid thinks that Reggie may have felt too guilty to see me after the destruction he'd done to my reputation. Reggie was never one for admitting fault. It was as if he thought that if he admitted any flaw, it would conquer him and he'd be lost to failure. He stayed sequestered in Muckle Skaill. Then he returned to the Front and died there."

Rose longed to reach for Thorfinn—to soothe him, to try to take away some of the rawness, to tell him that Barbury had been *wrong*. Thorfinn's words shook her perception of the viscount . . . but they brought stunning clarity to her conversation with Thorfinn under the northern lights. No wonder he felt such shame over not fighting. Barbury had been inexcusably cruel to spread lies about his half brother, but could his perfidy have pushed Thorfinn into spying? Rose doubted it, but she had to know for certain. Too much depended on her being right about whom she could trust.

"What do you know about this key?" Rose held it up. Although it was tarnished and scarred in more than one place, it still managed to catch the faint light. Just for a moment. But it was enough for one wink.

Thorfinn glanced back at the key, and a faraway mist clouded his gaze. He reached into his shirt and withdrew an identical one. "It was our secret, Reggie's and mine."

Rose held herself completely still as she stared at the piece of metal hanging against Thorfinn's chest. She wanted so badly to reveal all to Thorfinn—to have every secret between them demolished. But she could not give in to her own wants. She had to know in both her heart and her brain that she was making the right decision. This was the time for logic, not for emotion.

"What secret?"

"The earl never approved of my friendship with Reggie, but my brother—he never cared. Reggie was the sort that once he'd made up his mind, there was no swaying him. He decided he liked me when he was six and I was four, and that was that, in his view. He taught me to write—shared all his books with me—and we'd exchange messages by slipping them into a metal box he kept in his room. We locked it so his Lordship couldn't accidently stumble upon our correspondence."

Unlocks. Notes. Give. Him. Finally those long-ago words made a semblance of sense to Rose. Tears sprang to Rose's eyes. Unable to contain the powerful relief pumping through her, Rose let the drops freely fall and roll down her cheeks. Thorfinn wasn't the spy. He was the person she'd been sent by Reggie to find.

"You're *him*!" Rose grabbed both of Thorfinn's hands with hers and squeezed. "You really are *him*."

"Him who?"

Rose pressed her fingers even harder against Thorfinn's knuckles. "I wasn't your brother's paramour. I was his ambulance driver on the night he died."

Reggie's *ambulance driver*?

The words exploded through Sinclair as he sat dumbly in the seat. At the revelation, his body went curiously limp yet rigid at the same time, as if it could no longer withstand the emotions clobbering him. The grief that always seemed just below the surface when it came to Reggie bubbled up and over until it threatened once again to swamp him. With that came fresh slices of new pain . . . and old guilt. Somehow Rose had been there for his brother when Sinclair himself had not. She'd dodged shells to bring Reggie to safety while Sinclair had been hundreds of miles away pushing a plow in the peace of Orkney.

Had Rose been with Reggie in those final moments? Did she know why he had suddenly returned to France despite resigning his commission from the British Army? How much had his brother suffered in the end? It was the last unknown that had plagued Sinclair the worst . . . and the one he was most afraid to find out.

"I have been looking for you since I arrived on Hamarray, and here you were, beside me all the time!" Rose gripped his upper arms now. Through his shock and the roar of his own emotions, he noticed that tears glistened in her eyes. She hadn't seemed this vulnerable even after her episode of shell shock when she'd been trapped in Fornhowe.

"I have a message from the viscount—two, actually." The words tumbled from Rose's mouth before Sinclair could gather his own thoughts enough to form a single question. Her next sentence only caused his mind to whirl even more as new emotions piled upon the already heavy tumult.

"First, Viscount Barbury wanted me to say that he was sorry. I believe now that he meant for how he reacted after you, for good cause, declined to be his batman."

The emotion that splintered through Sinclair was so raw that he could scarce identify it. Reggie had rarely allowed himself to acknowledge his regrets even to himself and never apologized. For Reggie to make such a statement . . . grief and pain choked, sliced, and pulled at

Sinclair with such force he felt as if he were being drawn and quartered by them.

Yet before he could begin to process the flurry of frenetic feelings, Rose spoke again, as if he would vanish if she could not deliver Reggie's message quickly enough. "Second, your brother wanted you to show me where he'd hidden notes on a spy ring that he claimed to have discovered."

"A *spy ring*? Here on Hamarray or Frest?" The theatrical absurdity of Rose's claim was so at odds with the remorse and agony clawing through his insides that Sinclair almost barked out a humorlessly bitter laugh. First, she was telling him that Reggie had apologized, and now that his brother had been hunting down German agents. None of this was making sense. None of it.

"I don't know who the spies are, where they're located, or how far they've infiltrated the American and British governments, although I suspect that there may be foreign agents connected with Hamarray and Frest," Rose said.

Her words would have struck more fear into Sinclair if he weren't already inundated with conflicting emotions . . . or if he hadn't known Reggie's propensity for making up a reality that suited him. After Reggie's capture when he'd been sent home to convalesce, perhaps his brother had been so desperate to still participate that he'd drummed up the idea of espionage. Then Reggie would have had a way to claim the honor that had always seemed out of reach to him. Growing up as Mar's son and subconsciously knowing how much evil could be hidden away would make anyone given to conspiracy theories.

"I have the key that the viscount entrusted into my care," Rose continued. "Barbury told me to give it to you and that you'd know where to find his reports about the espionage."

"Me?" Sinclair started to reach for Reggie's key again but belatedly realized that it rested against Rose's breasts. Awkwardly, he dropped his hand to his lap. "Reggie didn't confide any of this to me. Are you sure he was in his right mind at the end? What exactly did he say?"

It occurred to Sinclair with an almost physical strike that perhaps Reggie had actually been referring to the earl's secret life of debauchery. Maybe impending death had finally forced his brother to accept the painful truths that he'd always swept aside.

Rose lifted the chain holding the key from her neck and laid it in his hand. Sinclair automatically folded his fingers around the warm metal, wishing the message accompanying his brother's parting gift were as solid. His hands shaking, he dropped the chain over his neck, and the two keys clanked together.

At the sound, Rose expelled a sigh, as if a heavy pack had been lifted from her back. When she spoke, her voice was tired, so very tired. "I wondered myself whether your brother had been hallucinating, but there was such conviction in his voice. There's also the fact I've apparently been ambushed, twice."

"You've been attacked?" Horror pulverized Sinclair's other emotions, and his muscles froze in preparation to defend against an unseen enemy. Lightly, he grabbed Rose's shoulders, instinctually scanning her body for scars. "Were you hurt?"

Sinclair's alarm only grew with each detail she described about the trap laid for her in Florida and the men Myrtle had spotted right after the *explosion* that had evidently caused the cave-in at Fornhowe. He wanted to gather Rose into his arms as he would one of the bairns and hold her there, keeping her safe and the world's peril at bay. But it wasn't in Rose's nature to be cosseted. She wasn't seeking protection or even comfort but assistance with her mission—a mission that had now become his.

He would not allow spies to threaten Rose or *his* people. He had *known* the cave-in at Fornhowe had been strange, and he should have inspected the damage further. He would not be so careless again. Now that he knew danger had found its way to Frest, he would root it out.

If it turned out that one of the islanders was connected . . . well, he did not want to consider that discovery . . . but if a crofter was a traitor, Sinclair would do his duty to protect the peace, no matter how much it would destroy him. He and Rose would need to discover concrete evidence of a spy ring. He, like her, had little faith in the authorities and knew their prejudices against his people.

"Are you certain that Barbury told you nothing—not even cryptically?" Rose asked when she finished her explanation.

"We didn't even write to each other, lass." The tragedy of that still tore at him. Over the past year he'd learned to deal with the gnawing, guilty ache, but now he had new reasons to regret their estrangement. "What else did Reggie mention?"

"I think he mentioned someone named Tamsin Morris." Rose sighed and started digging through her satchel, which she'd found on the seat between them.

"Who?" Sinclair vaguely recalled her inquiring about that name when she'd first come to Orkney.

"So you really haven't heard of her?" Rose pulled out a cigarette and jabbed it in his direction.

"Nay. Morris is not a common surname in Orkney, and like I've said, Tamsin is Welsh—not Scots or Norse."

"Maybe we don't need her." Rose flipped the roll of tobacco between her fingers. "We know where the key fits now."

"But I haven't seen that box since before the war. It could be anywhere. What exactly did my brother say?"

Rose stopped moving for a second, and then she leaned back. Sighing, she stared up at the circle of daylight.

"If it is too hard . . . ," he said softly, not knowing what memories threatened her. He did not want her to suffer like she had that night in Fornhowe.

"No. It's necessary," she said softly, "and I don't know for sure if it will trigger my shell shock. I can think about the war, but I try not

251

to concentrate too hard . . . to put myself back there in the moment. Would . . . would you mind holding my hand, being my anchor to the present?"

Her bravery nearly undid Sinclair, as did her unspoken trust. He tenderly cradled her right hand between both of his and sat there silently as she allowed herself to drift into the past. Her pupils seemed to dilate ever so slightly, and her fingers shook. Sinclair ached thinking of the images she saw—images that included the death of his best friend and older brother.

"He told me to come here, to Hamarray Isle. That you'd know what to do. And he mentioned a name. I could make out *Tam* clearly but not the rest of the first word. Then he said a surname that started with Mor or maybe even Nor. He . . . he was hard to understand by then."

Pushing away the clawing emotions at why his brother's voice would have been garbled, Sinclair instead focused on the message Reggie had been trying so desperately to send to him. *Tam. Mor. Tam. Nor.*

The screech of a guillemot interrupted his thoughts. A *guillemot*. Cousin to the puffin.

Realization traveled through Sinclair with such force that his own limbs started to shake. It seemed as if his body could no longer contain the revelations pummeling him, one after another. "I know where he hid the metal box we used as boys."

"Where? How?" Rose excitedly threw her arms around him. Although they were slender, there was no denying their strength as she squeezed him.

"In another sea cave—this one in the middle of a gap between the cliffs. The only way to reach it is to climb down from the headlands. It was one of our favorites because it was a roosting place for puffins." Old memories crowded alongside new, urgent fears. Sinclair knew where his brother must have secreted his notes on the spy ring, but what would those records reveal? And what would their contents do to the strongly woven social fabric of Frest? Would it cause it all to fray?

"Puffins? The bird you just mentioned. The one you said I'd like."

"Aye. The ones I said were called tammie norries by us Orcadians."

The gold flecks in Rose's topaz eyes deepened as she realized why he was so certain as to where his brother had hidden the old steel box. "It wasn't Tamsin Morris after all. It wasn't even a woman."

"Nay. Just a comical little auk with bright-orange feet and an even more colorful bill."

"A bird. I've been searching for a *bird* this whole time. Perhaps I shouldn't have been so dismissive of Astrid's naturalists."

"I'm glad you came looking, lass." Sinclair cupped her cheeks, the feel of her soft skin against his palms a steadying balm against all the feelings battering him. She was real and warm and solid.

"So am I."

Their gazes held. Despite everything that had just transpired, the heat between them immediately began to swirl. But this wasn't the time to get lost in the flames. And mayhap the interruption was for the best. Rose had a way of setting every fiber of him alight, and Sinclair didn't want to be left as a pile of cinders when she inevitably departed Orkney and returned to her own glittering world.

His stepda was right about one thing—in this relationship Sinclair *was* the mere mortal. And he needed to keep all his wits about him if he and Rose were to defeat a group of violent traitors intent on reigniting the Great War.

<hr/>

Rose's foot slipped, sending a pebble skittering over the edge of a narrow path and down into the ravine below. Her body tensed as her heart slammed uncomfortably against her chest. In front of her, Thorfinn carefully pivoted, concern etched into his face. "I can go myself. We don't need the two of us to retrieve the box."

Resolutely, Rose pushed back her nervousness and shook her head as she clutched one of the ragged outcroppings of rock as she descended. "I've spent months searching and crossed an ocean twice. I'm not giving up when I'm this close."

"I promise I won't open it. I'll leave that honor to you." Thorfinn stood as boldly as if he were standing in the middle of a flat plain instead of on a tiny sliver of rock barely large enough to hold his two feet. He reminded her of the bighorn sheep she'd seen out West that could gracefully bound up or down any sheer cliff at will. Perhaps the mild-mannered crofter had more adventurer in him than either of them had realized. He was clearly at home on these outcroppings, the wind whipping around him sending blond tufts of his hair flying.

"I have never backed down from a challenge, and I refuse to allow some jagged old sandstone to intimidate me."

"Keep minding your step, though," Thorfinn warned. "It only gets trickier from here."

Delightful.

He slowly moved forward, showing Rose how to place each foot. She concentrated on the rocky ledge, wishing she could instead take in the stunning views. They were situated in the center of a ragged gash between the cliffs. Before them, the turquoise-blue sea beckoned, stretching far into the horizon. Water rushed through the narrow channel below, echoing off the walls. Waves crashed with such violence that the spray reached Rose and Thorfinn and doused both sides of the split in the rocks. Delicate flowers grew in the sandstone crevices, their pink buds dancing in the breeze. The ever-present seabirds swooped to a perch on the rocks and then darted back out into the air.

The drama of the landscape echoed the emotions tumbling through Rose's own soul. Excitement wheeled through her in an intoxicating dance, but she could not quite shake the sensation of danger. It wasn't just that she was currently perilously perched on a narrow, craggy promontory or the sense of nervousness that had pervaded her since she'd returned from the Front. Until the viscount's notes were delivered safely to the British authorities, she and Thorfinn were at risk of real attack. Once she completed Barbury's mission, she would be standing on an altogether different kind of precipice as she confronted the emptiness still lurking inside her since even before the war. And that . . . that frightened her more than anything.

Time both crawled and raced by before Thorfinn and Rose reached a wide shelf of rock big enough for at least five people to gather comfortably. Thorfinn ducked into a gaping maw, and she followed quickly, her heart seeming to beat harder with each step. He paused near the entrance and picked up a rusting lantern. After withdrawing a match from his pocket, he lit the wick. "I'm glad there was enough old oil left. It's darker than I remember."

"You haven't been here for a while?" she asked, finding herself whispering. This place, their mission, everything felt hallowed.

"Nay." He reached up and rubbed the scar on his cheek. "I . . . well, I couldn't. Not after how Reggie and I left things, and then after he died . . ."

The broken quality of Thorfinn's voice threatened to shatter Rose too. She started to reach for him, but Thorfinn cleared his throat. He was obviously burying the pain, but being a champion of that herself, who was she to stop him?

Thorfinn resolutely hoisted the light to reveal a comfortably sized chamber about ten yards deep. A jumble of rotting books lay on a makeshift shelf cobbled together out of driftwood. Two mismatched wooden chairs with patched legs sat on either side of an old crate. A moldy ball rested against the back wall, along with what looked like a jar of marbles and one of jacks. There were drawings on the walls of faraway lands, pirate ships, and epic battles. They certainly were not masterpieces, but they gave the place a certain charm . . . or at least they would have if everything had not been covered with mildew.

The melancholy of lost childhood seeped into Rose, and she could only imagine how Thorfinn felt. He had indeed brought her to a sacred place. Even given the importance of their mission, his choice humbled her.

"You spent a lot of time here as children, didn't you?" Rose's voice still remained soft, low, reverent even.

"Aye," Thorfinn agreed quietly, rubbing his hand over one of the seats—Reggie's, she assumed by the bittersweet quirk of his mouth. "It was just the two of us when I still lived at Muckle Skaill. Astrid sometimes joined us later after my ma married my stepda. Reggie would sneak her books on birds. In his defense, I think he truly was sweet on her, but it never would have amounted to anything. He knew it, and he shouldn't have played with her emotions. They were of two different classes, and Reggie wouldn't have married her. She is like a sister to me, and I couldn't see her hurt by anyone—even my own brother. It was my duty to protect her, even if it meant fighting with him."

But who had defended Thorfinn's mother from Mar like Thorfinn had shielded Astrid from Reggie? Clearly Thorfinn had never been acknowledged by the earl—when any man should have been proud to claim someone solid like Thorfinn as his son. Part of Rose wanted to reach out and place a gentle hand on his shoulder, but she wasn't used to extending comfort.

Instead, Rose walked over to the books. She would have drawn her finger over them but was afraid of causing them to further disintegrate. Some were the type one would expect young lads to read, but the others were heavy tomes on agriculture, drainage, boating, and other topics central to operating a croft on a small island.

"Your brother was training you to be his estate manager, wasn't he?" Rose watched Thorfinn's face closely and saw him briefly shut his uninjured eye.

"It was the plan as soon as the earl shook off his mortal coil."

"Your father wouldn't have approved?"

"He wasn't my father." Thorfinn ground out the words. "He had no use for me—the offspring of one of his maids."

One of his maids? Not even the earl's mistress, then? He'd been raised as a servant in his own father's household? The pain of that reverberated through Rose. Her parents might have been absentminded, but they'd acknowledged and cared for her in their own way.

"He does not sound like a very bright man," Rose said casually, and Thorfinn rewarded her with a small chuckle.

"It is not an unusual decision for one of his rank." Thorfinn shrugged too nonchalantly. "In fact, it might have been easier on us all if he'd been lacking in intelligence instead of decency."

The statement caused a chill to slip through Rose that had nothing to do with the dampness of the cave. Memories of her first night in Muckle Skaill slammed into her. "Until I went searching for information about Viscount Barbury, my social circles and the earl's never aligned. I always felt there was something off about him, but I was just starting to uncover it when I chased him away from Hamarray."

Thorfinn's mouth twisted, and he touched his damaged cheek. "That is for the best, Rose. You do not wish to ever be in his presence for long."

"What kind of a man is—" she began to ask, but Thorfinn turned from her and cut off her inquiry.

"We should be looking for the metal box." Thorfinn brushed his hand along the back of the cave, his fingers flitting over the fading artwork. "It's getting late now, and we don't want to climb up the cliff in the dark."

Rose allowed the change of subject. "At least we don't have to worry about the rising water. This doesn't appear to be a tidal cave."

Thorfinn shook his head. "There are a few of those tucked into the cliffs of Hamarray, but this one stays dry . . . or rather relatively so. It was one of the reasons we met here. That, and the earl disliked precipices. Reggie always said his father was afraid of heights and didn't want to admit to his weakness."

Before Rose could ask another question, a scraping sound bounced through the deep alcove. Rose watched as Thorfinn slowly removed a long thin rock from where it had been jammed into a narrow crevice in the back wall. Reggie and Thorfinn had cleverly obscured the hiding place by making it look like one of the gunports in their hand-drawn pirate ship.

"You hid your treasure in a buccaneer's vessel?" Rose asked.

"We were just lads when we first made our hidey-hole." Thorfinn chuckled. "I, for one, wasn't expecting it to be used for actual espionage. Now, Reggie—Reggie was always dreaming up some sort of an adventure, so he might have considered it."

"I just think a Viking longboat would have been more apropos, that's all." Rose waved her hand in the air.

"Ha ha," Thorfinn said dryly as he pulled out a metal box.

"Is that it?" Rose excitedly rushed to peer over his shoulder.

"Aye." Thorfinn blew off a layer of dirt.

"It is smaller than I'd imagined. I was hoping for a big chest." Rose tapped her finger against the steel, making a pinging sound that echoed through the small chamber.

"It's where the keys go, at least." Thorfinn shrugged and carried the container toward the opening. "It'll be easier to see it in the light."

They knelt in tandem at the front of the cave. Thorfinn lifted the viscount's key from around his neck, where it hung next to his own, and returned it to Rose.

"You open it," Thorfinn said. "This is your quest. I'm just the late-coming squire."

"Fellow knight," Rose corrected, not liking how he'd once again made their statuses uneven.

"Did we find our grail, Sir Galahad?" Thorfinn asked.

"Oh, I'm not the saintly one," Rose said as she inserted the key and twisted. She had a bit of trouble with the rusty latch, but within seconds she had the lid off.

Fiery excitement rushed through her as she lifted out a single letter . . . and her heart plummeted.

"It's in code."

<hr/>

The disappointment in Rose's voice echoed through Sinclair. This . . . this was part of Reggie's legacy. Sinclair hadn't been there to protect his older brother during the war, but he *would* see to it that Reggie's last mission was accomplished. In the past hour, Sinclair had felt that a bit of his sibling was still alive, still fighting.

"Is it in some sort of secret language that you developed during childhood?" Rose asked, handing him the scrap of paper.

"Nay." Sinclair scanned the nonsensical jumble of alphabetical letters. "I have never seen the like in my life."

"Could he have given you the cipher?" Rose asked.

Sinclair idly rubbed his scar, feeling the puckered, silvery skin beneath his thumb. "Nay. Like I said before, Reggie didn't contact me after he first left for France."

Rose bounced to her feet and began to pace. "I suppose I should be happy that we at least found your brother's letter. Between the two of us, we can figure out a way to crack it."

"Did Reggie say anything else to you in the ambulance?" Sinclair asked. "Did he explain what had brought him back to the Front?"

Rose sank down beside him on the rock shelf. "No. He just warned me that there were spies everywhere and to trust no one but *him*, who is apparently you. It never made sense to me why the viscount was with a French regiment. There were no British troops in the vicinity and certainly not in the trenches. He was wearing the uniform of a poilu, not that of an English officer."

Sinclair fisted his hands as he thought about Reggie. He'd always been theatrical and so desperate to prove his honor. Everything had been a quest to him—even setting off to battle. Reggie had always had a singular way of swaying others into participating in whatever mad romp he'd cooked up. And Sinclair had followed his lead . . . until the war.

Pain sliced through Sinclair as an image of his brother standing on this very cliff blasted through him. *Come with me, Sin. Between the two of us we'll lick those Germans and kick them back to their precious fatherland in no time.*

"At the end, did he . . ." He trailed off, not knowing what to ask about his brother's death—how to ask. It wasn't just his pain but hers as well.

"His last thoughts were of you." Rose reached for his hand, her touch gentle. "His final words were to instruct me to tell you that he was sorry."

Sinclair's good eye burned. Turning his palm upward, he clasped Rose's slender fingers. His throat thickened until he thought his muscles might flatten his esophagus.

"I wish I'd been by his side like he'd wanted." Sinclair managed to squeeze out the words. "Reggie was always hotheaded—racing into situations without any strategy in place. I would have made sure he'd had one."

"We don't know that he didn't have a plan. Even if he did, it probably went awry." She dropped Sinclair's hand and leaned forward so her chest was flush against her knees. Rose always looked like she was ready to slay her own dragons, but now she seemed not defeated exactly but weary, terribly *weary*. "It was chaos near the Front, especially at the end. After years of the trenches not moving more than a few yards, nobody knew how to handle an actual advance."

Rose paused then and slowly stretched out her palm. Sinclair recalled how she'd asked him to hold her hand when she'd spoken of Reggie's last words. His fist closed over hers as he marveled at her courage—not just to face the past but to reveal to him her own vulnerability.

One by one, Rose's delicate, gloved fingers pressed against his skin as she spoke again. "Roads were blocked with trucks, carts, vehicles, men. Everyone was trying to get somewhere—whether forward or back. The . . . the shelling was terrible."

She stopped, her grip almost painful. He brushed his thumb over her knuckles, his own heart feeling as if it were between the grindstones at David Craigie's mill. "You do not need to continue, Rose, if you don't wish to."

She shook her head—a fierce, emphatic movement. When she spoke, her voice was stronger and determined, and Sinclair's respect for her swelled even more. "German observation balloons lurked in the sky—these silvery, bloated menaces. The Luftstreitkräfte were trying desperately to stop the Allied advance. Their quick, nimble planes strafed us constantly."

Rose swallowed hard, but she resolutely continued. "When the fighting was very intense, we could only traverse the roads at night without any headlamps to give away our location. We never knew when the Germans might release mustard gas to suffocate us all."

And Rose hadn't run from that. She'd stayed and kept driving through that hellish landscape. To save whom she could. To rescue men like Reggie. "You are one of the strongest people I know, Rose. Thank you for what you did for Reggie, for *all* of them."

Rose lifted one of her arms from her legs and reached into her pocket to withdraw her cigarette case, which she'd placed there before their climb. "I'm not strong, Thorfinn. I relive that scene too often."

He reached for the hand twirling the roll of tobacco. Gently, he removed her glove and traced his hand over her skin. "That doesn't make you weak, Rose. It makes you human, compassionate."

A harsh sound exploded from her lips. "I'm not the sentimental type, Thorfinn. Don't mistake me for some sort of angelic feminine ideal."

Despite the seriousness of the conversation, Sinclair felt the wisp of a true smile touch his face. "I would never do that, but you don't have to be a dreamy sonnet writer to care for people, Rose. To *feel* for them."

Rose shifted, but she did not tug away from him. "I didn't tell you about the war to discuss me. I wanted—*want*—you to understand that what happened to your brother wasn't something your presence could have stopped. I don't know why he was in the French trenches, but I do know that our ambulance was kicked over by an injured horse. That wasn't something you could have accounted for, Thorfinn. War *isn't* predictable. It refuses to follow order, or sense, or reason, or even justice. Even if the 'good side' prevails, there is a cost paid that is never equitable."

It was a price they were all paying—all the world—pulled into a conflict that they were now trying to put to rest. But would it ever lie quietly in its grave, or would it always haunt every one of them in some way?

"I am glad you were there," Sinclair said and realized how true his words were. "That Reggie was not alone."

"I was with him at the end, holding his hand and the key." Rose's words had softened, and she laid her head against Sinclair's shoulder. "And his mission became mine."

"Now I'm part of it as well," Sinclair said quietly.

"We might never know why he'd returned to the Continent, but we *will* ferret out this spy ring. For him. For the Allies." Rose no longer appeared worn down, but she instead nearly vibrated with intensity. This—this was the lass he'd come to know.

"And for you," Sinclair added. Rose needed the resolution that would come from finishing Reggie's mission, not just for her safety but for her inner self—for the woman who'd tried to save the men brutalized by the horrors of trench warfare.

"And also for you, Thorfinn."

Aye. He needed resolution too. But what would happen once they found it? Would the guilt inside him ever truly dissipate? Would Rose find a degree of peace? He truly hoped she would, even knowing that its discovery would lead her to depart from Hamarray. Rose belonged to the wider, glittering world and he here.

Rose lifted her green skirts, revealing a shapely leg covered in silk, but there was nothing seductive in the economical gesture. A sapphire-blue garter secured both her stocking and a dainty sterling-silver flask. After retrieving the alcohol, she lifted it into the air. "To breaking your brother's code!"

She took a swig and then handed it to Sinclair.

"To cracking the cryptograph!"

Chapter 11

"You want the rights to dirt on Hamarray?" Rose asked Sinclair as they sat together at the Flett dinner table five days later. The children had already cleared off the dishes and were outside playing in the long golden May evening with Miss Morningstar. Sigurd had set off on his daily walk earlier so he could make it back in time for the meeting with the crofters to discuss the distillery, the upcoming ceilidh and race, and the potential of turning Muckle Skaill into a hotel. What the islanders didn't know was that Sinclair and Rose were also planning to use the gathering to gauge everyone's reactions when Sinclair announced that he was going to investigate exactly what had caused Fornhowe to collapse. He sorely hoped no one acted suspiciously, but he could not rule out that one of his neighbors might have turned traitor.

Rose waved her fingers near Sinclair's face, drawing him back to the present. "I know sod is not the most scintillating of topics, but you *did* bring it up."

Sinclair gave her a rueful expression. "Sorry I was woolgathering, lass. Just thinking about that 'announcement' we're planning on making tonight."

Although he doubted that anyone was listening to their conversation, they were careful not to openly talk about the spy ring in case someone could easily overhear, including the children. So far, they'd had no success in breaking Reggie's bloody code and were continuing

Rose's original efforts at reconnaissance. But prying into his neighbors' lives was weighing on Sinclair, even though he knew that it needed to be done.

"I don't like it either," Rose whispered softly, and her hand slid into his—being his anchor this time. It was odd and wonderful—this partnership that they were slowly forging. For the past five evenings, Rose and he had huddled at the dinner table and then outside on the strand as they'd talked late into the night about improvements for Frest. But the most remarkable thing was that she, who'd dined in the finest restaurants in Paris, Milan, London, New York, Istanbul, San Francisco, and beyond, had chosen to sup with his family. He liked having her, even if it meant that Sigurd glowered at him for the intrusion throughout the entire meal.

Miss Morningstar—who'd rarely let Rose out of her sight after the latest ambush—would also come for dinner, and afterward she would set off to categorize the contents of Fornhowe. Freya and Hannah would join her, and Miss Morningstar was teaching both of them how to use her camera to document the findings. Either Sinclair or Miss Morningstar would walk Rose home. To his surprise, Rose barely protested the arrangement, but then again, they were all taking the threat against her seriously.

Sinclair was not fool enough to think that Rose might become a permanent fixture in his life. For now, he understood her true purpose for buying Frest and Hamarray. It had been to access Muckle Skaill and to give her a reason to question the crofters. Even though he sensed in her a true interest in his people, a society woman like her would never stay once she'd achieved her mission of uncovering the espionage. But he hoped that she might gain enough affection for the island to not sell it after Miss Morningstar's digs were completed but to keep it as an investment and allow him to run it for her. He wanted to show Rose that it could be profitable, and he and the other crofters had always been more than willing to work to make it so.

Sinclair cleared his throat, trying to push down the wisp of loss at the thought of Rose leaving. "Well, to return to the discussion on mud—"

"Which is very muddy, indeed." Rose squeezed his fingers, and he couldn't help but chuckle. He loved how she could find humor in the most mundane.

"Which is actually about peat harvesting," Sinclair finished. "We have nearly depleted our allotments on Frest, even with being very careful to replace the upper layer of sod when we are done. The ground has been overused for more than a century now."

"How dependent are you on peat?" Rose turned serious. "I imagine it is very important, since there doesn't seem to be any other easy source of fuel."

"It is our lifeblood. It heats our homes and cooks our food," Sinclair said. "We'll be needing it more than ever if we're to increase whiskey production."

"Well, we mustn't do anything to sacrifice that earthy, smoky flavor," Rose said, her voice that curious mix of light and somber that he'd begun to realize carried much more truth than he'd first given her credit for. "The intensity of peat and the uniqueness of the bere barley is what makes Frest Whiskey so utterly memorable. Do you think there are sufficient peat bogs on Hamarray?"

"Aye," Sinclair said. "I took a walk there yesterday to make sure."

"It looks like we need to take a stroll together, Mr. Sinclair, so I can see these fields myself." Rose winked, and he nearly groaned. Although they'd been spending every evening together, it was hard to find time for stolen kisses with his family constantly about. Rose and he, unfortunately, had not had an opportunity to resume their aborted tryst in the sea cave. But that didn't stop Sinclair from feeling like his body was a constant inferno fueled by the few embraces that they did manage.

Just as Sinclair thought his very bones were finally going to melt from the heat, Rose sobered again. "We'll also have the land surveyor that we have scheduled to visit the island draw up a proper map. You and Mr. Lewis can then work together to draft a lease."

"At least there will be one concrete benefit from the surveyor's visit. I still doubt that his findings will show us any spots I haven't considered that could be used for spying."

Rose shrugged. "The land has not had a proper review in years—you said so yourself. Can you wait, though, until the leases are drawn up to harvest the peat?"

"Nay, not if we want it to dry in time for winter. We need to start in a few weeks," Sinclair said. It was surprisingly easy to raise issues to Rose. She approached with logic, not the bluster of Mar, the apathy of Mr. White, or the wild jubilance of Reggie. Reggie had always been good at dreaming but not the execution. But Rose—Rose was a rare mix of creativity and practicality.

"Then this year we'll need to rely on everyone's good faith," Rose said. "We'll make sure at this evening's meeting that the crofters are in agreement that a necessary percentage of harvest will go toward whiskey making."

Sinclair nodded. "I will see to it when I talk to them directly that there are no hidden complaints to surprise us."

"Speaking of avoiding unpleasant shocks, I have been thinking about the guest list for the upcoming ceilidh and race." Rose's words caused Sinclair to instantly tense. He hated talking about the bloody speed trial, but he agreed that the crofters should have a chance to see what tourism would mean for the island.

"Aye?"

"It may be a good chance to draw our non-Frest suspects back to Hamarray."

The statement caused Sinclair's stomach to twist even though he understood her logic. "You mean the Earl of Mar and Mr. White."

"Yes, but I know that you and the crofters do not seem fond of either man."

That was an understatement. Sinclair somehow stopped his body from reflexively coiling for action . . . or attack. "Under normal circumstances, I would ask that you not invite them, but I can see how it would be useful—especially if you do not ask the earl directly."

"How do you mean?" Rose asked.

"When the earl wants to do something, he does it. If he is intent on using the race as an excuse to return to Hamarray, he'll either try to coerce an invitation or just show up. If he goes to that effort, we'll know his interest is strong."

Rose arched an approving brow. "And it will make it more likely that he is one of the spies! I can have my friend Percy make sure that the earl hears the gossip about the race."

"Perfect." As much as Sinclair didn't want the earl to ever return, he couldn't help a slight twinge of satisfaction that he was the one doing the manipulation after being at the mercy of Mar's machinations for so long.

"We make excellent partners, Thorfinn." Rose squeezed his hand, but he could have sworn it was his heart that she'd touched with the way it contracted. He *knew* she meant partners in the business sense, but he could not help but think of the word's broader, more romantic meaning. He had no idea why, but she'd seemed to slip so neatly into his life. It was surprisingly and perilously easy for him to forget sometimes that she was an American heiress and not a lass from the isles.

"I have the information on the thresher manufacturers whose sales agents you and Miss Morningstar can meet with in Edinburgh," Sinclair said quickly to remind himself of why they were really here together at this table: to improve Frest and catch the spy ring. As they simply could not make headway on breaking Reggie's code, Rose was heading to the Edinburgh Central Library to research cryptography. Miss Morningstar was traveling with her—both to serve as bodyguard and to do her own digging into tomes about Scottish antiquities, especially those connected with the Northern Isles. Rose would also meet with her friend from London named Percy, who was helping her organize the race.

"I wish you were accompanying me," Rose said.

"I do as well." Sinclair did not wish to stifle Rose, but he was worried about the attempts on her life. "You will stay close to Miss Morningstar and, if she is not around, to this Percy fellow?"

"You are as bad as Myrtle with her fretting. And yes, I promise I shall not go wandering about the city on my own." Once again Rose's faint protest seemed more reflexive than annoyed.

Sinclair did not press the issue further, as it was not really his place. If it hadn't been for the planting, he would have gone with Rose, even if he wasn't entirely sure how he felt about navigating a big city like Edinburgh. But he and Rose had both decided that he, as the estate manager, was needed on Frest to help oversee the critical spring chores.

"But you do realize that when you do accompany me on estate business outside of the island, you will need to acquire a suit." Rose leveled a challenging look in his direction. She had been after him to use his land agent salary to purchase new clothes.

"No amount of coin is going to make me look like a toff. I'll still be a simple crofter, and I'd rather be honest about that."

Rose arched an eyebrow. "You are running an extensive estate spanning two islands. If that does not qualify you to wear a premade suit purchased in Kirkwall, I do not know what would."

Sinclair shifted in his seat, uncomfortable that she had so easily divined the reason for his reluctance. He *felt* like an imposter. Even though Reggie had prepared him for this role, it seemed . . . wrong and arrogant.

"Are you sure I should be the one to initiate the meeting today?" Sinclair asked. "You are the laird, not me."

"But you *are* the land agent, and the people of Frest will respond better to one of their own."

Sinclair pulled his palm from Rose's grip and scrubbed at his entire face with both hands. "I am not exactly one of them, any more than I am a bloody gent."

Rose tugged gently on his wrists, and he allowed her to guide his fingers to the rough, scarred wood of the table. She was not wearing gloves, and her warm flesh pressed against his.

"You belong here, Thorfinn, to this island, to these people. You're like the standing stones by Fornhowe and on the headlands—sturdy, strong, part of the landscape."

Sinclair barked out a laugh, wishing it were so. "I wouldn't say that too loud, lass. You'll horrify the crofters."

Rose shook her head. "The islanders respect you."

Now Sinclair was chuckling in earnest but not from mirth. "They see me as a coward."

"They all rely on you, Thorfinn, and part of them resents that a bit. It must have been frightening for them to know how dependent they all were during the war on one single person. And now with you being estate manager, you will be the boss, which carries with it a whole other set of tensions. But the crofters wouldn't have anyone else in the position—I guarantee it."

Hope and pride clashed with disbelief. Sinclair had sought acceptance all his life, but it had always eluded him. Neither his sire nor his stepfather had ever regarded him as a son. And his very best friend had never been able to openly acknowledge him as his brother.

"Thorfinn, you're not that little boy hiding in a cave and reading about how to manage an estate anymore. You're doing it. You *are* the land agent—and a good one who cares. Once you see that, fully see that, your eyes will open to how the crofters really regard you."

A swell built inside Sinclair, and his breath grew short. He felt like he was standing on the strand as a great wave arose before him. Yet he did not flinch, did not try to run as the white frothy breaker started to descend. He had no idea where the current would lead him, but he was too enthralled to struggle against it.

"Thorfinn! Thorfinn! Thorfinn!" Margaret's excited voice seemed to physically wrap around him and pull him back from the beckoning deep. He and Rose sprang apart, as they had both by unspoken agreement chosen to hide their relationship from the children. It was too new, too vulnerable of a connection to expose to others, and Sinclair knew the bairns would read too much into it. His siblings were already enamored enough of Rose without dreaming of a fairy-tale wedding that would never be. And Sinclair would do well to heed his own warning. He'd never experienced a relationship like this afore, and he was sore afraid of tumbling headlong into an intensity that Rose would neither reciprocate nor desire.

He and Rose had shifted apart just in time, as Margaret careened into the room followed by Alexander, who was pumping his knobby legs as fast as he could to keep up with his older sister. When Margaret stopped short, the little lad slammed into her, but luckily neither of them took a spill.

"Myrtle told me to tell you that the crofters are starting to arrive for the meeting!" Margaret puffed out her thin chest in pride of being entrusted with the announcement. "Freya and the twins are showing everyone where to set out their blankets. Hannah's gone to fetch Da, as she knows he won't want to miss a moment."

No, because Sigurd clearly expected Sinclair to mess up and wanted to be there in case he needed to fix his stepson's blunder. As if she sensed his thoughts, Rose nudged his foot—the encouraging gesture obscured from the children by the sturdy table.

They stood up together, and the bairns danced around them excitedly. Sinclair heard his siblings' raised voices as if they came from a far-off distance. His blood seemed to whoosh through him like a riptide. He slowly fisted and unfisted his hand, but even that gesture didn't alleviate the pressure inside him. He really shouldn't be feeling so anxious. He'd previously led meetings like this.

But you weren't the bloody land agent afore. The words, dripping with disdain, sneaked through him like the taunt of the schoolhouse bully.

As Sinclair and Rose exited the cottage, people came up and greeted them. Trying his best not to sound stiff, Sinclair automatically responded.

The wind was gentle today, and the horizon glowed in a rainbow of orange and yellow. The air wasn't hot, but it was a pleasant mix of chill with a healthy hint of warmth. It felt like any other evening as the crofters gathered as they had for Sinclair's whole life. But women and bairns now came instead of just the menfolk—a change the war had wrought. The lasses were just as vital to the land, and they deserved their voice too.

No, it wasn't Frest or the people gathering that were different. It was *him*.

"Everybody's here!" Hannah's cry seemed far away. "Even Da. We can start now."

Feeling like he was moving against a powerful gale, Sinclair plodded down the bank to the sand below. The gentle slope of the island formed an almost natural amphitheater, and he stood within sight of all the crofters as they gazed down at him . . . waiting.

He spotted Sigurd's lined face and saw what he always did—not just the expectation that Sinclair would blunder but the mixture of satisfaction and disappointment that accompanied his stepfather's certainty of his failure. For although the older crofter had tried to accept Sinclair for his wife's sake, Sigurd could never completely stop seeing Sinclair as the offspring of the man who had worked to destroy the people of Frest.

Sinclair's steps faltered, and he felt curiously hollowed out, like an empty husk of wheat tumbling in the wind. Then he saw her, *Rose*. She gave him a nod, crisp and short, and he swore he felt himself take root. *She*—who had Edinburgh, London, and New York lawyers on retainer—believed in *him*, thought *him* capable.

And hell, wasn't he? He understood life on Frest—every bit of it from which lichens made the best dye to how to navigate the skerries to find the best place to drop crab pots. His childhood and adolescence had been spent reading and preparing to become estate manager one day.

Sinclair straightened and marched straight to the rock that the crofters had centered themselves around. After climbing on it, he exchanged a brief affirmative glance with Rose, and when he spoke, he felt like a modern Demosthenes.

"By now, I assume that all of you have heard about the collapse at Fornhowe. Our operations were not harmed, as only the entrance was affected. However, no one should currently go inside."

Miss Morningstar had reluctantly agreed with Rose and Sinclair that she would halt her current preliminary work in Fornhowe until he could make a reasonable show of studying the infrastructure.

"I will be thoroughly investigating why the cave-in happened and if the structure remains sturdy," Sinclair continued. "I'll stabilize it as necessary. Any questions?"

He paused, carefully scanning the familiar faces before him. Did any of them seem guilty, perhaps anxious? He saw nothing, though, to raise his suspicions. Aye, more than one visage showed concern but no more than one would expect, especially given how the islanders relied on the proceeds that the still made. Sinclair knew that Rose and Miss Morningstar would be studying the reactions too. And mayhap they could see more clearly than him, since they would not be blinded by years of knowing and working alongside these people.

"What's to happen next?" David Craigie asked, while Kilda Gray, who was a maid at Muckle Skaill, added, "How long are we to wait until we can start producing again?"

More questions poured from the islanders, which Sinclair readily answered. All of them were perfectly reasonable and raised no alarm until Astrid cupped her hands and called, "Are you sure it's necessary to shut everything down? You said that all the damage was concentrated in one area."

Sinclair knew that Astrid and her grandmother sorely relied on the illicit money—perhaps more than even the other crofters. For the last two years, Astrid had finally managed to avoid traveling to another island during herring season to make money preparing fish as a gutter girl—a job she'd always detested. It made sense that she would worry about any delay in production, but she was the only one to question his decision to halt operations to investigate the Fornhowe collapse.

"Aye. I'm sure. Is there any reason you think we should not?" Sinclair kept his voice casual without a single hint of sharpness.

Astrid, who'd been standing on tiptoe to be better seen, sank back to the ground. "I . . . I suppose not as long as we don't get too far behind. It just seemed like you were so certain that only the beginning of the tunnel was affected immediately after it happened. But you are probably right that we should be cautious. We do not want anyone hurt."

Sinclair waited a few beats to see if Astrid would expand upon her statements. When she did not, he asked, "Does anyone share my cousin's concerns? This is the time to talk it over if you do."

The islanders all shook their heads. Most of them seemed to understand the need for precaution. Sinclair's stepfather's face had sunk into an impressive glower, but it normally did during these meetings.

Sinclair glanced surreptitiously over at Rose, and she briefly inclined her head—their prearranged signal to move the discussion along. He returned his gaze to his people. It was time to begin the discussion about their future.

"As you have all heard, Miss Van Etten and Miss Morningstar have agreed to keep the contents of Fornhowe a secret for now. What you might not know is that Miss Van Etten has agreed to be our silent partner in a legitimate, *licensed* business. Eventually, instead of hiding our production in the mound, we will be able to build an actual distillery."

An excited murmur arose. The questions now punched through the air like blows in one of the boxing matches that Mar had forced his servants to hold to entertain his drunken guests. But unlike then, Sinclair didn't need to dodge or block or even strike back. He handled each inquiry easily—from the details of the arrangement with Rose to the logistics of the new operations. The crowd's wariness grew into excitement.

David Craigie shifted his broad shoulders and asked, "I do not wish to sound like I am not in support of the idea, for I think it is a fair plan, except for one thing. The Grand Fleet is gone. Who are we to sell all this whiskey to?"

Sinclair stepped back and glanced at Rose. Although he still did not like her idea of a hotel, Widow Flett and Astrid did. It was only right for him to allow Rose to present her case to the people of Frest. After all, this impacted all their livelihoods.

"Miss Van Etten is in a better position to address that question than me." As Sinclair gestured for her to step onto the rock, he thought he saw a flicker of hesitation in her eyes. The sight of it stunned him. She was always in perfect command, and he was certain she'd spoken before crowds much bigger than this.

He did what she had done for him only a half hour before. He jerked his chin down in a nod to indicate that he had faith in *her*, even if he was not keen on turning Muckle Skaill into a retreat for the rich.

She smiled then and strolled forward with such confidence he wondered if he'd mistaken the self-doubt that he'd thought he'd seen lurking in her eyes. She swung around, her expression warm and friendly, the perfect hostess or, in this case, lady of the manor. He could feel her power bestowed by birth, wealth, and education, but unlike the earl, she wasn't lording it over people but using it to welcome them.

"I am sure you have heard rumors of an auto race to be held here on Frest. I am planning to use the event to test the viability of turning Muckle Skaill into a hotel. It will not be my decision alone but all of yours, as you will be active participants in the running of the retreat."

Immediately, the crowd broke into factions, some loving the idea, some hating it.

"But why will people come?" someone called out.

"That is a question many are asking, but as an outsider, I can only say that your home has so much to offer—natural beauty, delicious food, a sense of seclusion—it is a place where a visitor can feel both thrilled and contented at the same time."

Rose's words reached down inside Sinclair and grabbed hold of him. Her love for the land was almost a palpable thing and something he instantly recognized, for he felt it himself.

"Are you planning to bring back the hunting? Will there be more hares imported?"

"No," Rose answered, "and I understand your concern. Orkney has enough stunning wildlife of its own. Mr. Sinclair and I have agreed that you may trap and otherwise take care of any hares eating your crops."

Sinclair nodded in affirmation. In that, he and Rose were perfectly aligned.

"It's never been a good thing for locals to work at Muckle Skaill." Sigurd spoke now, his gravelly voice silencing everyone.

Although Sinclair agreed with the sentiment, he did not particularly like his stepfather's delivery. It seemed personal, but then again, it was to him and to Sinclair. They both knew how Sinclair's mother had suffered nightmares long after she and Sinclair had escaped from the mansion's walls.

"I will not run things in the same manner as the Earl of Mar," Rose said, calm in the face of Sigurd's ire. "This will be a business operation."

"I like working at Muckle Skaill." Young Thomas spoke up. "I'm earning good money helping fix up the mansion, just as good as on the herring boats. Miss Van Etten is less demanding than a lot of the old sea captains."

"You've only just started, and you are a lad taken by a pretty face." Sigurd scoffed and shifted his eyes toward Sinclair. "There seems to be a great deal of that lately."

Doubt pricked Sinclair like he'd run headlong into a briar bush. Was he allowing his attraction for Rose to obscure his better judgment just as his mother had fallen for Mar's deceit? But Rose was not the old earl, and Sinclair wasn't his mum. And he wasn't swayed by her looks but by her spirit, her words, even her practicality. Still, the sting remained inside Sinclair—faint but still there.

Sigurd's words also hit Young Thomas. The poor lad's face turned as red as a scarlet sunset, and his shoulders slumped in embarrassment when titters arose from the crowd.

"Shhh!" Kilda Gray called out. "Ann Inkster has something to say."

Everyone immediately stopped speaking and swiveled to stare at the young lass. She was notoriously shy and had never spoken at a meeting.

"I . . ." Ann Inkster's throat worked up and down, as if the word had become stuck there. Some murmurs began to arise, but Rose waved them into silence. She gave the girl a warm, encouraging smile, and Ann's thin shoulders relaxed ever so slightly.

"I . . . like working for Miss Van Etten too. She is very nice." Ann spoke so softly that no one would have heard her if they all hadn't been perfectly silent.

"Thank you, Ann." Rose's own voice had grown thick with emotion. "Your words mean ever so much to me. Experience like yours at Muckle Skaill is key to this plan, and I am so glad that you shared it with all of us."

Ann lifted her chin and beamed at the compliment. Sinclair had never seen the lass looking so confident. Beside the young woman, her mother, Janet, watched her daughter proudly. And Rose had done this. She'd known what an effort Ann had made to speak, and she'd acknowledged, cultivated it.

Aye, Rose was meant to be a leader. She was even halfway to convincing him of the merits of her plan for a hotel.

Rose had organized thousands of parties before, yet none had felt quite like this. When she'd first climbed onto the rock, she'd felt like she was playing her old role of Belle of the Ball, Hostess of Hilarity, Denizen of Drama, and Motoriste of Mayhem. But as soon as she'd started addressing the crofters' concerns about the hotel, that feeling had slowly begun to fade. Ann Inkster hadn't just found her own confidence; she'd inspired Rose's as well.

Even now as the conversation transitioned into preparing for the race and the ceilidh, Rose didn't feel the empty futility that she'd experienced when planning the Armistice ball last November in Daytona. Thorfinn had convinced her not to pay the crofters for their contributions to the ceilidh, but she hoped the event would show off island life and convince guests to return.

"I can make my lamb stew," Widow Craigie offered.

"And we can show the guests how to dance!" Barbara and Mary shouted as they bounced up and down.

"I can organize those with fishing boats to help ferry the guests staying in Kirkwall back and forth," Ron Inkster suggested.

"Those are all perfect ideas!" Rose said. "And if you wanted to take some of the guests on tours of Scapa Flow and the interned German fleet, I am sure you can charge a fee if you desire."

"Now that's a fine idea," Ron said.

"We'll want to make sure there is plenty of drink available. I'd love every guest to take home a bottle. Once the world gets a taste of Frest Whiskey, the orders will keep coming," Rose promised.

"How long will you be in Edinburgh planning the race?" Astrid asked.

"I think about a week or so," Rose said carefully, hoping that Astrid was only being curious. It was a natural question, but it also was something a spy on the island would wish to know. Rose hadn't failed to notice that Astrid was the only one who'd expressed concern about Thorfinn shutting down operations at Fornhowe to investigate the collapse. Rose didn't like suspecting the young woman, whom she was starting to think of as a friend, but she also couldn't ignore the trickles of worry seeping through her.

"We shall miss you!" Ann Inkster said in a surprisingly loud voice. The young lady blushed, seeming more shocked than the rest of the crowd at her loud exclamation.

"And I shall miss all of you too," Rose said, and she was surprised how choked up she'd become from both Ann's words and her own emotions. "But I'll be back before we know it."

With that, she stepped away from the flat rock to let the crofters talk among themselves. The sun was below the horizon now, and the meeting would be ending shortly.

Breathing in the salty air, Rose turned toward Scapa Flow. The water shimmered silver and gold, reminding her of a Christmas ornament illuminated by flickering candlelight. The beauty of it struck her so forcefully that it almost hurt.

"You make a good laird." Thorfinn's deep voice rumbled through her like one of the glittering sea waves.

"You were the impressive one today, Mr. Land Agent." Rose turned to him. "I've always been able to plan a good party."

"It's much more than that, and you know it," Thorfinn said roughly, sending a pleasant shock through her.

"You mean you approve of the race and the hotel?" Rose lifted both her eyebrows, as an unexpected sense of triumph roared through her. It was not so much that she craved this man's approval but the fact that she'd *earned* it.

Thorfinn squinted out into the brilliantly illuminated sea. "I am still hesitant, but the young folks who work at Muckle Skaill seem enthused. It's also clear that you're not just trying to host some grand festivities. You're set on establishing a business."

"A frivolous one?" Rose kicked at a clump of sand as she voiced one of her greatest fears about her proposed venture.

Thorfinn gave her a hard stare, as if he could see all the doubts, all the emptiness swirling inside her. "You have taught me that just because something shines brightly does not mean that there is not something solid beneath it. The two are not the contradictions we sometimes think they are. There can be strength in brightness that I never considered before."

Strength in brightness. The words touched something inside Rose, and she felt possibility awaken like a bud unfurling toward the sun. She'd never considered her blitheness as a powerful thing, even if she'd always wielded it to protect herself, to *identify* herself. Rose was not sure if she felt entirely comfortable with connecting cheer with grit, but she didn't dislike the notion either. Perhaps . . . perhaps it was something she needed to explore further.

Chapter 12

"I never thought I'd find plowing so invigorating to watch." Rose's teasing voice carried through the spring winds. Sinclair pulled Charlie's reins and turned to find Rose sitting on a drystone wall. His heart kicked up at the unexpected sight. He hadn't seen her in over a week, and it seemed like he'd yearned for her more each day. He'd missed their nightly planning sessions so sharply that he'd started a notebook full of suggestions he wanted to develop further with her. But it wasn't just her keen mind that he'd yearned for. It was everything. Her laugh. The faint floral scent she wore. The way her eyes flashed when she had a brilliant stroke of an idea. The touch of her hand. The feel of her lips.

He had another list in mind—one he wouldn't dare write down and not just because it was filled with secret places to explore where Reggie might have stowed his actual report or where spies might be meeting. The sites possessed a second benefit of being decidedly private and perfect for a kiss or two or three.

"You're back two days earlier than you thought you would be," Sinclair called, unable to keep his mix of excitement and concern from his voice. As glad as he was to see her, he hoped that trouble hadn't driven her back to Hamarray. "Did you walk here from Muckle Skaill yourself? Are you sure it's safe for you to be by yourself?"

"My friend Percy flew me back on his seaplane," Rose said. "It saved us the ferry ride, and I wanted to make sure that I was here for the inaugural peat cutting on Hamarray. Myrtle is staying on in Edinburgh for a few days more. She's knee deep in research, and she wants to poke around the National Museum of Antiquities of Scotland a little more. And no, I didn't waltz over here myself—as I knew you and Myrtle would have my head. Percy was with me as far as Widow Flett's. Astrid is taking him on a bird-watching tour."

A new hint of unease slipped through Sinclair's happiness. It was not the mention of Rose's male friend but of the aircraft. Aye, he'd seen the contraptions in the sky since the British Navy had conducted test flights in the vicinity, but he'd never even thought of flying in one himself. He and Rose were of two worlds, like billiard balls on a collision course that would ultimately lead them to ricocheting away from each other. Yet in this moment with her in front of him, perched on the stone wall like a lass from the isles . . . their being together just felt right.

"I'm glad you're back early, then. I've missed you, Rose."

A beautiful smile broke over her face at his words. "I've missed you too, Thorfinn."

Charlie stamped one of his fringed feet, clearly not impressed with the humans' flirtations. Sinclair patted the horse's withers. "Now, Charlie, you know you've been after me for a peedie break from cutting the sod."

The pony tossed his head and glared.

"You're never one to be satisfied, are you, boy?"

Charlie wheezed out a heavy sigh, and a moment later, Rose's laughter floated over to them.

"Perhaps it's time to stop wasting your charm on a cantankerous equine," she called.

Charlie whinnied and stuck his speckled nose into the air as Sinclair began to walk away. He ignored the pony's theatrics. The old boy might put on a bit of a show, but he was too lazy to do anything but stand there until ordered otherwise.

Sinclair glanced around. They were in a pasture surrounded by two gentle hillocks. Although not steep, the slight swells did obscure them from view. Stepping up to Rose's knees, he bent over and pressed a quick kiss against her lips.

Rose wrapped her legs around his waist despite her heavy skirts. Her hands looped around his neck, pulling him close. The smell of the overturned soil mixed with the sweet perfume she always wore. The odors should have warred against each other, but instead they meshed— mud and flowers—the harbingers of spring awakening.

Sinclair had spent his whole life searching for a place to belong, and he'd never thought he'd find it, even temporarily, in the arms of an American heiress who treated seaplanes as a matter-of-course method of travel. But being with Rose just felt natural to him—exciting, to be sure, but also miraculously ordinary.

"I can only rest for a brief spell, lass." He laid his forehead against hers, wishing she could whisk them away on *The Briar* to the sea cave or to another secluded location on his secret list. "I want to finish plowing this field before sunset. I hope to get the corn in soon with the weather being so fine."

"Corn?" Rose wrinkled her nose. "I thought you were going to plant bere barley. I didn't know you grew an American crop."

"It's our general word for grain," Sinclair told her, and because he couldn't resist, he lifted one of her hands to his mouth. After flipping it over, he pressed a kiss to the sensitive skin at her wrist. She rewarded him with a shiver.

"Mmmm, if this is how you teach me your language, please continue." She closed her eyes and tilted her head heavenward. The bright sunlight caught her, and she looked like the very angel she was always claiming *not* to be.

Sinclair groaned, wishing he could give in to temptation just this once. But he didn't have that luxury. "When the planting is done, lass, when the planting is done."

Her eyes fluttered open, and she smiled. "I will hold you to that, mister."

"Mayhap you can spare some time to visit us for dinner tonight. Freya always is happy to set an extra plate for you and for your friend Percy if he wishes to join us like Miss Morningstar does. Afterward we can discuss *all* of our ventures." Even if Sinclair couldn't touch her, he liked having Rose near, and he wanted to learn what she'd discovered about cryptology in the Central Library.

"My research regarding our *project* has proved fruitful, and there are a few tricks I want to try." Rose hopped off the wall to stand next to him. "As the message was left for you, then the path forward must also be connected to you."

Clashing duties once again tore through Sinclair. He wanted to drop everything to finish his brother's last quest and root out the spies, but his family needed the spring crop in the ground if they and the animals were to eat this winter. The weather was fair today but might not be tomorrow. "I can assist as soon as the sun sets, although I can pause long enough to see you safely back to Muckle Skaill."

"I've arranged for Young Thomas to plow for you. He's just finishing up the work he was doing at the mansion. He should be here shortly."

Sinclair adjusted his eye patch, loath to accept help, especially since Young Thomas was making good money helping with the renovations. "Don't guilt the lad into helping me just because I did his family a couple of good turns when he was away last year. His parents are relying on those wages you've been paying him."

"I'm still giving him his salary for today."

Sinclair didn't know how he felt about that. "That seems a bit too much like giving me charity, even if it's indirect."

Rose crossed her arms and dipped her chin. "Thorfinn, it is a division of labor, one you may need to get accustomed to. Right now, I require your expertise. It happens to involve our other *project*, but another time it could be purely about the estate. Consider this part of your compensation as land agent."

"But—"

"Besides, Young Thomas was thrilled. He's tired of being stuck inside painting and hanging wallpaper, and I'm sure he won't mind being a stone's throw away from Freya's home. I suspect he's sweet on her. Come her birthday they'll only be two years apart, and he gets this funny look on his face every time—"

"Do you really think that's an inducement for me to give them a chance to be alone together without a proper chaperone?"

Rose rolled her eyes. "Your stepda will watch them like the proverbial hawk, and besides, Freya is a smart young lady who can make her own decisions about these things."

"Aye," Sinclair grumbled reluctantly. His little sister was slowly becoming her own woman, whether he liked it or not.

Just then Young Thomas appeared, whistling "It's a Long Way to Tipperary." He looked so cheerful and hale—a sharp contrast to the wan lad he'd been upon his return from the war. Rose was right. The nineteen-year-old needed to be out in the spring sunshine.

"Are you coming?" Rose cocked her head in Sinclair's direction.

"You know I am, lass." Sinclair then turned and called over to the pony, "Charlie, don't you go giving Young Thomas a hard time. You listen to him."

The horse shook his flank in Sinclair's direction and showed his teeth.

"I don't think your horse likes you." Rose linked her arm with Sinclair's as they headed over to the beach. The tide was low, so they could simply walk to Muckle Skaill.

"The beastie doesn't like anyone."

"I could charm him." She grinned at Sinclair. Then, after peering around just as he'd done to make sure no one was watching, she planted a kiss on his cheek. His left eyelid drifted closed for a moment as he savored the innocent sweetness of the gesture.

"Aye, that you could, lass. That you could."

As they reached the front steps to Muckle Skaill, Sinclair hesitated. The few times he'd called upon Rose regarding the estate, he'd always used the staff entrance. The side door was near to Rose's office, so he'd used the servants' corridor to get there. He hadn't been in the main part of the structure since he and his mother had fled all those years ago.

"What's wrong?" Rose asked as he began to slip his arm from hers.

"This isn't proper. I'll go in my normal way. Are we gathering in your study?"

"Which way have you been entering my house?" Rose knit her brows together.

"The servants' entrance, of course."

"That's absurd." Rose held on to Sinclair's arm as she started to march up the first step, leaving him no choice but to follow. "From now on, come in the front door. You *are* the estate manager."

His stomach roiled as he ascended the grand stairs to the ornately engraved wooden door, and he swore that his scar burned as much as when the wound had been fresh. The oak—rare to Hamarray—was carved with romanticized images from Orcadian folklore. Selkies transformed into beautiful maidens. Coquettish mermaids beckoned. Cheeky trows peeked out of corners while mysterious finmen paddled in their animal-skin boats. The carpenter had turned their harsh stories into some damn fairy tale.

Rose pushed on the heavy wood, revealing a foyer at once familiar and foreign. The mansion always had a musty odor about it—a decay that seemed rooted in its very walls. But fresh scents greeted him—the smell of new paint, a whiff of wallpaper glue, even the crisp scent of sea air. The formerly dark, imposing space was starting to be transformed into something airy. Gone were the thick draperies that choked out any light brave enough to try to enter the mullioned windows. Instead, gauzy fabrics drifted in the breeze. The gruesome statues showing Zeus with his various conquests had vanished.

Sinclair had expected to find the specter of the earl lurking in Muckle Skaill, but he saw only the touches Rose had made.

"What do you think?" Rose asked, and Sinclair realized he'd been staring slack jawed, his feet rooted to the freshly polished parquet floor.

"I wouldn't have believed that anyone could even begin to change this place," Sinclair admitted.

"Perhaps I can convince you yet that turning Muckle Skaill into a resort is a capital idea!" Rose gave him a flirty nudge.

But her words only released ghosts of the past. Cruel laughter drifted through the halls. A scream. The breaking of glass. Drunken guffaws. The clink of dice. The smell of liquor. Fists hitting flesh. A rifle shot. The cry of a wounded animal. The snarl of a dog. The screech of a cock.

Memories like that could not simply be painted over.

"Are you sure nothing is bothering you?" Rose asked as she brushed her hand over his bicep while she led him through the main corridor.

The hall retained more of the earl's overly masculine influences, including the dark-bloodred rugs, but Sinclair could already detect subtle influences from Rose. The most apparent was the removal of the salacious artwork that Mar was so fond of. In its place were rough, economical sketches of the broch, which he supposed that Miss Morningstar had drawn.

"Thorfinn," Rose asked again. "It seems like something *is* wrong."

"No, I'm just focused on cracking Reggie's code," Sinclair half lied as they arrived at the library. He hadn't been in the two-story room for over a decade. Even when he'd lived in the house, he'd been forbidden from entering it except to deliver coal or to sweep the fireplace. But Reggie had never listened to his father's rules, and he would often meet Sinclair there in secret.

But Sinclair saw neither his grinning half brother nor the preening earl but an empty space. The ancient glass windows overlooking the sea might have been freshly polished, but the musty smell of old books remained the same. Rose had not gotten around to replacing the furniture, but he noticed that pillows and lace doilies had been strategically placed over old cigar holes and port stains. Yet it still felt like a museum piece—a horrible diorama of a battle Sinclair had never stopped fighting.

"Do you wish to go to my office?" Rose asked, her head cocked as she worriedly watched him.

Sinclair sucked in his breath, forcing his thoughts away from the past. "I assume there is a reason you chose here."

"There is. The codebook may be hidden somewhere in the library. It certainly would be easy to overlook. There are plenty of dusty old tomes that probably haven't been touched in a hundred years. I thought you might be able to recognize which volume it might be."

Sinclair drew his thumb against his puckered scar. "I told you that we didn't have any code as boys. Reggie spoke of making one, but other adventures always stole his attention away."

"I believe he created one later when he was on Hamarray before he returned to France. It would make sense that he'd select a book to write it down in that would stand out to you but to no one else," Rose said quietly. "Unfortunately, before we even get to the code, we need to figure out what your brother used as a cipher."

Sinclair indicated for Rose to sit. If staying in this bloody room would help them find answers more quickly, he could endure it. Every minute the spies remained free meant more immediate danger to Rose and long-term peril for them all.

"Aren't a code and a cipher the very same thing?" Sinclair asked.

"That's what I thought, too, before my research at the Central Library." Rose chose a settee, and she patted the plush seat next to her. As Sinclair sank down, he was glad she'd chosen a place that forced them to press together. Touching her, even innocently like this, helped to drive away the memories.

"Evidently," Rose continued as she laced her fingers through his, "a cipher is a key of sorts to a pattern involving the switching around of letters or numbers or something of that ilk. A code is a compilation of words that mean something else."

"It is not completely clear to me, lass, but I think I understand the gist of it," Sinclair said. "How are we to go about figuring out that key?"

Rose turned in her seat and pulled open a drawer in the end table next to them. She extracted a journal and a fountain pen. Then she reached inside her ever-present reticule and retrieved Reggie's coded letter.

"One of the easier common ciphers uses a date. Are there any that were important to your brother? We'll start with his birthday and then yours."

Sinclair provided the numerals, and Rose slowly applied them to the first few words. Unfortunately, she produced only more nonsense.

"I suppose that would have been too easy," Sinclair said, trying to ease both of their disappointment. The knowledge of the spy ring had been bearing down on him for days, sometimes pressing down so harshly he swore it was hard to breathe. He could only imagine the urgency that Rose felt. After all, she'd been searching so much longer than him, and she'd been ambushed twice. He could not bring himself to think of what would happen if the villains were successful on their next try. The pain of it was searing.

Rose put her pen and the papers on the end table and then reached for his hand. Her touch was light but steadying. "What was your brother like? I realize that it might be hard to talk about him, but if we focus on who he was, perhaps it will become apparent what he would have chosen as a cipher."

Sinclair shifted on the soft cushion as he stopped himself from reflexively increasing his grip on Rose's hand. "Passionate. Dramatic. I

remember Reggie used to stand on the edge of the cliff as a young adolescent and practice the grand speeches that he was going to give when
he finally took his seat at the House of Lords. They were all exceedingly
progressive—about righting past wrongs, giving more assistance to the
poor, improving justice. Of course, he never finished one of them. He'd
always get bored somewhere around the middle and announce that we
should go fishing or have a footrace."

Rose shifted as she studied him intently. "You keep mentioning
how Lord Barbury never completed what he started. It is very different
from the impression I received from him. He seemed so . . . so determined, so focused. I talked to him before the ambulance ride in the
poste de secours. It was light out, and we were under heavy fire, so we
couldn't leave. He told me he had a mission beyond No Man's Land but
didn't mention the spies until . . . later . . ."

Rose trailed off, and Sinclair knew she meant the conversation she'd
had with Reggie as he'd breathed his last. Rose and Sinclair were silent
now, both united and separated by their pain: she lost in the memories
of a dying man she had only just begun to know, and he in those of a
living man who had become a stranger in the end.

"Reggie was always looking for something that would make him
the hero—an atonement of sorts."

"An atonement for what?" Rose asked softly. Her eyes sought his
undamaged one, but he could not meet her searching gaze.

*For never asking how my face came to be bloodied . . . not even when
the earl blinded me. For staying in his room at night with the gramophone
playing so loud it drowned out the sounds of the dogfights and the matches
between the servants. For never confronting his father, even when I almost
died under his blows for defending my mother.*

But those weren't the truths Sinclair wanted to voice . . . perhaps
because he was a bit like his older sibling, hiding the pain and the
shame he did not wish to accept. The old hurts mixed with the newer,

rawer pain of losing Reggie. Sinclair missed every damn bit of his older brother, even the flaws.

"I suppose he was trying to compensate for possessing all the trappings of nobility without really having earned the label of being *noble*," Sinclair said.

"Like Mar?" Rose asked, once again showing her surprising insight despite not knowing the details of the earl's horrible reign on the island. "He certainly seems like a *noble* in name only—a pretty shell of a man with nothing inside."

Oh, Mar had something inside him all right—a festering, rotten, moldering mess. But Sinclair only said, "Aye. Reggie was afraid of becoming his father." And his older brother had also felt a need to pay for the man's sins.

A new bolt of pain sizzled through Sinclair as he realized that both Reggie and he had suffered from Mar's depravity while Mar himself lived in impunity. Receiving the earl's affection had not saved Reggie from the same fate as Sinclair. The earl had irrevocably damaged both of them—leaving them feeling . . . broken, unsuitable for any place in society.

"My word, the viscount was just like *me*. He was just as empty and lost." Rose's self-reproach sliced through Sinclair's own horror.

He turned toward her, rubbing his hands across his face, as if he could scrub away the haze in his soul. How could Rose—bright, wonderful, caring Rose—regard *herself* as hollow?

"You do not have a void inside of you any more than Reggie did." Sinclair's voice was harsher and fiercer than he intended, but Rose seemed to understand that the rawness was not directed at her. "My brother could be irreverent at times and loved a practical joke, but he was as sentimental as they came."

"Love," Rose said, rubbing her forehead. "I'd forgotten that part."

"What part?" Sinclair asked. His brain was already saturated with emotion, and he could not follow her logic.

"Your brother had told me that his purpose was about love. I mentioned lovers, and he corrected me and said *loved ones.*"

"Aye." Sinclair rubbed at his chest as the pressure in his heart became almost unbearable. "That sounds like Reggie. He always cared deeply."

"He said he was fighting for those we let into our hearts."

The poetic words were exactly something Reggie would have said, and the shock of hearing them caused tears to burn in the back of Sinclair's left eye. He clenched his hands into fists, letting his blunt nails dig into his flesh—as if the external pain could distract him from the internal.

"Reggie was always protective of who he loved."

He knew Reggie had never forgiven himself for not stopping the earl from pushing Sinclair into the fire grate that fateful night.

Disobedient whelp. The earl's slurred words shot into Sinclair's mind. Suddenly he was no longer sitting beside Rose on the settee but standing in front of Mar, using his thin ten-year-old body to block the large brute's way.

Sinclair had not spoken—as he'd long since learned that the earl never really heard his words. They only made him angrier, as did any lift of the chin. So Sinclair just stood there, firm, his eyes downcast. He molded his hands into fists, but even though he was already a proficient fighter against lads older than him, his defensive maneuvers never deterred Mar.

The first blow sent Sinclair reeling backward, and his mother screamed. Somehow, he managed to stay on his feet. But he didn't the second time. He pitched to the side, pain exploded in the right side of his face, and everything went dark.

And then there was Reggie at his side, crying, helping him up. Sinclair didn't think he could move, but Reggie wouldn't let him stay down. *Hurry, Sin. He won't stay asleep for long. We've got to get you away from here. You and your mother.*

They'd never spoken of that night again—never mentioned how the earl hadn't been sleeping but passed out from too much drink. Again. And most of all, they never discussed how Sinclair had lost his eye. But neither of them had ever forgotten it.

"The twenty-third of November, 1902," Sinclair gasped out. Even saying the phrase physically hurt, but if Reggie wanted to choose a date that Sinclair would remember, that was it.

Dimly, he watched as Rose blinked away her own memories and reached for the pad of paper. She didn't ask him about the date. She must have realized from the tone of his voice that it was something he did not wish to share.

Slowly, methodically, Rose worked. Although Sinclair followed the movements of her hand, he did not actually see the letters she wrote.

"We . . . we have the first two words," Rose said, her voice shaky, as if she also had too many emotions boiling inside of her to fully grasp the enormity of what they were about to accomplish.

"How did you use the numerals?" Sinclair did not ask the mundane question out of curiosity but because hearing something mechanical, mathematical, would give him space to wrestle back the past.

"I wrote down the date the way you Brits do: twenty-three, eleven, 1902. For the first letter, I moved back two spaces in the alphabet, three for the second letter, one for the third letter, and so forth." Rose's words were efficient, as if she, too, needed the distance from her emotions.

Sinclair barely heard Rose's explanation as he forced the old ugliness back where it belonged—buried deep within him. He'd rather purge it from him entirely, but that was not possible.

"Are you okay?" Rose asked, her voice so low and soft.

"I will be." He cleared his throat and rolled back his shoulders several times. Rose's hand slipped up his arm, resting on his bicep. She gave him a squeeze, and a bit of his equilibrium returned. He hazarded a glance at Rose and found her golden-brown eyes boring into him. She was worried. About him. It was odd having someone fuss over him.

"What . . . what are the words?" Sinclair asked. He hoped he was ready to hear them.

"Puddle rumpus," Rose said.

Sinclair shook his head, trying to clear everything from it so that he could focus. "That makes no sense."

"That's why we need the codebook," Rose said. "The words are standing for something else."

The codebook—the one Rose thought only he could find. It meant more soul-searching he did *not* want to engage in.

"Perhaps," Rose said as she started to rise from the settee, "we should take a little break, maybe even have a sip or two of whiskey for figuring out the cipher."

Sinclair knew Rose's suggestion had nothing to do with celebrating and everything to do with her concern about him. She might not understand the nightmares plaguing him, but she sensed them.

"No." The rough word rushed from Sinclair as he gently tugged on Rose's hand. He didn't want to delay this. Rose was in danger, and he didn't want any further harm to anyone. "You said you thought I could recognize the codebook. How?"

Rose sank back down and studied his face. When she spoke, her tone was careful, as if she was afraid of pushing him too far. "You said that Reggie taught you to read. Was there a particular book that you used in the beginning? One that you remember?"

A bittersweetness choked Sinclair as he thought about huddling with his brother at night in this very room, a single candle shared between them. "Yes. It was a thin book no bigger than the width of my smallest finger. The cover was a blue linen fabric, and it had silver lettering. We accidentally dripped candle wax on the top left corner one evening, but other than that it is unremarkable."

"Well"—Rose stood up and brushed out her skirt—"let's split the room into two and find this code."

About thirty minutes later, Sinclair stroked a finger over a familiar worn cover before he called out to Rose. It was odd touching it now—this tangible connection to a time long gone. Sinclair closed his hand around the book as he pulled it gently from the shelf. His thumb brushed against the smooth wax. He and his brother had been arguing over whether the fictional Long John Silver or the real-life Blackbeard made for the more fearsome pirate. They'd been too distracted to notice the melted tallow dripping onto the book.

He could hear Reggie's childhood voice coaching him, helping him through the tangle of letters. Once again, his heart felt near bursting. Before it could explode with more unwanted emotions, he climbed down the ladder he was standing on and called to Rose. She immediately dashed to his side.

He opened the book with Rose leaning over his shoulder. As he flipped through it, she sighed heavily. "There doesn't appear to be anything written in it, but it does smell remarkably like a lemon tree."

A sense of bittersweet accomplishment filled Sinclair. He recognized the odor immediately and its significance. "Reggie always likened the scent to lemon meringue pie. We used to exchange messages with each other by writing in lemon juice in case the earl intercepted them. Do you have a candle handy?"

"Do you think Reggie wrote in disappearing ink?" Rose asked, her voice a bit stunned, as if she could not believe they were finally this close to solving Reggie's message.

"Aye," Sinclair said, understanding all too well her conflict as he battled back a cluster of mixed emotions.

"Fortunately, Myrtle and I have several tapers stashed in this room. We've had a devil of a time getting the old generator working again." Rose hurried over to a side table and opened a compartment underneath it to retrieve a candle and matches.

Drawing in an uneven breath, he accepted the lit candle from Rose. The flame bobbed a bit as his hand shook with all the sensation barging through him. Steadying his fingers, he carefully brought it behind the first page. Both of them froze, and he swore neither of them breathed as they waited a beat. Then another. He doubted either of them could completely describe the emotions clashing around them.

Slowly and then quickly, his brother's bold scrawl appeared. He'd always penned his letters with extra flourish. Reggie had drawn lines to certain words and phrases and then written alternative ones in the margins. It was, no doubt, the codebook.

Rose pressed her palm to her mouth and let out a sound halfway between a giggle and sob. The incongruous sound echoed the reaction burning through Sinclair—joy and pain, anxiousness and relief.

"It's all a bit of a jumble." His voice sounded like he'd swallowed a fistful of dry sand. Trying to hold the maelstrom inside, he handed the thin volume over to Rose and focused on the logical steps. "But it is definitely Reggie's writing and his style. He wasn't one for organization."

Rose swallowed audibly, and he could see her seeking refuge in the practical too. She tapped her finger over the exposed words. "It *is* rather a messy hodgepodge. I can go through and organize this into a proper form—a dictionary of sorts. It will take a few days, but I do not see any other solution."

"Don't tell me that you've rushed back from the delights of Edinburgh only to create a lexicon, Rose Petal." The cultured male voice seeped into the room like honey through a crack in a jar. "That would be a terrible bore. Worse, I feel complicit in confining you to these doldrums since I flew you here. You're in danger of becoming just as much of a bookworm as Myrtle."

Sinclair whipped around. The past and future slammed into each other with such force that he took an involuntary step backward. Some might have said that the blond-haired man in the doorframe looked like a gilt Renaissance statue come to life, but Sinclair saw only a monster. He tried clearing his gaze with a blink of his left eye. After all, the earl's favorite crony should have aged through the years. But no, the chap before him still was the very spit and image of the Duke of Newsberry.

The newcomer sauntered into the library and slung his arm around Rose's shoulders before bussing her cheek. Defensive rage ripped through Sinclair. He stepped forward, his hand fisted, ready to protect Rose from the man's overly familiar grip. Sinclair wasn't a lad anymore who had to stand by and watch nobs just take what they unjustly thought they deserved.

However, Rose merely laughed and patted the man on the chest. "Not everyone prefers a party to a textbook, Percy."

Percy—the Percy—not the Duke of Newsberry. Sinclair tried to force himself to calm down, but it was more than a trifle difficult with the interloper's arm still slung over Rose's back like a possessive mantle.

"Thank the good lord for that. The world has enough hellions running hither and thither—although I never thought I'd see *you* sequestered in the Orkneys of all places and compiling *dictionaries.*"

"Orkney." The correction slipped out of Sinclair's mouth before he could stop it.

Percy turned toward him. His light-blue eyes widened, as if registering Sinclair's presence for the first time. "Ah, very well. *Orkney.* But whatever you call this place, it's deuced far away from civilization—not to mention it's terribly windy. I cannot understand, Rose, why you are so dead set on establishing a retreat here of all places."

Sinclair waited for Rose to correct the pompous man—to explain that nothing had been officially decided about the future of the hotel. But she did not. She allowed the ass to prattle on, and a flame of worried anger flickered to life inside Sinclair. Had she made a final decision regarding Muckle Skaill during her time in Edinburgh in contradiction to her promises to the islanders to leave the decision to them?

"Although I can see how it is wonderfully private and away from all the hubbub and gossip of London," the nob added with a smile that most people would have regarded as charming, but all Sinclair saw was a sneer. But it wasn't the man's facial expression that made Sinclair nearly retch. It was the words themselves—a torturous echo of how Mar had crowingly described his island estate to his cronies.

News never leaves these shores, fellows. This is our Valhalla, where we rule as gods and can do whatever we desire.

Rose had promised it would be different—that she *was* different. Why was she not challenging the bruck spewing from this toff's mouth?

But Rose didn't counter it.

She *affirmed* it.

"The remoteness from Society *is* its alluring charm, darling. I find it all terribly dramatic here and good for the soul beleaguered by the demands of cosmopolitan civilization. You and your friends will love it here. I promise," Rose said gaily, as if Sinclair and she both hadn't been steeped in seriousness only moments before.

Pain ripped through Sinclair akin to a vicious backhand from Mar. He even physically stumbled, but both Rose and Percy were so focused on each other that neither noticed.

Rose's demeanor had changed around this nob, reminding Sinclair of when she'd first arrived on the island. There was flippancy to each word—as if everything were simply a grand lark for her private amusement. Aye, Sinclair knew she used blitheness as a shield, but it jarred him. It reminded him too much of the earl's cruel cavalierism. He felt like a boy again, trapped within these walls, every inch of him bleeding.

"You have changed, darling," the Newsberry look-alike said. Sinclair agreed with the man's observation but likely not for the same reasons. He'd thought he'd seen the real Rose. Hell, he'd even begun to *trust* her, a toff, not to lie and manipulate. But she was a chimera—nay, not that—a selkie sent to tempt him but always destined to return to her ilk.

"I'm not the one who went and became a stuffy old *duke*." Rose lightly flicked the man's arm, the gesture both familiar and intimate. A new slimy, sickly emotion slipped through Sinclair's innards, ripping away at his calm rationality.

"My change in station is merely the consequence of my uncle failing to do his duty and beget an heir before he thoroughly pickled himself in liquor. I may be the new Duke of Newsberry, but I'm still the same ole Percy."

Newsberry. He *was* the fucking duke, just the new generation come to wreak pain and misery like the legendary finmen in their fast watercraft—only this one had arrived by plane.

Rose laughed, the sound nearly shredding Sinclair. "An irrepressible rakehell?"

"No one uses that word anymore, but I find a title does lend a man instant polish." Percy suddenly lifted Rose's hand. Bowing over it, he pressed his mouth to her knuckles. Sinclair's hand fisted, and he had to remind himself that Rose wasn't his mother. This man's touch *wasn't* being forced upon her, but the past and present seemed to blend so thoroughly he couldn't tell where the old pains ended and the new ones began.

Still in the courtier position, Percy glanced up at Rose. "Do you think your parents will approve of me now that I am a genuine peer of the realm?"

Rose chuckled again, removing her hand. "You were the heir apparent to a dukedom. My parents were always ecstatic over you. And when Mother is happy in social matters, Daddy is as pleased as punch."

Sinclair breathed in and out, trying to separate himself from the tableau playing out before him. He needed to walk away. He needed to leave, but the duke's next words seared Sinclair to the ground, and he felt like a charred smudge on the floor.

"Then why are we not married, Rose Petal?"

Rose lightly bopped one finger against the golden crown of the toff's head, as if everything were a silly pantomime. "Because neither of us is the marrying type, Percy."

Rose's words shouldn't have shocked Sinclair, yet they seemed to vibrate throughout his very core, reaching through all the other darkness churning inside him. He had purposely refused to contemplate the future of his relationship with Rose—because it was obvious there would be none between a sophisticated society woman and a provincial crofter from Orkney. But part of Sinclair—a very foolish, reckless part of him—must have had unrealized hopes, for he felt them being dashed now. He was indeed the daft mortal who had succumbed to the charms of a selkie.

"Unfortunately, my change in circumstances necessitates that I settle down—eventually, of course. There is no need for me to instantly get fitted for a ball and chain." Percy finally straightened and no longer looked as if he was about to pledge his troth, but the pressure inside Sinclair did not release. The man was the same heartless cad that his uncle had been, and this rotter was the type of guest that Rose wished to infest Hamarray and Frest with.

"Not when there are so many pretty young ladies yet to meet?" Rose lifted an eyebrow, and that cavalier arch gutted Sinclair. Did she not understand the pain that dukes and their brethren inflicted on lasses who didn't have fortunes and powerful families to safeguard them?

"Precisely, my dear." Percy's lips curved into a devilish smile. "I must thank you for arranging to have the delectable Miss Flett show me the glories of avian life here on your fair isle. I have never been so enamored of feathered creatures."

Protective rage ripped through the very last vestige of Sinclair's frayed control. He could tolerate his own pain but not that of someone he loved.

Sinclair forgot his manners. He forgot his audience. And most of all, he forgot his place. But he did *not* forget the past.

"You introduced *him* to Astrid?" Sinclair advanced a step toward Rose, betrayal scourging him. He'd trusted her. Trusted her not to be like the earl, like the others. He'd even started to listen to her claims that once again turning Hamarray into a retreat for the wealthy would help the islanders, not bring them a return of old griefs.

Rose turned in his direction, clearly startled. "Why, yes. I mentioned it earlier. Percy is very well connected in sportsmen circles and adventurer clubs. A good word from him is sure to bring a number of bird-watchers to Hamarray, and if we start the ho—"

Sinclair barely heard her explanation. Instead, he turned to Percy, who was watching him with his mouth agape. Clearly the man did not expect a mere peasant to voice any opinion.

"Astrid is under my protection." Sinclair stepped toward the slighter man. Although Percy possessed an athletic build, it was a lithe one that hardly compared with Sinclair's bulk.

"I didn't know Astrid was spoken for." Percy gave Sinclair a congenial smile. "My apologies."

Heat flared through Sinclair as he realized what *under protection* meant in the upper circles of London Society.

"Astrid is my cousin," Sinclair said. "She is like a sister to me. She is not without those ready to defend her honor."

"Sinclair, no one is threatening Astrid's honor." Rose touched his arm, but he shook her off.

Guilt pelted him. He'd done this. He'd allowed the vipers to once again nest on Hamarray.

Bloody hell, he'd *helped* them dig their dark den.

Somewhere a bit of sanity returned. Sinclair had to leave this room—this *house*—before he acted on the anger surging through him. He was not thinking clearly. *Could not* think clearly. He was a child again—hurt and ready to strike blind, undirected blows.

He opened the obscured door to the servants' corridor and stalked through it. He'd almost made it to the exit when he heard Rose call his name. And by some damnable instinct, he turned around.

Chapter 13

The sheer rage on Thorfinn's face caused Rose to falter. He was normally so even tempered, so . . . congenial. But now. Now he truly looked like an ancient warrior.

"You are all the same." He spat the words at her.

His words ignited the doubts already seeping through Rose, like a match dropped in gasoline dripping from a punctured tank. Thorfinn's earlier revelations about the viscount had unbalanced everything she had been painstakingly erecting since that November night on Daytona Beach. She'd made Barbury's purpose her own. Yet if what Thorfinn said was true, his half brother had been just as desperate as her to create meaning in a world that seemed to have none. The viscount had seemed so self-assured, so certain. But so had she—gathering false confidence and bravado around her just as she'd donned the shimmering costume of Nike when she'd felt no victory.

What had she done when faced with Barbury's own fallibility? As soon as Percy had popped into the library—all irreverent nonchalance— she'd assumed the identical false shite that she always did.

"Who are the same?" She stuck her chin out, both daring him to answer and fearing his response.

"You nobs."

"I'm not a nob." But the protest felt weak. Because, thunderation, wasn't she despite all her efforts and protests to the contrary?

"You aren't?" Thorfinn advanced on her, his fist bunched so tightly his knuckles were white lumps against reddened flesh. But she didn't flinch. Even with him puffed up like a damn bull rampaging through Pamplona, she didn't fear him.

"No." Rose tossed back her bobbed hair. The feel of it striking against her cheeks gave her strength. She wouldn't crumble. "I'm an American. We don't have titles."

"But you want them," Thorfinn pointed out. "You certainly seem chummy with the duke back there."

"That's because we *are* chums! We raced in the same circuits before the war." And they'd been lovers on more than one occasion, but she wasn't about to discuss that in the servants' hall with her voice raised like a damn harpy, her insides splintered like wood strafed by bullets.

"What about Astrid? I thought you considered her a friend, but are we all just peasants to you? Hares to throw to your real pack when the wolves run low on entertainment?"

"Are you insinuating that I am some kind of Wild West madam?" Rose had thought she'd been accused of all the depravity there was— but being likened to a brothel owner was a new and unpleasant charge. Thorfinn's words seemed to blast apart the remains of the purpose she'd been trying to build. He had always seen more in her—challenged her to be more. And now he was not just voicing her innermost fears; he was damning her more than she'd even damned herself.

"That would be too gauche. You probably envision yourself as some female Dionysus, leading us all in hedonistic glory—not caring about the price that others pay for your pleasure."

The words sheared through Rose, nearly slicing her in half. She had called herself that so many times, but hearing Thorfinn say it, witnessing the contempt in his face, and feeling his distaste like a palpable blast against her skin left her shaken.

She'd been wrong.

Thorfinn Sinclair was more than capable of hurting her.

Rose stumbled back and felt like she was truly falling backward into the abyss. It was a yawning dark chasm she'd sought to avoid by running off to war. But it was here to swallow her up—the meaninglessness that she'd become, perhaps that she'd always been. She'd spent her whole life racing with no destination in sight. She'd thought she'd found purpose on Daytona Beach, yet she had only been clinging to another lost soul's desperate gamble to make his life mean *something*. The spies were real, but her mission . . . her mission was an illusion. It would not bring her peace or even a sense of consequence.

But she would not allow this man—any man—to see her crumble under the incongruous weight of emptiness. She wouldn't show shame, and most of all, she wouldn't reveal her pain. Rose straightened and stared straight at Thorfinn. "You asked me to be a laird."

"I didn't expect you'd take to the role so completely." The words were an ugly sneer. In the midst of all the pain, Rose realized that Thorfinn wasn't angry just at her but also at himself.

"What do you want from me, Mr. Sinclair? I have done my best to make Hamarray and Frest better for the folks who live here." And she'd liked doing it. She'd felt *good* even. She'd never laughed as much as when she'd sat around the table with the Flett children or even when she'd herded sheep with the crofters. And she'd never *felt* as much as when she'd kissed Thorfinn in a sea cave or when she'd lingered with him over a candlelit table while planning new schemes to foster prosperity in the isles.

"Parties, toffs, fast cars, and speedboats aren't going to bring life back to this island." Thorfinn crossed his arms over his chest. "They aren't real, Miss Van Etten. They are fantasies for those who've never known want."

"Are you calling me spoiled?" The last word tasted bitter on Rose's lips. The world was forever calling her that, and she'd always said she didn't care. But . . . but deep down she couldn't escape the truth—something was dead inside her or rather had never lived at all.

Thorfinn stood before her breathing hard, not answering at first. With each second that ticked away, a rawness grew inside Rose.

"You've faced down demons on the Western Front that I can never fully comprehend, but there are things that you will never understand about people like me. We are not playthings for you to move about on a game board as you wish."

"Do you truly believe that is what I'm doing here on Frest and Hamarray?" Rose's voice cracked, and the show of weakness caused her fury to kindle.

A bit of Thorfinn's own rage dimmed, and what she saw in his left eye stunned the ire straight from her. He looked . . . lost, wounded even. As if *she'd* been the one hurling insults, instead of the other way around.

"I don't know what to trust, lass. I can never think properly in this bloody house."

And then he turned and left. Quietly.

Rose stood frozen in the hallway, staring at the door that Thorfinn had so carefully shut behind him. She felt as hollow and empty as the spartan corridor surrounding her. Then she turned, and like a floating phantom, she slowly retreated to the library. It occurred to her as she pushed on the camouflaged panel door that she'd entered the servants' area only once before to search for the formerly elusive keyhole. If it hadn't been for her pursuit of the spy ring, she never would have entered the passage that Thorfinn had automatically chosen for his escape.

When Rose reentered the library, Percy was standing in the middle of the room, his distinguished nose buried in a book—an *upside-down* book. Surreptitiously, he edged toward the proper exit. Despite being a decorated RAF pilot known for his almost suicidal attacks on German observation balloons, he was clearly looking for a quick retreat.

Rose swept her gaze around the room one more time and made her choice. The choice she always made in the end. Oh, she'd tried her darndest to find a purpose, to fill the nothingness, but her "mission" here on Hamarray had left her only more hollowed out than before—for now she truly knew what a shell she was. It was time to stop fighting and accept she would always feel adrift. Oh, she would see this spying mission through. It was too important to the world. But she was going to stop regarding it as some shining goal that would magically transform her into something she was not and never would be.

Tomorrow she would relentlessly begin compiling the viscount's codebook into a usable format. But tonight . . . tonight she was going to fill the abyss with champagne and dancing and bright laughter. The ephemeral bliss would fade away by morning, but it was time for her to embrace the illusion while it lasted instead of searching for something solid always beyond her reach.

"Percy!"

The book bobbled in his hands. He made an attempt to catch it but missed. As it clattered on the wooden floor near his feet, Percy glanced warily in her direction. "Yes, Rose Petal?"

"Does your offer to take me to a party tonight in Edinburgh still stand? If we leave now, we can make it in time, and I suddenly find myself in the mood for a little bit of high society."

"I can have my seaplane ready in an hour or so." Percy grinned, his relief apparent.

"Perfect. That gives me ample time to prepare." And without another word, she walked from the room, ready to don her flashiest ensemble. If she was destined to be a female Dionysus, she was going to be the best bloody Bacchus of the bunch.

<hr />

"How is a connection between souls formed?" Rose tipped her champagne flute toward her audience of one. "Is it this grand metaphysical experience or just an opportunistic relationship that we wrap in layers of sentimentality?"

Rose hiccuped a bit, but thankfully her listener didn't appear to mind. "I've always considered love—all forms of it—hogwash. It's just some pretty lie to make the world less harsh. Even friendship is based on getting something in return . . . or on fulfilling some need."

Her companion remained silent.

"And belonging. What is that? Can any of us truly fit anywhere, or do we just reshape ourselves until we think we do? And what do we get in return? Is there really any escape from emptiness, or do we just fool ourselves into thinking there is meaning? Are we just guarding a grave, hoping someone or something will arise from it despite them being long dead—or perhaps they never even existed at all?"

Her confidant regarded her with kind but penetrating eyes. Rose sipped from the glass again, trying to gather her thoroughly sodden thoughts.

"And purpose? How does one find *that* when one has every material comfort? Is anything truly meaningful? Our bodies all turn to worm food in the end. Is that our true calling—to be fodder for the earth? Is that any less silly than some of the things that we attach significance to? Are we just sentries over our own ultimate demise?"

"Rose, darling?" Percy's hesitant voice broke into Rose's monologue, causing her to jump. Sighing, she swiveled in his direction as he crossed the street and walked toward her. Some of her champagne splashed to the ground, and she regarded the splotch on the pavement with a pout. She really did not want to return to the stuffy benefit inside the Royal Museum of Scotland to retrieve another refreshment.

"Rose Petal." Percy called her name again, his voice gentle, patient. She lifted her chin to regard him.

"Why are you outside in the dark streets and talking to a dog instead of enjoying the party and human company?" Percy asked. "I promised Myrtle that I would keep an eye on you when she begged off tonight's festivities in favor of reading another dull book."

Myrtle and Thorfinn—no, scratch that—*Myrtle* would scold Rose for endangering herself by being alone, especially at night, with spies after her, but Rose didn't care.

She hiccuped again. "Technically, I am addressing the statue of a Skye terrier."

"I don't think that improves matters, darling."

"Greyfriars Bobby is an excellent listener," Rose protested defensively as she swung her glass toward the effigy.

"It is a bronze likeness of a dog mounted on a drinking fountain near a rather scurrilous section of Edinburgh. Don't you think speaking to a sentient creature might be a bit more beneficial?"

"Are you volunteering?" Rose teetered toward him. She really should have worn lower heels. "What advice do you have to spare about devotion and loyalty and belonging and finding a home?"

A *home*? Thunderation, where had that ridiculous notion sprouted from? She wasn't some poor but cheerful waif looking for a place to belong like the inexorably optimistic heroines that haunted the pages of children's literature today. She'd been looking for a purpose, not Green Gables or Sunnybrook Farm.

I thought . . . fighting . . . was . . . for glory . . . but it's for . . . them . . . those . . . those . . . we let . . . into our hearts . . . loved . . . ones. The viscount's—no, *Reggie's* words popped into her mind, taunting . . . no, *challenging* her.

As she tried to concentrate on them, she hiccuped quite loudly. The sound caused her barely formed thoughts to flutter away like butterflies . . . or, given her dark mood, like bloodsucking vampire bats.

Percy shoved his hands into the pockets of his evening pants, causing his tuxedo jacket to bunch. "Perhaps it *is* best that you consult the inanimate terrier."

Rose laughed shortly, the sound ugly to her ears. She couldn't mask the self-loathing—not tonight. She'd come to Edinburgh to lick and hide her wounds, but instead she'd just ripped off the scab and forced herself to bleed. "We're two of a kind, aren't we, Percy? Living life one distraction after another, never pausing for long-overdue self-reflection."

Percy plucked the glass from her hand and downed what little champagne remained. "If you want to engage in philosophical drivel, I am afraid I'm not the right companion. But if you are interested in indulging in another diversion, I know a rather pleasurable pastime that we both enjoy."

Rose sighed and leaned against the tall base upon which Greyfriars Bobby was perched. She'd asked to come to Edinburgh for just such an evening as Percy offered. Dancing. Drinking. Merriment. And more *private* entertainment.

But she'd found she'd lost the taste for it. For all of it.

It should have been depressing, realizing that she could not even glean a moment of sparkle from the glitteriest of events. But it felt . . . liberating? As if she were no longer held under its thrall, no longer drawn to it, no longer an integral *part* of it.

She was a separate entity from the high society she'd been born into . . . which meant she was free to find her own place—to *establish* her own place. Where she chose.

"I think I shall just retire to bed. *Alone.*"

Percy heaved a melodramatic sigh. "I was afraid that would be your answer."

"Sorry I'm such a bore."

Percy gave her a fond grin. "You are never a bore, Rose Petal. After all, it is not every day a man can watch a beautiful woman engage in a philosophical debate with a statue of a dog."

"Shhhh. You'll insult Bobby. He takes these matters very seriously." Rose gave the old boy one quick goodbye pat on his bronze snout.

"I'm sure he does." Percy crooked his elbow in her direction. "Shall I accompany you back to the hotel before I attend another function?"

"I would be delighted to have your company." Rose linked her arm with his as they headed toward the Royal Mile. "But don't stay out too late. I plan to leave bright and early in the morning. I want to go to Hamarray."

Percy made a face. "I really cannot see the hold that windy, desolate place has on you. I admit it has a certain charm in the spring, but can you imagine it in the winter? Whyever do you want to go back there so soon?"

"It's home."

Those two words—so innocuous—slipped from Rose's mouth. In her drunken state, she almost didn't notice. When she did, she jerked to a halt and nearly turned her ankle. She would have fallen if Percy hadn't held her steady. She had never, ever considered a place *home*. Even in childhood, she'd always thought of where she lived as the New York residence or the Daytona house. Those edifices of brick and mortar (or, in the case of the Florida residence, coquina) were the domain of her parents, and Rose had just happened to be a temporary occupant.

But Muckle Skaill . . . Muckle Skaill was *hers*. Not because of a title, or a deed, or any claim of ownership. But because of how she felt—not about the building but about the land and the people. About shy Ann Inkster and earnest Young Thomas. About the proud David Craigie and his windmill. About the wonderful Flett children and their excited questions and never-ending enthusiasm.

Percy scuffed his shoe against the street and then lifted his head to face her. "Rose? The question that you asked Greyfriars Bobby about connection? I think you've just answered it. Home is a rare thing for creatures like us. If you've found one, do not allow a stuffed, pompous prig to chase you from it."

Rose looked at Percy, but she saw Barbury standing before her. She hadn't been wrong about the viscount. Reggie *had* found his purpose. It hadn't been about rooting out the spy ring—at least not directly. He was trying to bring peace to "those we let into our hearts." Back then, she'd automatically assumed that he'd meant lovers, but it was so much deeper than that.

Rose didn't need a mission to give her life meaning. She needed connections, and she was beginning to forge them with the people of Frest. Sinclair might have dismissed her, but she would *not* dismiss herself from the place she had begun to care deeply for.

Myrtle had been right when she'd asked Rose if she was falling in love with Orkney. And this time, Rose was no longer afraid of her answer to her friend's question.

———◆———

"Can you circle the islands before you land?" Rose shouted at Percy as she caught a glimpse of Fornhowe from the window of his Short 184 seaplane.

Percy glanced at her and nodded, his light-blue eyes unreadable instead of brimming with his normal joviality. He'd done all the talking on their flight, yelling over the motor in an effort to make conversation. At one time, Rose would have been bellowing right back at him, not wanting to endure the silence or, in this case, the constant roar of the engine. For discourse meant distraction from thought.

But Rose had found herself wanting the opportunity to think, craving it even. Watching Aberdeenshire and the foothills of the Cairngorms hadn't soothed her. The pink castles seemed too perfect—like a sugared confectionary that would dissolve in a single spring shower. Even as the landscape beneath them had grown more ragged, she still had not been satisfied. She wanted back to the drama and peace of Frest and Hamarray. She had a race to plan, a legal whiskey distillery to found, and a spy ring to root out of *her* home.

Something opened inside her when she saw the round crest of Frest. Although she couldn't tell who was who, she could see the Flett children running about their croft. The pony, Charlie, glanced skyward, and Rose could just hear him snorting in disgust. A figure sat under the eaves of Widow Flett's cottage—most likely the woman herself engaged in knitting. There were the other homes of the islanders, neat tidy plots of land. She knew each of them now . . . and their stories too . . . those who had braved wartime on the isle, those who'd returned, those who were still making their way home, and those who never would. She'd heard tales about selkies, trows, mermaids, and finmen, along with the more recent stories of sailors, soldiers, fishermen, weavers, knitters, and cheese makers.

Everywhere Rose looked, she saw the people of Frest. A wonderful sense of homecoming filled her, and she hoped that these welcoming, hardworking people would come to embrace her as much as she did them.

"Did you know that I'll be assisting with the peat cutting tomorrow? Not only do the crofters need it for their homes, but we're planning on increasing whiskey production by leaps and bounds over the next season," Rose shouted as Percy dipped toward the rocky cliffs. Puffins, skuas, fulmars, and other seabirds hopped about, some with fish dripping from their mouths, others arguing among themselves. Below, she caught the brief flash of a seal's head bobbing in the gentle waves.

"You? Cutting bits of mud?"

"Technically, I will be helping to stack it."

"An even more ludicrous image."

"I'm going to do it," Rose said, and a sense of rightness dropped over her. It was *not* up to Thorfinn Sinclair to declare who or what she was. She was laird of Hamarray, and she had a duty, from helping with the peats to ousting a dangerous spy ring—even if the latter meant turning in a resident of Frest. For her responsibility was to all the crofters—not just one but the people as a whole.

"Play in the dirt? It is full of crawly things." Percy feigned a shudder.

"I've never been squeamish."

"Wouldn't you rather try your hand at racing? My plane versus your speedboat?" Percy asked.

"Nope. I know exactly what I want to do on the morrow, and that's arranging peat to dry."

When a gal set out to find some purpose in her life, there was no shame in starting out small.

Chapter 14

"Is there a reason I am assisting you today while Rose is over yonder working with Young Thomas?" Astrid asked as she lifted out one of the bricks of peat that Sinclair had just cut from the earth with the tusker.

The people of Frest were spread out on the hillside of Hamarray as they worked in pairs to remove pieces of wet sod to dry into fuel. Rose's generosity of reopening the peats on Hamarray had invigorated the islanders. Despite the backbreaking work, the mood was jovial, and the old songs filled the air.

Sinclair, however, did *not* share in the high spirits. Not only did he feel like an utter lout about what he'd said to Rose, but he was also worried about the German agents. Would Rose risk her life and try to unravel the spy ring without him?

Sinclair grunted, not exactly sure how to answer his cousin's question about Rose. He hadn't expected the lass to show up for the harvest today—not with the awful words he'd spewed. She hadn't deserved it. He still didn't approve of her inviting guests like the Duke of Newsberry to the island, but he'd acted like his stepda, making up his own mind without taking time to consider the other person's side of things.

The more Sinclair reviewed the conversation in his head, the more he realized that Rose hadn't actually *said* that she'd decided definitively to open the hotel. He'd been so raw after both reliving the night Mar had blinded him and unraveling Reggie's cipher that he'd unfairly imputed duplicity he shouldn't have.

"Si-in-clair." Astrid drew out his name. "Did you act like a gappus?"

"Maybe," he huffed out as he sliced through the layers of soil.

"Is this perchance related to how you stormed my house asking if the Duke of Newsberry had besmirched my honor?"

"I didn't phrase it that way." Sinclair jammed down the thin blade so hard it got stuck.

"That is precisely what you said. It was dreadfully melodramatic," Astrid pointed out. "Also, when cutting peat, the point is not to beat the ground into submission; it is to slice it."

"You know how my mum was treated." Sinclair wrestled with the tusker and succeeded only in wedging it into an even more difficult angle.

"I am not your mother, Sinclair," Astrid said softly. "And Rose is assuredly *not* the earl presiding over lawless debauchery. A ceilidh and an auto race are not the same as an orgy and cockfighting."

Sinclair glanced around to make sure no one had heard them, especially the children. "Astrid."

"Well, that's what you're concerned about, isn't it?"

"The previous Duke of Newsberry was one of the earl's most frequent guests. His nephew looks exactly like him. Acts like him too. He called you *delectable*." Sinclair twisted the handle so hard for a moment he thought he'd broken the blade.

Astrid reached up and touched his hand. "He's a rogue, Sinclair, but he is not a monster. He *did* shower me with pretty words and clever quips, but I suspect he flirts with every woman he encounters. I have led enough male bird-watchers to know who are the harmless ones and who are dangerous. The duke only teased me as far as I was comfortable. He was a very pleasant client who actually listened attentively to my descriptions. He certainly did not view me as his for the taking just because he paid me some coin to direct him to seafowl."

A coldness settled deep inside Sinclair. "And others have?"

Astrid smiled wickedly. "Why do you think I carry a knife in my boot? There has never been a man that I could not handle."

"Why didn't you tell me this before?"

Astrid reached up and cupped his face. "Because I knew it would worry you and you'd fash yourself over it. Reggie and you both saw to it that I could defend myself. I'm only telling you now to say that I think you misjudged the duke by conflating him with his uncle. Rose wouldn't have sicced a lecher on me."

Guilt churned inside him. "I practically accused her of operating a brothel."

Astrid's eyes widened. "No wonder she is working with Young Thomas instead of you. You're lucky she allowed you to walk away from an insult like that."

"I could only think about all those times the earl 'introduced' my mother to his cronies. I was in that house where it all happened, and my mind—"

He trailed off when Astrid's fingers brushed against his hands fisted on the handle of the tusker. "I understand, Sinclair. I know your past, the whole island does, but Rose does not."

He stopped struggling against the peat cutter and rested a moment. "Do you think I should tell her?"

"If you don't want her abandoning the isle thinking you're a jealous gappus, aye," Astrid said.

"Rose is going to leave Hamarray eventually. She's not one for staying in the back of beyond."

"She's making a lot of improvements for someone who doesn't intend to stay," Astrid pointed out. "And she's still here, with us, cutting peat even after you insulted her. That says something, doesn't it?"

Aye, it did. He'd misjudged Rose sorely.

"Even if she would set her sights on a crofter like me, she's not the marrying kind. She's said so herself."

"Then maybe it's up to you to prove there's some value in it and that there's something here on Frest worth sticking around for."

Sinclair scanned the peat field until he found Rose. She was standing in a ditch, her practical skirt stained with mud. A smudge of it spread across her cheek and onto her nose. Her red-painted lips were parted as she laughed, her white teeth a contrast against the bright color. Her tam-o'-shanter had mostly slipped from her hair, and the black strands stood in wild tufts. Young Thomas must have said something amusing. The lad's smiles had been rare since he'd returned from the trenches, but he was grinning now and looking as proud as a peacock.

Rose could do that—make a body feel good about themselves. All the islanders were growing to like her. Although his stepda would never embrace an outsider, he grumbled less and less. Rose wasn't trying to change their ways. Hell, she wanted to *celebrate* them.

"No matter what, she deserves an apology, Sinclair," Astrid said quietly.

He nodded. This time when he pulled on the tusker, he easily freed it.

After walking over to Young Thomas and Rose, he stopped a few feet away. "Mind if we switch partners for a peedie bit?"

Young Thomas looked between him and Rose, clearly sensing some sort of tension between them. He tugged on his flatcap nervously. "Whatever Miss Van Etten wants is fine by me, sir."

Rose shielded her eyes as she gazed up at Sinclair from the hip-high pit she was standing in. "Is there a particular estate matter you wish to discuss?"

He nearly winced at her cool tone, but truth be told, he deserved worse. "More of an apology."

Young Thomas's eyebrows flew beneath his strawberry-blond bangs, but he wisely didn't say anything. He just lifted his tusker and slowly retreated.

"All right." Rose waved toward the exposed soil where Young Thomas had been working. "Dig away."

Sinclair sliced through the layers of sod, wishing he were as proficient at cutting through the muck he'd made of things. "I was in the wrong."

"About which point exactly?" Rose spoke with a politeness so sharp she could have used it to break through the peat if she'd wanted.

"Both in what I said and in how I said it," Sinclair answered. He glanced around, wishing he could say more, but this wasn't the place and time.

"I am still holding the ceilidh and the race next week, and Percy is here to help me. Those plans cannot be stopped, and the people of Frest *are* looking forward to it—with the exception of you and your stepda." Rose stabbed her shovel at the clump he'd just loosened with such force it crumbled in the center.

He still wasn't ready to fully embrace the ideas of rich toffs making Hamarray their playland, but he resolved to give it a chance—for Rose's sake and for the crofters'. "I truly hope it will be the success that you think it will be."

"Do you still believe I'm delivering sin to Hamarray?" Rose asked with brittle sweetness.

Sinclair stopped the motion of the tusker. "I know you intend to bring good, Rose. But I have my reasons for feeling the way that I do—reasons I should probably tell you."

Rose lifted both of her hands. "We have a long, tedious day ahead of ourselves. What better time is there?"

"If it is all the same to you, it's a conversation best held in private." Sinclair was going to have to reopen a lot of old wounds, and he'd never been one to bleed in public. Even the mere idea of talking about his past made his body tense, as if preparing for a devastating blow. He dreaded revealing the old horrors more than he'd ever feared entering the boxing ring.

"Okay," Rose said a little less stiffly than before. "I can wait if it's important to you."

"Thank you."

She whacked the exposed shelf of mud. "Before we continue working together in any capacity, I want to make one thing clear."

"Yes?" Sinclair asked as both tension and relief swirled through him.

"I cannot abide jealousy, if your reaction had anything to do with that. Percy is my friend, a good friend."

"My reaction to him had very little to do with that emotion," Sinclair promised. "And Astrid has made it exceedingly clear that I was being an overprotective arse."

Rose's lips twitched slightly on the last. "Astrid is very insightful."

Sinclair laughed as some of the pressure inside him lifted. "Aye. I won't argue with her on this observation."

"I suppose we should get back to work. I don't want it bandied about that the laird doesn't pull her own weight," Rose said with her old humor.

"I don't think anyone will accuse her of that." Sinclair couldn't stop the fondness that crept into his voice. Rose lifted her chin, and their gazes met. A connection shimmered between them still—he hadn't severed it completely after all. Weakened it? *Aye.* But destroyed it entirely? *Nay.*

"Rose Mae Van Etten!" a woman's horrified voice called out. "What in heaven's name are you doing in that ditch? You look a fright!"

Sinclair turned to find a man and a woman sitting in the back of Rose's touring car with a smartly dressed chauffeur in front. Sinclair had been so focused on his conversation with Rose that he hadn't heard the vehicle's approach. The female visitor wore a tight-fitting velvet hat with a brooch and a single feather pinned to it. Her mink-fur coat looked even more luxurious than the ones Rose wore. The man in a wool overcoat beside her stayed mostly hidden from view, his face partially obscured by an open newspaper.

"Mother?" Rose shielded her eyes. "Whatever are you doing here?"

Sinclair nearly dropped his tusker on his foot. He'd been bracing himself to reveal his past with his mother and the earl, but he hadn't been girding himself to meet *her* parents.

The horror on Mrs. Van Etten's delicately boned face did not diminish. "You have been rusticating too long, and I'm worried about the rumors I'm hearing that you intend to open a hotel on this godforsaken isle. It is bad enough you're holding a race here. You have social obligations back in civilization now that the dreadful war is over. And I see that I had every right to be worried. A true lady should always look her best. Living on a desert island is no reason to . . . to . . . ." The woman waved her hand wordlessly in the direction of Rose's mud-soaked skirt.

Sinclair stiffened. The woman trilled the words brightly, but that didn't make them less of a public dressing-down. He wanted to defend Rose, but he simply did not know how. If he tried speaking, it would inevitably make matters worse.

To his surprise, Rose seemed entirely unperturbed. Instead, she laughed, not bitterly but with true amusement.

"Mother, dear, it is hardly a desert island. And I think the mud is rather becoming. Don't you?" Rose spun gaily around in the trench.

"Rose, stop that this minute! You must hurry back to the house and change before anyone recognizes you."

Rose stopped her dancing, but she made no move to lay down her shovel. "I gave my word, Mother, that I'd help for the day."

"Mr. Van Etten!" Her mother turned frantically to the gentleman, who hadn't looked up from his periodical during the entire conversation. "Mr. Van Etten!"

When the man still did not react, Mrs. Van Etten shook his arm. Blinking owlishly, he slowly pivoted toward his wife. He gave his head a quick little jerk. "Yes, my dear Mrs. Van Etten?"

Rose's parents still referred to each other by their surnames, not their Christian ones? That felt terribly cold. Even his crotchety stepda had not only called Sinclair's mum by her first name but had even used a few pet ones.

"Your daughter is digging in the mud!" Rose's mother clutched her husband's arm so hard that his coat bunched up.

Mr. Van Etten peered around his wife. "So she is."

"Please tell her to stop. You know the Duke of Newsberry is on the island."

Mr. Van Etten sighed and leaned over his wife. "Rose, dear, would you please stop causing your mother to fret? You know how easily overset she can become."

"I made a commitment, Daddy." Rose flashed a winsome smile.

Her father nodded absently and turned toward his wife. "Evidently, she's obligated."

"But the duke—" Mrs. Van Etten began to protest, but her husband interrupted.

"Rose, does this future hotel of yours have a telephone?" The industrialist's thin mustache twitched impatiently.

"I'm afraid not, Daddy."

He exhaled heavily. "Telegraph line?"

"A dinghy bringing mail comes by once a week," Rose offered cheekily.

"Bah." Her father slapped his paper downward in a dismissive motion. "I do not see how you intend to run a proper hotel without modern amenities."

Sinclair's hold on his tusker tightened. Despite his own misgivings about the hotel, it meant a great deal to Rose, and her father was dismissing it sight unseen.

"Daddy," Rose said with fond exasperation untouched by hurt or anger, "if I even decide to open a hotel, it will be a *retreat*. People will come here to get away from the pressures of their lives. Those who want to stay connected wouldn't travel here in the first place. We're too remote."

Guilt peppered Sinclair as he realized how wrongly his mind had twisted Rose's similar statements to Percy two days before. She did not mean to take advantage of the island's solitude to hide sordid behavior, but rather she intended to create a peaceful escape. Given her experiences in the war, it made sense, and Sinclair should have understood what she'd meant. He would've, too, if he had been thinking properly.

Rose's father frowned thoughtfully. "Perhaps you're right, kitten, but isolation does not suit me. I have pressing matters to attend to. I will stay in Kirkwall, but your mother can enjoy our room at your place. I'll stop by in the afternoon."

"I shall love to take in the sea air here," her mother added as her husband returned to reading his paper. "I may, however, be joining your father on the main island on the day of this dreadful race. You know I cannot abide the sound of those wretched motors all firing up at the same time. And the smell! My nerves just cannot accept that my darling girl chooses to risk her precious life in those horrid contraptions. A proper touring car is one thing, but those machines you drive are positively nightmarish."

Sinclair inwardly winced at Mrs. Van Etten's almost cruel dismissal of her daughter's passion. Worried, he glanced at Rose, but she looked only mildly exasperated.

"I'm sure you will find plenty in Kirkwall to distract you, Mother," Rose said, her voice pitched to be soothing.

"Good." Mrs. Van Etten fluffed her hair. "Now will you please change into proper, clean clothes before the duke espies you?"

"I can assure you that Percy will not set a foot near muddy work, especially if there is any chance that he might be commandeered into doing it," Rose said.

"He is not the only noble who will be visiting Hamarray. Your father and I invited the earl we met in London. Didn't we, Mr. Van Etten?"

"Yes, darling," the man said absently as he flipped a page.

"Exactly *which* earl did you invite, Mother? You have a habit of collecting their friendships." For the first time, Rose seemed actively annoyed.

Mrs. Van Etten's lips pursed at Rose's words. "Why, the Earl of Mar, of course."

Even though this was what he and Rose had planned, Sinclair felt an old familiar panic rise within him. Anger came, too, hot and swift. But mostly he was filled with the need to defend as his grip instinctually tightened once again on his tusker, preparing to fend off an enemy not yet there.

All around them the people of Frest stopped pretending that they weren't listening to the conversation. Mrs. Van Etten, however, took no notice of the audience, probably viewing them as beneath her consideration.

Rose shot Sinclair a brief but pregnant glance before she returned her focus to her mother. "The Earl of Mar, you say. I can't see why you'd invite him."

"I know he's a bit older, darling, but he still cuts a fine figure. He was very interested in hearing about the improvements you were making to his old home. He cannot wait to see it and you again. You must have made *quite* the impression upon him earlier this spring."

"Mother, if I had desired the Earl of Mar, I could have married him months ago rather than buying this island from him."

"Nonsense, dear. He's got a title. Of course you want him." Mrs. Van Etten turned suddenly toward the chauffeur. "Harrold, I am feeling quite peckish. Proceed to the main house, please."

The lumbering touring car ambled away, leaving utter silence in its wake. Sinclair could feel the stares boring into him. Everyone knew what the return of the Earl of Mar meant to him . . . everybody but Rose. Now when Sinclair confessed the truth to her, he wouldn't just be talking about specters from the past. She would bear witness to his current pain . . . and fears. It was a deeper vulnerability than he'd intended to reveal but one that he now had no choice but to fully expose.

And that left him even more shaken than Mrs. Van Etten's announcement of Mar's imminent return.

＝◆＝

Rose fiddled with a cigarette as she waited in the library for Thorfinn to arrive. She had just finished organizing the words in the codebook into an alphabetical list.

It wasn't just the knowledge that soon she might know the answers that had been eluding her for half a year now that made Rose edgier than normal. Thorfinn had promised to apologize to her yesterday, but they hadn't had a private moment between her finalizing the organization of Reggie's codebook and Thorfinn overseeing the spring planting. As if the friction between Thorfinn and Rose weren't ample enough, she was also dealing with her parents' unexpected visit and Mar's impending return.

Leave it to her mother to personally invite a creature like the earl. All Verity Van Etten ever saw was the outside packaging, never the inside, while her father always paid attention to the details and not the whole. Although Rose supposed that her mother's attempt to see her daughter married into a title was benefiting the investigation by bringing Mar back, Rose would rather not have to deal with the man who tried to force his attentions on her and who'd treated his own son like a mere servant. The entire situation made Rose want to scream, but then again, her parents often had that effect on her. They had an inglorious knack of making her feel like a specimen simultaneously splayed open on the dissecting table and also shoved into a jar of formaldehyde and forgotten.

Rose shifted, trying to get comfortable. It didn't work. She had worn her most sinfully comfy clothes—loose silk, balloon-like trousers and blouse created by none other than Paul Poiret, but even the paja-ma-like creation did not inspire relaxation. She wanted to jump up and prowl. Or race. Or shoot through the sea.

"You didn't need to wait until Young Thomas fetched me to start translating the letter." Thorfinn burst into the room, each word coming out in a huff. It took quite a bit to get Thorfinn Sinclair out of breath. Clearly he'd not only rowed across the water using his full strength, but he'd likely barged straight up the hill as well.

"The letter is addressed to you," Rose said pragmatically as she forced her conflicting emotions toward Thorfinn aside. "Your brother wanted you to be the recipient, and a few minutes' delay didn't matter. Besides, it shall be faster with the two of us working together."

Thorfinn nodded. When he stepped over to the chair next to Rose, he paused, as if not sure of his reception.

Frankly, Rose was not positive of it either. She was still cross with him over his harsh words toward her and Percy, but his initial apology *had* felt sincere.

Deciding to gamble on Thorfinn providing a good explanation for his behavior, Rose patted the seat next to her. He gave her a grateful look and sank down.

"Why don't you call out each word from your brother's letter?" Rose suggested. "I'll look it up in the guide I created and tell you what it means. Then you can write down the correct term. That way, you'll be the first to see Reggie's message."

"Thank you."

The rough emotion in Thorfinn's voice made Rose soften toward him just a little bit more. Nothing about this was easy for him. She needed to remember that as much as her emotions were stirred up, Thorfinn's were exponentially more engendered. This *was* his brother's last letter to him.

They conducted the translation with a solemnity akin to a memorial service. Each word that they called out sounded like part of a somber Gregorian chant. With an air of reverence, Thorfinn recorded each word on a fresh sheet of paper until they reached the end of Reggie's original letter.

Neither of them spoke for a long moment as Thorfinn stared down at the revealed message. His eye did not flick across the page, and Rose knew that he was gathering the strength to read the contents.

"I can leave," she told him softly, instinctively reaching for his hand and giving it a squeeze.

"Nay," Thorfinn said, his voice low and unfathomably deep. "Stay, please. I'm glad you are here."

An encompassing ache filled Rose at the words. Despite the anger that had passed between them a few days ago, she wished she could help alleviate his pain . . . and felt a bit honored that he wanted her by his side during this intensely private moment.

Thorfinn needed *her*.

Which was an odd feeling. No one had ever really needed Rose before. Yes, her patients had relied on her to bring them to safety. But that was a physical thing. An interchangeable thing. But Thorfinn needed *her* presence, *her* words, *her* comfort.

And that . . . that frightened Rose. For it meant acknowledging that she needed him too—that they'd formed a bond. And a connection like that opened a body to pain . . . and to love.

But Rose didn't run. She gripped Thorfinn's hand even tighter.

He drew in his breath, his muscular shoulders rising nearly to his ears as he began to read in a deep, slightly unsteady voice:

> Dear Sin,
> I'll begin with the classic line—if you're reading this,
> I'm afraid that I am dead.

Thorfinn broke off with a faint bittersweet twist to his lips. "That was Reggie. Irreverent to the end."

"Even in the poste de secours, his wry humor was obvious." Rose's eyes burned as she remembered the brave man whose hand she'd held as he'd breathed his last.

"Reggie always liked to make people smile." Thorfinn's voice seemed on the verge of breaking as he rapidly blinked his left eye. He drew in air, and even Rose swore she could feel its raggedness rumble in her own chest. Resolutely, Thorfinn gripped the paper and began again.

> I hope it was a heroic death at least. If I had to die
> young, I pray that it was for a good cause. I used to
> want to die in glory, but I have learned that this dam-
> nable war holds little of that. You did the honorable
> thing, the brave thing by choosing to stay to provide
> for your younger siblings.

Thorfinn's voice did crack then. As he took in gulps to steady himself, Rose rubbed his arm with her free hand. She knew the doubts he faced and could only imagine how much he'd needed to hear his brother say that.

"He's right, you know," Rose whispered fiercely, tears burning in her own eyes.

A jerk of his head seemed to be the only acknowledgment that Thorfinn was currently capable of giving before he continued on.

> My behavior toward you was not only selfish, but childish. I cannot tell you how many times I thanked God that you were not at my side.

Thorfinn swallowed hard, and Rose knew he was taking a moment to absorb Reggie's words. He seemed to gather strength from them before he plowed on.

> One of those occasions was when I was captured by the Germans. I was badly wounded from shrapnel and sent to a hospital in German-occupied Belgium. I was fortunate to be placed under the care of a nurse whose father was English, and who had grown up in Kent. She'd been working in Belgium before the hostilities and had kept her position. At great risk to her own life, she helped British prisoners of war escape. Once I was capable of moving under my own locomotion, she arranged my perilous dash to freedom. Before I left, she told me that many of the wounded Allies had mentioned that it seemed as if the Germans had known their plans beforehand. I was the most well-connected prisoner that she had helped, and she urged me to uncover more.

While I was recovering, I formed connections with men from the War Office. I managed to secure a desk position there, and I began to unravel a spy ring. Not knowing who I could trust—and how high the problem went—I traveled to Hamarray to sort out my findings. I wished terribly to call upon you, but I was ashamed, and I did not want to bring danger to you and your siblings.

"Astrid was right that Reggie had felt too guilty to see me." Thorfinn's voice was thick as his throat muscles seemed to work double to get the sentence out. Rose wrapped one arm around him and squeezed.

"Despite the fact I knew him so briefly, even I saw that he sorely regretted how he treated you," Rose said. "He cared deeply for you, Thorfinn. You were one of the loved ones he gave his life to protect."

Thorfinn's head bobbed in an almost reflexive action—as if he needed to move to release some of the emotional pressure bearing down upon him. Rose stopped talking, and the two of them sat for a beat or two in silence. She wished again that she could ease some of Thorfinn's pain, but the best she could do was sit quietly, offering support.

When he was able to go on, Thorfinn began to read again.

But I felt safe here—too safe. In my foolishness I told a single person about how I escaped. It was only after that I began to notice strange things. Odd things. I thought it was just my damnable imagination that had me thinking that spies were everywhere. But it wasn't.

I began to secrete my work in caches about the island—insurance for my safety and protection of my research if I approached the wrong person with my findings. Then before I placed everything in motion, I received news that the nurse who had saved my life had been discovered and was being held captive by the

Germans. I instantly wondered if I was the cause of her capture—if I had confided in the wrong person about her.

"Does he say who?" The question burst from Rose's lips before she could stop it. Immediately, she clasped her hand over her mouth. She needed to allow Thorfinn to read the letter at his own pace, but the nervous fear rumbling through her made her anxious. It sounded dreadfully like someone on Hamarray or Frest *was* involved, and the confirmation shook her more than being rear-ended by another automobile.

Thorfinn, however, did not seem annoyed by her outburst. Instead, he scanned the letter. When he spoke, he sounded weary . . . defeated. "No, lass. He's only left us more blasted clues to follow for the rest of his notes."

"There's more searching to be done?" Rose's eyes fluttered shut as overwhelming exhaustion swept over her too. She had so hoped for answers, but she and Thorfinn had just found more pain and questions.

"He does explain away one of the mysteries that's been plaguing me," Thorfinn said, but he didn't sound relieved . . . just fatigued. In a tired voice, he read on.

As I write this letter, I am about to return to the Western Front in an attempt to free my former nurse. I doubt I shall return, but I must try—even if it means dressing as a French poilu, crossing No Man's Land, and then finding a German officer's uniform to wear. I can tell no one of my plans. I know not who to trust. I am sorry that I used that date for the cipher, but it is the only one that just the two of us would know.

I dare not lay out my findings in this missive, as I fear it is still too easily discoverable even with all the precautions I made. I leave for you more riddles to determine the locale of my conclusions.

Signets mark the king's great stand.

Centuries of rocky love doth keep the heart.

Pitch 'twas game where north winds doth swept the dust.

Surgeons slice and operate nigh the shade of rest.

Yours until the sea stacks,

R

"Do you know what he means?" Rose asked softly.

"Nay." Thorfinn shook his head as he reached for the translation. "I haven't the foggiest idea at the moment, Rose."

"It'll come to you in due time." Rose gave him an understanding squeeze. "The letter was a bit of a deluge of emotion for you—for both of us. We both need time to mull it over."

"Reggie was close to Astrid. And if she was involved . . . well, that casts suspicion on Widow Flett, my stepda, and . . . just about everyone—although I cannot see Astrid's grandmother and Sigurd taking up spying. The two of them wouldn't bring danger to Frest—no matter how much money they could make. But Astrid is young and has had such a hard life of it already. She always swore she wouldn't be a gutter girl preparing fish forever." Raw pain laced Thorfinn's words as he squeezed and unsqueezed his left hand. An echoing sadness filled Rose, and she wished she could deny his suspicion about his cousin—both to him and to herself. But she could not.

"What about the earl?" Rose asked. "Was he in residence at Muckle Skaill at the time?"

"Aye." The barest hint of life came back into Thorfinn's voice. "And Reggie could never see his father for who he was. He might have told him."

"Mar *did* take our bait," Rose pointed out. "It will give us the perfect opportunity to watch him. We'll unravel this spy ring one way or another."

"I just wish I could figure out Reggie's riddles so we could end this once and for all." Thorfinn didn't look at Rose as he spoke. Instead, he stared down at their translation of his brother's letter, his neat, precise handwriting so different from the viscount's brazen scrawl.

"Maybe we should go somewhere else. You said that you don't think well in Muckle Skaill."

His head snapped in her direction. "You remember that?"

"Yes."

He glanced away and rubbed at his puckered skin. She'd noticed he did that when working through something that upset him. It was the same as her cigarettes. What did that say about the two of them that he automatically sought an old wound and she an old vice?

"There's a lot of specters floating in these hallways, but it's time I told you about them. They're all tied up in this whole bloody thing," Thorfinn ground out.

Rose swallowed, wondering how she could make this easier for him. Maybe a simple, direct question would help. "The date. What is the significance of the date between you and your brother?"

Thorfinn's undamaged eye fluttered closed. When he reopened it, the sheer pain and turmoil in his gaze tore at Rose.

"It was the day that the Earl of Mar blinded me."

"The earl!" Pinpricks of cold dotted Rose's skin. His own father had maimed him?

"I don't think he intended to inflict the extent of the damage that he ultimately did, but the fact that he'd almost killed me didn't much bother him." Thorfinn's voice was hollow, mechanical. "He wasn't just laird here on Hamarray or even a mere peer of the realm. He was a god—leading the hunt, the excess, the merriment, the ruination."

"A Dionysus." Rose had never thought about the term from the other side—those who did not command the party but were forced to make it happen. Guilt awoke inside her again as she thought of the frivolous life that she'd led.

Thorfinn swallowed. "Aye. But he was a cruel one, Rose. You are not. But three days ago when I said those awful things about you in the servants' hall—you and the earl blended in my mind. It was likely the shock of seeing the duke."

"Percy?" Rose asked in disbelief. Percy was no candidate for moral propriety, but she could not imagine him associating with the type of debauchery Thorfinn was hinting at. Besides, Percy would have been a child himself. "Had you met him before?"

"Nay, but physically he is remarkably like his late uncle, who was a frequent visitor to Hamarray. He was . . . especially fond of my mother."

Rose had no trouble understanding his meaning. She felt as if someone had dunked her into an ice bath as the horror spread through her.

"When the Earl of Mar first took notice of my mother, he considered her just his. He said pretty things, gave her a trinket or two— nothing that a real mistress would receive, but my mother grew up with nothing, so it meant a great deal to her. He—as he would boast— groomed her. He was not particularly happy when I was born, but he allowed her to keep me, provided I would be a quiet presence and that I would work when I was old enough."

Pain for Thorfinn blistered inside Rose.

"Mar . . ." Thorfinn swallowed. "He—he grew bored with my mother . . . or perhaps less jealous of her. It amused him to share her. With the duke. With the others. They liked suffering. All of them. They had illegal cockfights all the time. I hated those. Hated the sounds. The dogfights were even worse. Sometimes . . . sometimes they'd pay the footmen to box or, if they wanted a laugh, us younger boys. They found it a grand lark."

"Oh, Thorfinn." Rose, who always had a quip at the ready, had nothing to say in the face of such brutality. She reached for him once more, and he accepted the embrace, pulling her close against him.

"When I got older, I would try to bar the gentlemen from seeing her, but I was still a slight lad. The earl would knock me about for my insolence, but it never stopped me from trying. Then one night—that night—he pushed me into the fire grate."

Rose tried to stop her gasp, but she could not manage it. She had witnessed the horrors of war—the damage that humans could wreak on each other. She'd heard the cries, the screams, the moans, the silence. But a father treating his own child in such a manner . . .

And this was *Thorfinn*. Steady, strong, good-hearted Thorfinn—the one who eschewed war to care for his siblings. The one who fought for his neighbors' livelihoods. The one who'd dug through rubble to bring Rose into the starlight.

"Mar passed out from drink, and another servant came to investigate. Not knowing who could help, she woke Reggie. He was only twelve at the time, but he was already more of a laird than the misbegotten earl—even if Reggie could never stand up to his da. My brother managed to secrete my mother and me away from the house. He rowed us to Frest and knocked on my stepda's door. He knew Sigurd hated the earl for ordering the sheep off Hamarray to turn the isle into game lands. My stepfather was also the only one on either island willing to stand up to Mar. Sigurd fell in love with my mum, and eventually she with him. It was a relationship born of necessity, but it made their feelings for each other no less real or strong."

"No wonder you responded the way you did when Percy mentioned Astrid." Hurt ripped through Rose, but with it came a greater understanding of Thorfinn. "I promise you that Percy is not his uncle. He is a shameful flirt, but he would never pressure any woman or take advantage of her situation in life. I wouldn't allow him anywhere near Frest or Hamarray if that was the case."

"I know that," Thorfinn said, turning in her arms so that they faced each other now. "I just . . . just couldn't bloody well think. I was already uneasy at being in Muckle Skaill, and then the new duke popped up like a congealed ghost talking about Astrid, and I lost all reason. From how your friend was talking, it sounded to me like you'd decided that the plan for a retreat was a foregone fact, although looking back, I realize I'd foolishly jumped to conclusions."

Rose cupped Thorfinn's dear face as his reaction made painful sense to her. "I promise you that no definitive decision on the hotel has or will be made until the people of Frest finalize it. Just as importantly, you don't have to ever come into this house if you don't wish it. We can conduct estate business at your cottage."

"I'm still the land agent, then?"

"I couldn't find a better one, Thorfinn. Your devotion to these isles, these people—it . . . it humbles me."

"Your tough kindness humbles me, Rose." Now it was he who framed her face.

The observation startled her. "Any toughness is mostly bravado, I'm afraid. And I am not known for my sentimentality."

"That's because you do not allow the people to witness the real you."

His simple statement made her feel more vulnerable than any physical nakedness ever could. Rose responded as she always did when real emotion threatened. "And you think you've actually seen the authentic me, do you, buster?"

"I know that you have more heart in you than your two parents combined. The compassion you have, I doubt they taught it to you. In fact, I suspect they're the reason you hide it. It's clear that they have no clue what to do with the brightness inside you, Rose. I imagine that hurt, and it was easier to shut it off than show it. I know a thing or two about burying pain and sweeping over rejection."

Tears Rose didn't know she had in her smarted the backs of her eyes. How had he detected the loneliness when no one ever had? She'd thought that she never wanted anyone to realize the emptiness in her . . . or maybe she'd really been waiting for someone to acknowledge it, to acknowledge *her*.

"You do know I'm considered terribly spoiled."

To Rose's surprise, he pretended to sniff her. "Nay. You don't seem rotten to me. In fact, you seem just about perfect."

She lightly punched his arm. "I mean by material things."

He sobered and lowered his forehead to hers. "You're not that either. I'm sorry it took me so long to fully see you, Rose. To fully appreciate you."

"How can you blame yourself when I don't even know who I am anymore?" The confession bubbled out of her, and she almost clasped her hand over her mouth. She could not believe she'd just voiced that. She barely even allowed herself to acknowledge it.

"What do you mean?" His thumbs drifted over her cheekbones, and warmth gushed through her, soothing her embarrassment.

"I've been . . . lost. Nothing gave me a thrill anymore. Not even racing," she admitted. "That's why I became an ambulance driver. I was running toward something I couldn't define."

"Rose, a satisfying life isn't to be found in endless escapades. Reggie falsely believed that. He was always searching for the next charge of excitement, and when he attained one, he was after another. You're more complex than that. You *know* you're more complex than that. And that's wonderful. You will find what your purpose is, Rose. That I do not doubt."

"I'm starting to," Rose admitted, remembering her revelations in Edinburgh and on the flight home. "But I think you're wrong about Reggie—at least in the end. He didn't go back to France for glory but to save the woman who'd rescued him. He was investigating the spy ring not for the honor of uncovering it but to protect *you* and the others whom he loved."

Thorfinn closed his left eye, and a bit of moisture seeped out. Rose felt as if the tear had fallen on her own heart as she said, "I'm sorry I've pushed to make Hamarray a retreat for the wealthy. I didn't understand what memories that would evoke for you."

Thorfinn shook his head. "It's time I stopped running from the past. There's no need for us to meet just in my cottage. You're transforming

Muckle Skaill. It's not the earl's domain anymore. It's yours. And I don't mind entering a sphere that you preside over."

A swell so strong and sweet swept through Rose that she couldn't help but lean forward and touch her lips to his. His mouth opened eagerly over hers, and heat blasted through her. The embrace was as wild and unpredictable as the wind whipping the seas into a frenzy. Her heart rose like water rushing upward against the sea cliff. Even sitting in the hard-backed chairs, their upper bodies began to move against each other in a rhythm older than Scapa Flow itself.

Abruptly, he stopped and jerked away. A pang of hurt rang through Rose's heart until she saw him struggling to retie his eye patch. Gently, she stayed his hand.

"You don't need to hide that part of you from me."

"It isn't a pretty sight, lass."

She lightly traced her finger along the pucker near his mouth. "Well, it certainly doesn't make you less kissable. You're a fierce Viking, after all."

A chortle of surprise burst from him. Allowing all the warmth in her to blossom into a smile, Rose pulled Thorfinn toward her. He dropped his eye patch to the floor and buried his hands in her short hair. The kiss had a rawness to it that went beyond lust to something deeper, something more emotional yet still elemental.

When they broke apart, they were both breathing heavily. The air felt like spring, laden with the sense of rebirth and beginnings. But before they could embrace the newness, there were still ghosts of the past to purge.

"With the earl returning, you should know that one of the reasons I chased him from Muckle Skaill is that he—*unsuccessfully*—tried to force himself upon me, but I stopped him. No harm was done to me." Although Rose tried to make it stupendously clear that she was not injured in any way, Thorfinn's grip on her tightened.

"What happened?" His voice was rough and desperate, and Rose let him hold her close.

"I pointed my gun at him, threatened to destroy his reputation with rumors of impotence, and forced him into selling Hamarray and Frest to me."

Thorfinn blinked, and a shaky smile slipped over his lips. "Rose, you are a marvel."

A marvel. She'd heard that before, but it had never felt right until now. Perhaps it was because she finally was starting to feel as if her boldness inside matched her outward show of strength.

"Are you certain that you are fine, though? Things like that—even if you fended him off—they linger," Thorfinn said softly, brushing his finger over her cheekbones, concern etched into his familiar, handsome face.

Rose didn't respond with blitheness but with the truth. "I was shaken in the moment, but it hasn't haunted me. I am not worried about him coming back to the island, but I thought you should know my prior history with Mar as well. That way, when he comes, we can face him *together*."

"I like the sound of you being by my side," Thorfinn said. "It's time that I confront him. He's just a mere mortal, not some boogeyman or god—and I need to stop treating him as such."

"He has no chance against either of us, Thorfinn." Rose gave him a squeeze. "Even apart, we each are much more than he ever could be. His machinations are that of a child, but we—we fight with hard-won power."

Thorfinn had called her strong, yet his resolve also humbled her. Rose knew what it was like to fight against memories—and how that battle could be even more bitter than a real one. With their strength combined, they could confront Mar and reveal the spies—no matter how painful it might be.

Chapter 15

Even with the Earl of Mar back on Hamarray and the riddles from Reggie's letter still taunting Sinclair, there was nothing like playing his fiddle at a ceilidh, especially one held under a golden sky. The music swelled up inside of him. Instead of only temporarily displacing the worries that came with crofting life, it now also offered him a brief reprieve from the increasing pressure of trying to discover traitors on Frest.

The songs didn't come from just Sinclair's instrument or even the other players'. They were also the sound of dancing feet hitting the floor. The rhythmic clapping of the audience. The peals of laughter. Even the smell of the whiskey and beer mixing with the lingering scent of the shared meal. In this moment they were one, the whispers of espionage temporarily silenced.

Rose's presence only intensified the wild, wonderful whirl of emotion inside Sinclair. She stood flanked by Barbara and Mary as the twins tried showing her, Miss Morningstar, and the Duke of Newsberry the proper steps. Rose missed most of them, but that made her seem all the more charming. She threw her head back and laughed each time she stumbled, her short black hair shining in the bright twilight of the simmer dim as the summer solstice drew near. She didn't quite look like an island lass, but she didn't appear like a toff either. She was simply . . . Rose. Exuberant, passionate, wonderful Rose.

She joined hands with Hannah, and the two spun madly about. It was an unfettered twirl—meant purely for fun and not for style. Sinclair felt that he, too, was caught up in the frenzied rotation. But unlike Ulysses's fear of Charybdis's whirlpool, Sinclair wasn't afraid of being sucked into Rose's vortex.

When his set ended, Sinclair stepped off the raised platform by the cliffs and started to make his way toward Rose. To his surprise, her posh attendees, including Miss Morningstar and the duke, were enjoying themselves along with several of Astrid's repeat bird-watching clients. Even Rose's parents were at the festivities—the expressions not exactly approving but not disapproving either. The younger guests were gamely trying to learn the proper footwork from the lasses and the newly returned lads, while the older tourists sat interspersed with the island's elders—although Mr. White seemed to have cornered Mr. and Mrs. Van Etten. Sinclair was not naive enough to believe Rose had felled social class strictures with a single blow, but this wasn't a hedonistic affair. It was a jolly, communal one. Frest and Hamarray hadn't rung with this much laughter since before the war.

It was a shame that Rose's parents planned to leave almost immediately after the race tomorrow. Business had allegedly called Mr. Van Etten back to the States, but Sinclair rather thought the hotelier and his wife were bored with Orkney and wished to escape. Either that or Mr. White's arrival and subsequent obsequious fawning over them had irritated them into leaving. No matter why they were to depart, their decision didn't seem to surprise Rose. Her matter-of-fact approach to their upcoming abandonment made Sinclair ache as he realized how alone Rose really was.

But she was strong. She hadn't dwelled on the shortness of her parents' visit but had focused on the race and on what information she and Miss Morningstar could ferret out of Mr. White related to espionage. Unfortunately, the man had not let any useful information slip to either woman . . . if he even possessed any knowledge of the spy ring to begin with.

When Sinclair once again spotted Rose among the evening's revelers, time shuddered to a stop and then suddenly seemed to rush backward and forward all at once. While he'd been weaving through the throng, the Earl of Mar had made not only his appearance tonight but also his way to Rose's side.

The man's blond hair was threaded with a few pure-white strands, and his mouth had fine brackets sketched around it. In his early sixties, Mar cut a handsome figure. Any signs of aging lent him only a false air of distinguishment. But then, he'd never looked like the monster he was.

Sinclair's first instinct was that of a child: his body tensed, and he eased back on his heels, preparing to pivot. To slink away. To escape.

His second instinct was that of a lad: his toes slapped back on the ground, and his hands balled into fists. He wanted to attack. To punish. To defend.

But he was no longer a youngster, and Rose was not his mother. She was well aware of the duke's true nature. Not only did she have the skill and the means to protect herself, but she had already bested the man. Sinclair, though, did not dismiss the danger the earl still posed, regardless of whether he was a spy. He was not about to stomp over and punch the man in the face, but he would watch him. Closely.

Sinclair debated whether to confront the earl or simply to remain in the background. Miss Morningstar seemed to have chosen the latter tactic as she pretended to watch Astrid and Sinclair's siblings show Lord Newsberry rather intricate dance steps. But both by the angle of Miss Morningstar's body and the fact that she had agreed to keep an eye on Rose in case the spies tried to attack again, Sinclair knew the archaeologist was listening carefully to Rose and Mar's discussion.

Before, however, Sinclair could decide upon the best course of action for himself, the lord's blue eyes lit upon him. A coldness slid over Mar's face as he took in Sinclair's eye patch and scar. Even without the telltale mark, it wouldn't be difficult for the man to recognize him.

After all, Sinclair always had possessed a striking resemblance to both his mother and the earl himself.

Mar's eyes flicked over him, and Sinclair was suddenly glad he'd finally given in to Rose's suggestion that he purchase clothes befitting his new station as land manager. Even with the generous salary she paid him, Sinclair had felt like a spendthrift when he'd purchased the ready-made suit in Kirkwall. But he was representing the Hamarray estate now, and Rose was right. He couldn't do that in a darned sweater and rough work trousers, and in converse, wearing a fancy set of clothes didn't make him any less of a crofter.

"Ah, finally, a servant." The earl's lips moved into a smile that would have looked polite if the ends didn't tilt with such smug superiority. Clearly, he'd mistaken Sinclair's simple suit for that of a footman or a waiter. "Could you be so kind as to fetch me a glass of sherry? I find I'm very parched."

Rose, whose back was to Sinclair, immediately corrected Mar even without realizing whom she was defending. "I'm afraid we have no servers tonight. This ceilidh is as much for my staff and the people of Frest as it is for the hotel guests. You'll all just have to grab your own refresh . . ."

Rose trailed off when she turned in his direction. Immediately, concern flashed over her face.

"I am Miss Van Etten's estate manager," Sinclair said evenly, wanting his position to be clear to Mar. He paused and then held out his hand. "Mr. *Thorfinn* Sinclair."

Bloody hell, it felt good to say his full name in front of this gappus—to stand as an adult, an *equal*, and hold out his hand. He would never, could never, attain the status of peer, but Sinclair didn't need a title.

"You inquired how I could possibly handle such a large undertaking of managing two islands on my own?" Rose wrapped her hand around the arm that Sinclair wasn't extending. "Well, this remarkable man is my secret. He has been an invaluable business partner."

The smug curl of the earl's lips drooped. He stared down at Sinclair's hand, as if being handed a rotten fish. He started to step back and then must have realized how that would appear to Rose. Clearly, the toff thought it was possible to force his way back into Rose's life—as if he hadn't tried to *attack* her. A man like the earl had never been made to even consider facing the consequences of his actions, let alone paying for them. Knowing Mar, he still probably wanted to lay claim to Rose's inheritance by wedding her. After the money was secured, the arse likely planned to punish Rose and then brush aside the pieces that were left of her.

Bright ire erupted inside Sinclair as his stomach contracted and twisted, but he managed to contain it. Now was not yet the time to annihilate Mar.

The earl's fingers closed around Sinclair's, his grip soft, weak even. They were the digits of a dilettante. Although Sinclair didn't pulverize the man's bones as he wanted, he applied enough pressure so there was no doubt who was the more powerful one now.

Mar withdrew his hand a peedie bit too quickly. His left nostril began to lift as it always did in anger, but it no longer triggered a rush of crippling fear inside Sinclair. The earl sniffed, clearly trying to maintain his poise.

"It is truly a tragedy that a young, vibrant lady has burdened herself with the upkeep of a holding like Hamarray. As the former laird, I would be happy to share with you the advice I have gleaned from running multiple estates." Mar bowed slightly at the waist—the position giving him the romantic air of a courtier as he tried to strategically move his body between Rose and Sinclair.

"How lovely!" Rose moved closer to Sinclair. "Then I suppose you can tell me the best time to plant the barley crop to ensure a maximum harvest for whiskey production? It has been such a trial trying to figure that out."

Mar cleared his throat. "Well, in the spring."

"Oh, the *spring*," Rose added with enough dry emphasis that Mar stiffened, apparently realizing that *he* was the one being mocked.

"But aren't these worries you wish to be free of? You made the decision to purchase these islands in such haste." Mar gave her a placating look that he probably thought would be viewed as heroic concern. "Wouldn't you much rather be in London thinking about dresses instead of corn?"

"Not really." Rose smiled. "I'm an heiress. I've spent my whole life around pretty frocks. It gets rather dull. But I am truly fascinated to know what kind of improvements you made to Hamarray and Frest that actually turned a profit."

Mar reddened, and his left nostril bounced up and down like a ball made from india rubber. Everyone knew that he'd had to sell Hamarray and Frest because he could no longer afford the luxury of the losses the upkeep required. His other entailed estates were failing miserably, and the earl did not have diverse investments to draw from.

"Thorfinn has given me so many ideas, and even my father had to admit our planned projects are sound. But Daddy would give me money even if I was being silly with it and frittering it away. I'm sure my mother has already hinted at the size of my allowance and my dowry. That is, of course, my most alluring attribute on . . . what do you Brits call it—the Marriage Mart?"

"After spending time with your respectable parents in London, I thought I would give you another opportunity to prove that you could act like a suitable lady. But if you again insist on American crudeness, then do not complain if I show mine." Mar reached out to grab Rose's arm, but Sinclair easily intercepted. To any observer, it looked as if he were merely shaking the earl's hand again. He wasn't. He twisted it nearly to the breaking point.

"Release me at once!" Mar hissed under his breath. "You might be as good a whore as your mother, but this Yankee trollop will kick you from her silken sheets if you start a scandal. You're a nobody, Sin, my lad. Never forget that."

A nobody. For years, Sinclair had believed that. Now, standing here, with Rose beside him, defending him, *believing* in him, Sinclair finally saw Mar's words for the absurdity that they were. They didn't make Sinclair flinch—not once. He felt only a rush of fierce, protective anger for the woman the earl disparaged, the woman Sinclair loved.

Increasing the pressure of his grip, Sinclair forced the earl to step closer to him. He bent close and whispered in his ear, "You forget, Mar, that you're on Hamarray. Scandals don't leave these shores. I'm the estate manager now, and it's my duty to protect the people. If you harm or even harass any man, woman, or child, I won't hesitate to hunt you down. Do not forget how easy it is to quarry game on this isle or keep dark secrets hidden."

"You're breaking my wrist, Sinclair," the earl gasped out.

"I'm aware, and it's Thorfinn."

"Thorfinn." Mar gulped.

"Do you understand?"

"Yes. Yes. I understand."

Thorfinn released the man and gave him a casual smile. "It has been a pleasure getting reacquainted, Mar."

The former laird stepped back as he adjusted the sleeve of his jacket with an indignant snap. "It seems that perhaps Hamarray no longer agrees with me. Please give my regrets to your parents, Miss Van Etten, but you are a—"

Thorfinn stalked toward the man just as the bully used to corner him. Mar immediately aborted his insult. The coward might have enjoyed inflicting pain, but it was clear he had no tolerance for it himself.

"You were saying?" Rose asked archly.

"Goodbye, Miss Van Etten." Mar bowed stiffly and then strode through the crowd.

"What a truly odious man," Miss Morningstar said as she turned with an intentional shudder and gave up all pretense of being absorbed by Lord Newsberry learning the local dances. "But the two of you handled Mar brilliantly. I wouldn't be surprised if he is, well, the person who we suspect he might be."

"If you'll keep Miss Van Etten company, I'll follow him," Thorfinn said quickly to Miss Morningstar in response to her veiled reference to the spy ring. "I'll make sure he does no harm and that he actually does leave with no clandestine meetings or furtive backtracking." Although Mar had clearly returned in an attempt to win Rose's fortune a second time, he could have also come to reengage in espionage.

"I'd say to stay safe, but I think you've made it truly clear who's the one in peril now on this isle." Rose gave him a gentle smile, and he realized then that she knew that he had finally stopped allowing the earl to haunt him.

"Aye." Thorfinn nodded as a sense of calm washed over him. He moved through the crowd and headed toward Muckle Skaill. Although it was getting late in the evening, a warm glow that the islanders called the simmer dim still lit the sky. The summer solstice was only a few days away, and there was barely any darkness this time of year.

Within a few minutes, Mar appeared with his valet carrying his valise. The man must have realized that Rose would never lend him the use of a driver. It wasn't hard to track the two. They went directly down the path and boarded the duke's yacht. In no time, the sleek vessel sailed away in the direction of Scrabster.

Thorfinn turned and headed back up the hill, a lightness inside him that he'd never felt before. The old memories would always be there. The pain of what his mother had endured would never be forgotten. And Mar, especially if he was a spy, could always try to return. But the man's power was gone forever. He held no sway on these isles gilded by the simmer dim. And he held no dominion over Thorfinn's soul.

As Thorfinn approached the ceilidh, his stepda's voice rang out as he wove one of his yarns. It was an old one passed down by Sigurd's da and his da before him and probably his da before that. Since the ancient hero shared a name with Sigurd, it was no wonder the epic was one of the older man's favorites.

In the tale, the famous warrior chief Sigurd helps the people of Frest defend against a group of vicious invaders who have forged an unholy pact with the finmen. When a giant emerges from the sea to assist the enemy, the islanders almost give up hope, but the mighty Sigurd charges the creature. He gives up his life to defeat the monster, but his sacrifice causes his people to rise up and fight off the attackers.

In a sweeping gesture, Thorfinn's stepda was raising both his hands as he reached the epic's conclusion:

"And even as the great Sigurd drew his last breath, he inspired his people.

"'For all time, I shall stand at the head of Hamarray, victor over this giant—a reminder to our people of our strength. When Hamarray and Frest shall need me to defend them again, I shall rise from my rocky tomb.'

"At the end of great Sigurd's final promise to his people, he and the giant turned to stone. And there they remain today—the sea stack forever guarding our home."

A faint smile touched Thorfinn's lips. Before, he'd always felt uncomfortable during the retelling of Sigurd's Rock. After all, he was the offspring of the usurper who'd ruled from Muckle Skaill. Even his mother's surname was of Scottish lineage, not of the older stock.

But Thorfinn belonged to Frest, to these people. He had chased off the cruel invader. Although the real-life Sigurd would never see him as a true son of Frest, Thorfinn rather thought the mythical hero would clap him on the back and offer him mead or whatever spirits they'd brewed back then.

Reggie would tell him it was about damn time. His half brother had always loved the old tale and its bravado. He'd never understood why Thorfinn hadn't. Shite, once Reggie had even convinced Thorfinn to crawl onto the stack using a rope so that they could "absorb the courage of the ancient hero." It had been a harrowing adventure, one that Thorfinn had refused to repeat despite Reggie's urging. His brother had always sworn he'd convince Thorfinn to return to the rock formation someday.

A shiver sliced through Thorfinn, and he thought back to his brother's list of riddles.

Signets mark the king's great stand.

His brother had been playing with homophones. He hadn't meant signets but rather *cygnets*. His brother used to call the gannets who nested on Sigurd's Rock swans. Locals called the birds solan geese, but as a child, Reggie had confused the terms and thought them solan swans. And *the king's great stand* referred to the sea stack.

Shite, Reggie, you and your damnable codes.

Thorfinn debated whether he should tell Rose, but knowing her, she'd want to climb over to the rock with him. There was no need for two of them to break their necks.

Thorfinn glanced skyward. Although it was getting late and the sun had begun to dip below the horizon, there was still enough light for him to crawl out to the rock. He'd rather do it in the low glow of dusk than with the noonday sun showing exactly how far the sea sparkled below him.

Noticing Freya standing by Young Thomas at the edge of the crowd, he headed over to them. The lad jumped nearly a foot high at his approach, but Thorfinn paid him no heed. The youth had only been chatting with Thorfinn's sister, even if the two might be sweet on each other as Rose suspected.

"Freya?" Thorfinn called.

"Aye?" she asked, looking just a bit cross at the interruption.

"Can you please tell Rose that our visitor has left and that I need to head back to the croft for a few chores I've been neglecting?"

Freya frowned. "Can't it wait until the morrow? You should be enjoying the ceilidh. You've worked so hard on the preparations for the festivities too."

"Nay, this must be done now," Thorfinn said. "Just tell her, will you, lass?"

Freya reluctantly nodded, and Thorfinn slipped away. With all the renovations to Muckle Skaill, it wasn't hard to find a good strong rope, a hammer, and some metal stakes lying about. After wrapping the sizable cord around his shoulder, he headed to the sea stack. The headlands curved around both sides of the structure, which made possible the stunt he was about to perform. Again.

"You always did say you'd find a way to persuade me to return to Sigurd's Rock." Thorfinn felt a bittersweet grin touch his lips as he pounded a stake into the ground. After tying one end of the hawser securely to the metal, he walked along the curved cliff until he was across from his previous position, with the stack directly between him and the far end of the rope. Pulling the thick cord taut, he secured it in place on the second stake. The rope now lay across the sea stack.

"Ah, shite, Reggie. Did you really need to pick this damnable rock?" Thorfinn asked as he gripped the rope with his hands, his head facing skyward. Looping his legs over the line, he proceeded to inch his way over the rope that hung 420 feet above the water below. He closed his good eye and tried to ignore the sound of the sea crashing onto the jagged rocks. The wind was relatively calm, but it still buffeted him, making him feel like a button on a children's string toy. The birds who made their home on the stack began to scream out warnings when they noticed his unorthodox approach. By the time he'd reached the grassy top of the rock tower, his arm muscles burned fiercely, almost masking the pain from his sore palms.

"Now, where did you hide it, Reggie?" Thorfinn asked as he searched the flat surface for a metal container. He doubted his brother would have left it where any sunlight could glint off its surface.

Sitting down on the loam, Thorfinn stared into the glow of the midsummer twilight as he tried to remember that long-ago day when he and Reggie had clambered over this rock. Well, Reggie had clambered—he'd preferred to sit like he was now, square in the center, taking in the view.

For a moment, he could almost see the adolescent Reggie bolting straight for the cliff's edge. *"Don't you want to look down and see how far up we are?"*

"Nay, I like it here where I am."

"Chicken!" Reggie called good-naturedly as he dropped onto his belly and stuck his head and shoulders over the precipice. "Good lord, Sin. You should see this. There are so many alcoves and caves. We have been missing great opportunities."

"That is a matter of opinion."

"There's even a shelf I can reach, right here! We should make this our new place for secret messages," Reggie hollered.

Thorfinn flopped onto his back. "I believe someone would eventually spy the rope. Besides, Mr. Flett will notice if my arms are always stiff when I do my chores."

"Gah!" Reggie suddenly appeared in his vision before he plopped down beside Thorfinn. "You think like an old man. If it wasn't for me, you'd never have a spot of fun in your life."

"Reggie, I really think I could do without this type of adventure," Thorfinn said as he stood up and walked toward the sea-facing edge of the stack.

Inside his head, Thorfinn heard his brother's reply. *You're having the time of your life, old boy. Why do you think I sent Rose your way? You need someone to remind you to stop being so sober and to have fun once in a while.*

"Maybe you're right. When Rose leaves, I suspect a bit of the joy she brought will linger, even if I will miss her like the dickens," Thorfinn said as he lowered himself to the ground and wriggled on his elbows to the very edge. It didn't take him too long, thankfully, to find a crevice he could reach. After moving away a pile of stones, he felt the cool smoothness of metal.

He pulled out the box and moved into a crouch. Luckily, the thin container wasn't locked. Thorfinn pulled out a sheet of paper and touched his brother's messy scrawl. There was just enough light to read it.

Sin,

I didn't have time to put this letter into code, but I doubt anyone will stumble across it accidentally. I firmly believe we are the only two humans who have ever conquered Sigurd's Rock. Didn't I tell you I'd figure out a way to lure you back here?

I wish I didn't have to write this missive, especially to you, but you are the only person I can trust to see this through. And I know you always choose the honorable course—the right course—no matter the personal cost.

When I first arrived at Hamarray after my capture, I was convinced that the strange lights I saw on the headland were part of my paranoia. But I kept seeing beams of reflective light during the day and odd flashes at night. Finally, at my wits' end, I asked the servants—and they too had witnessed the phenomena. Those who maintained the house year-round swore it had been going on all through the war.

I began to record the lights, along with who visited the island. I discovered that the highest occurrence happened when Astrid brought bird-watchers to Hamarray.

Regardless of who is creating them, I believe the lights are a way of communicating with German U-boats, giving them the details of the Grand Fleet's movements in and out of the Flow. The servants did say that the flashes were more active right before the HMS *Hampshire* was sunk.

Before I could discover more, I received news that the nurse who had saved me had been captured. Upon my arrival on Hamarray I had told Astrid of her. My brother, I fear that she may have conveyed the identity of my savior to the enemy.

Unlike my other findings at the Home Office, I have only weak evidence of a plot. And I do not wish to accuse your family of such dastardly dealings. Yet if they are giving information about the movement of the Grand Fleet to the Germans, they must be stopped—even Astrid, who I still hold dear despite everything. I know you have the strength to see my final investigation through, and to take the proper action if my horrible suspicions are correct.

Your best friend and brother forever,

Reggie the Bold

The paper in Thorfinn's hand shook. He read it again and again . . . until the light failed him. He knew it would not stay dark for long. The sun would rise shortly and begin the next day.

A day Thorfinn didn't want to face.

Because it meant discovering whether his cousin was a traitor.

He could not, would not, risk false accusations without consideration. It would destroy all of them. But he could not deny that Astrid's bird-watching clients were once again visiting Hamarray—just as they had on and off for the past five years. If he found out that Astrid was indeed involved, he would expose her. The peace of his family was not worth that of the world.

Late spring in Orkney was absolutely divine, Rose decided as she, Myrtle, and Percy walked among cars lined up on the drive in front of Muckle Skaill. They'd purposely scheduled the race for low tide, allowing for a quasi-road and quasi-closed-circuit extravaganza. The drivers, including her and Percy, would begin at the top of Hamarray. After shooting down the bouncy hillside road, they were to dash across the exposed strand, zip around Frest five times, and climb back to the big house to the grand finish.

Old friends Rose hadn't seen in years waved to all three of them, eager to chat. In some ways, it was as if the intervening war years had never happened. In others, the change was heartbreakingly clear. Comrades who should have been there smiling and pulling on their goggles weren't. Some lay in France, some in Italy, some in Russia, some in Turkey, some in Africa, some in Britain, some in the United States, some in Germany, and some in places no one knew. Others had become the enemy, separated perhaps forever by country allegiance.

And Rose wasn't the same.

She was no longer the blithe, carefree girl who cared only about speed—who'd never known deprivation or true fear or sacrifice or even real, honest love.

But who she *was* now . . . well, that—that was something she was just now beginning to define.

"Miss Van Etten?" Thorfinn's voice broke into her oddly philosophical musings for a race day.

"And now we make ourselves scarce," Myrtle said as she tugged on Percy's right elbow. "Why don't you show me your latest race car? Is it as fancy as the speedboat you had me bring from Stromness to Frest for you?"

"Fancier," Percy told Myrtle. Then he untangled his left arm from Rose's and gave her a wink. "I'm sure you have important *estate* matters to discuss with Mr. Sinclair."

Laughing at her friends' thinly veiled matchmaking efforts, Rose waved goodbye to them before she turned toward Thorfinn.

"You can call me Rose in public . . . ," she began and then trailed off when she caught sight of Thorfinn's face. He looked . . . gaunt. Despite his pallidness, his white scar seemed even more predominant while light bruising marred the skin under his bloodshot left eye.

"Did something happen with the earl?" Rose rushed to him. "I thought he'd parted peacefully by the way Freya phrased your message to me. Did he do anything to raise alarm—on any front?" She should have gone looking for Thorfinn last night instead of staying to the very end of the ceilidh, but she'd been having so much fun, and Freya had assured her that her brother had been in a fine mood. Had Thorfinn been hiding something from his sister and her? Perhaps Mar had attacked Thorfinn again or had done something suspicious that could tie him to the spying.

"The former laird sailed away without looking back. He never even noticed I was following. There was nothing particular about his behavior to note. I just had a peedie bit of trouble falling asleep. That's all."

If there was nothing for Thorfinn to report on Mar's exit, his unspoken worries must be of a personal nature, then, and not about the espionage. Rose glanced around at the well-dressed crowd swarming the front lawn. "Do you wish to discuss your confrontation last night?" She thought he'd handled it marvelously, but that didn't mean that he agreed.

Thorfinn jerked his head toward her wristwatch. "Isn't your big event about to start?"

Rose uttered the words she'd never thought she'd say. "Never mind the race. I can skip it."

"You would miss it. For me?" Thorfinn looked as poleaxed as her by the revelation.

"Yes." Rose cocked her head. "Gollyyy, it wouldn't even bother me one iota. How oddly refreshing."

A smile momentarily breached Thorfinn's otherwise grave expression. "You don't know how much that means to me."

"Well, it had better, buster," she teased, gently poking his arm. "I wouldn't cheerfully give up a race for just anybody."

"Is that true, lass?"

"Yep."

A charge arced between them before Thorfinn sobered. "It's not necessary for you to pass on it, lass. I'm just overtired—that's all."

"You don't have to stay. I know you're not keen on upper-crust soirees."

"Racing is important to you, Rose. I want to be here when you cross the finish line."

If Rose weren't worried about embarrassing Thorfinn, she would have reached up and kissed him. Her parents had already broken their promise to her and had left even earlier than planned. They weren't here to see her at the starting line, but somehow, their leaving didn't bother her as much as it would've in the past. Not when she had Thorfinn, her friends, and the islanders with her.

"And," Thorfinn said, moving a shade closer to her, "I enjoyed myself at the ceilidh. Mrs. Flett told me that she's sold all of her current stock of sweaters and that she has orders for more."

"At least two of the racers are wearing her designs," Rose said, "and they're known as very snappy dressers. Once photographs of them start showing up in the news rags, I suspect Mrs. Flett will have more work than she knows what to do with."

"I've heard compliments about the whiskey too," Thorfinn said. "And Young Thomas is enjoying working as an honorary 'bellhop,' as you called it. You were right about rich tourists bringing money to the isles."

Joy shot through Rose, sweeter than she'd ever felt before. It wasn't just a sense of happiness but one of *accomplishment*. She was starting to build something here in Orkney, something strong, something lasting, something *permanent*.

"You're really on board, then?"

"Aye." Thorfinn nodded. "I'm sorry it took me so long to accept your vision and to see how truly grand it is."

"You had your reasons." Rose couldn't resist patting the sleeve of his coat.

"You didn't just help me chase the earl from Orkney yesterday. For weeks now, you've been loosening Mar's grip on Hamarray and Frest . . . and on me."

A sense of pride rippled through Rose again, warm and pleasant. She was just about to ask what Thorfinn intended to do with his new-found freedom when the sound of a shell hitting the ground nearly blasted her from her feet.

Rose was back amid the ruination, her patients crying out in pain, begging her to move faster, pleading with her to stop. The sunny day had plunged into a dark night full of shadows. Warhorses snorted. Her Tin Lizzie rattled as an explosion hit close . . . too close.

"Rose."

A hand touched hers—warm, solid, real.

"Rose, lass, it was just an automobile backfiring. You're fine. We're here on Hamarray. Remember."

The hallucination slowly drifted away as she focused on his heat. Thorfinn's heat. She slid her thumb over his calluses to reach his wrist. His pulse beat under her flesh. Strong. Steady. Rhythmic.

Letting that ground her, she brought herself back to reality. This time, instead of reaching for a trusty cigarette, she wrapped her fingers around his.

"Hi there," she said, her voice only a little shaky.

"Hello, Rose." His husky, honeyed tone triggered a shiver through her already shaky body. But unlike the tingling sensation in her legs and arms, this quiver helped right her, not undo her.

"All drivers to their racers!" Ron Inkster called in his booming voice. Thorfinn had recommended picking him as master of ceremonies, and the man had done brilliantly so far.

"I suppose that is my cue." Rose sucked in her breath and steadied her thundering heart.

"You don't need to race if you don't wish to," Thorfinn said, watching her with concern.

"Oh, I always desire to race." Rose sent her short hair swinging, but as she said the words, she realized something wonderful. She did *want* to race, but she felt no desperate urgency to depress the accelerator and call upon the wind to whip away her troubles.

"Why don't you join me?" Rose asked. "My mechanic won't mind."

Thorfinn glanced over at her sleek Raceabout with its fenders and headlamps removed for weight. "I wouldn't want to make a mistake, lass, that costs you a win."

"I don't care a fig if I come in first or last." And for the first time, it was true. She didn't *crave* the victory.

"You're certain?"

"Absolutely, sure as shooting." She tugged on his hand as the tension in her body returned to the amount of energy that Rose normally experienced before a race. "Come on. I might not mind losing, but I *do* mind forfeiting."

Luckily, they managed to get situated before the starting gun was fired. As Rose shifted gears and steered around the sharp bends, she shouted instructions to Thorfinn. With his seafaring background, he instinctually understood how to throw his body to balance the speeding vehicle through the curves. When he hung out the side to balance them as she whipped the wheel to the right and left, she heard him holler in pure excitement.

Once they reached a short straightaway, Rose glanced over at Thorfinn. He was grinning and shouting, his blond hair blowing wildly about his face. He was loving this just as much as she was. Focusing on the road once again, she released her own whoop, and a heady, intoxicating emotion burst forth.

This . . . *this* was racing at its best!

Chapter 16

The glow from the simmer dim made it both easy for Thorfinn to keep an anxious lookout for Astrid and her bird-watchers and harder for him to obscure his presence. With a heart heavier than the standing stone that he crouched behind, Thorfinn warily watched the entrance to the old broch where Astrid often brought naturalists to see the fulmars. It made a relatively large and comfortable spot for secret rendezvous. Even if Astrid and her cohorts met instead in the sea caves, Thorfinn's hilltop hiding spot gave him an excellent view of both the headlands and the rolling countryside that stretched down toward Frest.

Remorse simmered through Thorfinn—guilt that he was having such thoughts about Astrid and pain at the knowledge that he *would* hand her over to the authorities if she was a German agent.

Nothing stirred except for the tammie norries and other auks returning from their day's hunt for sand eels—leaving Thorfinn alone with the thoughts that burned through him like a thousand funeral pyres.

Unable to bear the agonizing doubts any longer, Thorfinn found the only release he could—he imagined he was back in the Raceabout with Rose, his body hanging over the ground rushing below, the gorse nearly scraping his face.

Oh, it had been glorious. And then, when they'd won, the cheers of the islanders had surrounded them. He knew now what propelled Rose to climb into the steel beasties.

Reggie was right: Thorfinn did need someone to drag him into adventures . . . at least those *not* involving the fate of the bloody world and the potential destruction of everything Thorfinn held dear. And Thorfinn wanted Rose in his life—not just now, not just for a moment, but forever.

Aye, he loved the lass, fully and truly. He'd known it for days, perhaps even weeks. He just hadn't had a moment to acknowledge it . . . or accept what it meant. For Rose did not desire marriage, and she had made him no promises of a future. When the time came for her to leave, he'd have no choice but to let her go. But he couldn't stop how he felt, any more than he could force her to change her opinions on love.

A flicker of movement by the strand connecting Frest and Hamarray caused Thorfinn to stiffen. He scanned the landscape, searching for the red blonde of Astrid's hair. Instead, he merely spotted Sigurd's familiar flatcap.

Thorfinn relaxed his body against the cool stone. It was just his stepda out on his nightly stroll. Ever since Sigurd's apoplexy, he had suffered bad dreams that drove him from his bed. The walks gave the older man not only a bit of air but also a peedie dram of his old independence.

Just as Sigurd's head disappeared behind the last dip before he would reach the crest of Hamarray, Thorfinn spied two figures slipping out of Muckle Skaill. Thorfinn's blood started to pound, and he frantically glanced back toward where he'd last seen Sigurd. He hoped to hell that the spies didn't catch sight of his stepfather. Scrambling to think of a way to warn Sigurd without scaring off the twosome, he glanced back toward the mansion. This time his heart was fairly rent into pieces. With the men closer now, he had no trouble identifying them as Astrid's bird-watchers.

Thorfinn swung his gaze back to his stepda, and he could just see the brown and green of his tweed hat. Thorfinn started to cup his hand to yell to Sigurd to flee down the hill, but before he could shout, his stepfather popped into sight. The two apparent spies immediately turned in Sigurd's direction, and his stepda waved in greeting.

Thorfinn tensed his muscles. He had no weapon. He hadn't really expected trouble even though he'd taken the precaution of leaving Reggie's last letter at the bottom of Freya's bed with a note on the sealed envelope to deliver the missive to Rose in the morning. Thorfinn had planned to stay well hidden and let the authorities take care of the arrests, but he couldn't allow his stepfather to enter a trap.

But just as Thorfinn started to dash to the rescue, Sigurd casually met up with the two men. The threesome then disappeared inside the ancient stone walls, whispering together like fast friends . . . or conspirators.

It wasn't just Thorfinn's heart that plummeted but his soul as well. Denial screamed through him, but he could not ignore the damning evidence. Sigurd—who hated all interlopers to Hamarray and Frest— had just willingly met in the middle of the night two individuals who had the perfect cover for studying Scapa Flow.

With pain and disbelief dousing him in equal measures, Thorfinn silently sped toward a crack in the back of the ancient structure. As he pressed his ear against the narrow slit, he prayed that he would hear nothing but talk of seafowl—yet he already knew in his gut that it was not birds that these men were interested in.

"The admiral and kapitäns are all aware of the plans, then?" a smooth British voice with occasional faint traces of an accent asked. "They will be at the ready when reinforcements arrive tomorrow?"

Thorfinn desperately fought against the yawning ache inside him. He could not allow it to swallow him up and dull his senses. Despite his relief that Astrid did not appear to be involved, the fact that Sigurd *was* nearly slayed Thorfinn. He'd always trusted Sigurd to do the right thing, the honorable thing; it was the closest he'd ever gotten to a father-son relationship. And the loss of that belief, that betrayal, felt worse than any blow that the earl had ever inflicted.

But Thorfinn had to remain sharp and ignore his personal agony. It wasn't just the people of Frest who were depending upon him but the peace of nearly every nation in the world.

"Aye." It was Sigurd's voice. "I saw their signal this morning. They are prepared. Five of the battleships and twelve destroyers have communicated that they will be able to raise steam."

Thorfinn could not think of Sigurd as his stepfather right now, or he could crumble. His stepda was . . . most horrifically . . . the enemy.

"So few?!"

"Most of the crews will no longer obey their officers. The engines have not been maintained for months. Still, it will be enough for the plan to proceed."

"No one noticed you with all of the activity at the mansion?" This accent was American.

"Nay. Nobody ever minds an old man with a cane. That's why you pay me to sneak about, isn't it?"

"I was afraid the heiress would be troublesome, but the race is giving us a cover," the American said.

"Let's review our part of the scheme one more time," the British speaker said. "We strike out for Minnstray at sunset. We'll only have a few hours after nautical twilight to plant the bombs. The explosion should create a big enough distraction to allow the *Engel* to sweep in from the Atlantic and break through the British guard ships. She'll transfer sailors to the interned ships, who will help them escape to open water. We will take our speedboats to the rendezvous and sail with the reborn Kaiserliche Marine to the Netherlands to free the Kaiser."

Each word seemed to dismantle something inside Thorfinn until he was left with nothing but raw horror. How could his stepfather be involved in a scheme that purposely aimed to bring death to so many?

Given the condition of the old imperial vessels at Scapa Flow and their half-starved, mutinous crews, Thorfinn doubted the overall efficacy of the plot. But no matter if it worked, there would be more loss of life in an already too-costly war. The people of Orkney would be caught in the fighting. And most damning, the bloodshed could crack the already fragile peace talks in France, causing the war to erupt again.

After all, the whole conflagration had started in 1914 with a single gunman in Sarajevo.

Their plans *had* to be stopped, and so did Sigurd.

Thorfinn had no choice but to turn in to the authorities the man who'd saved him and his mother. His stepda would most certainly die for his treason.

How would Thorfinn explain to his sisters and brother that he had sent their father to the executioners? Hell, how would he tell them about Sigurd's perfidy? The bairns loved their father, *respected* him . . . and Thorfinn did too—at least the latter. In regard to the former, he had always cared for Sigurd, and part of him used to dream of a real father-son relationship. But now Thorfinn was destined to be Sigurd's betrayer, but hadn't his stepfather betrayed them first by spying for *Germany*?

Broken but resolved, Thorfinn quietly backed away, only to feel a small hard circle of steel.

"Going somewhere?" The new speaker possessed a heavy German accent.

Splinters of ice tore through Thorfinn's every major organ, but he didn't freeze like the man expected. Thorfinn pivoted and swung hard, his fist connecting with the German's arm. The spy let out an aborted shout of pain as his gun went flying to the ground. Thorfinn dived for it, but something hard and heavy slammed into his kidneys. The blow caught him off guard and sent him sprawling toward the ground, his chin glancing painfully off one of the partially exposed rock walls of the ancient circular homes surrounding the old broch.

But Thorfinn had learned never to stay down long in a fight. He pushed with his arms and legs and sprang his body into the air. But before the soles of his feet landed flat against the ground, pain slammed into his stomach and then his chest. Gasping against the agony, Thorfinn forced his eye open just in time to see the butt of a rifle smack into his face. He reeled back, his feet catching on the stone wall. He almost steadied himself, but another strike from the weapon drove him backward. His back cracked against the old wall, and the uneven rocks tore into his spine and flesh. But worse than the pain, the air shot from his lungs, immobilizing him.

Two sets of hands roughly rolled him over onto his stomach. As he helplessly hung there with his head dangling over one side of the pile of rocks, his feet over the other, the two men roughly bound Thorfinn's wrists. A cold circle of steel once again dug into his skull.

"We shall try this again," the conspirator sneered. "It's time I introduce you to my other compatriots."

Thorfinn tried to struggle when the men yanked him to his feet, but their collective strength only pushed him forward. Every time he scrambled for purchase, the fourth conspirator, who was as big a giant as Thorfinn, would forcibly shove him forward until he had stumbled around the broch. When Thorfinn reached the ancient entrance, his larger captor prodded him roughly while the other viciously jammed his boot into Thorfinn's backside. The brutal combination sent him sprawling into the open room. His already sore chin smacked down on the hard-packed ground, and a searing, bright-white light scorched his vision. His teeth clanked together, and the reverberation traveled through his jaw. He tasted blood, but he could not yet open his mouth to spit it out. When he finally was able to focus his left eye, he could see only three sets of boots and his stepda's well-worn shoes.

"One of the locals was sniffing around." The giant kicked Thorfinn in his already aching kidneys. Agony ricocheted through his body. Before he could fully absorb the blow, his tormentor reached down and grabbed a fistful of his hair, causing his entire scalp to burn. The abductor forced Thorfinn's face straight in the direction of his stepda. Sigurd's gaunt, weatherworn face had changed from its normal florid color to a pale ash gray.

Anguish besieged Thorfinn as he gazed into the eyes of the man who had shown him how to be a crofter. Betrayal, anger, dismay, terror—they all seethed through Thorfinn, and he did not try to hide them from Sigurd. To his surprise, his stepda flinched.

"How much did he hear, Heinrich?" the man with the British accent asked as each spy except Sigurd drew weapons.

"Enough." Heinrich smashed Thorfinn's face into the ground with his foot. Thorfinn's bottom lip burned as it cracked open, and the flat taste of dirt mixed with the salty tang of blood. His already sore teeth ached in protest while spikes of agony shot from his nose and through his cheekbones. Heinrich stamped his foot into Thorfinn's shoulder blade, and for a moment it felt as if his spine would crack. He hadn't felt this much pain since his last beating at Muckle Skaill. Still pinning him down, Heinrich sadistically ground his rifle against Thorfinn's scalp, seeking to cause the maximum amount of agony.

"Stop!" Sigurd's voice rang out, surprising them all.

"Are you afraid the rifle will make too much sound?" Heinrich asked, as if amused by Sigurd's qualms at seeing a fellow islander summarily executed. "Shall I slit his throat instead?"

"He is my stepson."

For years, Thorfinn had waited for his mother's husband to acknowledge him, to call him just that. *Son.* He'd worked hard and never complained, hoping to earn the stubborn man's respect. But he'd never achieved more than mere tolerance.

And now that Sigurd had acknowledged him, all Thorfinn could feel was the urge to vomit.

"If he's heard our plans, we have no choice," the first American speaker said.

"You promised that my family would not be harmed." Sigurd's feet moved closer to Thorfinn's nose.

Was . . . was his stepda *shielding* him? Was that even possible?

"You're not in the position to negotiate. We got what we want from you." Punctuating his point, Heinrich whacked the butt of his weapon against Thorfinn's skull, and white-hot daggers flashed through his vision, burying themselves deep in his brain.

"Now, Heinrich, Mr. Flett has been a valuable asset," the British speaker said. "We owe him our respect. But Mr. Flett, despite your service to our cause, we cannot allow your stepson to go free and jeopardize the entire mission. We're too close."

"Will"—Sigurd addressed the Englishman—"by this time morrow, it won't matter if he tells the whole island. You and the German fleet will be gone from here. Your role in freeing the Kaiserliche Marine will be sung far and wide. There's no need to kill my stepson. There are plenty of caves around here where you can leave him tied up. I can release him once your plan is executed."

Faint hope flickered inside Thorfinn as he vainly fought against his bindings. Sigurd might never accept Thorfinn as one of his own, but he'd saved his life twice now . . . if the spies listened to his pleas.

"But won't he just rat you out?" the first American speaker asked. "Look how he is still struggling."

"That is my concern," Mr. Flett said simply.

"It makes the most sense to kill him, Mr. Flett," Will said quietly. "Whatever your feelings toward this man, are you willing to trade your life for his?"

"Aye." His stepda shifted his weight from his cane to his strongest leg and then back again. "I cannot provide for my family anymore. He can."

And that was the harsh summation of their fraught relationship. Sigurd wasn't saving Thorfinn; he was protecting his real children. But even if that knowledge still managed to cut out a piece of Thorfinn, he wasn't going to quibble over his stepda's reasoning right now.

"Let the captive up, Heinrich," Will ordered. "Keeping him alive is a bloody foolish mistake, but it's Mr. Flett's consequence to confront."

Heinrich didn't protest verbally, but he delivered a vicious kick to Thorfinn's face. Once again blades of pain exploded across his nose and over his cheekbones. Despite the black and gray dots momentarily filling his vision, Thorfinn immediately pounced to his feet, and his loosened eye patch fell to the ground. Hot blood dripped from his nose and mouth, but he'd already managed to shake the cobwebs from his good eye. His early life at Muckle Skaill had taught him how to take blows.

His gaze met his stepda's icy-blue one. For once Sigurd didn't look either judging or impassive. There was true fear in him now and something else Thorfinn had never expected to see. Defensiveness.

But Thorfinn could feel nothing but sick horror toward this man who had sheltered him once upon a time.

"I made good . . . coin," Sigurd said, a pleading note in his voice. There was no doubt that his stepda was upset. His words even sounded slurred as his mouth worked soundlessly for a few beats. "It wasn't . . . for me but . . . the bairns. I couldn't provide . . . for them, and I . . . wanted . . . no reliance . . . on you. I've hidden the money . . . to be used when . . . needed."

"The HMS *Hampshire*? Over six hundred souls? Lord Kitchener? *Reggie?*" Thorfinn couldn't stop the accusation from passing his bloodied, cracked lips despite Sigurd's visible struggle to speak. His stepda had helped plan the deaths of so many because he'd made good coin? Because he'd wanted free of his stepson? Agony—sharper and more penetrating than all the physical hurt—serrated Thorfinn.

"He was never . . . *our* Lord Kitchener," Sigurd spat out as he rubbed his head, the one side of his mouth drooping. "Do not act . . . as if . . . *I* am a traitor. I owe no . . . fealty to the king of England or any of its leaders. We are not . . . British or Scottish. We are . . . *Orcadian*. Why should I fight for . . . the people who have subjugated us . . . and charged us fees for farming our own land? As a boy, I saw people . . . whose ancestors are buried in our howes . . . being forced to leave for No . . . Nova Scotia and New York . . . while English lords made themselves a pleasure ground here . . . on *our* isle. When King Christian . . . I of Norway pledged this land to King James . . . III of Scotland as surety for

Princess Margaret's . . . dowry payment, Orkney was to remain in the possession of the people who tilled it, but that promise . . . was broken tenfold. Who is . . . traitor . . . I ask you? The pretender who sits on . . . throne is . . . German himself—cousin to . . . Wilhelm!"

It didn't matter that Sigurd was choppily talking about a transaction that had occurred in the 1400s, a conflict from the 1700s, and a marriage from the 1800s. The old islander had never considered himself Scottish, let alone British. He had watched his neighbors suffer starvation during the Enclosures. He had worn his body down tending a land owned by a rich, cruel noble. And he'd held his sobbing wife as she'd recounted life in Muckle Skaill. Thorfinn could never, would never, accept his stepda's decision to spy for Germany, but he could see how the man could wrongfully persuade himself that his deeds were somehow justified.

"You two can discuss this later." Will lashed a rope to the bindings on Thorfinn's wrists. "For now, Sigurd, you can return to your croft. We have matters well enough in hand. We'll leave your stepwhelp in the cave that we used for sending signals."

With one last charged look in Thorfinn's direction, Sigurd slowly and unsteadily ducked under the broch's entrance. The other spies stayed as they discussed the details of their upcoming assault on the supply depot.

A whisper of unease inside Thorfinn burgeoned into a frenzied roar. Why were these men spewing more particulars about their scheme if they planned on keeping him alive? Wouldn't they just have shepherded him to the cave and then had this discussion? They had rid themselves of Sigurd's presence. Why not *his*?

"Should I take the prisoner to where we told Sigurd that we'd leave him?" Heinrich asked, giving his rope a particularly vicious tug.

Will glanced over at Heinrich, his expression stern. "I only wanted to ensure that Sigurd does not cause trouble. We still may need the old man before this night and day are out."

The sentence of execution fell upon Thorfinn's last hope like the blade of the guillotine. He would not give these men the pleasure of a shout of protest, but it roared silently through his every fiber. Who would care for the children? And Rose, passionate, fierce Rose? Would she blame herself for his disappearance since she had told him about the spy ring?

Aye, she would. She shouldn't, but she would. Thorfinn fought like old Clootie himself against his bindings, but the cruel, unforgiving rope only cut deeper.

"So can I kill him now?" Heinrich withdrew a rather wicked-looking blade.

"No," Will said. "We'll bring him with us to the sea cave in case we need to keep Sigurd in line. We can leave him tied up there. When the tide returns, it will kill him for us."

Although Thorfinn did not intend to make a sound, his throat convulsively clenched, and a choking sound emerged—like a cry from his soul. The waters would start rising soon, and before anyone was awake to save him, he'd be dead—and with him the chance to preserve the fragile peace. His death would be followed by so many, many more.

The frantic knocking on her bedroom door woke Rose with a terrible start. It felt late or early or both. Light peeked through the drawn curtains, but then again it was a constant presence this time of year. Pressing her hand against her speeding heart, Rose debated whether she should get up or try to quiet her body for sleep once again. If one of the guests staying at Muckle Skaill instead of in Kirkwall had an issue, one of the staff could handle it. She even had Young Thomas on duty tonight, working both as front-desk man and bellhop to test if he liked the work. Ann Inkster had taken the earlier shift.

The thumping increased exponentially.

"Miss Van Etten?" It was Young Thomas's voice.

"Please, Miss Van Etten!" Freya's high tones came next.

Rose popped from her bed like a cork. What in the devil were the two youngsters doing together at this time of the night? Heaven only knew what kind of trouble they could have gotten into.

Ignoring the cottony feeling inside her head, she whipped a robe over her lingerie. Securing it tightly with the sash, she jerked open the door to find not just the adolescents but Astrid as well.

"What is going on?" Rose demanded.

A distraught Freya pushed her way into the room, tears glistening in her blue eyes. "Something is wrong with Thorfinn. I know it. I just know it."

Astrid bustled in after the girl and threw her arm around her. "Freya, darling, we don't know that for sure. We haven't even read the contents of the sealed letter he left for Rose."

"Is Thorfinn in danger?" A ripping sensation tore through Rose's chest. Despite Astrid's reassuring words to her cousin, Rose couldn't help but absorb the child's panic. Something suddenly *did* feel terribly wrong, and unlike the trio half in and half out of her room, Rose knew exactly what peril Thorfinn might be facing.

"He left this at the foot of my bed!" Freya waved an envelope with Thorfinn's neat penmanship on the outside.

"Let's not rouse all the guests," Rose said nervously, shepherding them into the center of her room, including Young Thomas.

"He wrote on the envelope, 'Freya, give this to Miss Van Etten if I'm not home by morning' and 'Rose, you'll know what to do with this. It's from a night ago. I had to know for sure before I told you,'" Freya said. "If that doesn't sound important, I don't know what is."

The cryptic message, so much like Reggie's dying one, rushed through Rose like an East Coast express train. Thorfinn was in danger! Around her, the conversation buzzed like the ominous shake of a timber rattler's tail.

367

"But it's not morning yet," Astrid pointed out. "Perhaps Sinclair just hasn't had a chance to return from whatever he was doing."

"Something odd is going on. I heard Da come in late—and it sounded like he was talking to Mum. He kept apologizing over and over and over. He was slurring his words like he was drunk, and Da never gets blootered," Freya told her cousin stubbornly. "That's why I slipped out the back window and got *you* to help me row over here instead of Da."

"I was manning 'the front desk' like you told me, Miss Van Etten, when they came in looking for you," Young Thomas said worriedly. "I saw how anxious Freya was, and I thought I'd better bring her straight away."

"You made the right decision," Rose quickly told the lad, trying not to let any of them see her own fear. She turned then to Freya and held out a hand that she managed to keep steady only through sheer force of will. "Let's see what your brother wrote to me."

But when Rose pulled out the sheet of paper from the envelope, it wasn't covered with Thorfinn's precise letters but Reggie's sweepingly dramatic ones. The viscount had suspected Astrid of espionage, and Thorfinn had clearly gone to investigate the claims. Now he was missing, Sigurd was seemingly begging forgiveness from his dead wife, and Astrid—Astrid was standing in this very room trying to discount their fears.

All sensation seemed to pool in Rose's now-icy-cold hands and feet, leaving her not bereft but *driven*. With her hand now unnaturally steady, she crisply folded the letter along the same creases that Thorfinn had. If she was to save her Viking, she could not afford to crack. She had to *think*, not feel.

"Freya, Young Thomas," Rose said, the words so disconnected from her, so automatic, that she felt like a ventriloquist's dummy. "Would you please go and awaken my friends—Myrtle and Percy?" Percy knew nothing of the spying, but if Rose was to rescue Thorfinn, she needed to trust someone beyond Myrtle.

"Yes, ma'am." Young Thomas lightly grasped Freya's hand and gently guided her from the room.

As soon as he shut the door softly behind him, Rose shifted backward to her nightstand, where she kept her reticule, keeping her eyes on Astrid the entire time. "I want to grab my reading glasses. I didn't want to worry Freya more, but I was having trouble deciphering it."

Astrid frowned. "You upset her more by sending her from the room. What is the poor child to think?"

Rose felt for the knob and yanked on the drawer. Patting around, she found what she was looking for. Pushing aside the fabric of her purse, her fingers closed eagerly around the mother-of-pearl handle. Rose whipped her Bull Dog revolver straight at Astrid's face and cocked it.

"Where is he!" Rose freed the fire—the utter rage—inside her, allowing it to blast through the icy stillness and erupt onto Astrid. She fed the empowering anger and buried her disabling fear for Thorfinn's safety and her anguish at Astrid's involvement.

"What!" Astrid clasped both of her hands to her neck and stumbled backward a step.

"Where. Is. He." Rose advanced.

"Sinclair? I don't know." Astrid's green eyes darted frantically around the room, as if she could find answers there. "Rose, have you gone mad?"

"I know the truth about the bird-watchers." Rose watched her former friend's expression carefully and saw nothing but frightened confusion. Had some of Reggie's suspicions been incorrect? Were just the naturalists German agents? Was Astrid innocent? How was Sigurd tied up in all this? Rose had no time to consider the answers. She knew only that she could not afford to trust Astrid or to let doubts weaken her.

"Bird-watchers? My bird-watchers?" Astrid's fingers clutched at her shawl. "What do they have to do with this?"

"You and I both know they have *everything* to do with this. Do not think you can toy with me, Astrid. I have no qualms about shooting you if I have to." Rose hissed out the words, and she jerked her gun, as if she could make good on her threat. She doubted, though, she would be able to put a bullet through this young woman whom she had once admired. But Astrid did not know that, so Rose added, "I know what I'm doing with a firearm. I was taught how to shoot by a Texas Ranger."

"Shoot me? Good lord, what did Sinclair say in that letter of his? I swear I have no idea what you are talking about."

Rose held out the missive to Astrid. The woman's confusion seemed genuine, but if Thorfinn's cousin had been working as a spy for years, she'd be very good at playing the innocent. And Rose wanted to watch Astrid as she read Reggie's letter.

Astrid fumbled the paper several times, but she finally managed to open it. "This . . . this looks like Reggie's writing. How—why—I don't understa—"

"Read it!" Rose fluctuated back to cold, her mind focused entirely on how to save Thorfinn, because he *had* to still be alive. Rose couldn't accept any other alternative.

"Good lord!" Astrid clapped her hand over her mouth now. "I told Uncle Sigurd about Reggie being saved by a nurse. He goaded me. He kept saying Reggie must be a German sympathizer with the way he managed to escape. But Uncle Sigurd isn't a spy! I mean, he couldn't be. He's *Uncle Sigurd.*"

Rose, however, had no difficulty believing it. The man expressed little love for the United Kingdom, and she could imagine him rationalizing away his treason. And it made the pleas to his dead wife that Freya had overheard all the more stark. What had Sigurd done to his stepson? And Thorfinn . . . how had he endured discovering that the villain was once again someone whom he should have been able to trust implicitly? Sorrow threatened to bubble up and drown Rose, so she shoved it down and forced herself to concentrate on facts.

Astrid sank to the ground, her hand fisted over the letter. Rose quickly snatched it back in case it was all a ploy to destroy evidence. But Astrid didn't look like she was acting. She seemed honestly stricken. Rose knew how to fake a tear or two herself, but Astrid looked . . . gutted. And Rose hoped the woman was truly innocent.

"I killed him. I killed Reggie. It's all my fault. I should never have told Uncle."

"If you truly know nothing of the spying, then you're not to blame," Rose said frankly. Under other circumstances, she would have gentled her voice, but she didn't have the ability right now. Nothing about Rose was soft. She was hard, fierce, steely—but not brittle. Brittle meant that she could break under her fear, and panic wouldn't save Thorfinn.

"Uncle Sigurd introduced me to some of the bird-watchers. I—I never stopped to think. They seemed truly interested in wildlife—like all my clients. Oh lord, were they *all* spies?" Astrid frantically rubbed her forehead.

"Doubtful," Rose said shortly. "That's why it was such a good ruse."

Suddenly, Astrid's shaking fingers stopped their mad dance as she glanced up at Rose, her green eyes horrified. "Freya said her father kept apologizing to her *mother*! Do you think he did something to Sinclair? Sinclair must have been following him! Why else would he leave the letter with Freya?"

"Exactly." Rose snapped out the word as defensive rage rushed through her. She latched on to it rather than the piercing, debilitating agony.

The door creaked open, and Myrtle stopped midstride on the threshold. Her eyes flicked from Rose to the gun to Astrid kneeling on the floor and then back to Rose again.

"So *she* is the spy," Myrtle—whose mind always worked faster than anyone else's—said.

"That has not been proved conclusively either way." Rose handed Reggie's letter over Astrid's head to Myrtle.

"I am *not* a spy!" Astrid cried.

"What's going on?" Freya's voice sounded from the hallway.

"Can anyone get a blasted bit of sleep around here?" a random male guest bellowed, his muffled voice sounding harried.

The group hurried inside with Percy and Young Thomas taking up the rear. They stopped stock still when they spotted Rose.

"Good lord, Rose Petal, what mess have you gotten into this time?" Percy asked.

"Is that a *gun*?" Freya asked.

"Aye," Young Thomas said as he quietly shut the door. Clearly, Rose had won the loyalty of at least one islander.

"But why is Rose pointing it at Astrid?" Freya demanded frantically.

"Freya, you must be very brave," Rose said sternly, her eyes still trained on Thorfinn's cousin. "Your brother is in danger and needs our help. There may be spies on Hamarray, and we must be careful who we trust."

"Spies! What spies?" Percy demanded. "Why am I just now hearing about this?"

Astrid silenced both Freya and Percy with a look as she slowly rose to her feet. Nervously, she smoothed her skirts, but her trembling fingers only crinkled the coarse fabric even more.

"What can I do to help find Sinclair?" Astrid asked.

"Where are the places that the bird-watchers showed the most interest? Areas that would be good for secret meetings? Hideouts with views of Scapa Flow?" Rose fired off the questions.

"Um, the broch," Astrid said hurriedly. "And there's a cave in the cliffs not too far from the ancient tower that's easily reachable from the headlands. You can see exceedingly far in all directions."

"What about the sea cave that's accessible by boat?" Rose questioned.

"You know about it?" Astrid asked, surprised.

"Thorfinn showed me." Rose tried not to think of what had happened in that sheltered alcove. How she'd felt. How he'd felt. How, after such bliss, she'd dragged him into this mess, this horrid, awful, deadly mess.

"I did take the bird-watchers to that secluded inlet. It's a good place to see seafowl."

"And to hide small, swift boats," Rose added. She pushed back on every emotion now, even the anger. Somehow, she found the preternatural calm that had allowed her to navigate her ambulance through the dark, crowded roads as men and horses screamed and shells fell. Holding on to that steely focus, Rose began to plan. "We should fan out. A group of us should check the rock outcrop on the headlands, the others the broch. If they're empty, we'll head to the sea cave. Young Thomas, do you know what cliff cave Astrid is referring to?"

"Aye, but shouldn't we first alert . . ." Young Thomas trailed off, clearly at a loss for who could help.

"There is no time. Even if we can contact someone, it would take too long to convince them that we're not mad." Rose began to pace, the movement helping to dispel the anxiousness that she refused to acknowledge. "We will tie up Astrid and leave her locked in my room. Freya can watch the door while the rest of us look for Thorfinn. Myrtle and I will go to the broch since we are familiar with it. Since you know where the other cave is, you and Percy can explore it."

"What about the other male visitors, ma'am?" Young Thomas now stood at attention, as if facing one of his commanding officers. "A lot of them were at the Front, too, and can help in the search."

"We don't know who to trust," Rose answered.

"I'll go retrieve my Colts," Myrtle said.

"You know how to handle a firearm too?" Young Thomas asked.

"One of my grandfathers was a Texas Ranger, and the other was a hired gun," Myrtle said. "They taught me, and they also showed Rose how to shoot when she visited the family ranch."

"Why are there spies?" Freya cried. "How is Thorfinn involved? What is in the letter he left on my bed?"

"All reasonable questions," Percy interjected.

"We'll explain as soon as we find your brother," Rose said quickly, not wishing to reveal to the girl that her father might have killed her half sibling. Until they knew for certain Thorfinn's fate, she did not want to upset Freya even more.

"But—" Freya began to protest.

Young Thomas seemed to understand that Rose was seeking to protect the girl. He wrapped his arm around her thin shoulders and led her into the hall. "We have a mission, Freya. We need to focus on that. Can you do that?"

"Aye." Her petite chin stopped trembling as she set it at a fierce angle.

"It is a good thing that I have a penchant for adventure, a cavalier regard to recklessness, a Webley revolver in my room, and an undying fondness for you, Rose," Percy said.

"Can't I help?" Astrid cried.

"You can by not trying to run," Rose said as she opened her closet and pulled out a thick cord that she usually used as a belt. Astrid looked stricken, but she didn't struggle or even protest as Rose bound her hands behind her back.

As Rose secured Astrid, Percy and Myrtle left to gather their firearms and coats. They returned shortly, and Myrtle handed one of her twin Colt army revolvers to Young Thomas. They had been a gift from her hired-gun grandfather. She also had a Henry lever action rifle from the Texas Ranger slung over her shoulder. As soon as the rest of the group was out of hearing distance from Freya and Astrid, Rose told Percy and Young Thomas as much as she could about the spy ring as they dashed to the stables.

Rose and Myrtle took the Raceabout while the men squeezed into Percy's Napier, which he'd had shipped over to Hamarray for the race. Engines roaring, both vehicles blazed out of the old barn and shot down the road toward the other end of the headlands. Percy swerved first into the grasses as he and Young Thomas bumped across the uneven land toward the cliffs. The Napier stopped yards from the edge. As soon as Percy killed the engine, the two jumped out and dashed toward the path that led to the cliff cave.

Ahead of Rose and Myrtle, the broch shone like a beacon in the golden glow of twilight. The gilded sky made Rose feel like she was trapped in a Klimt painting . . . or, more correctly, *The Scream* with its swirling orange colors and surreal terror oozing from each deft stroke.

Dust flew and tires skidded as Rose yanked the Raceabout's hand brake and spun the wheel over. The right-side tires briefly left the ground and thumped back to earth as the car screeched to a stop, feet from the ancient tower. Rose jumped out, leaving the motor running, with Myrtle racing beside her. Every step seemed to send a spike of pain through Rose's heart. She almost dashed headlong into the broch, but Myrtle roughly grabbed her arm. After practically thrusting Rose aside, Myrtle ripped off her tam and placed it on the end of her rifle.

"Here," Myrtle hissed, handing Rose the long arm. "Use this to check if anyone is inside before you go barreling in. I'll be right behind you, bending low and getting ready to fire."

"A trick you learned from your outlaw grandfather?" Rose whispered as she grabbed the improvised decoy. She had to say something, *do* something, to ease the horrible tension, or she *would* make a suicidal dash straight inside.

"No. Grandpa Jack—the Texas Ranger."

Rose steadied her breath, just as if she were preparing to leave a poste de secours. But instead of getting behind a wheel, she pressed her back against the inner wall of the thick stone entrance, holding the hat in front of her to draw any fire. Slowly, her heart so tight she swore her blood would stop pumping, Rose slunk farther along the broch's deep doorway and poked the lure inside.

Nothing happened.

It was one of the hardest things that Rose had ever done, but she waited. Despite the cool night air, sweat saturated her, and her muscles threatened to tremble. Still, she held firm. One. Two. Three.

Then with her heart screaming silently in her chest, Rose peeked into the broch, her Bull Dog revolver ready to shoot.

But she didn't.

She shouted out the pain inside her.

For there, in the center of a hazy beam shimmering from the open ceiling, was a heartbreakingly familiar swatch of black material. Just as Astrid had done earlier, Rose collapsed to her knees. With a shaking hand, she reached for Thorfinn's eye patch.

Cradling it in her hand, she could only say, "It's his."

"But it means he was here." Myrtle squeezed her shoulder. "We're tracking him. There's still the sea cave that you mentioned for us to check."

"There's blood on his eye patch, M."

"I know, darling," Myrtle said. "But Mr. Sinclair's a tough man. He's your Viking, remember?"

But Rose had witnessed so many strong men felled by violence. Muscle and sinew could not withstand blades, bullets, and bombs. Rose's shoulders began to sag, and a soul-deep wail ripped from her chest and started to claw through her throat.

But before she could give in to the encompassing grief, Myrtle roughly tugged on her arm. "Get up, Rose."

"What if he's dead?"

"What if he's alive and trapped in a sea cave? You know how unpredictable the tides are around here. You're a motoriste, Rose, and you *need* to race right now."

Like a roar of fire through a previously dead furnace, renewed energy shot through Rose. Jerking to attention, she jumped to her feet. "We have to get back to the Raceabout!"

"Yes. Yes, we do," Myrtle agreed as they both tore from the broch. Percy and Young Thomas were nowhere in sight, but Rose had no time to wait to learn what they had discovered.

Even now as Rose slid into the driver's seat, her hands shook. But by the time she grabbed the wheel, they were steady.

Then she was off, bouncing over the hills, but Rose felt no thrill in the wild ride. Myrtle had accompanied Rose on enough rough trips that she automatically moved her body to balance the vehicle through the hairpin curves. Rose felt like she was back in France—only this time she was racing to save not a faceless poilu but the man she loved.

In the distance, Rose thought she heard a horse scream, followed by a man's groan, which she instinctually knew was from Viscount Barbury. She scanned the landscape for supply wagons. Where *was* that equine? Would its massive hooves send her Tin Lizzie tumbling? How could she save them?

"Rose! The pier!" Myrtle's shriek miraculously penetrated the nightmarish haze. Rose blinked and slammed on the Raceabout's brakes. Sea, not road, stretched before them. The car skidded to a stop only inches from the edge of the ancient jetty.

Rose didn't have time to contemplate that she'd almost driven over the brink. Ignoring her shaking muscles, she jumped from the Mercer before it fully stopped. Pounding over the dock, she leaped into her speedboat. Myrtle bounded in behind her. As Rose sped through the water, Myrtle placed her hand on the butt of her pistol tucked inside her coat's pocket. Recklessly, Rose tore through the waves as they bashed against Hamarray. She'd always relished the power of the sea, but it had never before threatened to carry away someone she loved. Now . . . now she despised each crash, each droplet of spray.

Whipping *The Briar* toward the maw of the sea cave, Rose tried to gird herself for the sight of Thorfinn's lifeless body. But how did one prepare for that?

Pulling back on the throttle, Rose slowed *The Briar* to a crawl, even though she wanted to storm the stony tomb. But with the current slamming them forward and the jagged rocks all too ready to greet them, speed wasn't possible. A mistake now would kill not only her but her best friend and the man who had become vital to her. Creeping through the entrance, Rose frantically began scanning the cavern's interior.

"There!" shouted Myrtle as she pointed toward the back of the cave, where Rose remembered a sizable rock shelf with stony pillars that the birds had circled through. Instead, she saw nothing but water and the faint glimpse of a flash of pale color.

Thorfinn's face.

Terror and relief both battered Rose until she was left light headed and nearly gasping herself.

Was he breathing? The anguished question nearly gutted her, but she did not falter.

Instead, she frantically drew *The Briar* closer. Her entire body sagged as she spotted Thorfinn's neck muscles straining as he defiantly fought to keep his head above the water.

The bastards must have tied Thorfinn to one of the rock formations, planning for him to die a horrible, prolonged death. But still he fought as the unforgiving sea pummeled him. He was every inch the Viking, battling with everything in him to the very end. Her heart seemed to strain along with Thorfinn, as if the mere organ could fly from her chest and lift her man from the waves.

"Thorfinn!" Rose shouted.

The tendons surrounding his throat visibly pulled even more as he somehow forced his chin up even farther.

"Minnstray!" he gasped out before a wave washed over his mouth.

"Just focus on breathing!" Rose said as she tore off her coat and robe and retrieved the knife strapped around her thigh. Her skin felt tight, as if it were straining to contain the urgency pulsating through her. The ropes holding Thorfinn must be underwater.

"Too strong!" Thorfinn protested, but she didn't heed his warning.

She plunged into the froth. It tried to sweep her back against the wall, and she could feel her body being shoved toward the unforgiving rock. But she fought—her muscles already burning in protest as she defied the power of the sea. Her hands brushed against one of Thorfinn's arms, and the unnatural chill of his flesh almost made her cry out. But she didn't. She had no energy to spare on fear or anguish.

"I'll free you," she vowed before she sucked in her breath and dived under the cold water. Her fingers found one of the hawsers wrapped around Thorfinn's body. Using it to anchor herself against the punishing waves, she braced her foot on the rock he was lashed against and began sawing through rope.

Her knife seemed only to rub against the fibers. Her chest grew tighter and tighter as she frantically worked the blade. With her lungs burning, she kicked her way up. As she broke through the surface, she wanted to sob, but that would take time and energy that she could not afford to waste.

She dived back down and attacked Thorfinn's bindings with all her strength. More water rushed inside the cave, slamming her against the rock. Her knife nicked her arm, and blood swirled in the water. She could feel Thorfinn's body straining against his bindings.

He was still fighting.

For both of them.

Rose's forearms protested as she again swam for more air. This time when she was topside, she could see only Thorfinn's nostrils and lips. Desperation fueled her now. Ignoring her aching body, she punched through the eddies and once again reached the rope.

Finally the knife sliced a hunk of fibers. She sawed again and again and again until she had nothing left in her lungs.

When Rose surfaced, she could not see any part of Thorfinn.

She transformed the rush of horror into motion. Fighting her way back to the rock, she wildly attacked the rope. She realized that she was just hitting stone only when pain shot up her fingers and through her arm.

Something brushed against her body, and she realized it was Thorfinn kicking toward the surface. Utter joy blasted through her exhaustion, giving her the strength to make her own way up out of the darkness.

Together, she and Thorfinn managed to swim to the boat. Myrtle, who'd been making sure that the vessel didn't smash into the walls of the cave, helped haul Thorfinn on board as Rose pushed from below.

He sprawled on the leather cushions, sucking in air as Myrtle threw a blanket around him. Rose clambered in and knelt beside him as her warm tears mixed with the cold rivulets of seawater dripping down her face. Sobs echoed from her as her entire frame shook with the intensity of her relief. Frantically, she ran her hands over Thorfinn, trying to both warm him and check all his injuries. Dimly, Rose noticed Myrtle laying a wool blanket over her shoulders as well.

"Are . . . are you wearing a peignoir?" Thorfinn asked, rather incongruously through chattering teeth.

Rose kissed his scarred cheek as she handed him his eye patch. A tremulous laugh escaped her chilled lips, and the sound felt good. It was not always wrong to use wit as a shield or a balm. Strength came from many sources.

Stroking Thorfinn's temples, she smiled at him. "I'm sorry, but I didn't have time to dress for your rescue. You gave us all a terrible fright. And when Perseus finally arrives, Andromeda doesn't get to complain about what he, or in this case she, is wearing!"

Bemusement crossed Thorfinn's face, quickly followed by a half smile and then a look of deadly seriousness. "A contingent of spies are going to attack the British supply depot on Minnstray. They need an explosion to divert the Royal Navy's attention while the Germans send a relief vessel filled with soldiers to man the interned ships. They're trying to free the German fleet and restart the war."

Muscles Rose had thought would not move for weeks tensed and prepared for action. There was no time for respite.

They had a mission.

"Hold on tight!" Rose shouted to Thorfinn and Myrtle as she jumped back into the pilot's seat. Gingerly, she guided the boat out of the cave, but as soon as she cleared the jagged rocks, Rose jammed the throttle forward.

She spotted Percy's craft just beyond the breakers. Swinging by the sleek speedboat, she shouted, "Percy! Young Thomas! Follow us. We're going to Minnstray. We have a peace to save!"

Chapter 17

The golden stage of twilight had darkened into layers. Most of the sky had turned a deep blue green with a yellow glowing band near the horizon. It was possible to travel the sea under such conditions, but with the tricky current of Scapa Flow, Rose normally wouldn't have attempted to take a speedboat out.

Luckily, Thorfinn proved an adept navigator. His mind was a virtual encyclopedia of each skerry, shoal, and sounding along the course, allowing them to tear through the inky waves.

Whenever Thorfinn wasn't barking out instructions, he told Myrtle and Rose as much as he could about the spies. It was hard to hear him over the roar of *The Briar*'s engine, but Rose understood enough to confirm that it had indeed been Sigurd who was meeting with the spies, not Astrid. Relief over her friend's innocence burst through her, but it was tempered with concern for the Flett children. But Rose didn't have long to dwell on the revelation—not with the low light and Scapa Flow's hidden dangers.

"Mind the crosscurrent here!" Thorfinn warned. "The sandbar off to port has been protecting us."

Keeping the vessel steady through the rough bumps, Rose sacrificed no time as they blazed toward the small outcropping straight ahead. Minnstray was more of a glorified rock heap than an island, but it had served as a naturally fortified location to store fuel oil for the British

Grand Fleet. With truce declared and the German vessels moored within sight, the small post was undermanned, and anyone could easily approach the tiny lump without the sailors stationed there noticing. But one single spark near the oil reserves could ignite the entire islet into an inferno that would draw the attention of the British guard boats, allowing the German relief ship to swoop in.

The dark forms of the conspirators' boats were tied to the rocks, well away from the main dock and guard post, bobbing up and down like ominous water beetles. It meant that the men were already scurrying around on the island, planting their bombs. It wasn't the first time Rose had dashed toward a potential explosion. But this time she wasn't stopping at a poste de secours but heading into the very fray. Nerves and fear bounced inside her—refusing to settle.

"Are you ready?" Thorfinn asked as he jumped onto the dock and Percy pulled up his boat to the shore.

"Are *you* ready?" Rose questioned, tossing him the rope to tie up the boat. He was the one who was covered in bruises and who had nearly drowned less than an hour before. She worried that he wasn't up to the fight ahead of them.

"I'm eager to return this favor." Thorfinn pointed to his swollen nose, and his confident grin made Rose feel a bit more steady.

As if Myrtle had been leading charges her whole life, she lifted another of her rifles from the boat's storage area. Turning, she held it out to Thorfinn. "I assume you know how to use this piece."

"Reggie taught me." Thorfinn took the weapon and inspected it with the air of someone accustomed to firearms.

"Which direction did you say we should head?" Rose asked Thorfinn. Despite the risk, they had decided that it would be best to disarm the spies themselves rather than taking precious time to try to explain the situation to the guards on Minnstray. Even with Percy by their side, she doubted they would readily believe a duo of female

Americans in their nighties, two local crofters, and a man in silk pajamas claiming to be a duke.

"A group of us should head north, to the closest oil stores," Thorfinn said, his strong jaw clenched. "The second should go south, where the farther reserves are."

"Percy and Thomas should go south," Rose decided, since the two men hadn't used up their energy fighting currents in a sea cave and could move faster. "Myrtle should come with us—she's the best shot."

"She is," Percy agreed as he checked his Webley. His perpetual smile was still in place but pulled tight at the edges. "I've lost a dismal amount of money betting that I could outshoot her."

"According to what the spies said after my stepda left, the men are supposed to signal with a light when they are ready to set their timers to make sure that every one of them has the chance to return to their boats before the blaze incinerates the island," Thorfinn said grimly. "Make sure not just to stop them from setting the explosives but from sending out the message."

A new chill spread through Rose at the unspoken reason for Thorfinn's warning. If the signal was transmitted and the fuses were lit—even by just one set of the oil reserves—they all would likely burn alive along with the British naval personnel stationed on Minnstray.

"We should move," Thorfinn said, his expression as gruff as his voice.

They all nodded sharply. Young Thomas squared his shoulders like the soldier he'd been, his facial muscles tight with concentration. Percy's grin had faded, replaced by a look more solemn than any Rose had ever witnessed on his normally irreverent visage. Silently, the two of them disappeared first, and Thorfinn led Rose and a determined-looking Myrtle over the rocky terrain.

The harsh landscape seemed to echo the dark, unforgiving tension inside Rose. Unlike the other, more fertile islands, this small swath of land seemed to be made of nothing but stones held together with bits of gorse.

Rose gripped the mother-of-pearl handle of her Bull Dog, surprised by how sweaty her palm had once again become. Her already abused lungs seemed to compress in her chest as they stalked through the desolate heaps of rock. Memories of another wasteland started to crowd into her mind—black chair stumps, smoky remains of century-old villages, a burned-out vehicle, the skeleton of a horse.

Men's voices sounded in the distance—one with a German accent, and one with a British inflection. The shock reoriented her.

She *knew* those voices.

The sea breeze might be heavy with different floral scents and the ground rocky instead of sandy, but Rose felt as if she'd returned to Daytona Beach. These were the men who'd ambushed and then stalked her. They'd even trapped her inside of Fornhowe, seeking to bury her with the ancient dead.

Reawakened terror rippled through Rose. But she would not allow these men—these *spies*—to cow her. This time if someone ran, it was going to be the German agents and not her, even if her heart was pounding so hard that she could barely hear.

Staying low to the ground, Thorfinn, Myrtle, and Rose used the landscape and the shadows to obscure their movements. Rose's blood thrummed through her, filling her ears with a fast tattoo. Like a Celtic fighting song, it urged her forward past her fear—not recklessly but steadily. With purpose.

Big circular tanks rose before them, reminding Rose of the stone monoliths on Hamarray and Frest. But these were less majestic and more brutally functional. Two figures were crouched down by one of the silos. They stood up and nodded to each other. A giant of a man began to lift something into the air.

An electric lantern! He was getting ready to signal. If he did and timers were set, they would all perish.

Thorfinn exploded into motion, knocking the massive German to the ground. As the second spy started to draw his weapon, Rose trained hers directly on his chest.

Myrtle fired a warning shot straight through the spy's bowler hat. He froze.

Something flashed in the prone man's hand.

"He has a knife!" Rose screamed.

Thorfinn rapidly slammed his fist into the villain's face three times, and the hand holding the weapon went limp. Grabbing the spy's lapels, Thorfinn slowly dragged the unconscious man up and slumped him against the oil tank.

Keeping her weapon aimed at the other man, Rose stepped out of the protection of the rocks to hand Thorfinn a piece of rope. The conscious spy shifted, and another bullet whizzed above his head.

"I wouldn't try that," Myrtle said. "The next one will be lower. I've killed a charging bull with a single shot. Your skull is considerably more fragile. I should know. I've dug up enough of them."

Once Rose bound the slighter agent's hands together, he became wonderfully compliant. She made sure to stand behind him and clear of Myrtle's line of fire.

By the time Rose and Thorfinn had cleaned out each of the men's pockets and removed hidden weapons, the giant fellow had regained his senses. He glared at Thorfinn. "I should've killed you instead of listening to Will."

"Hush, Heinrich," the man with the British accent snapped.

Thorfinn, however, merely shrugged. "I'm rather glad you didn't."

Rose couldn't stop the chuckle that rose up inside her. Fueled by nervous energy, it spilled out. Thorfinn's response to the German agent was just so . . . calm and so utterly and completely him.

"Good lord, they're completely mad," Will said.

Myrtle stepped out from behind the boulders, her rifle snug against her shoulder and aimed at Will's heart. "Come on, gents. Let's stop lollygagging about and head to the guardhouse. I'm sure the British Navy will be very happy with the presents we're bringing them."

"Should we tie them in a bow?" Rose asked as they marched the men toward the center of the islet.

"They're already decked out in ropes," Thorfinn observed.

"But the hemp isn't pretty. Gifts should have shiny ribbons on them," Rose complained, feeling more like herself than she had in a long, long time. Her wit didn't make her empty or frivolous. It could be so much more than a protective mask. There could be a deepness in humor. It could expose truths otherwise ignored, help process the harshness of the world, or provide a balm when nothing else would ease the pain. Rose didn't need to live a somber, dull life to find meaning. What she needed was a *full* one—one where she embraced the quiet moments *and* the exciting ones.

"In this case, I don't think the packaging matters," Thorfinn shot right back, and Rose smiled.

Her joy, though, proved short lived.

Moments later, three figures appeared in the dim light. Young Thomas had Myrtle's Colt trained on two German agents as he marched them in the direction of the guardhouse. But Percy—the softhearted scoundrel—was nowhere to be seen.

"Where's Percy?" Rose asked, fear rushing back.

"He's fine, Miss Van Etten," Young Thomas called. "He just twisted his ankle in a rock crevice a few dozen yards back. He's hobbling a peedie bit, and he didn't want to delay me in getting the prisoners to the guardhouse. He told me to go on ahead, and he'd catch up for the celebration."

A celebration. The words rushed through Rose, and for once the idea didn't make her cringe.

They *deserved* to celebrate.

"I cannot believe those puffed-up fools did not want to believe us! They even chastised us for firing our guns and causing *them* alarm!" Rose flopped angrily against the upholstered seat of *The Briar*. "They only started to listen to us when Percy showed up, and *he* barely even knows what's going on."

"He is a duke," Thorfinn pointed out.

"Any Tom, Dick, or Harry could be a duke. It certainly doesn't mean they have godlike knowledge." Rose crossed her arms.

The light had just transformed back to gold, and the world appeared gilt. Minnstray's docks were directly across from Mainland, Orkney, and the bucolic, rolling hills looked like the Elysian Fields. The seas were calm, the glistening water lapping against the shores. It was a glorious early morning—a perfect one to celebrate the defeat of a plot to end peace.

But the British sailors on Minnstray had ruined the stunning sunrise with their refusal to radio their commanders on the guard ships until they could "confirm" the evidence of the plot. Of course, the spies had pleaded their innocence, pretending to simply be bird-watchers set upon by a duo of crazed females aided by two poor, deluded crofters. The daft Brits had even come within a hairbreadth of believing the conspirators. Not only had the whole scene been horribly annoying, but the guardsmen had wasted precious time by failing to immediately direct the British ships to intercept the German relief vessel.

Fortunately, Percy—the *duke*—had limped up in his silk pajamas and signet ring and convinced the men of the Royal Navy to actually rouse themselves enough to venture out and see the indisputable evidence of the bombs that had so nearly ended all their lives. Rose had been so disgusted with the entire proceedings that she'd left as soon as the men had begun finally conveying the information to their superiors. Unfortunately, it seemed their bosses were being equally slow to accept the idea of a conspiracy being stopped by negligee-clad women and two locals. It appeared that the British Navy was intent on writing off the saboteurs as a small cadre of madmen. After all, how could a broken enemy *possibly* sneak anything by the oh-so-mighty Royal Navy?

"Should we set sail for Hamarray?" Thorfinn asked as he joined her aboard *The Briar*.

"No," Rose said grumpily. "We'll wait for the others in case His Majesty's Navy deigns to ask either of us a question."

"I might take a peedie kip, if you don't mind." Thorfinn wriggled down into the cushions, looking incongruously like a schoolboy despite his massive physique.

An undeniable swell of love burst through Rose as Thorfinn's golden eyelashes swept downward over his left eye. "If anyone has earned a rest, it's you."

He gave a sleepy nod that ended in a massive yawn. Thorfinn tucked his head against his chest, and his breathing almost instantly slowed into the measured rhythm of sleep. Rose reached for a dry blanket and tucked it around him.

Her Viking managed to look both vulnerable and fierce in slumber—this strong man she'd almost lost. Now that the urgency had ebbed and the plot was foiled, the emotions she'd kept at bay streamed forth. Rose *cared* for this man in a way she had not believed possible. Love had been a concept for naive dreamers . . . until Thorfinn had nearly been taken from her. Now it had become real to her—a palpable force, stronger than any she'd ever encountered before.

It frightened Rose with its power, as it left her with no shields. She had denied love for years, protecting herself from craving the one thing that her parents had difficulty showing in abundance. She'd let herself go hollow and empty—thinking that to *not* feel affection was surety against disappointment, rejection, and even hurt. But it had led to its own soul-biting pain—a constant ache of feeling loss and of *being* lost.

But here in Orkney, Rose was found. She had connections. Not just the incredible one with Thorfinn—as powerful and magnificent as it was—but with all the islanders, from little Alex and Margaret to Widow

Craigie. Yes, opening herself to them meant accepting the sorrows that invariably accompanied deep attachment—for one could not share just joy but must share agony too. But bonds of community, of *family*, made the rough times bearable and the good times more meaningfully joyous.

Oddly contented, Rose trained her eyes on the biggest island in Orkney. The entire island chain was a fierce place yet a calm one too. Harsh but bucolic. It suited her—this land of contrast and beauty. She could see herself—

Was that a flash?

Rose bolted upright and grabbed Myrtle's binoculars as she stared at a cove on Mainland. There it was again. A reflective wink of light off glass. Then another. Binoculars? Spyglass? Or something innocuous?

The red nose of a speedboat appeared next as it shot out of the secluded inlet and headed toward the Atlantic Ocean, exactly where the conspirators had said the German relief vessel would be. Unlike in the closely guarded North Sea, a ship could sit undetected in the open waters, awaiting the signal to steam in and unleash the interned fleet that could keep the terrible war alive.

At least one other spy must have been watching to make sure the explosion occurred on Minnstray and realized that the mission had failed. Rose had to head off the speedboat before it could warn the *Engel*. She had no time to enlist help from the British fleet. Not only would it take too long to run to the guard station on Minnstray, but she'd lose even more precious minutes trying to convince them of the peril.

After leaping from *The Briar*, she quickly untied the craft. She vaulted back inside, fired up the engine, and reversed her vessel.

"Wha . . . ?" Thorfinn came awake with such a violent jerk that he almost toppled overboard.

"We have to stop that speedboat!" Rose cried out.

Without questioning her, Thorfinn instantly straightened. Ahead of them lay two of the many skerries they'd need to navigate around.

Rose started to nose *The Briar* toward what appeared to be the shorter passage around the obstacle, but Thorfinn stopped her.

"Turn starboard," Thorfinn shouted. "There's a rock in the middle of the channel where you're headed."

She obeyed without hesitation, steering toward what visually appeared like the longer route. Despite the dangerous shoals of Scapa Flow, Rose gunned the engine and barreled ahead. Flicking her eyes over the surface of the water, she forcibly narrowed her world to nothing but the obstacles ahead of her—just as if this were any other race, any other competition, any other lark.

But it wasn't.

She wasn't racing just for herself and certainly not for glory. She was doing this for the people of her island, her *loved* ones, for the world, for each nation, and for every person who would suffer if peace was lost today.

Rose gave her senses over to the Flow and its tricky currents. The only person—the only *thing*—that she permitted to enter her sphere of focus was Thorfinn. With a steadiness that mirrored her own, he barked out directions and warnings. He wasted no words, and she wasted not a foot on overdoing any maneuver.

Like the pistons and rods in *The Briar*'s motor, Rose and Thorfinn worked seamlessly together as they powered through the water. Their quarry was not so knowledgeable of the Flow. By the time the conspirators reached the open ocean, Rose and Thorfinn were only mere yards behind them.

"Duck!" Rose screamed as she caught the glint of light off a long metal barrel. Thorfinn flopped down just as bullets whizzed over them. Rose scrunched down the best she could.

One slug, then a second, hit and shattered the windshield. More sounds of war boomed at the edge of Rose's senses. But she gripped the wooden wheel tighter, concentrating on its polished finish made smooth from oil and not from constant use as the one on her ambulance had been. She was on the sea in the golden light of dawn, not on land motoring through the blackness.

As she forcefully held herself in the present, Thorfinn popped up holding the rifle Myrtle had given him. He fired off his own shots, forcing the conspirators to take cover. Unlike in the war, Rose wasn't alone on this mission and solely responsible for the wounded men in her care. She had a partner, an *ally*.

"Not bad!" Rose shouted. She still felt the sting of fear, but it was purposefully directed into action.

"I can point and pull the trigger," Thorfinn yelled back, "but nothing fancy like Myrtle."

"It's sufficient for what we need! Just keep their heads down!" Rose was in top racing form now, her body and mind channeling everything inside her into stopping the spies.

The gunman tried raising his head, but Thorfinn sprayed more bullets, working the lever action on the Henry like a machine. After dropping the empty weapon, he grabbed another left on the seat by Myrtle. The helmsman must have realized that he couldn't outrun them. Sharply, he turned the boat in an attempt to ram.

His mistake.

Rose let the German agent believe that he had them in his sights. Then at the last minute, she jerked *The Briar*, bringing the old girl alongside the other vessel. Thorfinn leaped into the air, and Rose's heart seemed to fly with him. He pounced onto the other speedboat like a Florida panther and landed directly on top of the armed man. With one terrific blow, Thorfinn knocked the German agent's long arm into the sea while his other fist smashed out like a howitzer. The fellow's head snapped back, and he slumped unconscious into the seat well. The panicked helmsman began to reach down for his gun. Before he could even touch it, Thorfinn slammed his fist into the spy's cheek. The conspirator desperately swung back. Thorfinn easily blocked the blow and then jabbed a left into the man's solar plexus. As the fellow began to slump forward, Thorfinn aimed an uppercut at his jaw. The man flew backward and sprawled over the back of the boat. Thorfinn's fighting style was quick and brutal.

With the conspirators unconscious, Thorfinn reached forward and flipped the ignition switch, bringing the enemy's motor to a sputtering halt. Triumph and relief pumped through Rose as she pulled even closer to the other boat and cut her own engine to a burbling idle.

"Rope!" Thorfinn called out, as if they were simply working together on the croft and tying up shocks of wheat.

Rose tossed him a coil stowed in the rear seat of *The Briar*.

"We make a good team," she said as Thorfinn hoisted the gunman from the bottom of the boat and draped him against the side to more easily tie his hands.

"Aye." Thorfinn grinned as he finished the job quickly and moved on to the last—and hopefully final—conspirator.

"Which do you think we do better together? Spying? Peat cutting? Estate management? Whiskey distilling?"

"You know, lass, there is a thing or two we haven't tried yet," Thorfinn said with a naughty wink that sent arousal sparking through Rose's already charged body.

"Such as?" she asked throatily.

He leaned over the gunwale, as if to plant a kiss on her mouth. "Sheep dipping."

Laughter bubbled up through Rose, rich and fine. Yes, Thorfinn Sinclair had the most wonderful way of awakening everything that had been dead inside of her. And better yet, she was going to let him.

"Is there a competition?" She arched her brow.

"Nay."

It was her turn to wink. "I bet I can turn it into one."

He threw back his head and laughed heartily into the sea breeze. "Of that, I have no doubt. Life is definitely more exciting with you around."

Rose became aware of a roar, and at first she thought it was the pounding of her own blood. But as it grew in volume, she realized that it came from the Royal Navy patrol boats as they surrounded them. Soon sailors were shouting orders. Within moments, the spies were hauled on board the sleek military vessels and the enemy craft commandeered.

Thorfinn climbed back aboard *The Briar* with Rose, and the commander of one of the CMBs tipped his hat in her direction. "That was exceptional piloting there, miss. We wouldn't have been able to catch them if it hadn't been for you. Their boat was too far out to sea when we got a signal to follow."

A rush of pride swept through Rose. Although she'd won races before, they hadn't been like this. And for once, there was no mention of her having done a capital job . . . for a lady.

"Thank you, sir!" Rose said, beaming at the man.

"Do you know what is going on? The signal from the flagship was rather brief," another commander asked her.

"These men are spies," Rose explained. As she and Thorfinn quickly recapitulated the espionage they'd uncovered, more and more of the British sailors gathered to hear. Instead of looking incredulous, they were all staring with various degrees of admiration. They *believed* her. Finally.

Satisfaction washed through Rose. The men on the vessels gave her and Thorfinn a mighty cheer before their commanders ordered the CMBs to return to the harbor.

"Well, that certainly felt wonderful," Rose said, smiling at Thorfinn. "I guess we're credible after all."

Thorfinn laughed, looking just as pleased as her. He winked and added, "You'd better believe it."

Joining in on his mirth, Rose was just about to turn *The Briar* around to follow the other craft when she spied British destroyers moving into the Atlantic in search of the *Engel*.

"Want to see this out until the very end?" Rose asked.

Thorfinn settled back in his seat. "Why not?"

Rose followed at a respectable distance, not wanting to disrupt the British Navy's plans. Just when she was beginning to think she and Thorfinn would need to turn around for lack of fuel, she spotted another ship on the horizon. Cutting the engine, she reached for Thorfinn with one hand and her binoculars with the other. Trading the instrument back and forth, they watched as the destroyers surrounded the German *Engel*.

The surrender was uneventful. After a single warning shot fired well over its bow, the *Engel* surrendered. But that made it all the more satisfying to Rose. They'd done it. They'd preserved the peace, and no more people had to die. No more shells tearing through limbs. No more mustard gas destroying lungs. No more bullets decimating organs.

"You never stopped fighting, Rose. Even when no one believed you," Thorfinn said, his steady voice deep with emotion.

"I couldn't have done it without you, Myrtle, Freya, Young Thomas, and Percy. It was time I started working with a family."

She'd meant to end the sentence with the word *team*, but the word *family* . . . it just felt right—strong, just like them. For love in all its permutations wasn't a transaction or even a barter. It was essential. It *was* the purpose she'd been yearning for all these years—the mission, the *meaning* of living.

Chapter 18

"Da's asking for you," Freya said quietly, the dark shadows under her cornflower-blue eyes making them seem even lighter than normal.

"Me?" Thorfinn asked in reflexive shock.

He, Rose, Freya, and Astrid had arrived at the croft late yesterday morning after Rose had freed Astrid from her bedroom and apologized for suspecting her. Due to the circumstances, Astrid had immediately accepted Rose's contrition, and they'd all taken off to Frest to confront Sigurd and to decide how and when to report him to the authorities. When they'd arrived, he had been nowhere to be seen. After questioning the children, Thorfinn had headed to the byre and had found his stepda collapsed by the milking stool. Thorfinn had been able to rouse the older man, but it was clear that he'd suffered another stroke.

Rose had quickly offered to take off in *The Briar* to fetch a doctor from Kirkwall, but even though Sigurd had trouble with his speech, his *no* had been emphatic. Unlike with the stroke after his wife's passing, Sigurd wasn't fighting death. He was not only accepting it; he seemed to be welcoming it.

Rose had stayed overnight at the croft, helping with the children, and Young Thomas had arrived in the morning. Astrid had gone home last evening to work with her grandmother to organize the islanders to bring meals. Myrtle and even Percy had dropped by earlier today. Over the last few hours, Sigurd's breathing had become more and more labored. Each intake of air triggered a terrible, rattle-like gurgle in his chest, and he grew ever weaker.

Thorfinn and Percy had moved him to the back room for more privacy, and Sigurd had asked to see each of the children separately, starting with little Alexander. It was clear that the older man knew his time was drawing to a close, and he wanted to make his last goodbyes. Thorfinn hadn't expected, though, for his stepda to request a final audience with *him*. After all, it was clear that Sigurd didn't need to charge his stepson with the duty to care for the bairns; they both knew Thorfinn would.

"Aye." Freya nodded. "Da said your name quite clearly."

Thorfinn glanced around the small front room as he wondered if the children could spare him. Little Alexander was nestled on Rose's lap, and Margaret snuggled against her side as Rose told the wee ones tales from her racing days. Thorfinn's siblings were somber, their eyes red and puffy. Rose was not just distracting them but giving them the warmth, the *comfort*, that they sorely needed. Thorfinn still did not know how long she would stay on the island once they finally discovered where Reggie had hidden the rest of his notes, but she was here now—for him and his siblings.

"We'll be fine, Thorfinn," Freya said earnestly as she laid her hand on Thorfinn's forearm. "We are all strong, and I can help Rose look after the bairns while you talk to Da."

A fine mist momentarily distorted Thorfinn's vision as he realized the truth of Freya's statement. Aye, she was still young, but she was tough. She'd be there to support their sisters and brother, just like he had when their mum had died and Sigurd had experienced his first stroke. They'd survived and then thrived when it had just been him running the household. There'd been pain and sadness then, too, but like before, the gladness would come again as well as the happiness.

"And I'll be here too," Young Thomas said as he came to stand beside Freya, his shoulders straight. Shyly, he reached for Freya's free palm, and she wrapped her fingers around his. Young Thomas was clearly sweet on Freya, but that wasn't the only reason the lad was standing beside them. The crofters always helped each other out, and Young Thomas wouldn't be the only neighbor literally and figuratively lending a hand to comfort the Fletts.

"Go to him," Freya said to Thorfinn, a slight catch in her voice. "Da hasn't much longer."

Thorfinn laid his palm over the hand that Freya had placed on his arm. "You are a strong lass. You have made us all proud—me, your da, and Mum up in heaven."

Freya's throat worked as she visibly swallowed. Her blue eyes grew wet and bittersweet. She pressed her fingers against Thorfinn's sweater and then released him. As she stepped back to allow Thorfinn to pass, Young Thomas slung his arm around her shoulders, pulling her close.

Drawing in his own deep breath, Thorfinn plunged into the back room. A breeze drifted in through the single window, bringing with it the scent of summer flowers and the smell of the sea. The fragrances mixed with the ever-present remnants of peat smoke, creating an aroma that was as uniquely Orcadian as the man who lay swathed in blankets.

Sigurd—who had always been an indomitable force—seemed heartbreakingly slight as he curled in a pallet meant for a child. Even after his first stroke, when he'd struggled against paralysis, he'd seemed like a warrior of old. He'd fought, clawing his way back to life. But now . . . now he was willingly sinking into death. For the first time ever, Sigurd appeared frail—his body a husk of weathered skin, brittle bones, and withered sinew.

"Sigurd?" Thorfinn called, not sure if the man had fallen into sleep or unconsciousness.

His stepda's eyes fluttered open. The light in them was faint, but still sharp and fully aware.

"Thor . . . fff . . . inn."

The word was slightly mangled, but Thorfinn had no trouble making it out. Since his stepda normally called him Sinclair, the use of his given name slammed into Thorfinn, causing conflicting feelings to cascade through him. He'd never known exactly how to feel about Sigurd, and now, after his betrayal, even less so. Sadness and sorrow crept through Thorfinn but also, ashamedly, a whisper of relief. His stepda's death would not only relieve him of the burden of turning Sigurd over to the authorities for certain execution but help protect the children from their father's misdeeds. But Thorfinn's sense of escape brought raw remorse.

"It . . . is . . . best." Sigurd's voice might have been garbled, but the message was clear. He must have sensed Thorfinn's guilt and was assuaging it.

"The . . . the . . . gold . . . is . . . buried . . . on . . . the . . . backside . . . of . . . your . . . ma's . . . gravestone." Sigurd glanced away, but not before Thorfinn could see the shame in the man's eyes. They both knew that he meant the coin that he'd made from spying. Sickness twisted through Thorfinn as he realized that Sigurd was delegating this knowledge to him because he trusted Thorfinn to use the treasure to support the children. Thorfinn could never touch the blood money, but he didn't tell Sigurd that. He only nodded sharply.

"Take . . . care . . ." Sigurd forced out the instruction before his last word was drowned out by a wet rumble from his chest.

"You know I will make sure the children are provided for." Thorfinn started to grasp his stepda's hand, but he didn't know if the man wanted to be touched. He awkwardly laid his palm near Sigurd's instead. Another rush of shocked emotion blasted Thorfinn as his stepda's fingers rested on his own. Sigurd had rarely touched him and never in any way like this—a way that carried meaning, affection even.

"You . . . will . . . love . . . them . . . too." Sigurd's gaze held Thorfinn's again.

"Aye." He answered through a swollen throat, even though Sigurd's statement hadn't exactly been a question.

"I . . . am . . . sorry."

The apology upended Thorfinn even more than the physical contact. He stared at Sigurd, momentarily unable to speak. What did his stepda mean? The espionage? Thorfinn's capture? The mess he was leaving Thorfinn to unravel?

"I . . . never . . . knew . . ." Sigurd broke off, his words drowned by a gurgling sound. The man coughed, but it did not seem to clear whatever was obstructing his breathing. When he spoke again, his voice was even wobblier. "What . . . to . . . do . . . with . . . you . . . son . . . of . . . the . . . enemy."

"I wasn't the enemy." Thorfinn couldn't stop the words. He did not wish to guilt the dying man, but he could not let that stand. Not anymore. Not when he'd spent so many years believing it himself. "And I was never Mar's son."

"I . . . know . . . but . . . I . . . fool . . . do . . . not . . . be . . . bitter . . . do . . . not . . . be . . . me."

"I will not," Thorfinn choked out, realizing what this was costing Sigurd and what it meant to the older man. He felt as if the air had been pummeled from him again, his body shaky and hollow.

Sigurd lapsed into silence. As Thorfinn searched for something to say—*anything* to say—an odd raspy rattle emerged from his stepda. Sigurd's fingers on top of Thorfinn's hand became slack and heavy. Even before Thorfinn checked to see if the man's chest was still rising and falling, he knew the truth. Sigurd was gone.

His eyes wet, Thorfinn bowed his head and prayed. When he finished, he still kept his chin tucked close to his chest, taking a moment to gather himself before telling his siblings.

Thorfinn would miss the cantankerous old islander. The man had taught him, shown him, so much. Even if Sigurd had never been able to bring himself to love Thorfinn as a son, he'd still helped to mold him into the person he'd become. And with his last breath, he'd tried to gift Thorfinn with the support that he'd never been able to show in life. It might not have been affection, but there'd been respect and advice too. Sigurd had been flawed—more than Thorfinn had even realized—but he'd imparted to Thorfinn the skills to survive on this harsh land. Sigurd had also given his children a love that would stay with them forever. The good of the man—the strength of him—would live on in Frest and in his offspring. And the bad—the bad could be buried with Sigurd.

<hr/>

"Could you please dig each divot a bit more shallow?" Myrtle asked as she hovered anxiously by Thorfinn's shoulder.

It had been only a week since they had foiled the plot to free the German fleet and a few days since Sigurd's burial. Although Rose had been by Thorfinn's side constantly, they hadn't had any time alone together. If they hadn't been with his family, they'd been answering questions during a flurry of interviews with the British Navy or working with Astrid, Myrtle, and Percy to decode where Reggie had hidden all his reports on the spies that he had rooted out in London and even the Home Office itself.

"My goodness, Myrtle, if Thorfinn took any smaller ones, he might as well use a spoon," Rose scoffed.

"But we're not even sure if the viscount's last notes are buried under this standing stone, and who knows what archaeological treasures we might be disrupting," Myrtle protested. "I am still not quite sure how Thorfinn came to the conclusion that 'Centuries of rocky love doth keep the heart' means this particular location."

"Thorfinn's conclusions have been sound," Rose said from where she was sitting with Astrid and Percy on a picnic blanket. "We know Reggie employed homophones, so it makes sense the *centuries* mean *sentries*, and the locals do view these stones as guardians. This particular one is thought to protect young lovers if they bury an object by it."

"Can you imagine what a treasure trove is under our feet?" Myrtle tapped the ground.

"Careful," Astrid called out. "You might squish the celluloid doll that I buried there when I was a child. I am sure it is of great scientific import."

Myrtle glared at her. "Are you absolutely certain you are not a German agent?"

"I couldn't be surer," Astrid said firmly.

"What was that?" Myrtle called out in a panic when Thorfinn's shovel struck something hard. Her attempt to push him out of the way resulted in nothing but her own near tumble. But before she could pitch toward the ground, Thorfinn obligingly stepped away from the excavation. Myrtle quickly bent down and brushed away the dirt with one of her tools. A few seconds later she sank back down on her heels. "It is just another rock. Thank goodness. I don't know why we can't do a proper excavation."

"Because British intelligence may need this information immediately," Rose pointed out. "Having Thorfinn dig is much less damaging than the naval deckhands rooting around with spades."

Myrtle sharply sucked in her breath at the image of eager sailors running amok through her future archaeological projects. "I just wish time weren't so important."

"It is the secrecy that I find a bother," Percy remarked in his laconic tone, which, for once, wasn't setting Thorfinn's teeth on edge. "We helped save the peace, but no one will ever know."

Astrid rolled her eyes. "Do you really think your chest is broad enough for more medals?"

"Ouch." Percy clutched his heart. "You wound me."

"You'll survive," Astrid told him.

"If we blab about the conspiracy plot, it could incite public out-cry for even more extreme punishments to be placed upon Germany. The negotiations in France could be entirely upset. And then we'd be responsible for destroying the peace that we fought to preserve," Rose pointed out.

Thorfinn also had his own personal reasons to be thankful that the British Navy wished to keep the whole event a secret. It meant that Sigurd's role would be hushed up as well, and the children could go on thinking their da a hero. Freya, unfortunately, knew most of it, but she seemed to be coming to terms. She had even managed to discuss her thoughts about her father's actions with Thorfinn and had, on her own, concluded that his treason had been a product of Sigurd's bitterness and the need to provide for his children. Freya had determined that they should give the hidden gold to war widows, and her decision seemed to grant her some degree of peace.

"I suppose you're right about the need to be discreet," Percy said with an exaggerated sigh, "if you wish to be precise about it."

"Speaking about precision." Myrtle drifted back in Thorfinn's direction. "You haven't hit anything else with your shovel, have you?"

"You do realize that Frest has been host to agrarian societies since the beginning. All this land you're standing on has been tilled and retilled by generation after generation for thousands of years," Thorfinn pointed out.

The glare the archaeologist sent him was deadly. Considering Myrtle's aim with a gun was apparently equally fatal, Thorfinn thought it wise to refocus on the hole in front of him. Despite his teasing words to Myrtle, he was being extremely careful.

It felt rather odd, digging with an audience, but their group had promised Myrtle that only one of them would work at a time. Since Thorfinn was the most proficient at shoveling the sod, he'd volunteered to go first. Hopefully, he'd picked the right spot, and they wouldn't have to dig around the whole damn stone.

The tip of his shovel scraped against something, giving the distinct clang of metal hitting metal. Myrtle hopped over like a hare, her nose fairly vibrating like the wee beastie's too. "Did you hit something again?"

"Aye, but—"

Myrtle shoved him aside and carefully scraped away the sod. Rose popped over too.

"It sounded clangy," Rose said as she peered over Myrtle's shoulder.

"Did Sinclair unearth something of great-great-great-great-great-grandma's?" Astrid asked.

"Should I contact the London Museum?" Percy inquired.

"This is not a laughing matter," Myrtle said sternly. "It could have been priceless."

"But it isn't?" Percy arched a brow.

"Well, not as an archaeological object," Myrtle said, standing up, "but I do believe it is the viscount's. Just stay close to the metal container. Don't churn up soil unnecessarily."

"We should all do the honors," Thorfinn said, holding out the shovel to Rose. "You should lead."

"That is a wonderful idea!" Rose hefted the tool and tromped the head so firmly into the loam that Myrtle winced with her entire body.

They ended up passing the spade around in a circle until the container was freed. It made the entire process take a bit longer than necessary, but it felt right, doing this together. And as much as Thorfinn wanted to hand the important information off to the authorities and fulfill his brother's last request, he also didn't want the search to end. Because when it did, Rose would no longer have a reason to stay in Orkney.

It was a truth that had lain between them this past week as they'd cared for his siblings and worked ceaselessly to decode Reggie's last clues—one that neither of them had wanted to mention, especially him. Thorfinn didn't want to ask Rose to stay. After all, he didn't have that right. A decision like that had to come from her. And he couldn't leave—at least not without the children in tow.

Thorfinn didn't even know if Rose wanted a future with him. Not like he did with her. After all, he'd always believed in love and she in just flirtation.

But as Rose and he bent down together to hoist Reggie's last notes about the London-based spies from the ground, he swore that the connection between them felt stronger than a mere summer dalliance. The mystery of the spy ring had brought Rose to Hamarray, but their partnership had always been about more than just unearthing the past. It had been about improving the island and building its future. Foundations were literally being laid for the new distillery.

"Who will have the honors of hefting it down to the jetty and delivering it to the navy?" Percy asked.

Thorfinn glanced back at the hole he'd dug—an ugly scar in the otherwise green carpet. It made him think of an open grave, and in some ways, it was. He'd just exhumed the last remaining link to his older brother, the boy and man who'd meant so much to him, *given* so much to him. And Thorfinn wanted to say goodbye.

"I'll stay here and put the sod back together. No sense in leaving a ditch one of our new tourists might trip into. They're not always the heartiest."

"Are you certain you don't wish to come?" Astrid asked him as she started to follow Percy down the hill.

"Aye. You all go ahead."

"Would you like some company?" Rose asked, surprising him.

"Don't you wish to see the handover?" Thorfinn asked.

She shook her head. "My role seems . . . complete, if that makes any sense at all."

"It does." Especially since Thorfinn felt the same about himself. "And it would be good to have you here."

Percy and Astrid said their goodbyes and headed down the slope to the docks. Neither Thorfinn nor Rose spoke as he quietly replaced the dirt. She seemed to instinctually understand the significance of his action.

When he replaced the top layer of grass, which he'd carefully cut like he did when extracting peat, he stayed kneeling. Rose joined him, her gloved hand finding his bare one.

Reggie hadn't just forgiven Thorfinn for not accompanying him to war—he'd somehow managed to ensure that Thorfinn had shared his final great adventure. And what an epic one it had been.

"I only knew Viscount Barbury briefly, but somehow, I think he's smiling down from heaven and watching us," Rose said softly.

Thorfinn chuckled quietly. "Likely he'd be giving us a cheeky wink."

"He was truly a remarkable hero."

"And man." Thorfinn stood, and Rose followed.

"Do you regret that we can't publicly share how he uncovered a spy ring?"

"Reggie would've been of the same mind as Percy. He'd want the world to know about his cleverness. In the end, though, I wonder whether he would have agreed it was for the best to keep silent."

Rose was quiet for a second. "Do you remember when I told you about how Reggie confided to me in the poste de secours? He confessed that he originally thought that he was battling for glory but that he was really fighting for those he let into his heart, his loved ones. He wanted to protect you and the people of Frest. That was his mission in the end, not fame. I don't think it would bother him one whit to remain silent about his role—not if it meant amity and protection for you and the children from any fallout triggered by Sigurd's treason."

The pressure of unshed tears swelled inside Thorfinn, but his emotions were not just grief . . . but a sense of gratitude and perhaps a peedie peace. Reggie had died as the man whom he'd always had the capacity of being—a man who searched not for outer validation but for inner. He had sought glorious deeds not to compensate for the damage Mar had done to his soul but for love, connection, and family. One of the best ways to honor his fallen brother was for Thorfinn to never again allow Mar to make him feel less or, worse, unworthy. For he *was* worthy, just as Reggie had always been.

"It's odd," Rose said quietly. "I've spent my whole life chasing notoriety, but I don't feel any need to shout our victory to the world. Peace has been secured, and that's all that matters. I do wish you could tell the islanders, though. They'd love the tale."

"That they would," Thorfinn agreed, thinking how they'd laugh and slap him on the back—as long as he left out the part about Sigurd. But he didn't need any accolades. Maybe some folks would always think of him as a coward for not going to war, but let them. He knew who he was, just as Reggie had discovered himself in the end.

Rose had been right when they'd talked about bravery and honor as the merry dancers had whirled above them in the night sky. Thorfinn was proud of what he'd done to stop the spies, but he had an equal swell of satisfaction whenever one of the children rushed up to him brimming with excitement to tell their big brother about their day.

For once, he was completely comfortable in his own skin. He was Thorfinn Sinclair, an honest crofter and an estate manager, with deep roots on Frest and Hamarray. The identity of his sire did not matter—only his own, which was his alone to forge.

Thorfinn also had no doubts about his feelings for the woman standing at his side. He loved her, and even if she decided to leave, those feelings didn't make him a daft mortal who'd been bewitched by a fae creature. Rose wasn't akin to an enchanting selkie or a sly mermaid. She wasn't her elegant clothes or flashy vehicles either. She was fierce, loyal, compassionate, adventurous, stubborn, brave, mischievous—aye—but most of all *solid*. She was someone a man could put his faith in, his trust in, his *love* in.

What Thorfinn wasn't sure of was the decision that Rose would make for her future.

He turned, and Rose mirrored his gesture. Instead of regarding the standing stone, they now stared at the sea beyond.

Lightly, he asked the question that was anything but casual to him. "Now that you've successfully solved the task my brother entrusted to you, unraveled spy rings here in Orkney and in London itself, and assured the continued peace, what shall you do next, Rose Van Etten?"

⸺⬥⸺

What shall you do next? The question swept through Rose as she stared out into the turquoise waters. Despite the northern latitude, the seas around Orkney often had a tropical appearance. Today, they were the deep, vibrant color of the harbor in Key West or the shoals of Cuba. At times they made her think of the Mediterranean too—of Greece, Italy, and the French Riviera.

The world—like her—was coming back to life. Rose could travel it again, endless ocean voyages and cross-country trips. There would be rich foods, new people, old friends, fast cars, even quicker speedboats . . . and the emptiness she could never fill.

Except she had.

Here.

In Orkney.

A wide-open, windswept place that somehow offered everything she needed.

Still holding Thorfinn's hand, Rose turned their bodies away from the sea until they were looking down the slopes of Hamarray to Frest. Here she could see the changes that she and Thorfinn were making. David Craigie, with loans from her, was expanding production, and a new millstone was being shipped from France. Folks on Frest were already talking about having another ceilidh when the peace treaty was finally signed. The broadsheets in Edinburgh, London, Paris, and New York had declared the auto race a success, and Rose had more than one inquiry about whether there would be future events on the island. Departing guests had asked when Muckle Skaill would officially open as a retreat and accept reservations.

Rose had sheep dipping to help with soon. And the harvest. And the peat wasn't properly dried yet. Widow Flett had promised to show Rose how to cast stitches on the knitting needle, while Freya was going to let her assist with the cheese making. Rose hadn't even *begun* to learn about the fishing industry yet.

And then there was Thorfinn. The man who made her believe not in fairy tales but in *love*. Companionship. *Until death do we part.*

Rose had been wrong to think a union was merely an exchange of necessities and wants—or perhaps she'd been wrong to think she had nothing to gain from a partnership. She was strong alone. *Sufficient* alone.

But with Thorfinn?

She felt right. They fit. The crofter and the heiress. It shouldn't make sense. But then again, he was not just a farmer, and she was not just a rich adventuress. They challenged each other to be more.

Rose had always loved a challenge. And this one was sure going to be thrilling.

"I plan to stay here on Hamarray," Rose finally answered.

Thorfinn's fingers flexed around hers—tight and strong. "For how long?"

"I'm thinking forever . . . after all, it is full of the people that I have let into my heart. That is the true mission that your brother left for me."

Another squeeze, and Rose swore she felt it in her soul.

"I find . . ." She paused as she swept her eyes over the islands. "I find I belong here."

"That you do, lass, that you do."

As if of one accord, they turned together, their mouths meshing. Hunger met hunger. Joy met joy. Need met need.

She had no idea how long they stood at the headlands, the winds gently buffeting them as they drank each other in. Even the cry of the birds seemed more joyous than scolding. Waves crashed against the rocks below, cymbals to this particular orchestra. High in the sky, the sun shone brightly. Midsummer was mere days away, and the land was awash in light.

Rose broke the kiss and spun them madly about until they both collapsed. Even Thorfinn was laughing heartily as they lay tangled together. Somehow, they both managed to sit up, and Rose laid her head against Thorfinn's shoulder.

"It was worth the wait," she told him as they once again looked over Hamarray and Frest.

"What was, lass?" Thorfinn asked.

"Finding a home." She swept one of her arms over the landscape. "It's right here. With the people of Frest. With you."

"You're going to make a fine laird."

"Hmmm. Does that mean I need to do my duty and marry and beget heirs?"

She felt Thorfinn's deltoids stiffen under her cheek. He held himself still. And she almost felt bad for being such a tease. Almost.

"But you know," she said, slipping her hand over his chest until it covered his heart, "I am an American, so I must also marry for love."

"Is that so?" The poor man practically wheezed out the words.

"Yes. Luckily, I have the perfect candidate in mind." She tackled him then, sending them both sprawling onto the grass.

He reached up and cupped her face. "I love you, Rose Van Etten."

"And I love you, Thorfinn Sinclair," she said. "We do, after all, make the perfect pair."

Epilogue

Satisfaction swept through Thorfinn as he circled the nearly complete walls of the distillery. The lads of Frest had done a top-notch job. Not even the faintest bit of wind would make it through the solid structure. The roof would be erected just in time for the barley harvest, which was on course to be the grandest in recent history. In addition to the peat fields, Rose had opened some of Hamarray to cultivation, and Thorfinn was overseeing a series of drainage projects to reclaim more land on Frest. They would need the ability for surplus production given the number of whiskey orders that they had already received from places as close as Kirkwall and as far as London, Copenhagen, Paris, and even Montreal.

Rose had been right that the race last year had spawned interest in the isles. The well-connected competitors had returned home wearing Widow Flett's sweaters and having a taste for Frest Whiskey. Percy—whom Thorfinn had begrudgingly begun to consider a friend—had insisted that all his London clubs stock their spirits, and he served it at all the events that he hosted.

Thorfinn had traveled with Rose to Edinburgh, England, and the Netherlands as they'd met with her contacts to find buyers. They'd brought the children along, and the twins had absolutely adored the hotels where they'd stayed. Margaret had asked question after question. Alexander had practically eaten his weight in fairy floss. Hannah had dragged her siblings to a long list of museums. And Freya had gone shopping with Rose and, to his initial dismay, had ordered Thorfinn more than one suit.

But he found that the tailored clothes not only fit but felt *right*. *He* felt right—walking into places of business and negotiating contracts. But even more extraordinary, he didn't feel out of place attending Society functions that came along with being Rose's husband. People were ultimately just people, and he wasn't confined to being the perpetual outsider. One did not have to be born to a certain station to fill it.

Even though Thorfinn did not mind visiting mainland Britain or even the Continent, his and Rose's home was here, on Hamarray and Frest. It didn't matter if he carried English blood or she American. They belonged here—both of them—working with the crofters, making the twin isles productive again.

A low whistle of appreciation attracted Thorfinn's attention, and he turned to find David Craigie studying the distillery. Now that Thorfinn was not only the estate manager but married to the laird, the islanders had chosen the miller for their representative. With his cheerful enthusiasm and mechanical knowledge, he was an important partner in the improvements.

"Now that is a fair sight." David patted one of the stones they'd repurposed from the multiple ruined crofts on Hamarray. It was good to give new life to the building materials that had been lying in the gorse since their owners had been pushed off the island during the Enclosures.

"Aye. All from local stone and built without a single worker from outside Frest." Pride swelled through Thorfinn to see his and Rose's vision brought to life. It had felt good to be able to offer jobs to the men returning from the war. Despite the United States enacting the Volstead

Act and prohibiting the sale of alcohol in that country, Rose and he had found plenty of markets for the island's whiskey.

"The sight of it warms my heart even more than that grindstone that your missus bought from France, and I'm not ashamed to say that the big rock made me bawl like a bairn when my son, Young Thomas, and I unpacked it."

Thorfinn clapped his hand over the older man's shoulder. "Speaking of Rose, I'd best head back to Muckle Skaill. Between the grand opening of the retreat and the ceilidh tonight, things are a peedie helter-skelter."

"Go on then, lad." David gave him a grin. "I'll make sure everything is put to rights afore the men head home to prepare for the evening festivities."

Thorfinn bobbed his head before taking off at a jog through the grasses. His relationship with the islanders had changed. Rose was right that once he started to see himself as land agent, he would realize how much the crofters accepted him as a leader. Instead of setting him apart, it made him feel more connected. He'd come to realize that he'd always regarded himself as more of an outsider than his neighbors on Frest ever had.

Thorfinn slowed his pace as he reached the area where tents were being set up for the archaeology students who were arriving today to help Myrtle excavate the broch. Despite Rose's financial backing, Myrtle had experienced a devil of a time getting her college and the British authorities to allow her to lead the dig. In the end, though, between her and Rose's determination, she had prevailed. Depending upon how the summer progressed, Rose and Thorfinn had agreed to erect more permanent but still rustic lodgings, separate from the more expensive hotel, for the students and the less wealthy bird-watchers.

Thorfinn was just about to pick up his speed again when he spied some Scottish primroses fluttering in the ever-present wind. It was a second—and last—blooming of the season, and they'd become a favorite of Rose's ever since Alexander had gifted her with the single blossom over a year ago. Thorfinn bent down and carefully broke off one sprig. Whistling softly to himself, he resumed his original pace.

When he reached Muckle Skaill, he didn't even pause as he bounded up the front stairs. His simple crofter's clothes were caked with mud, but Rose wouldn't scold him. She'd accepted the dirt and sweat of his life as much as he'd learned to become comfortable with the gilt and perfume of hers.

Rose had replaced the heavy wooden doors with stained glass ones inspired by the sea cliffs of Hamarray with tammie norries flying above, sea pinks blooming on the rocky crevasses, and seals bobbing below. They were bright and light and celebrated the island's real beauty, not some sexualized, inverted version of their folklore.

He burst inside and smelled the faint trace of roses that his wife preferred. Everything sparkled, from the freshly washed windowpanes to the polished parquet floors. Ann Inkster, who was currently manning the front desk, smiled at Thorfinn, her chin straight, her eyes bright. She would never be the boldest of lasses, but she possessed a quiet confidence now, and her serene demeanor was exactly the kind of welcome Rose wanted their guests to experience.

Semicircular, silk-upholstered seats that Rose called *art nouveau club chairs* had replaced the brutish furniture of the earl. The curved pieces seemed ready to wrap around weary travelers and offer them a sense of privacy as they rested their feet or chatted a bit with their companions. The whole of Muckle Skaill had been transformed into this peaceful yet stunning haven. And it never failed to make Thorfinn think of Rose.

As if conjured by his thoughts, the Lady of Muckle Skaill herself appeared. She wore the flowy poppy-red trousers that he'd become eminently fond of. The bold, unconventional outfit with its fluid lines suited his wife perfectly, and his heart always seemed to flutter right along with the lithe material.

"You brought me a primrose!" Rose exclaimed as she stood on tip-toe while he bent down to buss her mouth. If it hadn't been for Ann's presence, he would have kept their lips together longer . . . a lot longer.

Rose must have sensed his thoughts, for she pulled on his hand and guided him into the nearby guest parlor. The room was as taste-fully appointed as the entrance hall with warm, inviting hues that felt homey and intimate. She carefully placed the flower in a vase on one of the windowsills and then wrapped her strong arms around his neck, pulling him down for a kiss. He eagerly obliged. When their mouths met, sensation, as golden and long lasting as the simmer dim, unfurled inside him. He drank in the marvel of their love.

Rose pulled back with a reluctant sigh and patted his chest. "I can't linger too long. More guests will be arriving soon, and I want to personally greet as many as possible, since this is the grand opening."

"What has the reaction been so far?" Thorfinn asked, cupping her face with his hand.

"Wonderful!" She beamed. "I even got a grunt of approval from my father, and my mother hasn't had one complaint—although I think Alexander nearly startled her to death when he showed her the vole family that he rescued from the plow. I've heard so many people say how much it felt like stepping into their own house, it was so pleasant."

"That's because you've managed the impossible, Rose." Thorfinn pulled her tightly against his chest as he brushed his lips over her temple. "You turned Muckle Skaill into a real home—not just for the guests who sojourn here for a day or a week or a month but for me and my sisters and brother."

"And me." A wondrous expression fell over Rose's face as she stepped back to stare up at him. "I never thought I'd have a home. But here I am. Here *we* are."

"Here we are," he repeated with a grin. They weren't anyone's idea of a proper laird and lady, but it was their very uniqueness that made them strong, steady, stalwart—like the standing stones that Rose had once compared him to.

⟺

"I couldn't imagine a better way to commemorate the official opening of Muckle Skaill Hotel and the first anniversary of the official end of the Great War than with all of you!" Rose projected her voice over the crowd of ceilidh attendees gathered in front of her. Myrtle and Percy stood together—glasses of Frest Whiskey in their hands. Next to them bounced the younger Flett children under the watchful eyes of Astrid, Freya, and Young Thomas. Beyond them stood Widow Flett, David Craigie, Janet and Ann Inkster, elderly islanders, the war heroes, the women who'd kept the crofts functioning during the war, children, toddlers, and babies. And interspersed among the people of Frest were Myrtle's archaeology students and guests of Muckle Skaill. Even Rose's mother and father were in the audience, looking almost . . . comfortable. Although the three of them would never be particularly close, it was enough for Rose that they were here, supporting her in their own way.

Beside Rose, on the temporary platform that had been erected on the headlands for the event, was Thorfinn. He had initially balked at joining her as master of ceremonies, but she'd pointed out that he'd need to get accustomed to it. After all, he was the laird to her lady.

"Today is both a celebration and a remembrance." Rose shifted her body slightly and gestured to Scapa Flow behind her with her tumbler. "We stand before a great natural harbor once filled with the British Grand Fleet and stalked by German U-boats. From these shores, men left to fight in Belgium, France, Italy, Russia, Africa, Turkey, and in the world's oceans; women volunteered and risked their lives to support the troops as nurses, couriers, and ambulance drivers. Men and women sallied forth to aid the peoples of France and Belgium against the German aggressor. All people supported the war effort. When a truce was finally declared, these waters were filled with the remnants of the German High Seas Fleet, a constant reminder that war could erupt again at any minute.

"But that threat is gone now—the once-fearsome fleet sunk by the Germans' own hands—a final act of desperation in a conflict that wrought so much hopelessness and pain. The dominion of Scapa has been returned to the people of Orkney. Trawlers and merchant vessels are once again the most common sight.

"Yet still we can see the masts of dreadnoughts rising from the water and the hulls of overturned destroyers resting on skerries. We know that beneath the turquoise waves lurk the sunken cruisers, their guns now pointing at nothing. These are both seen and unseen reminders—scars, if you will. We shall all carry them—whether it be inflicted by shrapnel, by bullets, by memory, or by loss.

"But we, like the Scapa Flow, will keep on moving, keep on changing, keep on sustaining life. Not just our own but each other's. We shall heal together, build together, create together.

"So let's not just lift our Frest Whiskey to toast the anniversary of the Treaty of Versailles. It is not only what that legal document granted us but what we do *with* it. To community, to healing, to growth, to the gift of a future."

Rose held the amber liquid high above her head, and the people erupted into shouts and cheers. The sound—both joyous and resolute—buoyed her. She did not feel like the cynical observer anymore but a part of this, a wonderful, connected part.

Beside her, Thorfinn nervously cleared his throat as he gestured for his siblings to join them on the stage as the children had requested. They wanted to tell a story in remembrance of their late parents, although they refused to tell either her or Thorfinn which one they had chosen.

Rose linked her arm with her husband's, and Freya took his other elbow. Her sisters followed suit and then little Alex, so they stood as one unit. Together.

"The past year has been one of great sadness and of great happiness for my family." Thorfinn's voice started out weak, but the more he spoke, the stronger it became. "As most of you know, my stepda passed away around this time last June."

Mr. Flett's death, in many ways, had been a mercy, and Rose believed the proud man had simply stopped fighting. He must have known that his passing would protect his beloved children. Despite the path his bitterness and desperation had placed him upon, Sigurd had been a loving father to Thorfinn's half siblings. For the latter, Rose mourned him, as did Thorfinn.

"Days later, Mrs. Sinclair and I announced our betrothal. Our engagement was made in the shadow of the standing stone known to bring luck and fortune to sweethearts." Thorfinn gazed directly at Rose now, and a sense of wholeness blossomed through her. "And our marriage, although it is still only a few months old, has been one of much joy."

Freya now spoke, her pale face flushed but her words confident and strong. "And to honor both our da—who always led the storytelling—and our brother and sister-in-law, the Flett children would like to tell you all a tale. It is a familiar one but also new. We have made it up ourselves, and no one has heard it afore, even Thorfinn and Rose."

Freya paused then and glanced at Rose with a huge welcoming smile on her face. "Our story begins with a selkie who decided to come ashore."

At the words, Rose clasped her free hand against her heart as the organ seemed to swell like a hot-air balloon.

"She was very, very bonny, of course," Alex piped up.

"And she could navigate a boat better than any mortal or fae creature—even the finmen," Hannah added. "For she had a knowledge of the currents, as she had traveled far and wide. There was naught of the sea that she had not seen with her own eyes."

Thorfinn glanced over at Rose, and his warm look made her feel like she was floating among the gold-drenched clouds.

"So she decided to explore the land," Margaret said. "Being a practical sort, she was very careful with her selkie skin when she landed on the shores of Hamarray. She folded it up and carried it with her. She didn't lose it or hide it in an obvious place or, worst of all, entrust it to a silly man for safekeeping."

"But she did meet a man," Mary interjected. "A nice handsome one with a big smile."

"He was a Viking!" Alex shouted, causing the crowd to laugh and Thorfinn to blush. Despite how many times Rose had called her husband *my Viking* in deliciously intimate settings, the appellation could still redden his cheeks.

"He was an islander, and he didn't know if he could trust a stranger—especially one so fair," Freya said. "But she seemed so eager to learn about the people of Frest and to try to help them that he soon found himself softening to her."

"He taught her how to dance," Barbara said, "and how to find cockles at low tide."

Memories of the past year rushed through Rose—Thorfinn's hand about her waist as they whirled through the library on a dark winter's evening, the children humming a song, the peat fire crackling in the hearth, a gale blowing against the mullioned windows. Bright summer days, the sand squishing between their bare toes, the wind softer but still present, Thorfinn's arms around her as they raked the strand for shellfish.

"While she took him out on her boat," Hannah added.

Whispers of Thorfinn's laughter filled Rose's ears—and as she stared at him, she knew he was thinking of her shouts of glee as they tore through the surf.

"She met his little sisters and brother, and was ex-cep-tion-ally kind to them," Alex said, carefully enunciating *exceptionally*.

"She still carried her skin with her all the time," Freya continued. "The man never tried to steal it. He never even asked her for it. For he knew it was hers and not his."

"But one day, she accidentally dropped it. He stooped down and picked it up. When he held it out to her, she took it, but she did not tuck it back under her arm," Hannah said. "Instead, she asked him if he had a chest with a lock where she could place it for safekeeping."

"For she had decided out of all the grand places she had seen, this was the one where she wished to make her home," Mary said.

Tears sprang suddenly to Rose's eyes, and she pressed her hand against her mouth. But still the emotion flowed from her, strong and wonderful. When she hazarded a glance at Thorfinn, she saw a hint of mist in his eye.

"She would still take out her skin from time to time when she wanted to revisit interesting locales," Barbara added hurriedly, "but she would bring her mortal husband along with her."

"And his siblings," Mary stressed before she clearly ad-libbed, "to places like Paris, Venice, and Bath."

A happy giggle escaped Rose's lips. Oh, how she'd loved the trips she'd taken with her husband and the children. All her family, including Thorfinn, had been filled with such wonder.

"But most important, she made her home here on Hamarray." Freya bent around her brother to smile at Rose as she spoke, and Rose wondered if a body could explode with utter contentment.

"And they all lived happily ever after!" Alex shouted. His voice was a bit overly loud but no less perfect.

Emotion swamped Rose as the little boy let go of Margaret and dashed toward her. She bent down and gathered him into her arms. Suddenly she found herself surrounded by the Flett children. Thorfinn lifted Alex onto his hip with one arm as he looped the other around Rose's waist. They stood in a clump, facing their neighbors and friends.

"Let the ceilidh begin!" Rose shouted, grinning through the tears that had escaped her eyes.

Behind them, the band began to play a rousing reel. As notes of the fiddles and accordions carried into the pinkish-gold twilight, Thorfinn swept Rose into a dance. Her feet didn't know all the steps yet, but her heart certainly did. And in the laughter and the merriment, Rose Van Etten was finally home.

HISTORICAL NOTE

While researching the roles that women held during the First World War, I came across articles about women who had served as ambulance drivers. Since my sister worked as an emergency medical technician (EMT) while she was going to college to become a physician assistant (PA), this immediately grabbed my imagination. Also rattling around in my mind was an online article by Jobe Close entitled, "Vera Brittain and the Shell-Shocked Women of World War One," which addresses how PTSD in woman volunteers in WWI went largely unnoticed, unstudied, and untreated—both then and in the popular historical records. Vera Brittain was a British VAD (Voluntary Aid Detachment) nurse and later an author who recounted her trauma and mental health struggles after the war in her book *Testament of Youth*.

I decided I wanted to write a story that addressed and honored the bravery of the women who served in WWI, the price that they paid for their contributions, and their continued strength as they readjusted to civilian life. When I was talking to my husband late at night as I rambled on about story ideas floating in my head, he suggested that I should make the hero a farmer (i.e., the bucolic, peaceful ideal generally embodied by the woman). He knows that I love a good gender-trope flip. Of course, Thorfinn is much more complicated than that—as he would be the first to tell you—but in many ways he is the one who represents domesticity and peacetime in *Velocity of a Secret*. I also thought it would be interesting to explore the thoughts and feelings of a male character who had chosen to stay and care for his much-younger siblings rather than to pursue glory on the battlefield as was expected of him.

As I began to gather background facts on Rose's character, I kept running into the age-old difficulty of researching women's roles—regulations and prejudices that kept them from pursuing their chosen careers and then, even more frustrating, the lack of documentation once they *did* manage to fight their way into alleged "male spheres."

Originally, I had intended Rose to be a race car driver primarily in the United States—but almost all prewar racetracks in the United States did not allow female drivers. Women who wanted to compete had to do so at fairs and similar events. They were daredevils, barnstormers, and entertainers.

Europe, however, was a different story. Women were allowed to compete in trials and other races there, including at the famed Brooklands in London. Dorothy Levitt was one of England's first race car drivers. She not only raced. She *won*. Like Rose, she also conned speedboats. She wrote a delightful book, *The Woman and the Car: A Chatty Little Handbook for All Women Who Motor or Who Want to Motor*—which is exactly as advertised.

Thus, Rose became an American auto racer in Europe, which ultimately worked for *Velocity of a Secret* since it gave her ties to the Continent. This made it more plausible that she would volunteer in the Great War at a time when most Americans not only wanted to stay neutral but did not particularly support those who did get involved— male or female.

As the United States entered the war only at the tail end of the conflict, I had always planned on Rose being part of a British ambulance unit. Even so, I once again ran into the issue of a sparse historical account of American woman ambulance drivers. The book *Gentlemen Volunteers* by Arlen J. Hansen addresses this issue head-on. Hansen points out that the US newspapers eagerly awaited and published letters from male ambulance drivers as a direct source of information since neutral US journalists were barred from the Front due to fears of espionage. But the stories of woman drivers weren't included. It wasn't as if there weren't any. Hansen mentions tantalizing snippets as the periodicals almost offhandedly mention that women were headed to Europe to volunteer as drivers.

In a rather showing demonstration of this lack of interest, Katherine Stinson—who was a famous aviatrix known as the Flying Schoolgirl before the war—volunteered as an ambulance driver when no one would accept her as a pilot. Despite her popularity, we know very little of her time serving overseas other than the fact that Stinson contracted influenza and tuberculosis, which seemingly so affected her health that she did not resume her flying career after returning home. Her illness was partially the inspiration for Rose's.

Britain, however, celebrated its woman ambulance drivers with greater enthusiasm, and the records of their bravery have been better preserved. We are also fortunate to have the letters of Mary Dexter, which were compiled and edited by her mother and published in 1918 in a book entitled *In the Soldier's Service: War Experiences of Mary Dexter, England, Belgium, France, 1914–1918*. Mary was an American and a very remarkable person. She first began her volunteer service as a VAD nurse in an English hospital, but she always wanted to do more, contribute more. First, she traveled to Belgium, where, at great danger from the advancing German troops, she worked in a hospital. After falling severely ill (another inspiration for Rose's sickness), she returned to England and studied psychology and the effects of shell shock. While still a student, she began to treat patients who suffered from PTSD. When she had a chance to serve in the Hackett-Lowther Ambulance Unit as a driver at the actual Front, she took a sabbatical from her studies and once again headed into danger. Unfortunately, her unit was delayed multiple times from being sent to the Front, but she still performed important jitney work and faced shelling. A back injury forced her to leave the unit right before they were finally deployed to drive wounded soldiers from a poste de secours right at the Front.

Often ambulance drivers in WWI are automatically associated with the Red Cross, but there were many different units and organizations (and even a sort of turf war often emerged). Some corps, like Rose's, were actually attached to French or Belgian military units. I never define Rose's, but it is a fictional one. Some of the real organizations with female drivers included the all-female Hackett-Lowther Ambulance Unit and the First Aid Nursing Yeomanry Corps (the FANYs). There was also the Munro Ambulance Corps early in the war, which included British heiress Dorothie Feilding. Two other members of the Munro Corps—Elsie Knocker and Mairi Chisholm—formed their own two-woman ambulance / field dressing station team. Both women were motorcyclists before the war. These brave women were called the Madonnas of Pervyse.

The spy plots in *Velocity of a Secret* are purely fictional. There is no evidence of a spy ring in the Home Office or one in the Orkney Islands. In fact, based on the historical record, it seems like there were more active German agents in the United States and in Mexico than in England. Throughout the conflict with Britain, some spies were apprehended, including eleven who were executed by a firing squad at the Tower of London in 1914. Some of the evidence that damned the conspirators included the fact that the nibs of their pens had been corroded by lemon juice used to write secret messages. The Home Office portion of my spy plot was partially inspired by one German national, Jules C. Silber, who appears to have single-handedly managed to get into Britain via Canada, wrangled a job at the British postal censorship department, and used that position to gather and transmit important secrets to Germany. He was never caught, and he made it home to Germany after the war. Later, he wrote an autobiography revealing his wartime activities.

The nurse who helped Reggie escape from Belgium was inspired by the courageous Edith Cavell, a British national working in a Belgian hospital before the German invasion. She treated men on both sides and helped over two hundred Allied soldiers escape to safety. When the Germans discovered that she was helping the other side evade detection, tragically they executed her by firing squad. She is quoted as saying the night before her imminent death, "Patriotism is not enough. I must have no hatred or bitterness towards anyone."

The Grand Fleet's home anchorage was indeed in Scapa Flow for most of World War I. The massive, naturally protected anchorage was hugely important to Britain. Lord Kitchener, Britain's Secretary of State for War, was killed along with 736 other people when the HMS *Hampshire* was sunk while departing Orkney. Today, it is believed that the vessel hit a mine planted by a German U-boat that had been recently seen in the vicinity. At the time, there were whispers of espionage and sabotage. Even today, the horrible tragedy is still shrouded by mystery. Of course, my explanation of a bird-watching spy ring is purely from my own imagination and not based on any fact or evidence.

After the Armistice, the German fleet was interned at Scapa Flow while peace negotiations were conducted in Versailles, France. There is no known attempt to free the fleet by German loyalists, and my idea is pure fiction. As the characters state, such an attempt would have been foolhardy indeed between the conditions of the vessels and the tired, weary, and often mutinous skeleton crews left on them. It could, however, have reignited the conflict, especially while negotiations were ongoing.

What did happen is that German admiral Hans Hermann Ludwig von Reuter ordered the scuttling of the Imperial Fleet on June 21, 1919, to prevent it from being handed over and divvied up among the Allies. This is the event that Rose refers to in the epilogue. Although many of the ships were eventually salvaged, parts of them were visible for years. Today, there are still WWI-era German ships under the waters of Scapa Flow—which serves as an important resource for low-background steel (i.e., steel produced before the detonation of the first nuclear bomb), which is used in the production of medical and scientific instruments.

Although the Orkney Islands and Scapa Flow are real, Hamarray, Frest, and Minnstray are wholly of my imagination. The crags of Hamarray are based on the impressive sandstone cliffs of Hoy, although the fictional islet is much smaller than the actual island. The sea stack in the book—Sigurd's Rock—was originally inspired by the Old Man of Hoy. Thorfinn's climb out to the formation, however, was based on the exploits of men from the Hebridean island of Lewis who rowed to Handa Island. Like my fictional Hamarray, the cliffs of Handa form a semicircle around a tall sea stack. Highlighting the harshness and resourcefulness of island life, the Lewis men attached a rope to either side of the headland so that the hawser stretched across the great sea stack of Handa for seafowling. They then crawled onto the massive rock formation to catch the birds for much-needed food.

The description of the landscape of Frest and Hamarray was drawn from my own visit to Mainland (the name of the biggest of the Orkney Islands) and the absolutely amazing Papa Westray, home to dazzling sea cliffs, inquisitive puffins, cheerful oystercatchers, seals, and more of the flora and fauna that I describe in *Velocity of a Secret*. Papa Westray is one of the few places in the world where you can find the Scottish primrose—although when I visited, it was, unfortunately, right in the middle of the two blooming times, and there was nary a one to be seen. The idea of Frest and Hamarray being connected tidal islands came from both the Brough of Birsay (another inspiration for the geography of Hamarray), which is connected to Mainland, Orkney, and the Irish island of Omey near Claddaghduff in County Galway.

I took a little bit of artistic license with the appearance of the merry dancers on the beach. As Thorfinn notes, it is quite late in the season to see them. However, I could not resist this touch—or the sense that Thorfinn's mother is watching from above and approving of her son's match. The appearance of the Scottish primrose that little Alexander picks is a bit early.

I have always had a great love for Neolithic structures, which is what drew me to Orkney in the first place. I could not resist adding a chamber tomb and some standing stones. Fornhowe is based on Maeshowe on Mainland, Orkney; Tomb of the Eagles on South Ronaldsay, Orkney; and Newgrange in County Meath, Ireland—all three of which I have toured.

Muckle Skaill is based on Skaill House, which is a sixteenth-century mansion overlooking the incredible remains of the Neolithic village of Skara Brae. It also has similarities to the nineteenth-century Sumburgh Hotel on Mainland, Shetland.

Myrtle's broch is a combination of the many that I saw in Orkney and Shetland. It is most similar to the Broch of Mousa, which I was able to see only from a distance, as it is on a separate island from Mainland, Shetland, and I did not have enough time in my schedule to take the ferry there and back.

The sheepherding scene is based on both my research of the seaweed-eating sheep of North Ronaldsay and my own experience at my in-laws' sheep farm in Western Pennsylvania. Although I was not trying to unravel a spy ring at the time (or any time except, of course, in my imagination), I did witness a poor sheep giving birth. Like the ewe in the novel, her herding instinct was greater than her labor pains. My mother-in-law noticed the sheep's distress, and my husband and father-in-law separated the ewe and assisted with the successful birth of her lamb. My husband then explained to me how the mother and baby bond and learn each other's voices by *maa*ing softly to each other— something that you may recall that Thorfinn tells Rose.

Although Rose's father is a minor character, his career was loosely inspired by the enterprises of the real-life Henry Flagler, who made his money originally as an investor in Standard Oil (of Rockefeller fame). Flagler later moved to Florida, where he was responsible for jump-starting the state's tourism economy as he built hotels and railroads.

GLOSSARY

afore. Orcadian word for *before*.

Bearcat. A sports car manufactured by the Stutz Motor Company; they were a status symbol and associated with the wealthy college set.

blessé. French word for *wounded soldier* but also used by English-speaking ambulance drivers.

British Grand Fleet. The largest formation of the British Royal Navy during WWI. The Grand Fleet comprised twenty-five to thirty capital ships and numerous smaller vessels. Its primary purpose was to patrol the North Sea and guard against attempts by the German High Seas Fleet to break out and harass British shipping or bombard England.

bruck. Orcadian word for *garbage*.

byre. Scottish word for *cowshed*.

calloo. Orcadian word for the long-tailed duck (arctic duck).

ceilidh. Gaelic social gathering with music, singing, dancing, and storytelling.

Clootie. Scottish word for the devil.

CMB. Royal Navy Coastal Motor Boats.

dreich. Scottish word for *damp and chilly*.

fash. Scottish word for *worry*.

feartie. Orcadian word for *coward*.

finfolk. Magical, shape-shifting seamen known for stealing away mortals as spouses.

gappus. Orcadian word for *fool*.

hen harrier. Bird of prey.

heuk. Sickle. Handheld curved blade used for harvesting grain.

howe. Orcadian word for *mound*. Often these howes contain Neolithic cairns or chambered tombs.

kye. Orcadian word for *cow*.

Mercer. Mercer Automobile Company or one of their cars.

merry dancers. Orcadian word for *northern lights*.

morrow. Orcadian word for *the next day* (not just the next morning).

muckle. Orcadian word for *great* or *big*.

nob. British slang for *aristocrat.*

Paris Gun. Massive German siege gun used at the end of WWI to bombard Paris.

peedie. Orcadian word for *small.*

peelie-wally. Orcadian word for *appearing pale, sick, unwell.*

poilu. French infantryman.

poste de secours. French term for field dressing stations near the Front.

puggled. Orcadian word for *tired* or *broken.*

Raceabout. A sports car (which could easily be transformed into a race car) manufactured by the Mercer Automobile Company. They were a status symbol and associated with the wealthy college set.

Scapa Flow. Huge natural harbor in Orkney.

simmer dim. Twilight around midsummer.

skaill. Orcadian word for *hall* or *house.*

skerry. Rocky outcropping in the water. A reef.

strand. British word for *beach.*

Stutz. The Stutz Motor Company produced luxury cars, including sports cars. Also shorthand for one of their cars.

tammie norrie. Orcadian word for *puffin*.

Tin Lizzie. American slang for a Ford Model T car.

tirrick. Orcadian word for *arctic tern*.

toff. Derogatory British term for an aristocrat or peer.

trow. Troll-like creature in Orcadian and Shetland myths.

whinge. British word for *whine* or *complain*.

ACKNOWLEDGMENTS

I want to thank my editors, Lauren Plude and Tiffany Yates Martin, for their invaluable insights, which have helped me craft a deeper and more suspenseful tale. Their probing questions and comments prompted me to delve further into my characters and their most carefully hidden dreams and pains. They encouraged me to take full advantage of the spy plot to not only challenge Rose and Thorfinn but to help them grow stronger, both as a couple and as individuals. The editing process, in some ways, is very similar to the growth of a character in a novel, and I am very thankful that I had not one but two perceptive editors guiding me and *Velocity of a Secret* through this journey.

The cultural reader provided key insight into the effects of post-traumatic stress syndrome and helped me with my portrayal of Rose's experience with shell shock (the historic term for PTSD). Any mistakes that I made in *Velocity of a Secret* regarding PTSD are unintended and mine alone.

Once again the Montlake art department has done an absolutely fabulous job on the cover! Caroline Teagle Johnson has captured Rose's indomitable spirit. The swirl of color in the sky perfectly embodies both the emotional journey in the book and the sweeping adventure.

The cover also has a story of its own—complete with sleuthing. I had really wanted a Mercer Raceabout on the cover. The fast cars of the teens possessed a very distinctive look that differed greatly from other vehicles of the time and of the 1920s. Of course, finding an image of a car that is over one hundred years old isn't easy. Emily Freidenrich, a photo researcher at Montlake, tracked down an image and contacted the owner of both the photograph and the car—Fred Hoch. Fred Hoch graciously agreed to allow his beautifully maintained Mercer to make a cameo on the cover of *Velocity of a Secret*. In addition to his generosity in sharing the image, I wanted to extend my thanks to Fred Hoch and other car enthusiasts who painstakingly restore, care for, and preserve the automobiles of our past—allowing us all to experience the thrill of history as they motor by on the road or display the vehicles at vintage- and classic-car events.

The rest of the Montlake team has been a huge part of this book— from the copyediting and proofreading process to distribution, market- ing, and publicity. There are so many people who have worked behind the scenes on *Velocity of a Secret* to make sure that it is highly polished, properly laid out, and available to readers.

This book also would not have been possible without my agent, Jessica Watterson, who encouraged me to consider writing a story about courageous women during WWI. Her suggestion led to my research discovery of the daring ambulance drivers of WWI—both male and female—who risked (and even, at times, lost) their lives to save the wounded. Her idea to keep the vestiges of the war in the background also immediately made me think of Orkney as a setting for the book, since I knew that the German fleet had been interned at Scapa Flow after the war.

I had the great fortune of traveling to Orkney and Shetland back in 2018 for research on another book. The inhabitants of both island chains were incredibly welcoming and patient with all my questions. The Northern Isles are truly magnificent, from their ancient Neolithic structures to their wildlife. I only hope that I was able to do them jus- tice in this story. Any mistakes that I made in *Velocity of a Secret* about

Orcadian and Shetland culture and language are unintended and mine alone.

My physician assistant sister (whom this book is also dedicated to) helped me "diagnose" what type of strokes Sigurd suffered in his final days. I gave her the plot points that I needed, and she helped me determine what symptoms would present that would work within my story structure. Mistakes, if any, that I made from a medical standpoint are mine and mine alone.

Once again, my husband has proved an invaluable technical resource on this book, from introducing me to the naval history of Scapa Flow to watching *Jay Leno's Garage* videos with me. He's always quick with an answer when I ask, "So what gun should my heroine have? And her female best friend whose grandfather was a Texas Ranger? What about a rakish duke who served in the RAF?"

My mother has continued to be my first beta reader who catches my grammar errors and plot holes. She is also, along with my husband and daughter, my biggest cheerleader.

I also want to extend my gratitude to my daughter for her support and understanding when Mommy has to work on her book. She has made me many adorable drawings as I sit and type or edit.

And thank you, readers—both returning and new—for joining me on Rose and Thorfinn's adventure. Knowing a reader connects and enjoys the characters makes the writing journey richer.

ABOUT THE AUTHOR

Photo © 2018 Skysight Photography

Two-time Golden Heart finalist Violet Marsh is a lawyer who decided it was more fun to write witty banter than contractual terms. A romance enthusiast, she relishes the transformative power of love, especially when a seeming mismatch becomes the perfect pairing.

Marsh also enjoys visiting the past—whether strolling through castle ruins or researching her family genealogy online (where she discovered at least one alleged pirate, a female tavern owner, and several blacksmiths). She indulges in her love of history by writing period pieces filled with independent-minded women and men smart enough to fall for them.

Marsh lives at home with Prince Handy (a guy who can fix things is much sexier than a mere charmer), a whirlwind (her toddler), and a suburban nesting dog (whose cuteness Marsh shamelessly uses to promote her books).

Find Marsh on Facebook at www.facebook.com/violetmarshauthor, on Instagram at www.instagram.com/violetmarshauthor, and on Twitter at www.twitter.com/vi_marsh_author.